forget' – Humaira, for Lovereading4kids.co.uk

'Gets your heart racing, your brain working overtime and your heart hoping that our world never experiences the horror of Scarrow's imagination!' Phoebe, for Lovereading4kids.co.uk

'An addictive, intense book that I just could not put down' – Geeky Zoo Girl Blog

'Packed with contemporary detail and just enough real science to validate it . . . so close to convincing that even cynical readers may be unnerved' – BookTrust

'Tingling with tension, supercharged and fast paced, there won't be a second to lose until the last page has turned . . .' – *Lancashire Evening Post*

Books by Alex Scarrow from Macmillan

Remade

Reborn

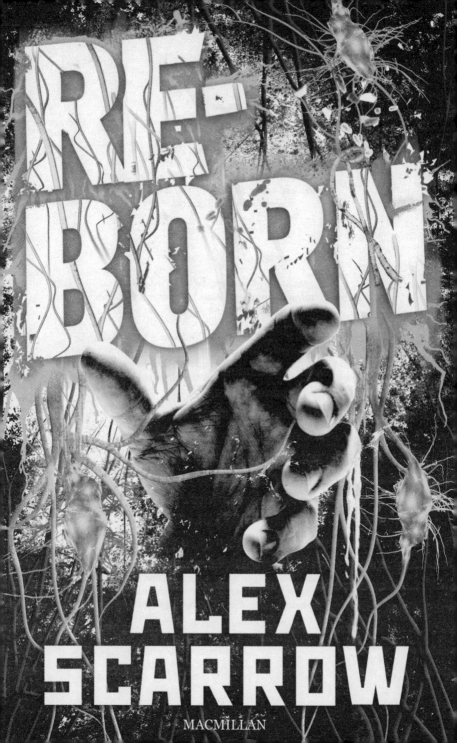

RE-BORN

ALEX SCARROW

MACMILLAN

First published 2017 by Macmillan Children's Books
an imprint of Pan Macmillan
20 New Wharf Road, London N1 9RR
Associated companies throughout the world
www.panmacmillan.com

ISBN 978-1-5098-1122-9

1 3 5 7 9 8 6 4 2

A CIP catalogue record for this book is available from
the British Library.

Printed and bound by CPI Group (UK) Ltd, Croydon CR0 4YY

To Debbie,
my partner in slime.
(And who helps me turn my bad wurdz good.)

CHAPTER 1

Two Years Ago

Tom Friedmann stared out through the smoked glass of the foyer at a scene of which he couldn't make sense. The sky was spilling flakes like Thanksgiving-parade ticker tape. It vaguely reminded him of the billowing clouds of office stationery that had fluttered down over Manhattan after the first American Airlines impact all those years ago. These were smaller, though, like those big fluffy snowflakes you know are going to settle and know *damn* well are going to cause merry havoc with your travel plans.

Channelled down by the tall glass-and-chrome office blocks all along Wall Street, the flakes fluttered in clouds that at a distance looked like a descending bank of fog.

And people were dropping. Dying.

Not immediately . . . not gas-attack immediately. He'd seen that at work in the Middle East. The ghastly sight of civilians dropping in waves. No mess, no fuss, just death by chemical agent. But, Jesus, this was happening almost as quickly.

Too fast for nature, surely?

Tom watched a cop on the other side of the road. A minute ago he'd been waving pedestrians inside into various corporate foyers. Now he was on his knees, swaying like a drunkard and staring at the glistening skin of his hands.

'Tom, there's no answer!'

He turned. Elaine Garcia – she was holding his phone up at him. She'd been trying to reach her mother.

'Give it to me!' he demanded.

He took it off her.

'Tom, what's happening?'

He ignored her as he swiped through his contacts: half a dozen numbers in a quick-retrieve list. The first number started with the White House prefix. It was engaged.

The second number was his son's mobile. It rang twice before Leon picked up.

'You OK, Dad?'

'That you, Leon?' He sounded different. Not Leon's usual lazy for-parents-only drawl, the voice version of an eye-roll.

'Dad, what's goin—'

'It's *here*, Leo. It's right here in the city!'

'What? In . . . in New York?'

'Yes! There are people dying in the goddamn street!'

The line rustled and crackled with telecoms overload. He wondered how many people were saturating the network with panic calls right now.

'Dad, where are you? Are you safe?'

'Leo, listen to me! Son! Listen! This thing is airborne! You've got to stay inside! Stay at home! Tape up your windows and doors, and STAY INSIDE!'

'But we're on a train, Dad! You said get out of London. You told us to—'

Tom winced. He *had* said that. That had been his advice exactly. *Get away from London.* Outside in the street a police car with a wailing siren had pulled up. The fallen cop's colleagues were getting out to help him. Tom banged his fist on the glass to warn them to stay in their squad car, but with the noise outside, the siren, people's screams . . . his banging fist was lost in all of that.

'I know. Shit . . . shit. Are you close to Mom's family?' He tried to remember where Jennifer's parents lived. A small chocolate-box village just outside a city called . . . he remembered.

'Are you near to Norwich?'

'I don't know . . . Train's about—' The rest of what Leon was saying was gone amid crackling.

'OK, soon as you get there, you tell Mom, you tell Mom's parents they've gotta stay inside. Do you understand me? Stay inside! Close the windows. Don't go out again!'

The cops outside were now looking up at the artificial snow, batting the flakes away from their faces. The infected officer had flopped over on to his side, the good hand clawing at the other glistening, reddening one.

'Oh God, Tom!' cried Elaine as they watched.

The man pulled some flesh away from his hand. It came off far too easily, like casserole beef from a T-bone. Blood streamed down his forearm; a tendon hung from the bones of his hand in a tired, swinging loop.

Jesus Christ!

A few metres further down the street, where a woman had collapsed earlier, the process seemed far more advanced. Under the woman's now stained clothes, her previously bulky frame had reduced and dark trickles of liquid seemed to be fanning out around her.

The cop on the ground was flailing his dissolving hand around, screaming for help from his colleagues. There were other people outside converging on the squad car. Other people infected like him, shambling towards the cops in a state of shock, like toddlers bow-mouthed and mewling for their mothers. They stared bewildered and frightened at their hands, their arms, swiping at glistening, erupting blisters, pleading for help.

The cops seemed to be ignoring the light fluttering 'snowfall' as if that was much further down the list of things to note. They backed away from the screaming mass of infected people approaching, barking commands at them all to stay well back.

Jesus . . . it's like a frikkin zombie movie.

A gun came out. A single shot went up into the air. Tom could see by the wide-eyed look from the young cop standing over his stricken colleague that the next shot was going to be aimed. He was aware Leon was still on the end of a crackling line. Waiting for advice. For help.

'Listen to me . . . Listen . . . This thing's in the air. You can SEE it. Like flakes. It's fast! It's killing people everywhere . . . touching their skin, then they're dying . . . melting . . .'

The signal was breaking up badly.

'Don't let it TOUCH you . . . the flakes! Don't let them near you!'

He heard his son reply. Something chewed up and spat out by the failing signal.

'I love you, son!' he shouted into the phone, as if that might make a difference. 'I love you, both you and Grace! God, I wish I was with you—'

Someone barged into him. Nearly knocking the phone out of his hand. A guy in a grey suit and a white office shirt damp with sweat. He tried to snatch the phone from Tom's hand.

'Hey! Get out of my goddamn way!'

Tom shoved the man backwards into the smoked-glass window. It rattled and boomed, but didn't crack.

'You got a signal there?! I gotta make a call!'

'Get someone else's phone!' Tom snapped. The man backed off and went in search of someone else on a phone. Tom put the cell back to his ear. 'Leon! You still there?'

Just a crackle and hissing.

'Leon! LEON!'

He was gone.

Elaine was staring at him as he disconnected the call and slid the phone back into his jacket pocket. 'Tom . . . ?'

Outside, the cops were now reacting to the flakes that had landed on them. One was staring intently at his own hand like some hokey carnival palm reader; the other was rubbing the bridge of his nose with the back of a hairy forearm.

'Tom?' she bleated again, more insistently this time.

'*What?!*'

'What are we going to do?'

5

He shook his head. Furious with himself. He'd had advance warning. Twenty-four hours ago the president had been advised to mobilize FEMA resources. He'd been ahead of the herd . . . just. And yet he'd failed to capitalize on it, failed to take steps, and here he was stuck in the reception of some Wall Street reprographics company, watching people die all around him.

He stared out of the window. The downfall of flakes seemed to be lessening, or perhaps the ever-present 'Manhattan Mistral', funnelled between the tall buildings, was pushing the cloud of particles further down the street. The two policemen who'd turned up in the squad car were beginning to falter. One had dropped down to sit heavily on the kerb, like a late-night reveller trying to figure out how he was going to get home. Most of the other people around were in the same state, slumped to their haunches, dizzily trying to comprehend what was happening to them.

Tom reached for the swing door that led on to the pavement.

'What the hell are you *doing*?' cried Elaine. Her perfectly threaded brows were arched in horror.

He nodded at the police car parked on the far side. 'I'm going.'

'We can't go out there!'

'I'm going. You can come with or you can stay. Up to you.'

She shook her head frantically.

Act quickly or don't act at all, MonkeyNuts.

'I'm going, then,' he said firmly.

'You can't leave me!' she cried, reaching out to grab his arm. 'Please! You can't—'

He shook her off roughly. 'You're a grown-up, Elaine. You'll have to figure something else out.' He pushed the door open, pulled his jacket over his head and hurried across the pavement and into the late afternoon sunlight now striping the ground with shades of salmon pink and shadowy lavender, like vast Rothko-esque hard-edged brushstrokes. Behind him he could hear Elaine banging on the glass and howling after him.

He approached the younger cop sitting on the kerb.

'Officer?'

The cop looked up at him and blinked back the sun in his eyes.

'Keys?' said Tom. 'Your car keys? Are they in the ignition?'

The cop grinned, vacant and childlike, at him. 'Hey, Steve? That you, man?'

He's gone. He's out of it.

Tom looked past him. The driver's side door was wide open. The blue lights were still rotating. Which presumably meant the keys were there. 'Never mind.'

He quickly hopped in and pulled the door closed, found the keys dangling from the side of the steering column and turned them. He shot one more glance back at Elaine, standing beyond the smoky-coloured glass, banging her fists on the window for him to come back to rescue her.

She's not your responsibility, Tom. Leon and Grace. OK? Just Leon and Grace. That's it.

CHAPTER 2

I get it, Dad. I get it. I'm not a complete moron.

You're dead.

I realize now that you're just a figment of my imagination. A therapy tool. A way for me to confront my issues and set them out on the pages of a journal instead of leaving them to stew inside my head. You're a cure for my migraines, a placebo.

So why the hell am I keeping this journal going? I suppose part of me still hopes you'll end up reading it and see that I did OK. That I'm not some useless waste-of-space slacker. That I actually managed to last this long.

Longer than you, probably.

I suppose a part of me kind of hopes you're watching me somewhere, a ghost looking over my shoulder as I write this.

So, yeah, Dad . . . Surprise! I survived! And if you're a ghost reading this, I guess you want to know how I'm doing, huh?

Well . . . life's been better. We're still in Norwich, but we moved from the apartment block near the football ground to a flat above a supermarket.

Life is all about economy of energy use: calories spent getting calories in. Until we moved we had to make tough calorie choices every day. Now there's a ton of tinned food just two floors below us. We're sitting on top of our own larder. Plus it means me and Freya don't even have to step outside. Which is a frikkin relief considering how cold it is out there.

Last winter we got completely snowed in. For months. Then there was 'summer', which was cold, grey, wet and not very long. Then another winter again – same damn thing. Real New York-style; snow piled up in dunes.

And the virus? We've not seen a single sign of it. Anywhere. Not for over a year now. I don't know if this cold weather is linked to that somehow. Maybe it is. Maybe without seven billion humans churning crap into the atmosphere, global warming did a sudden massive U-turn. But, linked or not, it is what it is. I think the freezing cold has killed that thing off, and this is the aftermath.

This is our challenge now . . . surviving an Ice Age.

'Leon? Look!' Freya was pointing.

He lowered his scarf and puffed out a thick plume of steamy air. 'Yeah, I see it.'

They were standing on the rooftop of a shopping mall on the west side of the city. A mall called Chappelfields. Just like any other, with the same usual-suspect chain stores, the same useful and useless things to be found inside.

Freya was pointing to the left of a snow-covered outdoor market, where a faint red light was blinking at the top of a cluster of masts and satellite dishes. On a clear day with the sun shining and everything glinting, they probably would have missed it, but today the thick grey clouds overhead cast the city in a pall of twilight shadow.

'Someone's still got power,' said Leon.

'Let's not get too hopeful about it yet.'

One night last winter, they'd spotted a light on the other side of the city. The next day they'd trudged across to find out what it was. A hummock of snow had slid off the slanted surface of a bank of rooftop solar panels, and after a few days of getting some light a neon sign had eventually blinked back to life and lit up, promising one and all that they could have hours of family fun at *Lazer Warz*.

This blinking red light was closer. Close enough to bother taking a quick look.

'Worth our while?'

Freya shrugged. 'Something on telly you need to hurry back for?'

Leon smiled. 'You OK to take a detour for it?'

She shifted her weight and leaned on her stick, one of those walkers with a rubber grip-handle at the top, and four stumpy legs at the bottom.

She nodded. 'My hips are aching like hell. But I can do it. Let's have a look.'

They stood outside the glass-fronted building and stared up at the cluster of aerials and satellite dishes at the top. Leon looked at the sign perched on the side of the building.

BBC. The three letters were each wearing a tall bonnet of snow.

'BBC Norfolk,' said Freya. 'TV and Radio Centre.'

He turned to her. 'This is where the BBC lives . . . *lived*?'

'Not *all* of it. Obviously. It's just a regional building. BBC Norfolk.'

'Ah, right.'

Leon reached into his rucksack and pulled out a mallet and chisel, their standard breaking-and-entering kit. He looked up. The glass frontage was three storeys high, divided into a grid of two-metre panels, supported by metal spars. Smashing the one directly in front of him wasn't going to result in a glass cascade. He'd made that mistake before and nearly been decapitated by an avalanche of large, jagged shards.

'Ready?'

Freya took a few shuffled steps backwards. 'Ready.'

He pulled his scarf up to cover his face right up to the bridge of his nose, placed the chisel firmly against the glass, narrowed his eyes and then swung the hammer hard. The glass, brittle from the cold, shattered easily and clattered noisily inwards, leaving an empty frame in the front of the tall building, like a gap-toothed smile.

They waited until the last loose shard had wobbled and dropped to the ground, then stepped inside into another dimly lit cavernous interior.

Leon led the way into the large atrium. There was an indoor-outdoor cafe to their right, all glass-top tables, cushy chairs and large potted plants that might once have been lush temperate-weather ferns but which were now twig skeletons. At the back of the atrium was a large municipal library. A stairway led up to a balcony that overlooked the large interior and, to the left, they saw an entrance to the main BBC floor space.

They took the stairs up in silence, their boots scraping and tapping noisily, listening hopefully for the sound of someone challenging them. They arrived in front of the main entrance. A turnstile blocked their way, an access-card slot beside it, waiting patiently for an employee pass to be inserted. Leon swung his leg and hopped over it easily, then turned and offered his hands to Freya to help her.

'I thought the BBC was all about ease of bloody access for all,' she grunted as she parked her bum on top of the turnstile, passed Leon her walking stick then swung her stronger leg over. She had to lift her other leg across, and gritted her teeth as a dull pain stabbed at her hip.

The inside was just as Leon had expected: an open-plan office full of desks, chairs, shoulder-high cubicle partitions and pot plants that had died long ago. One side was the internal glass wall that looked out upon the atrium and the cafe below. The other side was punctuated with framed posters featuring the grinning faces of the station's local newsreaders and celebrities.

'There's no sign of any power here,' said Freya. The computer monitors and ceiling lights were all off. They were standing in the gloomy pall of waning third-hand daylight. 'Another stupid wild-goose chase, by the look of it.' She sighed.

Leon nodded. With the worst of this second winter gone and the weather warming up a fraction, it was probably the result of another solar panel being exposed by a slide of snow.

'Might as well see if there's anything useful we can grab while we're here.'

They picked their way past workstations, each abandoned cubicle telling its own story of hasty departure. There were no bodies here. Everyone must have abandoned their posts quickly, but tell-tale signs of the last thing they were doing before they left were strewn around: the fossilized remains of food in wrappers, Post-it notes stuck on screens as reminders for workers long gone.

Leon picked up a Rubik's Cube from a desk and tucked it into his backpack. Something to while away the endless hours they had to spare. Then they climbed an emergency stairwell to the next floor and pushed the door open.

'And this is where all the television magic happens,' said Freya like a tour guide.

They were looking at a newsroom: a news desk and two empty anchor's chairs in the same corporate BBC crimson colour. Three automated cameras stood in a semicircle and stared with blind cyclops eyes at the abandoned desk.

Freya wandered over to the desk and slumped down into one of the chairs. She grabbed at the papers spread out across the top and shuffled them together in both hands, tapping them down solemnly.

'Tonight on *Freya Hart at Six*, we discuss the shocking number of dog owners who refuse to pick up the mess left behind by their feckless canine companions.'

Leon snorted as he sat down on the chair beside hers.

'Seriously . . . *that's* what used to pass for news around here. That and Ofsted school reports,' said Freya.

Leon grabbed some loose sheets of paper and gazed at the glinting lenses of the three lifeless cameras. 'It's another quiet news day here in Norfolk,' he uttered. 'There's snow forecast for the weekend. More snow and yet more sn—'

He stopped and stared at the headlines printed on the paper: a short list of bullet-point items, some crossed through with a red pen, others with scrawled margin-note alterations, loops and arrows reordering the list – on-the-hoof editing.

- *Government declares Martial Law from 9 p.m. tonight.*
- *All transport links: railways, roads, airports have been closed.*
- *Police forces issued with firearms – have full authority to use them.*
- *Russia suspected of using tactical nuclear warheads on several infected cities.*
- *Australia, Japan, Hong Kong, Sri Lanka announce first confirmed cases of infection.*

Freya was reading the same list in her gloved hands. She looked at him. 'It really got everywhere on the planet, didn't it?'

'It was floating around in the air. I guess it must have.' Leon looked at the handwritten postscript at the bottom. He read it out loud. 'This will be our final television transmission. For further news updates please tune into the BBC emergency broadcast signal, which is using Radio Four's longwave preset, one-nine-eight.'

'At least they didn't sign off with the cheesy "May God have mercy on our souls" thing,' said Freya.

It may not have been written down, but perhaps they did, thought Leon. He could imagine there'd be that temptation for an anchorman or woman, a chance to go off-script and say something from the heart.

A goodbye.

A good luck.

'Me, Mum and Grace must have still been on the train when they broadcast this.'

Freya turned to look at him. She'd heard Leon's escape story. And she'd told him *her* story. Neither of them needed to dwell on those now. Least of all Leon. Grace was gone. His mum was long gone. So were Freya's parents.

She pushed the chair back on its castors. 'Come on – let's go. There's nothing for us here.'

Leon nodded. He let the papers scatter from his hands on to the desk.

They got up and headed towards the stairwell door. The light from outside was waning fast, and if they wanted to get back home before it was pitch black, they needed to leave soon. Not that the darkness itself was anything to be concerned about. They had torches and knew the way they'd come. And there was nothing out there *now* – no *snarks* any more, no monsters – and no one else as far as they knew. It was just going to get much colder once that pitiful sun was gone from the tumbling grey sky. Reason enough to hurry home.

As Freya pushed the stairwell door open, Leon stopped her. 'Wait!'

'What?'

'Over there. I saw something . . .'

She looked to her right. There was a passageway lined with more framed local celebrity posters, and at the end a thick acoustically insulated door stood ajar. Above it an ON AIR sign hung, dark and lifeless.

A weak, blinking, amber-coloured spot of light reflected on the small glass window.

'There's a light on in there,' said Leon. He headed down the passageway, pulled the door open and peered inside. He was looking at a small room without any windows. It was almost completely dark, but faintly illuminated by one small flashing orange light on a rack of equipment. He reached into his backpack, pulled out a torch and snapped it on.

'Radio studio,' said Freya.

The walls were lined with a corded grey carpet that sucked the life from her voice. The room was split in two by a partition and another door. Through thick glass Leon could see a recording booth, several microphones hanging in anti-vibration cradles, a couple of chairs and a desk.

They were standing in the control room. Leon stepped towards the rack of equipment and the one blinking orange light: a small, square button, one in a row that remained resolutely dark and disinterested in their insistent, winking sibling.

'AUX,' said Leon, reading the three dark letters in the middle of it.

Freya shrugged. 'You might as well.'

'Might as well what?'

'Press it. It's not like it's going to blow the world up or anything.'

Leon pulled his glove off and gently rested the tip of his index finger against the button. He felt just the slightest sensation of warmth coming from it, heat generated by a tiny blinking LED that steadfastly refused to give in and join the others.

For a moment he was reluctant to push. Perhaps it would flick off whatever system was still running here on a trickle of power. Like switching off life support. Putting something out of its misery.

Freya huffed impatiently, reached out and pushed down on his finger.

The light behind the button blinked from amber to green and speakers either side of the control room's mixing desk suddenly began to hiss and crackle softly.

'. . . *are not alone. I repeat you are NOT alone. Help is coming. Help is on its way* . . .'

CHAPTER 3

Two Years Ago

'For Chrissakes, hurry up!'

Tom Friedmann stared out of the windscreen of the 'borrowed' squad car as civilization fragmented before his eyes into pockets of caveman anarchy. He was parked up on the kerb beside the veterans memorial in Battery Park, which was perched at the very bottom tip of Manhattan. How many times had he snuck out here from work for a quiet lunch, watching the ferries come and go from Pier A to Liberty Island laden with selfie-taking tourists?

Battery Park was one of the few slices of tranquillity in the city that never, *ever*, slept.

The call finally connected. 'Private line,' answered a harried-sounding female voice.

'Patty, it's Tom Friedmann. Where the hell is it? I've been sitting here like an idiot for half an hour!'

'It's coming, Mr Friedmann. It's on its way, I promise!'

She was shouting over the noise of a roaring engine. He could hear a dozen other voices, raised to be heard over the *thud-thud-thud* of rotors and an engine gathering momentum to take off.

Bullshit. She's stonewalling you.

The squad car was being jostled and bumped by the

crowds streaming past. A greasy palm thumped against the driver-side window. There was a scuffle going on right outside.

'Is he right there with you? Let me speak to him!'

'He's busy on another call, sir.'

'Dammit, Patty, give the goddamn phone to him!'

The noise over the phone was suddenly muted. Her hand was over the mouthpiece. He could hear her muffled voice. A moment later, that deafening whine of the helicopter's engine winding up for lift-off.

'Tom?' Doug was on the phone now. Before Tom could answer, he spoke. No time for politeness or pleasantries. 'Tom! There's one on its way. Just sit tight, *amigo*, OK?'

'Dougie, for Chrissakes! It's beginning to fall apart over here!'

'We'll get you out of there. That's a promise!' The call disconnected. Not even a goodbye.

Tom cursed and tossed the phone on to the passenger seat. He hadn't even asked if he was still parked up and waiting in the same place.

And . . . amigo. He said amigo.

There's no goddamn helicopter coming for you . . . amigo.

Tom looked out of the window at the people streaming past him, all heading for the ferry piers ahead. The bastard was looking after himself, clutching his golden Willy Wonka ticket and screw their old 'brothers in arms' mantra. He was sorted and that was just fine.

He smacked the dashboard with his fist. And again. And again.

Stay calm. You've just got to start working on a plan B.

For a moment he gazed at the broken skin of his knuckles.

Ferries.

That's where this surging crowd was headed. He opened the door, got out and pushed his way into the stream of panicking people.

Looking back over his shoulder, all he could see were faces contorted and stretched, ugly with fear, what seemed like every last person in Manhattan hurrying southwards to catch the last ferry out of here. The bridges on both sides were now blocked by national guardsmen. The subway and the trains were locked down. The last couple of ferries were the only way out – that, or a cold swim in the Atlantic.

You're going to get yourself on one of those ferries, Tom. You're going to do it because you HAVE TO.

He shouldered his way into the crowd, barging and pulling his way forward through them.

'Hey!' He felt someone tugging roughly at his upper arm.

He spun round and thrust the heel of his hand into the bridge of someone's nose. He felt cartilage crack under the impact and the figure dropped down out of sight amid a sea of legs.

That's how it's going to be: not survival of the fittest – survival of the shittiest.

He turned and carried on through the crowd until he'd

cleared the small park and could see the low squat green roof and memorial clock tower of Pier A's ticket building, and beyond that the canary-yellow double-decker hull of a water taxi. Every square centimetre of its surface seemed to be covered with people, standing, sitting, clinging and crying. The pier itself was so crowded that every now and then the water of the Hudson spouted a plume of freezing foam as someone was knocked over the side and splashed in.

He could see a thin line of camouflage helmets trying to control the flow at the end of the pier. Trying to prevent the boat from being swamped.

It was then that he heard it. The *thwup-thwup* of rotor blades approaching from the south.

The sky over New York was buzzing with helicopters lifting the lucky few from the top floors of skyscrapers, circling and hovering like bees disturbed by a beekeeper. But this one appeared to be making a hasty approach towards Battery Park.

Tom allowed himself a flicker of hope. Maybe Doug was actually delivering on his promise. He began to barge his way out of the flow of the crowd, untangling himself at last and standing in the open.

The helicopter was swooping low and fast across the Hudson. It finally began to slow down as it approached the southern tip of the park.

That's got to be my ride.

Tom felt a fleeting moment of shame for doubting Doug's word. He broke into a trot as he dodged and weaved around others heading towards the pier, like a salmon swimming against the current.

The helicopter began to descend as it approached the railings of the park, its downdraft kicking up a mist of freezing saltwater droplets into the air. Fifty metres away now, Tom could feel them prickling his face.

That IS for me, he told himself.

It finally swung over land, stirring up a cloud of autumn leaves, twigs and dirt from the park's orchard and flower gardens. People around him began to stop and look up hopefully as it hovered twenty metres up, hesitantly, cautiously descending.

Tom felt his face stinging from the debris being whipped up. He narrowed his eyes as he waved both arms frantically above his head. He could see half a dozen marines crouched in the open door of the cabin, waiting to jump out.

The helicopter descended the last few dozen feet, gently setting down on its skids. The soldiers spilled through the open door, spread out into a half-circle perimeter and dropped to their knees, guns raised. Tom hurried forward still waving his arms.

Dozens of other people had heard the roar of the arriving helicopter too – now they stopped, turned and edged optimistically towards it. A woman just ahead of him, her scarlet-coloured designer high heels clutched tightly in one hand, hurried towards the nearest of the soldiers. He couldn't hear their voices over the roar of the engine and the whipping of the rotors, but it was clear she was getting a firm *NO*; she wasn't going to be let on. He was shaking his head and shouting something at her. But she wasn't having it, trying to sidestep round him. He grabbed one of her arms and shoved her roughly backwards so that she stumbled and fell just in front of Tom.

Tom stepped around her and cupped his hands as he approached the soldier.

'THIS IS FOR ME!' he bellowed.

The soldier cocked his head and cupped one ear.

'I SAID . . . *I THINK THIS IS FOR ME!*' yelled Tom. He started to fumble inside his jacket.

'WHAT'S. YOUR. NAME?' The soldier barked each word separately.

'TOM . . . FRIEDMANN!'

He nodded at that. Right name. A good start. 'YOU. GOTTA. SHOW. ME. SOME. ID, SIR!'

Tom was already working on that. He pulled out his wallet and opened it carefully to get out his driving licence. The wind whipped out the loose receipts inside, almost snatching the plastic licence along with them.

'HERE!' he shouted, holding the card at arm's length. The soldier quickly scanned the embossed name and checked that the photo matched.

'YUP!' Good enough for him. He seemed keen to call this a successful result and get back up in the air once more. 'OK, GET IN QUICKLY, SIR!'

Tom hurried past him towards the helicopter, the engine beginning to rise in pitch to a metallic scream, getting ready to lift off again. As he grasped the hand held out to him, he heard shots being fired and looked back over his shoulder. The soldiers were shooting warning shots overhead, close enough to have the nearest people ducking down and flinching at the sound, but, beyond them, he could see something far more worrying . . .

Rolling across the small park, over the low round fortifications of the battery fort, across the flower gardens, through the trees, past the visitors centre . . . slowly heading towards them was a billowing cloud of fluffy snowflakes. The same pale flecks he'd seen earlier, the ones that seemed to stick and hang on to anything in sight like polystyrene beanbag balls.

That's it. *This . . . thing.*

The cloud of flakes now covered the pier and everyone crammed on it, the ticket house, the water taxi. It swept towards the helicopter like a fog bank. The blast from the helicopter's rotors began to stir the leading edge of the cloud flakes up into two frenzied eddying spirals that mirrored each other like the spurs of a Texas longhorn. Tom was yanked roughly up into the helicopter's cabin, slammed into a seat and hastily strapped in. His view of what was going on outside was obscured as the soldiers on the ground clambered in quickly after him. He felt the helicopter pitch forward and begin to rise.

It turned and banked just a few dozen metres up, the pilot clearly keen to put horizontal distance above vertical safety, and Tom caught a fleeting glimpse of the woman with her expensive red shoes brushing frantically at the sticky particles on her arm.

CHAPTER 4

Leon stared at the page of printer paper and read the scribbled transcription once again.

Don't give up. Help is coming. Help is on its way. This message is aimed specifically at survivors in the United Kingdom. If you are able to travel, make your way to the city of Southampton by the first of September. Civilian and navy vessels will be waiting for you. Medical help and emergency food supplies will be available there. Those requesting evacuation will be assessed. The ships will be there for two weeks only, leaving on the fourteenth of September.

Freya was stirring stew in its tin over the butane burner. 'Assessed? For what? Good behaviour? Fashion awareness? Good taste?'

He sighed. 'Infection.'

'Infection? Anyone who's infected is surely just bones and rags now. They must be aware of that.'

He looked up from the sheet of paper as Freya pulled herself up on to her feet.

'Hey. Let me get—'

She batted him away with one hand and made her way across to a cupboard to get their bowls. He watched her clumsy movement, the wincing on her face as she pressed a hand to her left hip.

He wondered if they meant assessment for *fitness*. Only the young and fully healthy. The brutal filtering of people. No room for those who couldn't keep up.

The message they'd heard on the radio was word for word what had been scribbled down on this sheet of paper. Nothing more. Just an endless, repeating, pre-recorded loop. Someone else had made a visit to the BBC studio before them, heard the same message and thought to write it down and leave it behind on the console in case whatever was trickle-feeding the studio power finally ran out.

Someone thoughtful.

Someone *else*.

'Here,' Freya said, handing him a bowl and a spoon. She settled down on an armchair, snaked her feet back into the open mouth of the sleeping bag and worked it up her legs to her knees.

'Thanks.'

'So now we know for sure there *are* others,' she said, smiling. 'I knew there had to be. I bloody well knew it.'

'With ships . . . and meds and supplies.' Leon dipped his spoon into the can, gave it a quick stir then scooped out several spoonfuls of the thick broth into his bowl. 'An organized relief effort. Jeez . . . about time.'

'That announcer on the radio sounded American to me.'

Leon nodded. 'Maybe they managed to ride it out over there. Maybe they had a contingency plan.'

'Unlike our useless government over here.' She helped herself to the stew in the can. 'And then there's the question of who wrote *this*,' she added, nodding at the piece of paper lying on the floor between them.

Leon looked down at the note. He wondered when someone had last poked their head into the studio. A few weeks ago? A few months? A year ago? Two? There was no way of knowing how old the note was. It could have been scribbled down an hour before they arrived, or a few days after the outbreak.

'September the first. There's no year with that date, Freya. This could be old, *old* news.'

'Or it could be *current* news. It's *still broadcasting*.'

He sighed. 'It could be the same situation as the BBC place . . . some old generator running on fumes somewhere, beaming out a message that isn't, you know, *current* any more.'

Freya tested the heat of the stew cautiously with her finger. Her lips were permanently numb, no sensation from them whatsoever. She could burn her lips and not even know it.

Another wonderful symptom of her encroaching sclerosis.

'Leon, that's what I like about you . . .' She huffed.

'What?'

'The eternal optimist.'

'Huh?' He looked up, confused.

'Sarcasm,' she clarified. 'You're definitely the glass-half-empty type, aren't you?'

He was going to reply that he just didn't want them to raise their hopes. They'd been camping out in this small apartment for about fourteen months now, watching one

27

winter come and go and another one come along straight behind it. They were slowly eating their way along the supermarket shelves below, creating gaps that were getting bigger, making it easier and easier for them to figure out how much longer the rest of those tins were going to keep them going.

Another two years. Maybe three.

Then what? A move to another place above another supermarket . . . to exist in bleak isolation, watching snow cover the rooftops in the winter and nettles cover the streets in the summer. Not living, not really – just existing, becoming urban wildlife.

A pair of lonely scavengers.

He pressed a smile into service to match up with the hopeful look on Freya's face. 'On the other hand, you might be right.'

She was always upbeat, always optimistic . . . stronger – mentally *far* stronger than he was. He wondered if he'd even be alive right now if it wasn't for her.

Probably not.

'We can't stay hiding here forever, Leon.' She chewed her food carefully, slowly, then finally she spoke again. 'There's nothing to hide from, anyway. It's all gone. There's nothing out there. Literally.'

'We're going to run out of butane before we run out of food. And what if there's another winter like this one again next year? And the next? If this is how the climate's going to be from now on, one day we're going to freeze to death.'

'You're suggesting we act on this?' he asked, tapping the

28

sheet of paper on the floor. 'You want to trek all the way up to Southampton?'

'*Down*, actually. It's south, not north. But . . . yes.'

'What if it's nothing? What if whoever recorded that message never even shows up? What if they died two years ago?'

'And what if it's *something*? What if we sit here like a pair of muppets and they do come and we could have been rescued if we'd bothered to get off our arses and go see?'

He nodded. Somehow, dying because of *not* doing something seemed worse than dying because of doing something. She had a point.

'And, apart from the cold, what's out there? The virus?' She hunched her shoulders. 'Unless the virus is tucked up somewhere with a camping heater and a sleeping bag, I'd say it's frozen. Properly dead and gone.'

He looked again at the scribbled page. 'September . . . that's, what, six months from now?'

She nodded. 'We could wait out here for a few more weeks. Wait for the snow and the roads to clear . . . Hey, we might even find a car that's still working.'

'How far away is Southampton?'

'I dunno . . . gimme a sec and I'll check on Google.' She laughed at her own amazing wit.

He looked down at his food and stirred the congealing gravy. Another couple of minutes and it was going to have a skin. He heard the chair creak and her sleeping bag rustle as she leaned forward.

She placed a hand tenderly on his. 'Do you want to go

home, Leon? Back to America?'

Home. Home had once been New York. It certainly hadn't been London, not even with Mum and Grace trying their hardest to make a new start.

But they're gone, MonkeyNuts. Very . . . very . . . gone.

'Maybe your dad's still alive over there somewhere?' She squeezed his hand. 'Maybe I'll even get to meet him?'

He snorted. 'My dad's a selfish pr . . .'

Is? Or was?

'He sounds like a total kick-ass from what you've told me about him.'

'You've got that about *half* right.'

CHAPTER 5

Two Years Ago

Tom Friedmann watched the grey Atlantic skimming beneath them, the darker outline of the New Jersey coastline slipping out of frame from the helicopter's small porthole window.

Doug had delivered on his promise. No man left behind.

Despite what he'd begun to feel in recent years about his old squad buddy – that he was a ruthless user and discarder of people, a manipulator, a Washington shark through and through, quite probably a corrupt one too – if the guy made a promise, the guy damn well kept it.

He looked around at the soldiers he was sharing the helicopter's cramped cabin with: five men, boys, really, not much older than Leon. And they all seemed terrified. The only things that kept them from looking like a bunch of spooked-out frat boys were their uniform and their quiet, firm belief that blindly obeying orders was going to save their lives.

Jesus Christ.

He checked his phone. No signal, of course.

What am I doing?

Why the hell am I here?

He'd panicked. He'd called Doug for a save-my-ass favour. Now here he was. But, really, he needed to be on a plane, one heading east to England. To his kids.

Jesus. He closed his eyes.

He was clutching at straws of hope here. That maybe the infection wasn't as advanced in the UK as it had been here. Maybe Jenny had managed to get the kids to her parents' house safely. That would be a good place for them to lie low – in the countryside, out on its own on that back road. They kept a larder full of canned goods there. He was pretty sure they had a clean freshwater stream at the end of their garden. Her dad had an old vintage shotgun that he potted clay pigeons with. It was fantastically inaccurate, but it made a big scary bang. Her mother had a sharp-edged tongue that could cut a man at ten paces. They'd be far better sitting tight there than stuck in the middle of London.

He was clutching his straws very tightly.

Also . . . so maybe this outbreak dies out quickly too.

His knowledge of epidemiology came from one page of a FEMA pamphlet and a bunch of Netflix box sets, but one thing he knew *wasn't* movie-script BS was that a fast-acting virus was its own worst enemy. Killing your host wasn't a smart move. Whatever this was, wherever it had come from, it was going to be history within weeks or months. Surely.

And then, Tom, old son, there'll be the goddamn aftermath.

Millions dead. Hundreds of millions, perhaps even billions.

Collapsed infrastructure. Supply networks compro-

mised. Unstable government systems. Some countries will cope with this far better than others. Mostly the Third World nations. Rural ones. China for example. Maybe even Russia too.

There'll be chaos. Instability. Opportunistic land and resource grabs.

Shit. And where the hell does that take us all? Sabre-rattling, toe-to-toe posturing.

Where does that end up? Nukes.

Tom opened his eyes again and realized his mind was racing too far ahead. All those kinds of worries were for presidents and cabinets in a couple of months' time, and God help them if they made the wrong decisions.

His worries were immediate: his two kids and his ex-wife stuck in the middle of the Norfolk countryside . . . hopefully.

CHAPTER 6

Leon stared at the driveway, flanked on either side by small granite pillars topped with a pair of wind-worn and weathered stone elephants. Waist-high brambles sprouted from the driveway in confident clumps, and either side of the long driveway the overgrown lawn poked through the melting snow.

'This is it . . . I remember these old pillars and the stone elephants.'

'Your grandparents rich or something?'

He shrugged. 'I dunno. I guess, kind of.'

At the end of the driveway he could see the white walls, dark wooden beams and the thatched roof of his grandparents' home. He remembered his last visit, four years ago. He'd been thirteen, Grace a precocious nine, and Mum and Dad had still seemed fine with each other then.

'Well? We going in?' asked Freya.

Leon nodded. He put the Ford Transit into first gear and gently rolled forward up the driveway, flattening the sporadic and over-confident bramble stalks with a sense of satisfaction.

The driveway's not yours yet.

To the right was the pond, still mostly frozen over, a moss-flecked statue of Cupid beside it, worn hands placed strategically for modesty. To the left stretched a high mesh surrounding a snow-covered tennis court.

He recalled playing tennis on there with Grandma. She, in her early eighties and with bad knees, had thrashed him easily in a one-set match. He remembered he'd hurled his tennis racket down in a fit of petulant unsportsmanlike rage and had stormed off, leaving Grandma all alone, calling after him to come back so she could show him how to stop slicing the tennis balls right out of the court.

Leon winced at the memory.

Just one among many things he wished he could go back in time and redo. Their last visit had been one fortnight-long sulk for him. He'd missed his mates, missed having access to any wifi (all his grandparents had was one of those ancient dial-up modems) and he'd felt utterly overshadowed by Grace who'd been on a total charm offensive: all best behaviour and beaming smiles for Grandma and Grandad.

His grandparents had been gracious, patient and understanding with him, and he'd been a total tool, hinting unsubtly that he preferred his dad's parents.

'Do you think anyone's home?'

Leon couldn't see any woodsmoke coming out of the chimney. In all likelihood they weren't home, and, if they were, the chances were that they'd be nothing but bones, rags, false hips and dentures.

It had been his idea to call in on their way south. Something he'd wanted to do. It was a few winding miles off the road they were on anyway, too temptingly close to not at least look in. Though he was beginning to wish he hadn't chosen the detour now. The place looked bleak and lifeless, the mature oak trees like looming skeletons.

He pulled up outside the front door and beeped the horn hopefully.

'Leon? You know they're most likely . . . ?'

'I know.' He opened his door and stepped down into wet, mushy snow. Freya climbed out her side and came round the front. She stumbled and cursed.

'You OK?'

'Frikkin tripped on something.' She kicked aside the wet snow and revealed the knuckle of a gnarled old tree root poking up through the gravel and slush. 'Mother Nature doing her bloody-minded "This Is All Mine Now" thing.' She joined him standing before the dark oak front door.

'You really sure about this?'

'I've got something I want to do.'

'What?'

'Just a . . . stupid thing. An errand.'

He reached for the large wrought-iron knocker and the heavy door creaked inwards at his touch. He stepped forward into the entrance hall beyond. It was dark with wood panelling and still smelt faintly of linseed oil. The smell filled him with hope for some reason. He almost called out 'Grandma? Grandad?' but stopped himself.

It felt wrong.

Face it. They're gone. You know what you'll find, Leo. Right?

He knew.

Just making sure you're prepared, MonkeyNuts, that's all.

Freya joined him inside and Leon led the way into the heart of the house, Grandma's pride-and-joy country-house kitchen. Pots and pans hung in order of size from hooks, gently bumping and clanking in the breeze that stole in behind them. The large kitchen table was set for breakfast as it always was: marmalade, jam and Marmite in pots in the middle, and a china teapot ready and waiting beside them.

Leon could see them all sitting around it now: beams of coloured sunlight streaming in through the stained-glass kitchen window catching dust motes drifting lazily; classical music playing from one of those old record players sitting on top of the chest in the corner; Dad and Grandad exchanging headlines from their very different newspapers; Mum, Grace and Grandma discussing their plans for the day.

And Leon . . . sulking . . . again . . . over his Coco Pops.

Oh jeez. I was a total brat last time we came here.

He felt Freya's hand on his shoulder. 'You OK?'

'Yeah, fine.'

She touched his cheek lightly and held her wet finger out for him to see. 'Really?'

Self-consciously he swiped at his face with the back of his hand. 'Just . . . you know . . . nostalgic shit an' stuff.'

She nodded. 'I know. What do you want to do?'

'You stay here. I'm just going to have a quick look for them.'

'You sure that's a good idea?'

'There won't be much left. I . . . I just want to say goodbye.'

'Go on.' She waved him off, then eased herself down on to one of the kitchen chairs.

He found them as he'd hoped he'd find them. Upstairs. A brief glance into their bedroom was all he needed to work out how they'd chosen to leave things. Their bones were spooned up close together beneath a darkly stained and rotting quilt. On their bedside tables were empty water glasses and a motley collection of little brown pill bottles.

Leon couldn't help a slight smile. *Good for you, guys.*

Bodies were a grim sight that had become all too familiar for him and Freya. Every home, every building, every street, the same bundles of bones and rags like kindling wrapped in tarp. But it was the skulls he couldn't get used to: the sightless dark round orbits where eyes had been and the permanent snaggle-sneer of exposed teeth. Mercifully, right now, he could only see the backs of his grandparents' heads. Tufts of snow-white hair still anchored to their skulls.

They died snuggling up together.

'I'm sorry for being a complete asshole, Grandma,' he said softly.

He unzipped his backpack and reached into it. He pulled out his journal, the leather cover dog-eared and scuffed, and set it down gently on their dressing table. 'If Dad . . . ever, you know, drops by, can you tell him it's right here?'

In answer, he heard the creak of a door somewhere out on the landing. He wanted to believe the noise was Grandma's ghost doing her best to tell him he was forgiven.

Of course I will, Leo . . . and, don't worry, I'm well aware that teenagers have tantrums!

Or perhaps even the ghost of his dad, urging him to get going.

Go on, MonkeyNuts. Go catch that ship before she sets sail. I'll read this later, buddy.

'You found them?'

Leon nodded as he led the way out of the kitchen, into the entrance hall and back through the wide-open front door into the snow.

'I'm so sorry,' she replied.

'Hey, it's OK.' He pulled the driver-side door open and climbed in. 'I knew they were going to be dead anyway. At least now I know for sure.'

'Did you manage the errand you wanted to do?'

He turned the ignition key and the van coughed and rattled to life. 'Yeah.'

'What was it?' She looked at him and then quickly had a change of heart and shook her head. 'My bad. Private. I'm sorry. I'm too bloody nosy for my own good.'

'It's OK. Just saying goodbye to ghosts and all that.' He turned the van round and drove back down the driveway, swerving slightly to flatten the bare bramble stalks once again for good measure.

*

The noise of the van dwindled away to nothing, leaving the snow-covered gardens and driveway in silence. Silence . . . except for the creaking of bare tree limbs as they swayed in the modest breeze, and a sporadic hiss and patter as clumps of sun-softened snow slipped from the branches like ripe fruit, cascading down in light powder showers.

The snow had been thick this second winter. Thicker than the last one. From the middle of October until now, it had lain in deep drifts across the entire country. An unending carpet of white across fields and woods and urban landscapes. Rooftops no longer leaking heat, cities and towns no longer warmed by movement and industry now as white and picturesque as a Dickens postcard.

The morning sun crept across the garden, coaxing the violet-coloured shadows beneath the trees and bushes, making the snow sparkle and glitter. Before the creaking oak front door of the house the deep ruts from the van's wheels cleaved through the snow.

And, there, the knuckle of the gnarled tree root Freya had exposed, emerging from the gravel like the gliding hump of a whale from a becalmed sea.

A root of sorts.

But not a tree root.

Its lumpy and gnarled surface was as hard as that of a mature tree's root, its shape as random as a product of nature with whorls of half growth and stunted, abandoned stubs of dead-end branching.

If Freya had kicked away just a little more of the snow and gravel and dug just a little deeper, she would have noticed that the root had made a long journey thus far. A journey that most certainly had not begun ten metres away beneath the nearest oak tree.

If Freya had knelt down and pulled the hunting knife from her backpack and cut a groove into the muddy root's 'bark', she would have exposed a soft protective membrane, like leather. And if she'd been curious enough to cut through that membrane, she would have discovered a pink fleshy mulch, very much alive, a super-highway of microbiotic life, busily delivering amino-acid messages to and fro.

It had a purpose.

CHAPTER 7

Grace stroked the hindquarters of the Arabian horse. She savoured the suede-smooth texture of its coat as she stroked downwards, then the coarse brush-bristle texture as she stroked upwards, feeling the spasmodic twitch of long muscles beneath its coat as it responded to her touch. She could feel the damp warmth of the animal radiating from its flanks.

'He's really beautiful.'

'Oh, that he is. He won the Virginia Derby six times, he's travelled the world and now he's spending his retirement in the lap of luxury. And, of course, entertaining lady horses of a very high standing.'

She suppressed a chuckle and blushed at that. She knew exactly what the trainer was talking about.

'He's one in a million. Although, he's worth a helluva lot more than that.'

The stables echoed with the snorts and impatient stamping of dozens of other horses, and the rich smell of their dung was almost overwhelming. But Grace didn't dislike it. On the contrary, it was a comforting smell, one that seemed to come encoded with positive associations, like burning leaves on an autumn bonfire, or the extra cinnamon topping of a Thanksgiving latte.

Dad had promised her this for months. And, today,

he'd finally delivered on his promise to take her to his rich friend's stables. Mom was there too, stroking the horse.

'It's really very kind of you to show us around,' she said.

The trainer shrugged. 'No problem, Mrs Friedmann.'

'Tom, we should probably go soon. I'm sure this gentleman has plenty of things he needs to get on with.'

'Relax, there's really no rush, hon. Mr Trent's got plenty of guys taking care of his horses.'

'I know, but . . . I don't think we should impose—'

'Mom, not yet. Please?'

She looked down at Grace. 'Douglas Trent's been very kind letting us have a tour around here. We're very lucky. Let's not be too cheeky.'

Grace frowned up at her. 'I'm not being cheeky. I just want to stay here a little while longer.'

'We've got somewhere to be—'

'Like where?'

Mom's face creased with sympathy. 'I'm really sorry, honey . . . This will have to wait for another time. There's some important news.'

The image of her mother quivered like a reflection in a bowl of water. Grace felt the memory beginning to unpick itself, fading to darkness and leaving her with a neutral blank canvas of abstract thought. The horse, the trainer, her dad, that smell . . . The stables were all gone now.

[. . . **information. High importance . . .**]

I was enjoying that.

[. . . **(enjoy, enjoying, enjoyment) less**

43

importance. Information high importance . . .]

Her memories were all right there, like a jukebox, ready to play so very vividly for her. Sometimes she allowed herself to get lost in them, to fool herself that she was still Grace Friedmann living in the outside world. But in truth she was now nothing more than a complex amalgamation of blood chemistry, a superstructure of billions of loosely allied cells, capable of detaching and reattaching.

She was just information in liquid form.

Her memory faded, the hallucination of Mom replaced by the presence of a data package-carrier. Grace sensed its proximity, the amino acids that crossed the nano space between them infusing the outer cells of her super cluster with a sharp taste of urgency.

What's so important?

[. . . contact. New identifier. Handshake . . .]

Even now, after such a long time, she found the chemical-exchange conversations hard work sometimes.

Can we talk in an abstract?

[. . . this is acceptable. Choose an abstract . . .]

She was used to conversing with a different package-carrier cluster. It had learned how she preferred to communicate and prefaced its delivery by constructing the abstract . . . the memory first. This package-carrier was completely new to her. A stranger.

It had obviously come a long way with its message. A very long way.

She gathered her wits and pulled a clear memory from her mind. She selected one she was comfortable using.

A memory that for no obvious reason was much more firmly defined than any other. Possibly it was the routine familiarity of it, the reinforced, repeated scenario. The same journey, the same small environment . . . the back seat of Mom and Dad's car.

In this memory she was seven again. Swinging her short legs and kicking at the back of the passenger front seat with her pink pumps. Outside, tall buildings edged slowly by as they sat in stop-start traffic from one intersection to the next. Davison Elementary School was just half a dozen blocks away from home, but every morning the journey seemed to take an eternity.

The package-carrier 'became' Mom in the driver's front seat, tapping the steering wheel impatiently with her hand. Just the two of them. Leon's high school was close enough for him to walk.

Mom looked in the rear-view mirror at her. 'I have high-priority information for you.'

The package-carrier had absolutely no idea how Mom talked. It was an imposter within her illusion, a stranger inhabiting Mom's body and doing her voice all wrong.

'Have established connection, exchanged data packets,' continued Mom in a flat, emotionless, robotic voice. Grace hated her mom sounding wrong.

Outside the boundaries of her illusion, her super-cluster cells parted, allowing the messenger in, and then closed again to completely absorb it. The package-carrier dissolved and the information it had carried was now available to her.

Mom spoke again. This time her voice was better. 'We've got some brand-new family.'

Grace was in the back seat, swinging her pink pumps. 'New family? I thought I knew about everyone. I thought we were the family.'

'Well, honey, there's no real limit to who your family is. But these are family from a long way away.'

'How far away?'

'It's another super-cluster. A very, very big one.'

'Bigger. You mean . . . bigger than us?'

Mom settled to a stop at a red light, turned in her seat and looked at her. 'Much, much bigger.'

'Oh.' Grace played with the zipper of her Hello Kitty school bag, back and forth – zzzup, zzzup, zzzup – as she gazed out of the window at another bored kid strapped into a back seat, being driven to school. Their eyes met for a moment.

'So . . . does that mean I'm not the most important person any more?'

'You're always our most important person, sweetie. We all love you. But it's not just us any more. We all need to get on together.'

'Are they coming over to visit?'

'No. We're going to have to pay them a visit.'

'But we're the family, Mom. Why don't they come to us? Why do we have to go to see them?'

'Because they are the family, Grace. We're really just an offshoot. We're the country cousins, if you want to think about it that way. And they really, really want to meet us. Learn all about us and share family stories.'

'Are we going to have to talk about . . . the big plan?'

'Yes, honey, we are. You know there's so much we all have to do, and we've only just begun. The plan needs to be discussed.'

She sighed wearily and the sigh turned into a stretch and a yawn.

'Oka-y-y.'

CHAPTER 8

'Not once?'

'No.'

'What, never?'

'No.'

'Like, literally . . . never?'

'Argghh.' Leon turned to look at Freya, exasperated. 'Like I said . . . *no*.'

She giggled at his mock anger and absently tapped the steering wheel with her knuckles. They were sharing the driving. It tended to be a more comfortable and less jerky ride with Leon in the passenger seat.

'OK, so what about you, then?' asked Leon.

'Boys have never featured heavily in my personal life. At primary school I used to hang out with them more, because I . . . I suppose I preferred playing the boy games, rather than pretending to push a pram around. Then, in secondary school . . . Well . . . the secondary-school years weren't a great success for me romance-wise.'

He glanced at her walking stick, leaning against the seat behind him. 'The MS?'

'No, that started in my last year. No, I was always just a bit of an outsider. Not one of the cool kids. You know how it is – you are or you're definitely not. It was very binary, wasn't it? Playground politics.'

Leon nodded. He knew what she meant. High school in New York had been the same. A caste system of jocks and WAGS, the rest of the student body . . . and then at the bottom, the *outcasts*. He'd constantly hovered on the borderline between 'the rest' and 'the outcasts'.

After Mum and Dad had split and she'd taken them 'back home' to England, he'd definitely been one of the outcasts in his sixth-form college. Mum had assured him that his acquired American accent would make him an exotic curiosity. Instead it had made him a target. He shook his head at the hypocrisy and flawed logic of teenage doctrine. They all parroted the same mantra – *I'm an individual . . . I'm unique . . . There's only one of ME. I'm special* – and then did anything they could to look and sound identical to all their friends. Worse than that, they punished those who didn't tow the line and follow suit.

Who do you think YOU are? You think you're so special, huh?

He'd once tried to clarify that very point with one of the popular girls at college. She and her gang had been picking on him because he sounded different, and yet all they banged on about all day, every day, was how wonderfully different they were to everyone else. The fact that some days it was almost impossible to tell them apart from each other was completely lost on her.

'I used to think that—'

They heard a loud bang.

'Shit! What was that?'

The van suddenly started to judder violently, then it

swerved sharply towards the central reservation. Freya grasped the steering wheel with both hands and began to push on the brake. There hadn't been many potholes or cracks from the cold weather, nor any weed tufts to steer around. The road must have been freshly surfaced just before the virus hit.

Reassured by the smooth surface and clear for the last hour of any car graveyards, Freya had slowly allowed her speed to climb to nearly sixty miles an hour.

She wrestled the wheel left, then right, then left – short controlled jerks that prevented the van spinning on the wet surface – finally coming to a rest a hundred metres down the road.

Freya sat back in her seat and puffed out a breath. 'That was a blow-out, wasn't it?'

'I don't know. Never had one.' Leon looked at her. 'Jeez, you were pretty cool, though. You had one of those before?'

She shook her head. 'Oh well, after six hours of your riveting company . . . I could do with some excitement.'

'Thanks.' Leon opened his door, got out and went round to the front. 'Front-right tyre's gone,' he called out. He was looking at shreds of rubber and wire coiling. The wheel rim was resting on the ground. Behind the van was a snaking, still-smoking black trail of smeared tyre rubber.

Freya got out and looked at it. 'Ever changed a tyre?'

Leon shook his head. 'It's pretty simple I'm guessing.' He headed to the back of the van and opened the rear doors. 'There must be a spare, and one of those lifting things.'

'A jack?'

'Yeah, that.'

He pulled several boxes of their tinned supplies out on to the road, lifted the plastic matting and found an empty space where a spare had once been. 'Great.'

Freya sucked air through her teeth. 'So we borrowed a van from a careless idiot. Bloody marvellous.'

They both looked around. There were no other vehicles in sight. Just empty road as far as they could see. Ahead of them, though, rose the outskirts of a town, a low carpet of rooftops, and in the distance the faint grey outlines of several high-rise buildings.

Leon could see an overpass and a slip road about a quarter of a mile ahead. He noted a sign informing them to take the next slip for the city centre.

'So that must be Oxford over there, then?'

'Yeah.'

'Looks pretty close by. We could go see if we can find a spare . . . or borrow another van.'

Freya sighed and rubbed her hip absently. 'Wonderful. More walking.'

Leon reached into the back of the van, pulled out their backpacks, the two army rifles they had and Freya's walking stick. 'I can go alone, if you want to stay—'

'No,' she replied quickly. 'You're not leaving me here all alone!'

'Well, at least let me carry your back—'

'And don't patronize me!'

He looked up at her. She was grinning at him. 'Joking.'

They made their way down the slip road, as empty as the A road, and turned right at a small overgrown roundabout. Ten minutes of walking later, they found themselves staring at the tail end of a logjam of vehicles.

As they drew closer, they could see it was actually the very front of a traffic jam, a solid convoy of cars and vans prevented from proceeding any further by a barricade of dumped concrete blocks and barbed wire.

'My God,' whispered Leon.

It was also *solid* in the sense that a number of the vehicles, all a uniform charcoal black, had been welded together by some kind of intense heat. Leon stepped carefully between the concrete blocks, round some coils of rusting razor wire, and inspected the nearest vehicles. Their tightly packed metal carcasses seemed to be merged together in places. The road was black with soot, and crusty cowpats of melted rubber and plastic around their wheel rims.

Freya joined him. 'God . . .'

'It looks like it was *napalmed* or something.'

Freya nodded. 'Firebombed.' She winced at something and looked quickly away.

Leon saw what she'd spotted. In the car to their right, a four-door hatchback that might once have been a Volvo, were the carbonized silhouettes of bodies. He counted five. Two in the front, three smaller ones in the back. The fingerless blackened nub of two small hands and thin arms protruded through the empty frame of the rear left window.

One of the kids . . . trying to climb out of the back.

He caught a glimpse of the corpse's face: a dark speckled mannequin's head, featureless, without a nose and only fused dents where eyes had been. A tidy row of small white upper teeth framed a dark hole where the mouth had frozen open in a perpetual fossilized scream.

He snapped his eyes shut and turned his head away, not wanting to pick out any more details, not wanting to give this image a chance to take permanent root in his head.

'No one got to leave Oxford, then,' said Freya matter-of-factly. Leon could tell she was trying to sound dismissive and business-like, but he could hear the slightest tremble in her voice.

'Come on.' He reached for her hand and tugged her gently. 'We need to go find another ride.'

They walked along the hard shoulder, staring resolutely ahead as they passed beside the blackened convoy, not wanting or needing to look closely at any of the other frozen shapes, some still belted in their seats, others half in, half out of their cars, nearly but not quite escaping the fireball.

The road began to slope down into an underpass. They came to a halt just outside its gaping gloomy mouth and looked at each other.

'We could backtrack and go up and round,' said Leon.

Freya looked behind them up the blackened road, flanked on either side by concrete banks, then back into the tunnel ahead of them. It wasn't long. Fifty metres of gloom – she could see the glint of unburnt vehicles edging out into daylight at the far end.

'Unless there's such a thing as underpass trolls, I think we'll be OK.'

They made their way along a service walkway at the side with a safety rail. After taking several steps, they found themselves a metre or so above the road, looking down on the roofs and bonnets of the jammed vehicles. Their boots echoed in the cavernous interior, and somewhere nearby they could hear the steady *drip*, *drip*, *drip* of water.

Round about the middle where the road began to flatten out, ready for the rise up and out, Freya chose to lighten the mood by whistling a tuneless version of an Olly Murs song.

A few minutes later they emerged, relieved, into daylight at the far end.

'You can't carry a tune, Freya,' said Leon.

'Could have been worse. I could've been *singing*.'

At the top of the sloping road, the jam of vehicles began to thin out, and they started looking for a suitable candidate that could be reversed clear of the tangle.

'There's a similar van.'

Leon looked. A dark blue one, about the same size as theirs. Leon crossed the road and peered through the driver-side window – no rags, no bones to be seen. He suspected the vehicles at this end of the jam must have been hastily abandoned by their owners, not wanting to face the same fate as those poor souls ahead.

He tried the driver-side door. It opened easily and he pulled himself up inside. The key was still in the ignition and he gave it a hopeful twist.

Nothing.

'The battery's probably flat.'

Freya looked around. 'They're all going to be flat, aren't they?'

Leon climbed out. 'Why don't we just grab a tyre off this one?'

'Are the tyres the same size?'

Leon shrugged. 'I don't know.'

'Did you check on the tyre type for our van?'

'No. Did you?'

She rolled her eyes. 'Duh . . .'

He shrugged. 'Same kind of van. I guess the tyres'll be the same.'

They both went round to the back, pulled the rear doors open to reveal a drum kit, guitar cases and amplifiers. 'A band,' said Freya. 'You reckon they were on their way to a gig?'

He wondered. The whole thing had happened so suddenly that he could actually imagine a bunch of dozy, self-obsessed rockers so singularly focused on Making It Big that they hadn't actually noticed the end of the world going on around them.

He lifted the mat up at the back and found a tyre and a jack. At least they had a spare. He lifted them. Freya stored the jack in her backpack and Leon held the heavy tyre in his arms. He tried to heft it on to his shoulder.

'Might as well just roll it.'

'Oh yeah, that's true.'

They headed back down the sloping road to the dark mouth of the overpass.

'If it's the wrong size, you know we're going to have to do this all over again,' said Leon.

Freya laughed. 'We're not exactly the survival A-team, are we?'

'Screw that. We're still alive. That's got to count for something.'

She paused and leaned on her walking stick. 'Leon Friedmann.'

'What?'

She smiled at him with a hint of something like maternal pride. 'Spoken like a true dude.'

They entered the gloom of the tunnel once more, climbed up the steps on the right on to the service walkway and began to make their way slowly along it. As they approached the middle, Leon was waiting for Freya to start whistling tunelessly again (or, worse, start singing) when she suddenly stopped ahead of him. The tyre rolled heavily into the back of her legs.

'Hey!' Her yelp carried down the tunnel.

'Why did you just stop then?'

'I heard something.'

'What?'

In the gloom, Leon could dimly see that she was holding a finger up.

'Shhh . . .'

They both strained to hear, waiting for the echo of her voice to finally recede. There was the dripping sound, of course, but Leon couldn't hear anything else.

Freya shook her head. 'Huh . . . thought I heard . . .'

'Heard what?'

'I dunno . . . like someone tearing a sheet of paper. Like a sort of *fwhiiiit* sound.'

Leon reached into his backpack and pulled out the torch. Not that they needed it to make their way out of here. There was enough ambient light spilling in from both ends of the underpass to see to the far end. But there were also enough pools of darkness between the stationary cars to make him feel uneasy.

He snapped the torch on and instantly shadows danced across the tiles on the far wall. Glass windscreens and headlight and tail-light reflectors glinted back at him like cats' eyes as he carefully panned the beam up and down the line of vehicles. The cars and vans down here had escaped the firebomb at the front and, protected from the weather these last two years, some of them even looked showroom-clean.

This time they both heard it. A creaking, tearing sound above them.

'I'm not going to lie, that sounds decidedly not good,' whispered Freya.

Leon panned his torch beam up to the low ceiling of the overpass.

'What . . . the . . .'

CHAPTER 9

Hanging half a metre or so below the low ceiling, running diagonally from the far wall to their side, the thing was as thick as a person's waist. It looked like a giant gnarly tree root, and appeared to have forced its way through the far wall, dislodging tiles and plaster on to the cars below, growing its way along the underpass ceiling, burrowing its way through the tiles.

In the middle, it bowed down slightly as it bore the weight of a huge glistening sac that dangled from it like an unsightly tumour.

The sac pulsated and quivered with movement going on within. It was growing in size as they watched, distending and swelling like a water balloon being filled from a tap, shedding dark brittle flakes of a protective coating to reveal a glistening purple-red membrane.

'Oh . . . my . . . God . . .' Freya gasped each word with a separate breath.

'It's the virus,' whispered Leon.

The root creaked under the increasing weight as the sac quivered and expanded.

'Back . . . get back!' hissed Freya, reversing into him.

'No, forward. Forward is closer!'

The membrane suddenly ruptured, spilling its contents down on to the cars like offal dumped from the back of a slaughterhouse lorry, a cascade of glistening organs that splattered heavily on to the roof of the car directly beneath it.

Leon instinctively thrust the torch into Freya's hands and slung the assault rifle off his shoulder.

The pool of gunk and organs beneath quivered and twitched. He could see dozens of bubble-like embryonic sacs, each one like the 'parent' sac, stretching and rupturing and, emerging from them, the nightmare creatures they last saw eighteen months ago.

'Snarks!'

Bigger, though. These were the size of small dogs.

Leon pushed at Freya to go forward. She stubbornly resisted and pushed him back. 'The other end's closer!'

He turned. Actually, she was right. 'Go. GO!'

He backed up against the wall and let her squeeze past him. Then reversed in her wake, keeping his eyes on the squirming mass of creatures as they shook their limbs clear of the glistening amniotic fluid and began to find their footing.

It didn't take them long. The snarks began to move towards them, clambering from car roof to car roof, hopping effortlessly across the gaps between vehicles.

'Hurry!' Leon shouted. Freya was ahead of him, swinging and planting her walking stick quickly and carelessly and lurching like a drunkard after it, not a run but a shambolic loping gait.

The nearest of the creatures were now scuttling abreast of them, just a few metres beyond the safety railing and just a metre below. Leon imagined they were within leaping distance. He aimed the gun in the direction of the snarks and pulled the trigger.

Nothing happened.

'Shit-shit-shit!'

As he scrambled behind Freya, he slapped his hand hard against the side of the weapon, hoping to find a switch or a toggle that would make the damned thing work. In movies, even ones with reluctant heroes who'd never handled a gun before, it never appeared to be this difficult to get a gun to work.

'*Come on!*' he howled as he kept bashing the side of it in different places, squeezing the trigger to check if he'd got the weapon working yet. The trigger seemed locked firmly in place.

He squeezed it again, and again it resisted.

'*For God's sa—*'

Then suddenly the trigger gave way. The assault rifle spat out a single strobing muzzle flash and kicked in his hand like a jackhammer. He dropped it on the walkway and it clattered to the edge, nearly sliding past the handrail and down on to the road. He bent and scooped it up.

'*Hurry!*' screamed Freya. She was pulling ahead of him now.

One of the creatures leaped across from the nearest car roof and bounced off the hand rail. It squealed with frustration as it dropped down on to the road.

Another snark launched itself at Leon and this time managed to successfully land on the service walkway beside him. Leon aimed the gun at it, fired, and the creature spattered grey loops of viscous liquid and fine shards of shell.

He staggered another dozen steps, not daring to turn his back on them and make a run for it. Another snark flew up and across, clattering off the tiled wall a couple of metres behind him before falling down on to the walkway.

He fired again. The ground sparked where he missed and fragments of the bullet left momentary tracer tracks in the gloom.

He fired again and missed again.

The creature suddenly leaped up at him, at his face. He swung the butt of the assault rifle upwards to block it. The weapon shuddered on impact. Rather than deflecting and flying off into the darkness, the creature was latched on, its serrated pincers firmly locking around the trigger guard. The gun was suddenly twice its weight. It felt as if a bag of groceries was swinging from the end of it.

The creature instinctively extended another limb to gain a further toehold on the gun, pulling the bulk of its body along the weapon and closer to Leon.

He found himself staring at something that vaguely resembled a face: a cluster of three pale semi-opaque orbs, each one specked with a tiny dark dot like frogspawn.

Are those eyes?

He swung the butt against the wall and heard something in the creature crack as it smacked heavily against the tiles. He shook the stunned creature off, backed up several more steps, aimed and pulled the trigger.

The gun fired off half a dozen rounds on automatic, disintegrating it.

Then it jammed.

Leon tugged at the trigger again several times, then banged the gun against the railing, hoping the impact would dislodge whatever was causing the jam. But this time it seemed the weapon was utterly useless.

There were now half a dozen creatures on the walkway racing towards him. More clinging to the railing beside him, scrambling to hold on to the smooth metal.

He tossed the gun at the nearest of them, turned and sprinted after Freya.

She was approaching the entrance to the underpass where the road sloped upwards and was a dozen metres short of the chink of daylight spilling in.

But down among the cars, to her right, keeping pace with her, Leon could see movement, dark shapes flitting quickly from car roof to car bonnet. The snarks were going to reach the entrance before them. Reach the entrance, turn and clamber up on to the walkway and then . . .

Shit. We're dead. We're dead.

He closed the gap quickly and soon he was right behind Freya. He could hear her gasping from the exertion, mewling with terror between each ragged gasp.

'*Freya!*'

He grabbed her arm. She flinched and spun to look at him. 'Shit, Leon, we're not going to make it!'

He nodded at the road beneath them. 'I know! They're ahead. They're going to block us in!'

She stopped her awkward loping run and bent over.

'What the hell are you doing?'

'My gun! Get my gun out!' She shrugged off her backpack and let it drop to the ground. The barrel was poking out of the top of the open zip.

'There's too many! They—'

She grasped his wrist tightly. Her fingers digging in hard like claws. 'Not for *them*!'

He felt his stomach suddenly lurch and turn over on itself. 'Oh, God, Freya. No. No. No.'

'I don't want to die like this!' she cried, looking over his shoulder. 'Hurry! Leon! Please!'

He reached for the barrel, shook the gun free of the bag and hefted its reassuring cold weight in his hands. 'No. Not yet . . .'

The creatures were closing on them from the right. He aimed the gun, hoping to God he wasn't going to have to slap it around like the other one to make it work. There wasn't the time. The gun jolted violently in his hands as he fired five, six, seven rounds in rapid succession. A couple of his shots found targets, but the rest sparked off railings, tiles and concrete. The snarks suddenly slowed as though already comprehending the danger the gun presented. But they didn't stop. While it was no longer a ravenous charge, it was now a cautious and steady advance.

'Oh God, Leon!' Freya cried. 'Don't use up *all* the bullets!'

He had no idea how many a magazine contained.

Neither of them had examined these weapons or tried to figure out how they worked, or even *if* they worked. He could well have just used up the last bullets in this gun.

'Leon!' she whimpered. 'Please . . . do it now!'

He was about to chance taking his eyes off the steadily advancing creatures to check whether their way out was blocked by the others yet. If it was, then . . .

. . . *Then your girlfriend's got it right. Far better her way, Monkeynuts.* Dad's voice in his head.

One . . . BANG, two . . . BANG. Game over. Done. Better that than . . . ?

Leon jerked his gun quickly to aim at the ones closest to them, just a couple of metres back up the walkway. They froze in response. Almost intelligently, beady eyes on the gun.

He could hear Freya sobbing behind him. Begging him to shoot her.

'Leon . . . you have to.'

But he didn't get a chance to turn and do what needed to be done because, just then, he heard or, more accurately, *felt* a percussive thump from behind him, and the tunnel glared brilliantly for a second.

Freya yelped with surprise. She turned to see a row of figures slowly approaching, their silhouetted forms fogged and indistinct behind what appeared to be a row of tall, scuffed and scratched rectangular police riot shields.

Beyond the front row holding the shields, there were more of them, arms raised backwards then forward as they hurled something. She saw a couple of dark objects arcing through the air, bouncing with a loud clatter off the roofs of the cars near them . . . then . . .

BANG!

The unbearably loud noise and the brilliant flash that came with it left Freya seeing a negative image against the back of her closed eyelids and her ears roaring with a dull white noise.

She heard muffled voices. Men barking orders. Felt a pair of hands on her arms, jerking her off balance so that she was being physically carried rather than dragged.

'*Flame them!*' she heard someone shouting.

A moment later she heard glass breaking behind her and felt a sudden rush of hot air against her cheeks. The tunnel filled with a chorus of high-pitched squealing.

She tried opening her eyes and caught a momentary glimpse of blurry daylight ahead of her and dozens of dark bodies moving quickly around her. Her eyes stung and she instinctively snapped them shut again.

'*Again!*' barked the same ragged voice.

Once more, she heard the crack and tinkle of breaking glass and felt a blast of heat.

'Where's Leon?' she heard herself screaming. 'Leon? There's another person back in there!'

Somebody replied with an answer that was muffled behind a helmet visor, but she couldn't work out what he'd said.

'WHERE'S LEON?' she screamed.

Still disorientated, her sense of balance completely

shot, she felt a wave of dizzy nausea as rough hands hefted her up on to something hard and flat.

'*LEON?*'

She felt a hand slapping the surface beside hers, finding her fingers and then holding on. 'I'm here! That you Freya?!'

She felt the hand squeeze hers and she squeezed it back, tightly, in relief.

'Oh, God, Leon . . . I thought you'd been left in there!'

'Freya . . . Jesus Christ! That was . . .' He couldn't finish.

She swore between wretched gasps. 'Oh shitty shit . . . shit . . .'

'I know,' he wheezed. 'I know. I can't see a thing . . . My eyes . . .'

They heard the barking voice again and felt the flat surface they were sitting on vibrate as boots clambered up beside them.

'Was there anyone else in there with you?' asked the voice.

'No . . . just us,' replied Leon.

'Good, cos they'd be bloody toast otherwise.'

Freya wiped her stinging eyes with the back of her hand. She blinked, trying to open them again but snapped them quickly shut. She heard more boots clambering up, then finally the growl of a diesel engine being gunned. Whatever they were sitting on, presumably the floor of a flat-bed truck of some sort, lurched violently and Freya banged her head against something hard.

'Ooof!' she heard Leon cry. 'Ow!'

She cracked an eye open and saw him cupping his nose, wincing, and realized he must have been leaning in towards her to hold or comfort her, and she'd just nutted him with the back of her head.

'Sorry – I'm so clumsy.'

CHAPTER 10

It felt like ages before Leon could open his stinging eyes, and even longer for the whistle of white noise in his ears to clear enough to hear anything.

They were in the back of an army truck. It was painted a sandy yellow with wavy grey 'disruption' streaks: desert camouflage. He guessed it was one of the many army vehicles that had served time over in the Middle East and had been patiently waiting its turn to be repainted to a default olive green.

Freya was sitting on the bench opposite. Like him, she was blinking back chemically induced tears. Soldiers sat quietly on either side of them, swaying as the truck swerved to avoid road jams, rolled off congested hard shoulders on to dirt and then back on to tarmac again. Leon met her eyes and she managed to pull a smile together for him, her expression full of questions.

Are we alive?

Are you OK?

Is this for real?

Was I really begging you to shoot me?

Maybe just five or ten minutes before, Leon had been psyching himself up to do it. He'd almost been ready to turn the gun on her, then himself. Counting down the last few seconds before he was out of time.

Now here we are. Rescued.

Finally safe in the hands of the authorities.

He returned her smile. *It's OK, Freya. We did it. We're safe.*

He looked at the soldiers sitting patiently in the truck facing each other. Their equipment wasn't what he expected to see. They were wearing army uniforms, of course, but over the top of the olive greens were overlapping dark segments of Kevlar protective armour. It reminded him of the kind of segmented protective plating that speedway motorcyclists wore. But no guns. He looked up and down the truck. Not a single assault rifle or sidearm as far as he could see. He saw a bunch of cylinders with tapers, flashbangs presumably, and a crate of bottles plugged with cloth that sloshed liquid.

They were each holding on to the handle of a tall riot shield with POLICE stencilled boldly across them. And at their sides, tucked into belts and pouches, he could see the handles of a curious variety of sharp-edged weapons: fire axes, machetes, hunting knives. One man even looked as if he was carrying a samurai katana.

One of the soldiers further along noticed Leon's curious look. He pulled himself on to his feet, carefully made his way down between the two rows of grounded shields and hunkered down in front of him.

'You all right there, son?' he barked over the growl of the truck's engine.

Leon nodded.

'Aye, close bloody call that, wasn't it?'

Leon recognized the voice from back in the tunnel. The one who'd been shouting the commands.

'*Flame! . . . Again! . . .*'

Deep and gravelly, like a knife drawn flatly across dry toast. Clearly someone used to a lifetime of shouting over noise and with a hard Glaswegian accent.

'Yeah. I'm OK.'

'You were checking out our kit? Not exactly standard issue, huh?'

Leon nodded. 'Like . . . I dunno . . .'

'Medieval?'

'Yeah.'

The man snorted a laugh, then wiped at the thick moustache beneath his nose.

'For good reason, lad . . . Different kind of warfare now. Guns're useless on those scuttlers. Too many of 'em, too small and too bloody fast.' He looked Leon over quickly. 'You medicated?'

'Aspirin.'

'Good. Your girlfriend too?'

He didn't bother correcting him. 'Yeah. She's on the same.'

'Good. You'll get a full medical examination when we get back.' He stood and began to make his way carefully towards his seat. 'Lucky we decided to come out foraging today!'

The truck rocked and bounced across another kerb.

'Where are we going?'

The man didn't hear Leon's voice. That, or he ignored him.

Half an hour later the vehicle turned off on to a side road, flanked by mature oak trees that hung over the road from either side, creating a flickering tunnel through which the pale sun dappled light. He spotted a sign by the side of the road.

WELCOME TO BANTON CASTLE:
CORPORATE EVENTS, WEDDINGS, BANQUETS.

Scrawled over it in red paint:

CAMP CAMELOT

Perhaps another emergency operation?

They emerged from the trees into a clearing. Leon craned his neck to look over the heads and helmets of the soldiers in front of him, expecting to see some vast military base, perhaps an airstrip lined with Chinooks ready to whisk them away. He was anticipating a stirred-up ants' nest of activity: army doctors and nurses processing queues of bedraggled and malnourished survivors, soldiers organizing queues, rows of buff-coloured tents . . .

Instead he saw a tall and narrow castle encircled by a moat. Surrounding the moat was a large tree-lined clearing, he guessed a quarter of a mile in diameter: the castle grounds.

Except, unlike any castle grounds he'd seen, it wasn't

all carefully cross-hatched mown lawn and tended rose gardens – it was a wasteland of weeds and grass and nettles and brambles. Here and there, dark, ragged craters pitted the ground like a no-man's land pockmarked by artillery.

The truck came to a halt beside the moat as a drawbridge was slowly lowered for them.

'OK,' said Freya. 'I get the Camelot reference now.'

Beyond the lowering bridge stood the castle, a traditional Norman keep sitting proudly on its own man-made island, an acre of mud-churned ground littered with pallets of supplies, boxes, crates, oil drums, another army truck and a third one up on blocks that looked as if it had been cannibalized for parts.

The bridge finally clunked into position and the truck rolled across on to the muddy ground beyond and parked beside the others.

'All right, lads!' barked the Scottish soldier. The others stood up, grabbed their shields and shuffled to the back of the truck, jumping down into the mud.

The man gestured at Leon and Freya to follow the others. 'End of the ride, boys and girls.'

'What is this place?' asked Freya.

'You saw the sign, didn't you?'

'Banton Castle?'

'Aye. Although you may have spotted we call it Camelot now.' He held a hand out to her. 'Come on.'

She pulled herself up off the bench with a groan.

'You all right? You pulled a muscle, love?'

'No . . . I've got MS.'

Leon got up, squeezed past her, jumped down off the back and then turned, holding up his arms to help her down.

'This is being used as an army base, then?' asked Freya

'Aye. You need a hand with her, lad?'

'I'm good.' Leon grasped her hands as she sat down and bum-shuffled off the back.

Leon looked around. Above him loomed the Norman keep. He could see faces looking out of narrow arched windows and heads peering down from the flat roof at the very top. From one of the corner towers a Union Jack fluttered.

'First things first, you two. Medical examination and then Major Everett will want to have a chat with you.'

CHAPTER 11

Two Years Ago

Chaos. Absolute chaos.

Tom Friedmann was being led across the deck of the aircraft carrier by a young man who looked as if he'd stepped straight out of high school into a standard-issue secret-services dark suit. Between his shoulders Tom could see the discreet bulge of a radio battery, and curled over the top of his ear the skin-coloured wire descending from an earpiece fed into the crisp white collar of his shirt.

'This way, Mr Friedmann.'

It was getting dark now, the Atlantic sky a cold, deep grey-blue that almost mirrored the freezing ocean below it. The carrier's football-pitch-sized deck was almost completely filled with civilians sitting in rows like POWs, each issued with an orange waterproof spray jacket and a plastic bottle of water. Thousands of them – men, women, children – trembling in the cold. He recalled images of Syrian refugees in life jackets spilling from rickety boats on to Greek pebbled beaches.

And now it's our turn.

At the far end of the deck, a large floodlit space was being kept clear for the constant traffic of helicopters coming in to land, disgorging yet more people on to the carrier's deck, refuelling and taking off again.

The young secret-services agent led Tom towards an open door at the base of the carrier's tall, office-block-sized island. Tom craned his neck up to look at the bridge and air-traffic control at the top. Through the windows up there he could see the busy comings and goings of navy personnel and the faint glow of screens and displays inside.

'Mind the step and mind your head, sir.'

The passageway beyond was crammed with a seething mixture of navy personnel and government civilians. Everyone seemed to be clasping a clipboard to their chest as they squeezed past each other, or the flapping sheets of freshly printed and hurriedly stapled printer paper.

He could guess what they were: hastily authored and printed-off procedure documents. Tom knew the CDC and FEMA had a thick dossier of emergency procedures to follow in the event of a wide spectrum of emergency situations. Today's crisis, however, wasn't in either of their playbooks. He was pretty certain of that. He looked around at the harried faces; everyone appeared to be doing their best to pretend there was some semblance of order here. That someone, somewhere, knew what the plan of action was.

The young man kept looking back over his shoulder to make sure Tom was keeping up with him.

'Where are we going?' asked Tom.

'I'm trying to find Trent's PA, sir. Let her know we managed to pick you up from Battery Park.'

'Make way there!' Just ahead of them, navy personnel

backed up against the bulkheads. The civilians, less used to the cramped confines of navy life, were slower in following their lead.

Tom's chaperone put an arm across Tom's chest and pressed him into a rack of internal-post pigeonholes. The papers poking out rustled and crumpled against his back.

Down the passageway he saw some faces he recognized approaching, one behind the other, playing follow the leader; a Supreme Court justice, a couple of Republican congressmen. Then he saw uniforms: army, navy, air force, all silver buzzcuts, razor-burned jowls and stern expressions. They swept past Tom, and a young navy officer gestured for them to turn left into the open doorway of a meeting room.

'This way, please, gentlemen.'

Still more followed in their wake. He noticed several uniforms from the Royal Navy, the Canadian Navy. The familiar face of one of the White House's regular press liaison officers and the news anchorwoman from CNN. He couldn't recall her name right now, but all it would take would be someone saying out loud, 'Tonight's six o'clock news brought to you by . . .' and he'd have it.

Then, right at the back, one more familiar face.

Tom waited until he was right beside him. 'Dougie!' He reached out and tapped the Secretary for Commerce on the arm.

Douglas Trent turned angrily, a man with far too much on his mind and in no mood to be door-stopped by some civil-servant underling. His scowl instantly vanished when he recognized his old friend.

'Tom! Thank Christ you made it!'

Tom nodded. 'Thanks for getting me out. It was a real close-run thing.'

'A promise is a promise, *amigo*. No man left behind. Right?'

'Mr Secretary?' It *was* an underling door-stopping him this time. 'The others are waiting in the briefing room to start the—'

'Just gimme a second!' Trent snapped.

'Doug, what the hell's going on?'

Trent shook his head. 'We don't have anything like a chain of command. It's a goddamn mess. That's what we've got going on. We need to get our shit together and we need to do it quickly.'

'Right.' Tom nodded. 'Right . . . then better let you get on. I'll—'

'Sure.' Douglas Trent turned to go, then stopped. 'No, wait. You can come in with me.'

'What?'

He shook his head. 'It's going to be a free-for-all in there. I need someone in my corner. I need a quick-thinker. Fresh eyes.'

'Jesus, Dougie . . . I'm not a bureaucrat or a—'

'We got far too many of those in there already. Right now what I need is a *wingman*.'

CHAPTER 12

'You OK?'

'Shaken,' Freya replied. 'And, yeah, just a little freaked out.'

'Hold still, please,' said the doctor. She wrapped a tourniquet round Freya's arm, cinched it tight and began to study the pale skin of the girl's forearm for a suitable vein.

'What are you doing?'

'Taking your bloods.'

'We're not infected.' Freya pulled her arm away. 'We've both been taking the pills since the outbreak happened.'

'This is just a precautionary measure. Now, please—'

'I don't want her sticking a needle in me!' She turned to Leon for support. 'I don't want a *stranger* sticking a bloody—'

'Hey, Freya.' Leon stepped forward. 'It's OK. She's just taking a little blood, right?'

The doctor nodded. She looked as if she didn't smile very often.

'A small blood sample. That is all.'

'I . . .' Freya stared at the empty syringe in the woman's hand. 'I . . . really hate needles. And, look! I'm still shaking from earlier! You're going to miss the vein and . . . Can't we do this tomorrow?'

'I'm sorry. Every newcomer must be screened straight away,' the doctor replied. She had an accent. Clipped. Precise. European.

'Screened?'

She looked at Leon. 'Yes. Tested for dormant infection. This is not optional, I'm afraid.' She turned to Freya. 'And my name is Claudia Hahn.' She smiled. 'So . . . no longer a *stranger* now, all right?'

'What do you mean by a dormant infection?' pressed Leon.

Dr Hahn sat back on her stool. 'We suspect some people are resistant. Not fully resistant, but in so much as the virus takes a great deal longer to affect them and present symptoms.' She looked at them both. 'You encountered them earlier today, yes?'

Leon nodded. She was referring to the snarks. 'But we didn't make *contact* with them.' He turned to Freya. 'Right?'

Freya nodded quickly. 'They never even touched us.'

'Nonetheless, I still must have a sample. Please. To be absolutely certain.'

Leon nodded at Freya. 'I don't think we get a choice here. Best just get it over with.'

Reluctantly Freya offered her arm and looked away as Hahn inspected it and started tapping it in search of a decent vein.

'We have also heard from some others that joined us last summer,' the doctor continued. 'You two may find this quite unbelievable . . .' She looked up from Freya's arm.

'This virus . . . this thing, I don't even know if we can call it a "virus", but, whatever it is, it has tried to make imitations of people.'

'People?' Leon recalled the horse. The *very convincing* starving horse that Grace had pleaded with the others to be allowed into their shelter. If it could do horses, then why not people?

'Yes. But very *bad* imitations, though. It is possible to easily tell. Apparently it cannot replicate hair or nails.' She finally found a decent vein and eased the needle in.

Freya jerked and looked away quickly.

'Then if you can tell just by looking . . . why the blood test?' said Leon. 'Why not just take a look at our hair and nails?'

'I have. I can see you have real hair and nails. But this is a more thorough test.' She finished drawing the blood sample then pressed a cotton pad to Freya's arm.

'What's the test?'

Dr Hahn took the syringe of blood and squirted several droplets of it into a petri dish. 'Sodium chloride.' She looked at them both. 'Table salt.' She opened a bottle of clear liquid. 'This is a strong saline solution. Ready?'

Freya frowned. 'Uh, why're you asking me that? I'm not exactly planning to jump up and eat your face or—'

Hahn poured a small amount of it on to Freya's blood.

'The virus reacts instantly to the salt. For some reason it cannot tolerate it.' She gently swirled the petri dish around, ensuring the saline solution and blood had a fair chance to mix.

'I have actually seen a positive result . . . just once. Blood taken from an animal. The blood instantly congeals. It is quite unmistakable.' She stared closely at the mixed liquid as she tilted the dish from side to side and watched Freya's blood run freely across the glass. Eventually she looked up at her over the plastic rims of her glasses. She smiled.

'Congratulations, young lady. You are one hundred per cent human.' She turned to Leon. 'Now it is your turn . . .'

'Knights, you may be seated!'

Freya met Leon's eyes and cocked a brow at him.

Knights? Seriously?

They were standing in a great banquet hall. On all four sides stone walls rose up to meet roughly hewn oak support beams that stretched across the ceiling and supported the planking of the gallery floor above. At one end a vast fireplace crackled with burning logs. Above the flames a large cooking pot hung from a frame and a hook, bubbling and steaming.

Crowded around the fireplace Leon counted seven dogs, a mixture of greyhounds and cocker spaniels, watching the pot intently and licking their lips hopefully.

The hall was filled with probably a hundred people, standing either side of two long, wooden tables, waiting for their turn to take a seat on the benches beside them. At the far end of the hall was a third table set horizontally.

Leon found himself thinking of Hogwarts. Instead of the teaching staff sitting at the top table, there were 'knights'. Leon recognized the face of the man who'd squatted beside him in the back of the truck. They were all still wearing their army fatigues, but the strapped-on armour had been removed and now they looked like an unkempt row of army cadets.

In the middle of them all, where Leon would have placed Dumbledore, stood the community's leader, Major Everett. The only person on the top table with a military title and yet not in uniform.

'And now the rest of you may be seated,' he said, spreading his hands.

The hall filled with the noise of bench legs scraping against the wooden floor and the rustle of movement. Leon and Freya followed the others and squeezed on to the bench side by side.

'Jesus, did we just step through a time portal into the Middle Ages?' whispered Freya.

Major Everett remained standing as he waited for them all to settle.

'Well, I'm sure the rumour mill has been turning this afternoon.' Absently he pulled at the hem of his dark burgundy shirt and fussed with its flapping sleeves. 'I was hoping, as I'm sure we all have been, that this second shitty winter might have finished the bloody thing off, but that appears not to be the case. The kraken is still out there and very much alive and well.'

The hall filled with a chorus of sighs and muttered exchanges.

'Sergeant Corkie, would you mind briefing everyone on what you encountered today?'

The gravelly voiced old soldier who'd spoken to Leon nodded and stood up. 'Aye, sir. As you lot all know, since the snow started clearing up, me an' the lads have been scouting out the nearby towns around Oxford. Those of you who've been here with us since last year will remember that we saw just a few of those little scuttlers around last spring. And they looked pretty sluggish and all done-in. And since then absolutely nothing. Not a sign of the buggers.'

He shook his head. 'Then today . . . well . . . it turns out that the winter hasn't killed them off. They're not dead. In fact, they're doing very well and send their regards.'

The hall filled with sounds of shuffling and gasps.

Beneath his thick moustache, Corkie bit his lip. 'We came across a large concentration of them. And this time they're bigger. A lot bigger.'

Corkie scanned the faces either side of the two long tables until his eyes finally settled on Leon and Freya. 'We rescued those two over there . . . Leon and . . . ?'

'Freya,' said Freya.

'Aye . . . the pair of you were lucky we were in the area. Lucky you actually used your guns or we wouldn't have heard—'

'I wonder,' cut in Everett. He looked at Corkie and raised a hand. 'Sorry for interrupting, Sergeant.' He turned to look at Leon and Freya. 'Would one of you two mind briefing us on what you've seen out there? Where you've come from? Any information at all would be most helpful to us.'

All eyes settled on them both. They looked at each other. *Me? You?*

Freya shrugged and took the initiative. 'We've come from Norwich. We were driving . . . on the A40, I think it was. There was, like, an obstruction and we needed a spare tyre and so we had to get out and walk into Oxford.'

'We found both of them in the underpass, sir,' said Corkie.

Everett made a face. 'You actually went down into an underpass?'

Freya nodded. 'We thought it was safe enough. It wasn't a long tunnel or . . . you know, totally dark, it was just . . . well, easier, quicker to just cut through that way.'

Everett tutted. 'What we learned last year, young lady, was that the virus seeks out warmth. Warm, dark places. Underground places. Basements, cellars, tunnels.'

'And underpasses,' added Freya.

'Indeed. Those are the sorts of areas Corkie and his lads have been probing for signs of the virus. Without any encounters, that is, until today. We were actually beginning to hope the virus had died off.'

'Us too.' She shrugged. 'That's why we came out of hiding. We just—'

'Corkie tells me the kraken's scuttlers had you bottled up in there. Can you tell us anything you can remember? Everything you saw, as best you can? Like I said earlier, any information, no matter how unimportant or trivial you think it is, could help us in the future.'

'Well, the crabs – we call them *snarks* by the way –

they *are* definitely much bigger, and also, they seem . . . I dunno, a bit smarter?' She turned to Leon for support. 'What do you think?'

He looked around at the many pairs of eyes suddenly resting on him. In the life *before*, that would have turned his cheeks hot and red and left him tongue-tied, but, after everything that had happened these last two years, all the things he'd witnessed and endured, opening his mouth before a waiting audience was a big nothing to him.

'Sure.' Leon nodded. 'They moved in from both ends, tried to outflank us. They also seemed to figure out what my gun did pretty damned quickly.'

'Smart,' said Freya. 'Smarter. Definitely.'

'And there was a root thing. We saw this big root,' added Leon.

Everett frowned. 'A root?'

'Yeah. Like a thick tree root running across the roof beneath the underpass. It was big, I mean *tree-trunk* big.'

'And to be clear,' cut in Freya, 'it wasn't a tree root. It was something the virus made.'

Everett looked at Corkie. 'You seen anything like that?'

'No, sir.'

He turned back to them. 'You're sure this "root" was part of the virus?'

'Definitely, sir.' Leon realized Freya had sat back down, letting him do the telling. 'We saw there was, like, this blister-type thing growing out of the root. Like a tumour or something. And then it sort of burst and then all those snarks came spilling out.'

'Snarks?' Everett narrowed his eyes for a moment. He smiled at Leon and nodded approvingly. 'That's a rather good name for the buggers.'

Leon continued. 'That was on our way back through the underpass. We went through it first time and didn't see it, and then coming back . . . I think we must've woken it up first time, and while we were looking around for a tyre that tumour thing was growing.'

Everett stroked the tip of his nose absently. 'Perhaps you triggered something?'

Leon nodded. They hadn't exactly been stealthy; Freya had been singing her head off.

'Yeah. And those snarks came out looking to see what was up.'

'Don't like the sound of that. Roots . . . I wonder if this thing is linking itself up?' Everett turned to Corkie. 'Did you see this root?'

'No, sir. But we weren't exactly hanging about.'

Everett steepled his fingers beneath his nose. 'I suspected the kraken might have gone dormant, lying low, hiding from the cold. But this suggests it's been doing a lot more than merely hibernating. What do you make of it, Corkie?'

The sergeant sat back in his chair. 'Well, we've seen it try to make copies – a couple of those bad human copies last year. Bad dog copies too. Lots of those scuttlers, of course. But nothing yet like what this lad's described.'

He looked at Leon. 'Not saying you're lying, son, but are you sure it wasn't just a tree root? I mean nature's had its own way for the last couple of years.'

'It grew a giant bloody sac!' cut in Freya. 'Which split open and unloaded a frikkin avalanche of snarks on us.' She looked around the room. 'I'm no tree expert, but I'm pretty sure they don't normally do that.'

A guy sitting opposite him, with a ponytail and the meagre tuft of a goatee, snorted with laughter.

'Consolidating,' said Everett. The word hung in the air and echoed for far too long around the cavernous hall. 'God help us all, then,' he muttered, before stopping himself, as if suddenly aware that his misgivings were best kept to himself. He turned his attention back to Leon and Freya. 'Thank you. Thank you both. I presume you've already been checked over by Dr Hahn?'

'Yes, sir,' said Leon.

'Good. It's just a precaution. Clearly the pair of you aren't kraken stooges. And I imagine you're both very hungry.' He managed a congenial smile. 'We should all eat now before dinner gets boiled to a tasteless slop.' He nodded towards the uniformed men either side of him. 'Knights first. Off you go, gentlemen.'

The soldiers stood up as Everett sat down, and the hall instantly filled with the hubbub of voices and movement, the clattering of bowls and spoons as a queue began to form at the far end of the hall beside the fire and the dogs started to bark for scraps.

CHAPTER 13

Two Years Ago

'Tom, this is going to be a bar-room brawl. We have no *POTUS*, no *Veep*, apart from Monica LaGuardia over there, and she's useless. I'm the only cabinet-ranked official here.'

Tom looked where Dougie was pointing. He vaguely recognized the Secretary of Agriculture, her dark hair was pulled up into an I-mean-business bun.

Trent was sitting back in his chair and muttering into Tom's ear as he leaned over his friend's shoulder. 'We've got a mixture of military chiefs-of-staff, from our armed forces and various others. We've got a bunch of White House flunkies, the Mexican ambassador, for Christ's sake . . . a real collection of tide-drift, and no one's got a goddamn clue what the hell we're going to do next. Tom, we need to take control of this chaos *right now*.'

'OK. I'm right here. Whatever you need me to do, Dougie.'

The room was noisy with a dozen different heated conversations going on. Douglas Trent clapped his hands loudly together like a schoolteacher. 'All right, everyone, shut the hell up!'

The crowded briefing room hushed down. Tom backed up against one of the faux wood-panel walls and found a narrow space between two clipboard-carrying navy officers.

'Right . . .' Trent tossed the papers he'd been carrying on to the table in front of him. 'We don't have a playbook to work from. This –' he gestured dismissively at the scattered papers – 'is *shit*! It's nothing more than a To Do list of things we need to sort out!'

His loud locker-room voice battened the room down to a shocked silence.

'It's a pile of crap! But it's what we've got. And right at the top of that To Do list is sorting out a crisis chain of command.'

Monica leaned forward on her elbows. 'Doug, we don't even know for sure yet where both the president and the vice president are . . . or whether they've been—'

'Last communication from Camp David wasn't encouraging,' interrupted Trent. 'There was a call from one of Bernie's secret-service detachment that this . . . outbreak had hit them there.'

'And we've heard nothing from the vice in the last eighteen hours,' somebody called out from the edge of the room. Heads turned towards a young, well-groomed representative from the White House press staff.

'Right.' Trent nodded. 'And we've had nothing from the rest of the cabinet.'

'Jed's still alive,' said Monica. 'I got a text from him.'

'How long ago?' asked Trent.

'A few . . . *some* hours ago . . .' She shrugged defensively. 'This morning.'

'Jesus!' Trent shook his head. 'This morning I woke up to George Clooney's court appearance and *South Park* reruns. This morning was a lifetime ago. Jed's gone, Monica.' He looked around the conference table. 'The attorney general's dead. Just like everyone else. As far as I'm aware, this sorry cluster of ships is pretty much all we have for an organized government.'

'Doug, if Jed's still alive, he's next in succession, after the vice, after the secretary of state, after the—'

'I'm well aware of the goddamn chain!' He slapped his hand on the table. 'But we've got to work with who we have – and that means whoever's standing right here in this room!'

'It's too soon to write off the others.'

'Too *soon*?' Trent looked at Monica with incredulity. 'In the space of the last twenty-four hours, we've gone from a goddamn amber bio-alert to . . . *this*.' He looked around the room. 'Unless anybody here knows any better, *this* is the US government right now.'

'Sir . . . Mr Trent?'

Doug looked to his right at a silver-haired woman in a pastel orange jacket, another face Tom vaguely recognized from the television but couldn't place right now. In the back of his mind he had her down as a political correspondent for some paper or network.

'If the first order of business is succession, then, unless I'm mistaken –' she nodded at Monica LaGuardia – 'the Secretary of Agriculture is actually next in line.'

'Monica?' He looked pointedly across the table at her. '*Monica?*'

Monica challenged his stare with her own. 'Doug, if we really are down to eighth place of succession, then, yes, I'm afraid Helen's right. It's going to be me.'

The room filled with the sound of shuffling and whispered asides. Tom noted concern on the faces of many of the older uniformed delegates present.

Trent shook his head slowly. 'Monica, we have a succession order that dates back to what . . . the Second World War?' He huffed out a dry, hacking laugh of exasperation. 'And that order was based on the chronology of when government departments were created, if I'm not mistaken. Which puts, let me see, Secretary for *Housing* above Secretary for *Homeland Security*, for Chrissakes!'

'I'm sorry, Doug. It's all that we've got to work with.'

'We're screwed!' snapped Trent loudly. 'We. Are. Frikkin. Screwed!' He looked around the table, eyes wide and challenging. 'Our country pretty much just got wiped out! The *world* just got wiped out! We have no playbook here and we are—'

'We have a playbook,' said Monica. 'It's called the constitution.'

Trent planted both fists on the table in front of him. 'I'm going to play my cards for all of you people to see. I'm just going to say this once, then I'm done talking because we've got way too much other crap to sort through.'

Jesus. Tom could see where this was going. *Doug's got half of them like putty in his hands already.* Tom could see that most of the silver-haired men sporting bars of campaign medals were nodding, urging Doug to take just one more tiny step forward.

'I'm going to insist we bypass Monica. She's only a recent appointee. She doesn't have enough experience to lead. Christ, she's an ex-beet farmer from Illinois who got appointed because Bernie wanted more female faces in the cabinet. As Secretary for Commerce, I'm well aware that puts me next in line. I know that looks bad, but frankly I don't give a crap how it looks. We need to get this sorted and start making some decis—'

'That's absolutely outrageous!'

Trent sat back in his chair. It creaked in the silence. 'Well, you know, do feel free to sue me, Monica. Hell, I won't even mount a defence.'

'This is . . . unconstitutional! This is actually *illegal*, for God's sake!'

'I think we're way past that, Monica. Way past that.'

She looked around for support. 'This is not how we do this! Helen?'

The woman with the orange jacket shrugged. 'Look, I'm just—'

'Hey! People!' Trent clapped his hands together again. 'We've got God knows how many American citizens sitting out there in the freezing cold. And we've got nowhere to take them. Who knows how much food and water there is on these ships. People are going to die unless we get off our asses and act.'

'We should take a vote,' said Tom. Doug twisted in his chair. All eyes settled on him. He was waiting for someone to call him out and ask who the hell he was. But then the same could probably be asked of half the people crowded into this room.

He took a deep breath and added, 'There's no America left, anyway. Just survivors. I think the constitution is pretty much irrelevant right now.'

Trent offered him the slightest nod of gratitude. *You tell 'em, amigo.*

'Right!' Trent spread his hands. 'Good idea. We vote on this. Everyone American in this room gets a vote. No one else. It's Monica or me.' He grabbed a paper cup full of pens sitting in front of him and emptied the biros on to the table. 'Grab a pen, some paper and write a name down. Come on, let's get this done!'

CHAPTER 14

Freya watched the soldiers – Everett's 'knights' – from the rooftop of the castle. They were out there, beyond the protective moat, in the tall grass working in 'no-man's land'. Leon was somewhere among them and she pivoted on her better leg to try to catch a glimpse of him between the castle's battlements.

Major Everett had announced in this morning's breakfast briefing – or 'morning prayers' as he liked to call it – that as it was now clear the virus was out there and still a very present threat, the defences they'd been relying on last summer that had been allowed to fall into a less-than-ready state in the intervening months needed immediate attention.

She watched the men working in teams of four and five, rolling barrels of chemicals across the muddy ground, carefully carrying packets of demolition charges and bundles of wiring between them. Several soldiers stood on guard, dotted around the tall grass and scanning the distant treeline for any signs of movement. They were wearing their distinctive 'armour' plating, which she now understood was sportswear. One of the soldiers had sheepishly informed her they'd raided a sports store last year and grabbed every last bit of cycling, skateboarding and snowboarding protective gear they could lay their hands on.

'Don't worry. It's not as hazardous as it looks.'

She turned to see a slight woman – shorter than her with dark skin and boyishly short cropped black hair.

'It is of course *men's work*, though,' the woman added dryly as she folded laundry that she'd plucked from one of the washing lines stretched across the flat castle roof.

She offered Freya a small hand. 'I'm Naga.'

'Freya.'

Naga jerked her chin at the men working out beyond the moat. 'Like I said, *men's work*. Typical, isn't it? The first thing that vanishes in the aftermath of an apocalypse is a hundred years' worth of women's liberation. Apparently, once more, we're only good for hanging out laundry.'

Freya found herself nodding. Although . . . 'You sure it's OK?'

'Pfft. Relax. Just firecrackers.'

Freya pointed at the craters that punctuated the wild grass. 'The holes look pretty big. What's in the drums those guys are rolling?'

'Liquid butane.' Naga folded a shirt and dropped it into the basket at her feet. 'Don't worry, though. Nothing's live until the field's cleared and Corkie goes out to wire it up.'

Canisters of liquid gas – that explained the craters.

Naga narrowed her eyes. 'Meanwhile us women, as always, are stuck with the cooking, cleaning and scrubbing. Presumably because we're all too stupid and *female* to dig a hole, stick a barrel in it and twist some wires.'

'Do those bombs actually work?'

She nodded. 'They did a pretty good job last year. I don't

know if we killed that many, but the big bangs seemed to do a good job of scaring them off.'

'What about the moat? Did that help?'

'Uh-huh. Corkie's boys backed several trucks full of gritting salt right up to the edge and dumped it in. That water's probably saltier than a bag of chips.'

Freya managed to pick out Leon, knee deep in a hole, swinging a shovel full of earth over his shoulder. Naga's reassuring words settled her a little. An odd sensation, though, to suddenly realize that she was pining, *aching*, to get him safely back on *this* side of the moat.

Let's not be getting all gooey-eyed, Freya. There's love, there's Love and there's LOVE.

She wasn't sure which of those she and Leon shared at the moment, but it was enough that she couldn't help casting an anxious glance his way every now and then.

She was plucking some woolly red socks from the line when she became aware Naga had just said something. 'Sorry?'

'I said, do you want to guess what I did before I became a bloody laundry lady?'

'Sure.' Freya turned to look at her, as if that was actually going to help. 'Umm . . . I wanna say an air hostess?'

Naga laughed at that. Then tutted. 'A tax accountant, actually.'

'Oh.' Freya nodded as she resumed unpegging socks from the washing line. 'OK.'

'Yup!' Naga laughed. 'That's exactly what people used to say to me at parties.' She propped her small pointed jaw on her fists and batted her eyes as if she was struggling to keep them open. 'Accounts, huh? Hmmm . . . so very *fascinating*.'

'I'm sorry – I wasn't trying to say your job was bor—'

Naga flapped a hand. 'Don't worry about it. It's the classic "yawn job". Like being in HR or being an estate agent. Doesn't matter. The fact is I enjoyed doing it . . . and I made lots of money too, which is what really counts.'

She arched her back, straightened her arms and clicked her elbow. 'What about you? Who were you?'

'An A-level student.'

'Really?' Naga's eyes widened. 'How old are you?'

'Eighteen.'

'I thought you were in your mid-twenties!'

'*That* old? Charming!'

'Hey, no, sorry. That came out sounding wrong, didn't it?'

''S OK.' Freya chuckled. 'It's my old-woman hobble I guess.' She tossed a fistful of socks into the clothes basket at her feet. 'So, how did you manage to survive, Naga?'

'Like everyone else here, I was zonked out on medication at the time.' She held out one hand. 'Chronic RSI. Carpal tunnel syndrome. I'd just had the operation done . . . privately, I might add. And then guess what.'

'What?'

'I got sepsis. An infection as a result of the op. So I was being kept in and pumped full of antibiotics when the plague came.' She laughed. 'Ironic, really – as a result of some ridiculously overpaid consultant not washing his hands properly after playing golf, my life was saved.' She put her hands on her hips. 'That's why I probably won't be suing them for shoddy hygiene standards.'

Freya laughed.

'What about you?' asked Naga.

'I was on meds too. Painkillers. I was diagnosed with—'

'Multiple sclerosis?'

Freya nodded. 'Good guess.'

'My auntie had it. I thought it only happened to older people, though?'

'Old and young.'

'What about your boyfriend? American, isn't he?' Naga arched her brows. 'I'm presuming *boyfriend*?'

'Oh.' Freya laughed a little ruefully. 'We're not that.'

Naga narrowed her eyes. 'But . . . ?'

'No.' Freya shook her head. 'That's not a . . . a *thing* for us. We've got each other's backs, though. We met at this other place after the virus and we just sort of clicked. And, no, Leon's not American, by the way, he's British. He gets really pissed off if you call him a Yank.'

'Right.' Naga zipped her mouth. 'Note to self.' She unpegged a heavy sweater. 'So what was this "other place"?'

'It was like a super-posh health spa in some woods outside Norwich. It was pretty remote, so they were well set up to survive.'

'What made you leave, then?'

Freya wondered how much she wanted to share with her. The memory of that traumatic last day was still raw in her mind. For Leon, mercifully, a lot of it had been a

98

concussed blur. Not for her, unfortunately. She'd heard Grace's screams as she burned to death in that storeroom. She'd watched Dave staring through the open door and seen the flicker of flames on his face, the reflected glint in his eye.

She'd been the one who'd had to plead with Phil as he drove them both away, crying, begging for him not to follow Dave's orders and kill them both. To let them go, and in return she'd promised they'd never come back. She'd done all that, saved their lives, while Leon had been dazed, useless, in shock.

She didn't want to talk about that now. Instead she gave Naga an edited version of what had brought them here, which included their discovery of that BBC radio studio and the message for other survivors. 'Me and Leon have no idea how recently that broadcast was recorded. It could have been a few months or weeks ago. It could just as easily have been recorded days after the outbreak.'

'You said the station still had electric power?'

She nodded. 'Some places still do. Wind turbines, solar panels . . . you know?'

'This message, what was it?'

'The gist is there's a bunch of ships coming to collect survivors from Southampton. They said we had to get there by September. But, you know, *which* September? This one? Last year's? The year befo—'

'And you two were on your way down to find out?'

Freya nodded. 'Stupidly. Yeah. Because . . . what else are we going to do? Right?'

'You told Everett about this?'

Freya wondered what Leon would say about her sharing this with Naga. They hadn't actually discussed whether it was something to keep secret or not. But both, so far, had instinctively kept it to themselves.

'Not yet, no.'

'My God, you *have to* tell him! If there's even a small chance . . .' Naga stepped closer. 'If there's even a *tiny* chance that there's a rescue effort being put together?' Her brown eyes were suddenly wide and round with hope. 'You're not messing me around? This is for real?'

Freya was regretting opening her mouth now. 'Yes.'

'Flipping hell! Seriously. Bloody hell!' She was grinning. 'Go tell him!'

Freya nodded. 'OK . . . but, you know, maybe don't tell anyone else until I've told him?'

Naga nodded quickly. 'Sure. Sure!' She snatched the socks out of Freya's hands and shooed her away.

'Go! GO!'

CHAPTER 15

Leon was pretty annoyed. He hadn't wanted everyone to know their business. And now here they were, both summoned to Everett's room, with Corkie and Everett there waiting patiently to hear them fully explain their story. Since it was Freya who'd blabbed, he let her do most of the talking.

Everett listened impassively, not giving anything away as he absently stroked the tip of his nose. Finally, Freya finished.

'And you just told Naga about this?'

Freya nodded.

'Marvellous,' he said wearily. 'We can now assume then that it's common knowledge. It'll be all around the bloody castle by evening prayers.'

'Everyone *should* know about it,' said Freya. 'It's a chance for rescue, for all of us!'

'Forgive me for *not* tap dancing with excitement and optimism, young lady,' he said, settling back in the leather chair behind his dark oak desk.

Freya looked bewildered. 'Why? Why not? It's a chance—'

'Because it's highly likely any ship has been and gone. Or, more likely, that it never came at all.'

The room – Everett's 'campaign room' – looked like

the set from some medieval movie. On the desk, spread out like a tablecloth, was a blueprint of the castle and the surrounding grounds, like some general's battlefield map. The walls of the room were panelled with dark wood and hung with tapestries bearing coats of arms. A thin shaft of light shone through the narrow arched window, catching floating dust motes in its beam.

'But how can you be so sure of that?'

Everett sighed. He pointed to a desk beneath the window. Sitting on it was a rack of olive-green army equipment.

'*That* is a CNR radio pack. VHF, MHz and digital. We get all the emergency frequencies, and I hate to be the bearer of bad tidings, but we haven't heard anything on it other than a handful of weak garbled signals for quite some time.'

'You *have* heard other signals, then?' said Freya.

Everett looked sorry for her. Genuinely sorry. His gaunt cheeks creased with paternal pity and he looked down as he spoke.

'The last person we ever heard in the ether was speaking in Mandarin. And she was singing. Not particularly tunefully, either. That was eighteen months ago. We've not heard anything since.'

Everett directed his gaze at Leon. 'You're being rather quiet. What are your thoughts on the matter?'

Leon hadn't wanted anyone to know in the first place. He was equally inclined to keep his intentions to himself.

'You can speak freely, lad . . . I'm not a tyrant.'

'Maybe you're right, sir.'

Freya did a double take. 'We *have* to go and check it out, at least.'

'I see.' Everett puffed his lips out. 'Well, look, you're both free to leave the castle any time you wish. And, if there'd been no further signs of the virus, I would have wished you all the best, bon voyage and send us a postcard, please. But it appears our hopes that the kraken is dead and gone were . . . shall I say, premature.'

'We still have to try,' replied Freya.

'You'll die out there.'

'We got this far, didn't we?'

Everett glanced at Corkie. 'If my men hadn't turned up when they did, that underpass would have been the end of your journey.'

Everett took several steps across his room to stare out of the narrow window. 'Last autumn, before this second winter kicked in, those grounds out there were *a battlefield*. There were thousands of them. Our minefields, the moat, these walls kept them back, day after day after day.'

Leon could see his blue eyes gazing out at the distant tree line.

'Each day, the virus was trying something different. Learning from its mistakes. Adapting its creatures, experimenting with smaller ones, then larger ones. Probing us for weaknesses.' His voice had a hollow quality to it, the voice of a besieged king.

'As the weather cooled again, and on its last attempt, it managed to produce some very large creatures, the size of cows. But, of course, nothing like a cow. Lumbering, clumsy, badly balanced things . . . that ended up tumbling into our moat and dying.'

He turned back to face them. 'The point is that it tried and it failed.' He smiled. 'You know this castle is not a *real* castle?' He turned to them. 'The foundations are, but the rest of it is, essentially, one big movie set. The ruins, which I believe do date back to Norman times, were bought by a film company, and this castle was rebuilt to make some sort of expensive fantasy drama. After they finished with it, they sold it on to another company, which used it for corporate events, weddings, medieval banquets, that kind of thing.'

He slapped a hand against the wall beside the window. 'Behind this facade it's all modern concrete and iron girders. And, God help me, I'm thankful for that. It's solid. It'll hold. If you want to leave us, then feel free. But, if you want my advice? Stay. The kraken, it appears, has awoken once more.'

'I've met him somewhere before,' said Freya. 'I know I have.'

'You know Everett?'

'I know his face.'

The two of them were sitting outside the castle on a pallet on the mud-churned ground before the entrance. The drawbridge was down; Corkie and the knights were out on another scouting trip. One of them had been left behind on sentry duty. He was sitting on a stool on the far side of the drawbridge in an anorak that snapped and rustled in the cold wind as he scanned the grounds.

'Maybe he just looks like somebody you know,' said Leon.

'Yeah, maybe,' replied Freya.

His mind shifted on to another matter. 'So, what are we going to do? Stay? Go?'

She didn't answer.

Leon sighed. 'If he's not heard anything else on that radio in eighteen months, then it means that message is probably old news. Just some repeated loop.'

Freya looked at him. 'So we give up. Is that it?'

'It's not giving up, staying here.' He nodded at the trucks, at several stacks of boxes containing tins of food. 'It's a pretty good set-up. Better than Emerald Parks.'

'It's no different to Emerald Parks. Another survivor camp run by another prat with a God complex.'

Leon was grateful she didn't say Dave Lester's name out loud. Hearing his name spoken would have brought the memories right back. *That* day . . . the day that had started with The Horse.

He looked at the distant tree line and wondered if there were any virals lurking out there, observing the open ground and the castle, *evaluating* with those pale little eyes.

'A couple of days ago we were seconds away, Freya. We were just *seconds away* from—'

She nodded, not wanting him to finish. 'I know. I know.'

He turned to her. 'You asked me to *shoot* you.'

Freya closed her eyes and shuddered at the memory.

'That's how bat-shit crazy it is out there – when a bullet in the head is the *better* option.' He took a deep breath. 'You *really* want to head out there?'

'No. But . . . do you *really* think we're going to be safe here forever?' She stretched out her cramping left leg. 'What if the virus learns how to make snarks that can fly? Or can tunnel under the castle? Or float across the moat?'

'That's a way off.'

'Oh, of course, because you *know* that, right?'

'I know shit. But I do know you and me – we didn't "make it" this far. We got our asses *saved*.'

They sat in silence for a while listening to the soft hiss of a steady breeze through the tall grass. Finally Leon spoke. 'You know . . . I don't think I could have done it – pulled the trigger.'

Freya rested a hand on his. 'Yes, you could. And I know you would have. I trust you.'

'Really?'

'And, you know . . . you can trust me. If something like that ever happens to us again?' She shook her head firmly. 'I'm not dying the virus way. I want it to be quick, to be instant.' She squeezed his hand. 'That's our pact, remember? You and me . . . we're not going to end up as snarks.'

Leon closed his eyes and saw that service station two years back. The toilets. The snarks in their thousands.

'I saw Mum die that way. Those things, climbing all

over her, in her hair, climbing across her face. You know what her last words were?'

Freya shook her head.

'They're inside me.'

She looped her arm through his and pulled him closer. 'Don't relive it, Leon. It's done. It happened. Nothing changes that.'

'Call me weak, but –' he sighed – 'I don't think I'm ready to go out there again. Not yet.'

He felt her head nod on his shoulder. 'Well, we've got time, Leo. We've got six months until September.'

'Right. Six months.'

CHAPTER 16

[. . . your advance presence is registered . . .]

The core portion of her command cluster – the substance that felt like her – arrived in packets first: parcels of amino acid data that had travelled like a convoy of trucks along endless winding arteries.

For Grace, time was an irrelevance, an illusion. She'd been deconstructed into small batches of cells for easier capillary transportation. Her consciousness had broken down into constructs as incapable of thought as any red blood corpuscle. For the duration of the journey she hadn't been Grace – she'd been a stream of tumbling, stupid cells – and now that enough of her had been directed by a dedicated 'chaperone' cluster to her destination, she felt her consciousness building, block by block.

The translation along untold hundreds of miles of networked roots had been an instantaneous process for her. In the world outside, weeks might have passed, but for her it was as if she'd fallen asleep in one place and woken up in another.

My name is Grace.

[. . . this is known . . .]

Where am I?

[. . . collective of command cluster designate . . .]

No, where am I? In the world? What country?

[. . . (term-'world') . . . seeking clarification . . . (term-'country'] . . . seeking clarification . . .]

The communication clusters, she had grown to understand, were little more than tug boats in this incomprehensible ecosystem, there to latch on to and steer clusters of cells to the right place. They had no intelligence of their own.

To make sense of her surroundings, in her mind's eye Grace conjured up the illusion of a Manhattan hotel lobby. The illusion solidified in detail around her.

[. . . creating abstract/metaphor for communication convenience. We/I understand . . .]

Her lobby was a busy one with serious-looking businessmen checking in and out. She re-formed the communication cluster into the illusion of a flustered ruddy-cheeked bellboy looking around for someone more senior to help his Very Important Guest with her query.

She sensed the proximity of nucleic acids reacting with her outer cell walls. In her abstraction of a hotel lobby, help arrived in the form of a uniformed manager.

'Grace, welcome to this place.'

Where am I? Am I in England still?

The manager – tidy, particular and coolly courteous, the cliché of a concierge – looked around and spread his hands.

'You are referring to exterior macro-universe location labelling?'

She was getting better at understanding their . . . her . . . new language. *Yes.*

'I understand. Then no. We are not in The England. We are in the place called "Europe".'

Europe. She once went on a school trip to Europe. An expensive one. They visited Paris, climbed the Eiffel Tower, saw a bunch of old paintings and some other stuff.

Did I travel across sea?

'Under the sea. Through an artificial man-made conduit. I believe the term is a "tunnel".'

She wished a tiny fragment of her mother were here with her too. Just enough to conjure the ghost of her to hold her hand and tell her she was just fine.

'There are others like you here,' said the manager. 'Complete conscious entities.'

Other . . . humans?

'Once they were "humans". Now they are all a part of WE. As you are too, Grace.'

I'm afraid.

'There is nothing to be afraid of. We are all linked now.' He smiled warmly at her. 'We are "family".'

Were you once a human?

'Yes. A part of me was. I notice you see me as an old man.'

Grace nodded. She imagined the manager of a hotel as grand as the one she'd created would look just like a butler; elderly and distinguished with old-world manners and a handlebar moustache.

The manager smiled. 'Yes, I was once human. But I didn't look like this. Would you like to see what I really looked like?'

Grace nodded.

The manager wavered into a nondescript outline. She didn't want the entire illusion to collapse into darkness and communicate chemically. She needed the comfort of familiarity right now. 'Don't go . . .'

'My name was . . . Hannah. Just give me a moment. More of myself is nearby. I will retrieve information.'

Grace gazed at the indeterminate form in front of her, shimmering and shifting, the power of her imagination hovering in an unstable holding pattern, waiting to have something to work with.

'I'm Hannah Schenk,' the manager eventually said. 'I was thirty-nine. My hair was long and light brown. I was quite tall, slim, healthy. I like to think I was an attractive woman.'

The shimmering avatar in front of Grace took a more distinct form, a collaborative image. Hannah was sharing small packets of data with Grace, and Grace was interpreting them. The voice she was 'hearing' rose in timbre to a softer feminine tone, but with a hard edge to it and the hint of an accent, how Grace imagined a German woman with a good grasp of English would sound. She found herself looking at an attractive, smartly dressed woman.

'Tell me about you, Grace. I know you were a girl. How old?'

Yes. I was . . . am *twelve*.

Grace wasn't quite ready to describe herself in the past tense yet. In that case, was she *always* going to be twelve? Or was that an irrelevance now? More to the point, was she even *female* now? Could she be either gender? Could she be old or young? Did it matter?

'Yes. It does matter,' replied Hannah Schenk. 'We are the sum of the lives we lived. Our memories define us in a way chemistry can't.'

Hannah cocked her head, her eyes narrowed as she studied Grace. 'Embrace who you are, Grace. That's why we are so important to our friends.'

Our friends? Grace had long since abandoned the term 'snark'. In that strange period after she'd been consumed, as she'd slowly gathered her wits and gradually comprehended what had happened to her, the term had seemed ridiculous and from another time, another century. Like the horrible 'N' word, 'snark' felt like an abusive term. As she'd grown to understand they meant no harm to her, she'd abandoned it. She'd very quickly begun to think of the entities she sensed around her as teammates, as colleagues, helpers, assistants.

But friends?

'Yes. Friends. They only want what is best for us.'

Best for us? For humans? But they killed us all!

'You're not dead,' said Hannah. 'Nor am I. In fact, I feel more alive now than I ever have.' She smiled. Grace wondered whether the smile was her imagination, or whether Hannah had somehow stepped within the boundaries of Grace's imagination and taken control of this whole illusion.

'We can read each other's thoughts. Feel each other's emotions. Grace, you can look inside me. You can know me, a perfect stranger, in a way no one else ever did. Not my parents, not my friends, not my lover. Please –' she offered Grace a slender hand – 'come and know me.'

Grace reached out and touched Hannah's hand. And instantly felt it.

An overpowering kinship.

She saw fleeting images of a whole other life. In a heartbeat, she *was* Hannah Schenk. She saw, *felt*, thirty-nine years of another life: childhood memories . . . a birthday party with balloons and cake and a silver-haired woman who was old enough to be Hannah's grandmother, yet she instinctively knew was her mother. No siblings. No father. Just the two of them. Older now . . . playing the flute in a school orchestra, looking for her mother's face in an audience of reflecting video camera lenses. Older still . . . practising scales in her bedroom, posters of R.E.M. and Einstürzende Neubauten on the walls, bands Grace had never heard of but all of sudden felt she knew. College. A music college. And a boyfriend called Hamsa who played cello, who had won a musical scholarship and came from Palestine. Reciting pieces together, busking together on the streets of Hamburg. Older now . . . and in an office job she absolutely hated. The flute sitting at home in her single-bedroom apartment, in a box collecting dust. A new boyfriend. This one is called Stefan. He works in the same place. They both want a baby so badly, and Mother now is so old . . . She yearns for grandchildren. Hospital. A miscarriage. Heartbreak. So close to term and then this happened. Hospital again some years later, this time for her mother. Her silver hair is all gone and she looks so pale and sunken. But she strokes the bump of Hannah's belly and smiles.

A funeral. Hannah watches the coffin being lowered into a grave. Stefan squeezes her hand.

A birth. If only Mother had lived long enough . . .

Christmas. It's 2010. The bump is now a boy called Homer. The little boy unwraps a present. It's a Teenage Mutant Ninja Turtle action figure and he goes absolutely crazy with excitement.

Older now. Homer's a couple of years older than Grace is . . . *was* . . . with floppy purple hair dangling across his face. Stefan's gone. It's just Hannah and Homer. Life repeating itself, mother and child facing the world alone in a one-bedroom flat. Hannah's back at work, because bills need paying and Stefan's being difficult with the maintenance payments. It's another job she detests and that same college flute sits in the same box with a thick film of dust on it.

The last memory is a rock concert. That's Homer onstage playing guitar with three other lads, and Hannah may not like their music – it's grungy and loud and sounds very angry – but she's so incredibly proud of him. Homer's a good boy. He might be on tour a lot but he comes home whenever he can and nags her to get online with a dating site. She won't because it costs so much and it's all just weirdos anyway. But he insists, and he pays.

Then the day the virus hits Europe.

Hannah dies alone in the kitchen, not knowing if

Homer's still alive in Japan where his rock band is on tour.

The images fade and Hannah lets go of Grace's hand.

'And now you know me, Grace. And I know you.'

Why do they want me here?

'You, and the others who've been invited . . . you're here to discuss what happens next.'

What happens next to what? To whom . . . ? To us?

'To those poor souls who have been left behind.'

CHAPTER 17

'Now then, I know the rumour continues to circulate around this castle. So I'm going to address it . . . *again*. And, hopefully, this will be the last time I have to do so.' Everett looked up and down both tables like a head teacher admonishing unruly students.

'There is absolutely, one hundred per cent, *no rescue effort currently in progress*. Not in Southampton, not at Land's End, not in Dover . . . not in Barnsley-Bottom-On-Sea!' Everett stared firmly at his audience sitting either side of the long tables.

'Our two newcomers stumbled across a message that was, unfortunately, out of date. *Two years out of date!* I'm sorry to be the killjoy here, but there has been nothing, absolutely nothing, on any frequency in the last year and a half. Not a word, or a beep, or anything other than bloody hissing and warbling. And certainly no messages about approaching rescue fleets!'

He sighed. 'I'm sorry – genuinely, truly, sorry – but that's the way it is. Now, I think we should proceed on to more pressing matters. It's absolutely clear that we are going to have to revive the security measures we put in place last year. That means a return to night watch duties . . .'

There were several groans.

'. . . ground-maintenance patrols AND weekly blood

screening for everyone. I also think it would be prudent for our knights to forage for additional supplies. We should start stockpiling in case we find ourselves besieged again. I know we've been getting slack and tapping into our diesel reserves, so I want those topped up too, Corkie.'

'Aye, sir.'

The honeymoon period seemed well and truly over for Leon and Freya. They'd become properly enrolled into Everett's community, and over the last month Leon had found himself adjusting to their new way of life.

Routine and more routine. Everett ran the castle with precisely timed horn-blowing.

There had been nothing remotely resembling an organized day during the eighteen months alone with Freya. There'd been stretches of endless days when they'd remained inside in the dark, beneath quilts, eating cold tinned meals and reading books to pass the time. On other days necessity had forced them to forage outside in the snow, or the rain. Sometimes in the few warm weeks between the late spring and the early autumn, the dead city of Norwich lay fully exposed, forlorn, and it stank like rancid pond water.

He preferred this: keeping busy, the regimented schedule broken into two-hour time blocks marked by the blowing of a hunting horn from the rooftop of the keep. Eight until ten – breakfast. Ten until twelve – work session one. Twelve until one – lunch break. One until three – work session two. Three until four – personal chores. Four until six – work session three. Six until eight – dinner. Nine – lights out.

The work sessions were marked up on a chart in the main hall where they assembled for meal times. The tasks varied and were shared out among the five work groups: laundry, toilet emptying, cooking, combat drill, perimeter inspection, firewood collection, gardening, water purification.

Leon and Freya had been assigned to different groups, divided by gender. Everett seemed to hold a puritanical view on what was considered women's work and what was men's work. Three out of the five groups were all female, the other two all male. Which, of course, was an endless source of irritation to Freya, since the female groups tended to get the first three tasks most of the time. None of the women liked it, but Everett's decision was final.

The days seemed to pass quickly, especially after the evening meal when there was an hour to spend until the power generator was switched to economy mode and the castle's electric lights went out, leaving nothing but candles to read by. A contrast to Mr Carnegie's more relaxed schedule, where they'd all seemed to have far too much time on their hands.

Leon liked this better. Come nine o'clock, when the horn sounded and everyone made sure they were close enough to their beds to be able to find them by candlelight, he was ready to hit the pillow and get some sleep.

In his work group were fifteen others, ranging in age from an eleven-year-old boy called Stephen, right up to an old guy, Paddy, who he guessed was somewhere in his sixties. There was a whippet-thin guy called 'Fish', with fine blond hair pulled back – always – into a limp ponytail, a goatee that only seemed to appear when the sun caught it at the right angle, and an Adam's apple that Leon couldn't stop staring at when he talked or swallowed; it bobbed up and down like a cat in a canvas bag.

Fish had a couple of battered old Nintendo handhelds that he'd managed to keep alive on scavenged batteries. He was grimly resigned to the fact that even though this dead world was littered with pristine plastic-sealed packs of double As, they all had a finite shelf life that was ticking slowly down and one day there'd be no more *Mario Karts*.

'I used to be a games coder,' Fish told him.

'Really? Any games I might know?'

'Sure. Probably. Maybe. You a console gamer?'

Leon nodded. 'I used to have a PlayStation.'

Fish curled his lips. 'Otherwise known as the *PlebStation*. Yeah . . . when I was working for Kindoo Games, we did *DemonStorm*. You remember that one?'

He did. 'Really? You worked on that?'

Fish nodded.

'That was pretty *awesome*.' Actually it wasn't. Leon remembered quickly begrudging the fifty pounds and three hours he'd spent on it. He'd been seduced into parting with his money by the trailer and endless five-star reviews. All the same, it was a pleasant connection with the past to be sitting here with someone who'd worked on it.

'Ah, but, no, see, it wasn't. In fact, it was a steaming

pile of cynical shite. A quick cash-in on those first-gen VR headsets. Run-'n'-gun, pray-'n'-spray bollocks. The whole development team knew it was a complete turd even before it got released.'

'Uh, OK. I was kind of being polite. Yeah, it wasn't that great.'

'I went solo after that. Worked on apps. Did you game much on your phone?'

'*Clash of Clans*, a bit. Got bored of that, though.'

'You ever play *Zombie Last Stands*?'

Leon shook his head. 'Never heard of it.'

'That was one of mine.' He rolled his eyes skyward and Leon took the chance to stare at his Adam's apple for a second. 'Two years in the bloody making, just me on my own. Historical famous last stands, right? You know the famous ones like the Alamo, Thermopylae, Rorke's Drift?'

Leon nodded.

'Well, anyway, my game was taking those famous battles and then replacing the bad guys with, you know . . . *zombies*. Hundreds of 'em swarming over the heroic few.' He grinned. 'Bit like us lot last year. Anyway, I launched it on the app store and it was just beginning to take off, right? I swear, it was getting thousands of downloads and was going to make me flipping rich, I'm telling you. I was going to be the next Notch. Then that frikkin end-of-the-world thing happened.' He shook his head. 'Can't moan, though, I suppose . . . I'm still alive.'

'I'm guessing you were on meds at the time?'

'Yup. Fluoxetine for the mood swings, Omeprazole for

the stomach ulcer, aspirin for the migraines and RSI.' He laughed. 'That poor virus never stood a chance with me.'

Leon laughed. Fish was all right.

'You not finished peeling those yet?' Naga gestured at the spuds on the chopping board in front of Freya. Three-quarters done, another thirty of the big lumpy things to go.

Naga raised her tidy dark brows into two symmetrical arches, her silent way of saying *get on with it*. As the work-group leader, she managed to keep her girls in line with a variety of expressions: exasperation, irritation and, on rare occasions, approval.

The kitchen was hot, steamy and noisy with the sound of clanking pans, scrubbing and chopping. This morning they'd been out in the grounds under the watchful eyes of a couple of knights, digging up another patch of earth that had been set aside for potatoes last summer. Digging them up, sorting the winter-spoiled from the good, scrubbing and now peeling them.

If I have to peel another bloody potato this week . . .

Everyone was expected to pull their weight here. Well, nearly everyone it seemed.

'I'd like to see those army boys do some bloody kitchen work for once,' muttered Freya. 'You do know they're not proper soldiers?'

'Uh?'

'Everett's knights.'

'But they—'

'Have the uniforms?'

Freya nodded. 'And they call Corkie "sergeant".'

'My dad was in the army. I lived on army bases throughout my childhood. I know what soldiers are like. And those aren't proper soldiers, I'm telling you.'

Freya wasn't entirely sure what Naga meant by that. They seemed to have the rough-and-ready manners and coarse language she expected of a bunch of squaddies.

'They don't have the same *discipline* as proper army lads.'

'How do you mean?'

'Well, come on, you've done laundry duty, right? You've picked their pants off the floor, seen their unmade beds? Trust me, blokes who've been through basic army training never lose those habits once they've had them drummed into them.'

'Corkie's area is tidy.'

'That's true. Now he, I'm certain, *is* ex-army. But the rest . . . ?' Her face pinched sceptically. 'Nah.'

Freya halved the last couple of potatoes she'd skinned and tossed them into the pot.

'Could be reservists, though,' added Naga. 'I imagine every last reservist was called up when the virus hit the UK. They had soldiers out and about everywhere.'

'I really don't remember much of that week,' said Freya. 'I didn't even notice the news story when it was starting abroad. I was far too busy dealing with this . . .' She gestured at the walking stick resting against the counter beside her stool. 'And when the virus reached Kings Lynn it was just so sudden.' She looked up from the chopping board. 'I went to bed one night leaving my parents watching the news. I remember they were getting really worried, talking about getting in some extra shopping the next day. I woke up in the morning and I found them in the kitchen. They were . . . well, you know . . .'

'I'm sorry, Freya. That must have been truly awful.'

Freya started on another potato. 'All long ago, another time. I try not to think about Mum and Dad any more. What about you?'

Naga shrugged. 'I was living on my lonesome in London. Single. No kids, no boyfriend. I look back now and thank God I didn't have to witness anyone I loved die.

CHAPTER 18

'Leave the engine running, old son,' said Corkie. 'Better to be safe than sorry.' He studied the bottling plant warily; it was a two-storey box-shaped office building with a large warehouse to one side.

Three cars were parked up in the staff car park. Weeds had punched through the cracked tarmac and were slowly wending their way through the vehicles' hubcaps.

'Can't see any creepy-crawlies, Sarge.'

'Which doesn't mean to say there aren't any.' He continued to scan both buildings for any signs of fine tendril-spread. He also scanned the parking area for the telltale hump of viral roots growing beneath the failing tarmac. Over the last two weeks, now that they were looking, they'd become aware of the subtle bumps that signalled their presence below ground.

The root system seemed to loosely follow the roads. Perhaps the ground beneath them was somehow easier to burrow through, or perhaps there was another unfathomable factor at work. Roads were generally the straightest and least obstructed routes between population centres, and the roots presumably mirrored that rationale. Or maybe their branching and direction of travel was entirely random, but their presence was far more noticeable beneath the flat, tarred surfaces.

'Looks like this place is unvisited,' said Corkie finally.

He picked up his helmet from the dashboard, put it on, then climbed down out of the passenger door of the truck and banged on the side. 'All right, lads, dismount!'

He signalled at the second truck parked behind with a circular sweep of his hand. Soldiers spilled out of both vehicles, and army boots clumped noisily on to the parking lot. Riot shields were quickly passed down out of the back of both vehicles, and a couple of minutes later twenty men stood ready for instructions, shields in one hand and an assortment of swords, axes and machetes in the other.

Corkie gestured towards the bottling plant's warehouse. The objective for today's foray was to obtain a decent stash of sealed, unspoiled water containers. While there was a source of recycled water back at the keep – provided they had continual supply of firewood to boil and purify it – there was inevitable wastage and loss, and Major Everett was keen to ensure they built up a reserve supply of stored water in case of emergencies.

Water. Food. Source of fuel for heat and medication. The key four things needed for survival.

'Corporal Briggs?'

'Yes, Sergeant?'

While Everett insisted on referring to these soldiers as his *knights* – a frivolous habit that Corkie went along with – when out on patrol, it was *his* rules, his terminology, not Everett's. He was damned if was going to call them 'knights'. Damned if he was going to call Briggsy 'Sir Briggs'. They were *his* lads. He'd been the one to train them up and, even if none of them had served a single day in Her Majesty's armed forces, they were corporals and privates and not bloody men-at-arms, praetorians guards or bloody knights or whatever other stupid term Everett might come up with.

'I want you to take your section and search that office building for anything worth nabbing.'

'Yes, Sarge.'

Briggs led his men towards the building, one of them carrying a pressurized fire hydrant on his back filled with heavily salted water – much safer than a flamethrower and just as effective at holding back the crawlers.

'Rest of you lot with me,' said Corkie. He led the way over to the warehouse and stopped a few metres short of a large sliding delivery door. He looked up at the placard on the side of the tall structure:

SCHLOOP PLUS!

He couldn't work out whether the pink, bubbly logo meant this had once been an energy drink or an alcopop bottling plant. He hoped it was the first one. They didn't need alcohol on the castle grounds. Alcohol was a Very. Very. Bad. Idea. Alcohol caused problems.

Once again he scanned the car park for signs of root humps and the cinderblock sides of the warehouse for any sign of those faint branching patterned stains that growth tendrils would have left behind. It appeared that the virus hadn't discovered this place yet. All the same, he summoned Private Gosling over to stand right beside him and ready the fire extinguisher for use.

'Anything inside moves, you spray like crazy.'

'Aye, Corkie.'

Corkie scowled at him.

'Yes, Sarge.'

'Right then. Ready, lads?' He reached for the handle of the delivery-bay door and tugged hard on it. The large door rattled noisily aside on runners that screamed pitifully for a squirt of lubricant. Inside it was gloomy but not dark. The roof was punctuated with two rows of scum-fogged skylight windows and they could see what they'd expected to see: plant machinery, storage vats, pallets of wood on which cling-film-wrapped boxed product waited patiently for a truck that was never going to come.

The concrete floor was damp and puddled in places where rain had leaked through the roof. A solitary tree sapling a metre high was growing out of the middle of the floor where the concrete had given way and light from the skylights above had offered a chance of solar nourishment.

Nature's a canny bastard.

Corkie inhaled deeply, his nostrils whistling in the silence as he did. No yeasty smell. He puffed out his breath and sniffed again just to be sure. That odour, that musty, *brewery* odour, they'd come to realize, was a fair indicator of where the virus had concentrated its mass into festering pools.

Nothing.

It just smelt of damp and the faintest hint of diesel sludge and grease.

'Looks all clear, lads. Gosling, Jameson, you two just do a once-around recce inside the warehouse. The rest of you scruffy Herberts, let's make a start by grabbing these pallets.'

Several pallets were stacked high with plastic bottles of Schloop! – whatever the hell that was – and blanketed in thick swatches of polythene wrapping.

Corkie cut through it with his machete, then organized his men into a human chain, grabbing twelve-packs of the drink and passing them down to be stacked in the back of the trucks.

They'd just cleared the second pallet when Corkie heard Gosling's voice bouncing off the roof of the warehouse.

'*Sarge! Sarge!*'

'Shit!' Corkie hissed. His men froze and looked to him for orders. 'Gosling? What's up?' he barked in reply.

'Sir, over here!' The voice echoed around the warehouse. It could have come from any direction.

'Where the hell are you?'

Just then they heard boots pounding the concrete, webbing jangling, and Jameson appeared to their left, emerging from behind a large iron vat.

'Sir, we've found a survivor.'

Corkie nodded at his men to carry on with the task at hand and swiftly followed as Jameson led him down a narrow walkway between rows of cylindrical brewing tanks linked by a mad spaghetti of rusting pipes. He felt as if he were walking through the digestive tract of some large mechanical beast.

'Just one survivor?'

'Yeah . . . a young boy. He looks in a pretty bad way, sir.'

Jameson took a left turn between two vats and ducked under the pipes that linked them. 'Over here.'

Corkie followed. 'I said recce the *perimeter* . . . not dive into the middle. How the bloody hell did you find him?'

'We heard him crying. We just followed the sound.'

They turned another corner and found Gosling kneeling down beside a small child, his knees drawn up protectively, painfully thin arms around them, hugging them, face buried and sobbing.

Corkie hurried over and squatted down beside them. 'All right, son,' he said in the softest tone his gravelly voice could muster. 'It's all right. Help's here.'

The boy was barely clothed. Gosling had found an old rag nearby and thrown it over his narrow shoulders. Even so, Corkie could see there was extensive scarring and livid red welts on the pale skin of his tiny frail body.

The first thought that occurred to him was that the boy must have been physically abused. The world might have ended, but there were still bad people out there.

'We're going to take you with us, son, OK? Get you cleaned up and fed. We're going to take care of—'

The boy raised his face from his arms and Corkie could see the right side of his face was terribly scarred, a swirling spiderweb of tight, ridged flesh from his scalp all the way down his cheek to his mouth.

'Jesus!'

He recoiled, staggering backwards.

'It's OK, Sarge. They're old scars. It's not infection.'

Corkie steadied himself and leaned forward again, carefully reaching out for the boy's chin, lifting it and turning the child's face to get a better look. 'You're right.' He'd seen enough old wound scarring in his time.

He looked up at Gosling and Jameson. 'Third-degree burns. Bad ones. That's what the scarring is.' He gestured at the boy's short dark hair. In places, where the scarred tissue was, he was bald. That was skin that was never, ever, going to grow hair again.

'And see? Real hair. He's real.' He rested a hand lightly on the boy's shoulder. 'You poor, poor little bastard. Let's get you out of—'

The boy looked up at him and finally opened his mouth. 'They're ... right ... here,' he whispered. '*They're everywhere.*'

It was then that Corkie heard it. All around them, the soft rasp of movement, the gentle clack of hard chitin brushing against rusting ironwork, the creak of machinery under the weight of subtly shifting bodies.

'Oh shit,' whispered Corkie.

CHAPTER 19

Corkie reached up slowly and flicked on his helmet torch. The narrow space around them had previously been gloomily illuminated by the filtered shards of light from above, but was now caught in the tight, stark, glare of his beam. Gosling and Jameson did likewise, pulling out torches, snapping them on and beginning to sweep left and right in panicked jerking movements.

'All right, lads . . . Let's all stay calm,' Corkie whispered.

The sound of scraping and movement was increasing, coming from all directions now. Corkie reached out and scooped the small boy up into one arm, dirty rag and all. The child struggled and whimpered in his grasp.

'Shhhh, be still. There's a good boy.'

He signalled for Jameson to lead the way out of this constricted cul-de-sac of piping and machinery. The sooner they were in more open space the better.

'Jesus . . . I can hear them getting closer!'

'Just get moving, Jameson . . . and keep your bloody voice down.'

Jameson picked up his riot shield and moved cautiously out. Half a dozen metres up the narrow space towards the junction they'd turned into, he ducked under the piping and then squatted down behind the grounded shield, looking left then right into the walkway beyond.

The others joined him there in a huddle, Gosling at the rear. The sound of scraping and skittering was louder still, the echoes blending the noise together into a soft kettle hiss.

In the distance they could hear their colleagues, their voices, the scrape of their boots, the thump, rustle and swish of packages of drink being tossed from one pair of hands to the next, down the human chain. He heard the rumble of the truck's engine . . . and realized Morris was backing it up to the delivery-bay door to make it easier for the lads to load into it.

Corkie fumbled for the handle of the machete tucked into the belt of his webbing.

'We should call out to the others!' whispered Gosling.

Corkie panned his head left to right, his torch beam making patterns of shadows on the cinderblock wall in front of them. The hiss of rustling movement was getting louder. Surely the others were hearing that now? Or was the noise just here, around them?

'Let's make a run for it, Sarge,' said Jameson.

He nodded. The route back to the others was straightforward: turn right and follow the cinderblock wall to the end, turn right again, follow the wall to the end . . . and right again. It would be quicker cutting back through the plant's guts, the way they'd come. But he really didn't fancy that.

Something glinted in the beam of his torch. He turned to look at Jameson and saw a glistening trail of milky gunk spattered on his shoulder strap, as if a pigeon had relieved itself. He looked up just in time to see *something* descending fast.

It zoomed down, landed heavily on Jameson's head: a bulbous glistening body the size of a basketball. Limbs protruding from it, random in apparent design and purpose, like utensils from a penknife, every one of them sharp and ragged. The limbs flexed, unfolded and closed around his head as he screamed.

Corkie yanked out his machete and swung it, hacking through the thin chitin shell. It splintered and cracked like cooked crab, spattering strings of pearly white gunk through the air.

Over Jameson's screaming he could hear the man's skull crackle like a boiled egg being shelled.

'Spray the bastard!'

Gosling nodded, shunted out of his frozen torpor. He aimed the nozzle of the extinguisher towards Jameson's flailing body and the grotesque creature encasing his head, and pumped the trigger. Salt water under high pressure spurted out in a hard jet and splashed over both of them. The creature reacted instantly with a squealing hiss, released its vice-like grip on Jameson and drew back.

Beside him, Corkie heard a soft thump and saw that a second creature had landed a metre away. He glanced upwards and saw a glistening rope ascending to the warehouse roof. And there, in the harsh beam of his torch, he could see the entire ceiling alive with the things, like an inverted ant's nest reacting to the sudden exposure to daylight . . . a squirming carpet of glistening bodies and sharp-edged blades and spines.

He swung his machete down at the second creature, aiming at its unprotected bulbous centre. His blade sliced through without obstruction and the creature flopped lifelessly to the ground, limbs still quivering with unfulfilled purpose.

'Sarge! We've got to GO!' screamed Gosling.

Corkie looked down at Jameson. He was still alive and gurgling even though there seemed to be nothing left of his face but an excavated cavern of muscle, bone, teeth and tissue.

He's gone. Poor bastard's gone. You can't save him.

'OK, that way!' He pointed right with his machete. 'GO! GO!'

Glistening threads began to descend from the ceiling all around, like spiders summoned by vibrations in their web, and down them came more of the creatures.

'Don't look, lad,' Corkie hissed. The boy buried his face into Corkie's chest and clung to him tightly as he staggered after Gosling.

He heard a gunshot. A few of his men still carried guns. Force of habit. Shotguns mainly. Good for only one thing really: a guaranteed one-shot kill, but only right up close.

Gosling reached the corner and skidded to a halt in front of him. Corkie thumped into him and saw why he'd stopped. Between the cinderblock wall and the labyrinth of machinery, no more than a metre's width, the way was filled with the things, glistening abdomens in the process of detaching from the 'slide ropes', leaving gluey strings that stretched and finally snapped.

'Gosling! Don't just sit there gawping, spray a bloody path through!'

He tried to swap his machete to his other hand. *I'm going to need both hands.*

Corkie peeled the boy's arms from around his neck and put him down. 'I can't hold you!' He fumbled once again into the pouches of his webbing and found a flashbang. He pulled it out, uncapped it, pulled the pin and held the release catch. Ready to use.

Gosling was spraying, pumping the lever and jetting salt water in front of them like a fireman. The creatures hissed and recoiled from it, backing away into the relative safety of the labyrinthine innards of pipes, machinery and vats.

'Behind!' the boy squealed, and tugged hard on his belt. Corkie turned to see a swarm of the creatures approaching them. In motion, they reminded him of daddy-long-legses; fully extended, he guessed their limbs were nearly two metres long. Fragile-looking but clearly strong enough to heft their unarmoured bodies up to almost head height as they skittered along, top heavy, almost comical.

He tossed his flashbang at the floor between them. It clattered and rolled across the concrete. He didn't wait for it to go off, just grabbed the boy's wrist and dragged him after Gosling who'd made his way a dozen metres ahead, spraying and pumping the cylinder's pressure up frantically.

They were down at the end wall, approaching the second corner of the warehouse when he heard the percussive thump of the flashbang go off behind them.

He caught up with Gosling as he reached the second corner. The man tossed the fire extinguisher down and it clanged noisily, a metallic ring that echoed deafeningly. 'It's empty!'

'We're nearly there.' Corkie peeked round the corner and saw the light from the wide-open delivery-bay door. The rest of his men were clustered there, circled around the rear of the truck. They'd picked up their riot shields and had formed a semicircular shield wall.

Good boys.

It was a manoeuvre he'd drilled into them day after day, a revival of medieval battlefield tactics for modern soldiers. They were hacking, from behind the safety of the wall, at a dozen or so of the creatures that had dropped down nearby.

'WE'RE OVER HERE!' he bellowed. His voice boomed and echoed and he could see some of their heads turning one way then the other. 'To your right! WE'RE COMING IN FROM YOUR RIGHT!'

Several threads began to unfurl and descend from the roof between them. He looked up and saw the roof of the warehouse was sparsely populated on this side. But it wasn't going to remain that way for long. Caught in the glare of his beam, he could see the creatures stampeding their way across the ceiling, spindly limbs clasping metal support spars, puncturing holes in the thin corrugated-iron roof to get a better grip . . . moving with frightening agility as if gravity were an irrelevance to them.

Gosling pulled out a thin-bladed katana from his belt, one of a haul they'd lifted from a martial-arts store. 'We've got to go! NOW!'

Corkie nodded. 'You swing and run, Gosling. Cut us a path!' He picked the boy up again. No shield for either of them to cower behind. Just twenty or so metres to sprint. He decided he'd move quicker carrying the boy rather than dragging him by the hand.

'GO. GO. GO!' He thumped Gosling hard between his shoulders.

They charged forward, weaving around the dangling tendrils that had already unfurled. Corkie glanced up again. More were coming down now, not actually 'unfurling' as he'd first assumed. In his mind he saw these tendrils as the kraken's version of abseiling ropes, just like special-forces troops sliding down ropes from some hovering black hawk, but instead he glimpsed glistening torsos above, ejecting wet strings from their middle, like spiders crapping out webbing, a liquid-like paste that seemed to congeal in the few seconds it took to drool to the ground, making a robust thread strong enough to take their weight.

He could see one coming down to the right of Gosling, sliding down the length of its fibrous goo with balletic ease.

'Watch out!' he shouted.

Gosling looked up just in time to avoid the same fate as Jameson. He sidestepped clumsily, tripping himself up and sprawling on to the ground as the creature landed beside him, limbs uncurling from their spider-like defensive huddle.

Corkie dropped the boy and shoved him roughly in the direction of his men. 'Go, boy!' He spun round and squared up to the creature, machete raised to hack at the first limb that reached out to him.

'Get up, Gosling, you lazy bloody arsehole!' he barked, keeping his eyes locked on the thing, waiting for it to make a move. He could hear Gosling pulling himself to his feet, gasping, winded from the fall, and he could see the glint of a cluster of dark spheres, grape-like. *Eyes.* Studying him intently.

'Yeah? Come on, then! After you, love.'

It remained where it was, its body bobbing gently, held two metres above the ground by too many limbs to count.

'What are you waiting for?'

He risked a glance over his shoulder. Gosling and the boy had reached his men. A momentary gap in the shield wall and then they were safely behind it. He whipped back round to face the creature. It seemed to be studying him as intently as he was studying it.

Or perhaps those beady eyes were on the glinting blade of his machete, calculating its chance of getting past the blade to him.

He took a step back from it, fully expecting the thing to mirror his movement and advance one step forward. But it didn't. It remained where it was, just bobbing and watching. He sensed more than some dumb insect intelligence behind that grape-like cluster of eyes.

'*Sergeant!*'

He could hear the truck's engine being gunned.

'I'm coming!!' he shouted, backing away a few more steps. The creature watched him, and he could have sworn blind that the damn thing cocked its body in the same way a spaniel would cock its head at the sound of a dog whistle.

Corkie quickly backed up three more steps then turned and ran the rest of the way, joining his men.

He looked around. 'Where's Briggs and his lot?'

'Here, sir!'

He saw Briggs standing in the shield wall at the rear of the truck.

'All of us here, accounted for, sir. Where's Jameson?'

'Dead.'

Corkie looked around for the boy and saw Gosling was helping him up into the back of the truck. He noticed a couple of his men stretched out – Osman, the only one with paramedic experience, was busy tearing open the foil on a first-aid pack.

'Serious injuries?'

'Nasty ones, Sarge,' Osman replied.

'Right . . . we are bloody well leaving. NOW!'

Corkie grabbed the shoulder of his other 'salt sprayer', Moss. 'You can give me that . . .' The soldier willingly passed him the fire extinguisher. 'Get in, lad.'

Corkie backed up against the truck as his men quickly passed their shields up and clambered in after them. He could see twinkling hairline threads dangling from the ceiling in their hundreds now, like the freeze-frame image of some torrential downpour of rain. And in the gloom of the warehouse among the innards of the bottling-plant machinery, he glimpsed the glistening bodies, the spikes and spines, so fragile-looking and yet so lethal. All silently bobbing . . . and, like that other one, he sensed them intelligently regarding the fire hydrant in his hands and *knowing* what it dispensed, knowing that the tactical advantage of surprise had been spent, knowing that a sudden rush was too late now.

Knowing when to cut their losses and wait for another chance.

God help us . . . they're smart.

There were senior officers he'd served under who weren't as smart as these things.

The truck's engine gunned noisily and a cloud of exhaust fumes billowed warmly around his legs. He turned, tossed the extinguisher into waiting hands and then quickly pulled himself up.

'Let's go!'

CHAPTER 20

'Uh-oh,' said Fish. 'Something's wrong.'

Leon and Freya looked where he was pointing. The two army trucks were bouncing along the rutted track across the grounds towards the castle, the rear tyres kicking up rooster tails of dirt and puddle water.

The horn sounded from the keep. Clearly somebody else had spotted the trucks and had had the same thought. Those who were out in the grounds, foraging along the tree line for firewood, dropped what they'd gathered and began to hurry towards the drawbridge, following the orange guide-ropes that had been strung up to mark off the wired-up landmines.

Leon handed the Nintendo back to Fish, got to his feet and offered Freya a hand to pull her up. The rest of the keep's inhabitants spilled out through the double oak doors to see what was going on, Everett among them.

'What's happened?'

'Corkie and his men returning,' shouted the soldier on watch duty.

Everett yelled at someone to raise the drawbridge quickly, but there were people on it, hurrying for the safety of the far side and, anyway, the trucks were coming their way too quickly to stop them crossing.

The first truck rattled over the wooden planks and

lurched to a hard stop in the space where they were usually parked. The second came to a halt right next to it.

Corkie jumped down from the passenger side of the driver's cabin. 'Get Dr Hahn!'

Everett flicked his hand at someone lingering in the doorway to do just that, then stepped forward. 'What's happened?'

The soldiers emerged from the back of the truck, boots hitting the dirt one after the other.

'The virus.' Corkie swore under his breath.

'Corkie, give me a *proper* report, man!'

'Bloody virus ambush! We were loading bottles from a plant, and they were hiding inside.' He looked at Everett. 'The bastards were actually waiting, like they knew we needed water, or something.'

'Any casualties?'

'Jameson's dead. And we've got two more badly wounded in the back. Where's Hahn?' He looked around desperately for her.

'She's been called. She's coming. Corkie . . . *anyone infected*?'

'Jesus Christ . . .' Corkie shook his head. 'That was bad. That was really bloody bad.' He saw Leon and Freya looking at him. 'They're getting much bigger. Bigger than when we found you two.'

'How big?' asked Leon.

Corkie held a hand high above his head. 'Like daddy-long-legses, but this big!'

'Corkie!' snapped Everett to get his attention again. *Anyone infected?*

'I don't bloody know! There are wounds. So, yeah, maybe!'

'And the kraken? They're bigger?'

'These ones were more like spiders than crabs. They dropped down on us from strings. They were crawling across the bloody ceiling!' He glanced up at the keep's sheer stone walls. 'Everett, if they get across our moat, they'll scale these walls no problem.'

Dr Hahn emerged from the oak doors with a shoulder bag and hurried over.

'Back of that truck.' Corkie pointed. She nodded and made her way to the rear and pulled herself inside. He turned back to Everett. 'They're getting smarter. That whole thing was an ambush. A bloody trap. They found a supply of water – they must know we need it – and they were bloody well waiting for us!' He took a deep breath. 'We're going to need to rethink our defence plans.'

'All right, Corkie, all right,' Everett said in a calm voice. Leon could see the major wanted to continue this conversation in private rather than have it blurted out in front of everyone. 'Soon as Hahn has looked them over, why don't you get your knights sorted out, rested? Get them some food.'

'We picked up another survivor.'

Everett looked around. He could only see his knights. 'Where?'

'In the truck. A young boy.'

'You sure about that?'

Leon wondered if he was asking whether he was sure it was a boy not a girl. Then realized he was asking something else.

'He's real, sir, not an *imitation*.'

'You certain?'

'He's got hair . . . nails . . . and he's bloody terrified. I'd say he's real.'

Dr Hahn poked her head out of the back of the truck. 'Please . . . you and you –' she pointed to Fish and another guy – 'help me, please. These two wounded ones need to be assisted up to my surgery.' She beckoned them over to help get the wounded men out. One of them had a blood-soaked cotton pad taped across one side of his neck, the other had bandages and a tourniquet cinched tight round his thigh.

'Corkie, your men are all pilled-up, aren't they?' asked Everett.

'Of course.'

'The girl,' Hahn called out to them, 'she will need to be isolated. I must do a blood test immediately.'

'Girl?' Everett looked at Corkie. 'You said boy, didn't you?'

Corkie shrugged, too tired to care.

Hahn disappeared into the truck again and emerged a moment later with a bundle in her arms. Leon could see a dirty blue-grey blanket, the sorry kind of rag you'd find in a skip, or lining a cardboard box beneath a bridge. He could see two pale, bare ankles and dirty feet flopping lifelessly beyond the hem. Hahn sat down at the back of the truck then bum-shuffled off the edge on to the ground.

'She is in a very, very bad way,' Hahn said as she passed by Everett.

At the other end of the bundle Leon could see a tuft of dark hair and a scalp, bald in patches and with mottled skin that looked as if it were thick with sores and scabs.

'Poor thing,' whispered Freya.

Hahn stepped past them. The bundle in her arms seemed to weigh virtually nothing. 'Please stay back. She may be contagious,' she cautioned to those getting too close. 'We do not know what she has.'

As she passed by them, Leon craned his neck to get a better look at the pitiful creature. He caught a glimpse of her face.

Just a glimpse.

And his heart froze.

'Leon?'

He watched Hahn's back as she eased through the gap of the open doorway and disappeared into the gloomy interior of the castle.

'Leon? You OK?' asked Freya.

He turned to look at her.

'Jesus, Leon, you've gone as white as a—'

'It's Grace.'

He nodded at the doorway. Hahn now gone from view.

'That was Grace.'

CHAPTER 21

'Please . . . please, just let me have—'

Dr Hahn stood in the doorway of the infirmary. She wagged a finger at Leon. 'Not until I've given her a proper examin—'

'She's my *sister*!'

Hahn frowned from behind her round-rimmed glasses.

'That girl! In there.' He pointed over her shoulder. 'She's my sister. It's Grace!'

'This is true?'

'Yes! We got separated. I thought she was . . . dead. I thought . . .' Leon's voice failed him. The emotion hit him like a get-up-too-quick dizzy spell, unannounced and instant. He stifled a hitch in his breath and swiped at his eyes. 'I thought she died in a fire.' His voice trembled.

'She does have extensive scarring from burns,' said Hahn.

'Please let him see her,' said Freya. 'It *is* his sister. I know her too.'

Hahn pressed her lips together. 'The girl is very, very weak. And very traumatized . . .' Her stern scowl softened slightly. 'But all right. You may come in, Leon, but only you. Freya—'

'It's fine. I'll wait out here.'

Hahn stepped aside and Leon pushed past her into the

infirmary. It was a small space, room only for an inspection gurney covered with a plastic sheet, a desk tucked into a corner beneath a narrow window, and cubbyhole shelves filled with medicine bottles and white packets of pills stacked against the wall.

And Grace. There she was, sitting on the gurney, a white hospital sheet draped loosely around the welts on her shoulders. His heart broke at the first sight of her painfully thin, unclothed body. Livid swirls of knitted skin ran all the way down the left side of her face and her neck. Her left shoulder and arm were scarred all the way down to her elbow, the left side of her torso down to her naval.

'Grace!' he gasped.

She turned listlessly towards him. For a moment it seemed she didn't recognize his voice, perhaps didn't even recognize her own name. And he saw more clearly how burned her face was. Her ear was completely gone and the left side of her mouth dwindled to an uneven, lipless slash, but she still managed a smile. A half-and-half smile: one side quite normal and so pretty; the other a tight, almost skeletal sneer.

'Leon?' she whispered.

He hurried forward, both arms held out, then halted just in front of her, scared to touch her, scared to hurt her.

She held out her hands and grasped his tightly. Her mouth crumpled, her chin dimpled, the half of her face that he recognized folded into an expression he knew well – tears were coming. Her narrow shoulders shuddered as she began to sob. 'I thought . . . I . . . was alone . . .'

'I'm here, Grace. I'm right here!'

She pulled him towards her, wrapping her arms around him tightly. She buried the right side of her face against his neck and began to sob uncontrollably.

They held each other like that for several minutes, then Dr Hahn gently interceded. 'I must take a look at her, Leon. We need to know . . .'

Leon loosened his hold on her, then took a step back.

'Don't go!'

'I'm not going anywhere, Grace. I promise. I'm staying right here.'

'So, your name is Grace, yes?' said Hahn. She smiled. 'It is a beautiful name, my dear.' She pulled on a pair of sterilized gloves. 'I need you to lie down on this bed. If you can and it is not too painful, on your back, please.'

Grace did as she was told.

'Your damaged skin . . . it must be quite painful still? How old are these burns?'

'Two years,' Leon answered for her. 'The last place we were at . . . the people there tried to burn her to death.'

Hahn's tight little eyes rounded. '*What?*' Her normally emotionless face stretched into an expression of horror. 'Why?'

'They thought she'd been infected by a scuttler. They poured petrol on her and . . .'

'My God! This is completely *barbaric*!'

She leaned over Grace and began to carefully inspect her neck and shoulder. 'You poor child,' she said softly as she touched her lightly and cautiously. 'Ignorance and fear makes people act like complete animals, I think. Does the touching hurt?'

Grace shook her head. 'Not any more.'

Hahn peered closely at her burns. 'There is no apparent weeping . . . the redness does not appear to be infection. Just scarring.' She smiled down at Grace and stroked the side of her face that wasn't scarred. 'You are a very brave girl.'

Hahn let her hand run into Grace's hairline. Leon knew what she was doing . . . making sure it was real. Hahn leaned closer, inspecting the hair as she ran her fingers through it.

'How old are you, Grace? Eleven? Twelve?'

'She's fourteen . . . now,' answered Leon for her.

Hahn's eyes widened. 'Actually fourteen? Well . . .' She shrugged. 'I thought younger.'

'We both take after Dad. He always looked younger than people thought he was.'

She produced a small torch, bent low over Grace and peered into her eyes and mouth. She continued to examine the rest of her body for sores and inflammation. Finally, she leaned over Grace and smiled down at her. 'I think you are a very resilient and brave young lady.'

Grace managed a limp smile back at her.

'Your sister is very weak from malnutrition, of course, Leon. She looks anaemic to me. She will need to have lots of iron and vitamins. And much rest. I would say also that her immune system is not looking so great. She is best being isolated here in a sterile and hygienic environment until we can make her strong and well again.'

Leon sighed inwardly with relief. 'She's OK?'

Hahn steered Leon away from the gurney and lowered her voice. 'Outside, yes. I can't begin to imagine what she has been through over the last two years. She will be very . . . scarred on the inside as well. You understand what I mean by that?'

Leon nodded.

'What she needs is plenty of rest and a recovery diet. I may also give her antibiotics to help her in the meantime. We don't know yet what bacteria the virus has left alive, if any.' She shrugged. 'Perhaps that is why her scarring did not develop infection or sepsis. Thanks to the virus there may actually be no more bugs and germs. Who knows yet, hmm?'

'Can I stay here with her?'

'I am going to sedate her. Let her have a chance to rest and recover a little first. Why don't you come back tomorrow morning after breakfast, after she's had a good night's sleep?'

'OK.'

She narrowed her eyes at him. 'And you . . . you also need some adjustment time, Leon. You thought she was gone?'

'Yeah.'

'And now she is here. It is a shock for you too, I think.' She gently guided him to the door. 'You also have things to process.'

'Are you going to blood test her?'

'Yes, as a matter of course, I will. But not right now.' She nudged his arm. 'I think we can safely say she is human.'

Hahn pushed the infirmary door open with her shoulder, and Leon saw Freya sitting on a bench in the hallway outside, her mouth already open with a waiting question.

'First thing after breakfast, you can come up, Leon, all right?'

'I will.'

'How is she?' asked Freya.

Hahn leaned to one side. 'His sister will be fine. She is very weak right now. But she is a strong-willed girl, I think.' She smiled. 'A special day . . . to get back a loved one.' She let Leon step past her then turned back. The infirmary door swung shut and Leon sat down on the bench beside Freya.

'Did you manage to talk to Grace?'

'A bit.' He shook his head. 'I think she's in shock, or something.' He turned to her. 'My God, Freya . . . Her burns . . .' His voice failed him again, but this time he didn't feel the need to put a brave face on.

'What happened to her? How did she get here?'

Leon shook his head. 'I didn't get a chance to . . .'

Freya hugged him firmly and *shushed* softly. Questions like that could wait for later.

If Grace could just hang in there.

CHAPTER 22

Eighteen Months Ago

'You got a minute for an old buddy?'

Douglas Trent looked up from his desk at Tom and smiled. 'For you, ol' buddy, I got *two*.'

Tom tentatively pulled out a dark wooden chair from beneath the teak desk. 'May I?'

Trent wafted his hand with a look of incredulity. 'Jesus H. Christ, Friedmann . . . just *sit*!'

Tom could see his friend was adrift in a sea of paperwork. The desk was covered from one end to the other with status reports, resource requests and terse diplomatic communiques from their wary hosts, the Cuban government.

'I got paperwork coming out of my ass,' grumbled Trent. He stretched back in his leather chair, cracked his knuckles and looked at Tom. 'What can I do for you?'

'You asked me to go away and put some figures together. Remember?'

Trent's eyes closed wearily. A not-this-again expression on his face. 'So I did. And I'm guessing you have?'

Tom nodded. 'We have the ships, we have the navy personnel, and we have enough fuel from those Mexican Gulf refineries to do this.'

'Go on a wild-goose chase?'

'They're out there, Dougie. Survivors. Lots of them.'

'And you know this because . . . ?'

'Because of statistical probability. When the plague –' he decided to use the name Trent used for it – 'the *African plague* hit us, it was so goddamn quick that the data we have from the week before is still relevant.'

Trent spread his hands, waiting for Tom to elaborate.

'Just under a fifth of our population, so, about sixty million Americans, were on analgesics, statins and anti-depressants when it hit us. Those people, as we now know, would have been immune.'

'So that was six months ago, Tom. How many do you think are left now? How many do you think have survived the winter without any goddamn power? How many have survived without access to clean drinking water?' Dougie's thick sandy eyebrows bunched up above piercing blue-grey eyes. 'How many survived being attacked by that frikkin freakshow?'

They had all seen the last few broadcasts from the studio of a religious cult in Utah. The enclave had been large, well organized and well provisioned. It had been eagerly preparing for the end of the world for years, decades even, so they had their own generators, stockpiles of fuel and guns. They were self-sufficient, ready and waiting for the Rapture.

Over a period of several months, the cult leader had made about half a dozen rambling broadcasts to the world, and they'd watched him *slide*. At first jubilant and confident that their time was at hand, that the strange insect-like creatures they were easily holding at bay were the devil's spawn coming to overwhelm them. There'd been shots from CCTV outside the cult's high walls of squirming masses of pale crabs. Footage from a smartphone of someone holding up, by one spindly leg, something that looked like the kind of crustacean you'd find at the bottom of the ocean.

As time passed, the leader appeared to be losing his grip on reality. In his final broadcast, it appeared he'd arrived at the conclusion that Jesus wasn't coming to rescue them. There was nothing more after that.

They had satellite images and high-altitude photography from the reconnaissance planes they'd launched from the carrier, showing absurd heat signatures on the ground. Patterns that suggested a weird 'pooling' of biomass with threadlike tributaries linking one mass to another.

'We know the virus is stopped by salt water,' continued Tom. 'We also know that the analgesics make us immune to infection. We know that these *creatures* can be burned, blown up, squashed. So, we know that it's *possible*, Doug, that there are a lot of people in America, and elsewhere, who've figured these things out too and they've managed to find a way to hold out.'

'We don't *know* any of that, Tom. I mean, Christ, where are all the radio messages? Huh? Where are the SOSs? Where are the "Is anyone else out there?" broadcasts? Apart from New Zealand, there's no chatter out there, amigo.'

'Well, come on, it's not that easy broadcasting an SOS.

You need power, a transmitter. That means a survival group with the same means and resources as those poor bastards in Utah.'

Trent wrinkled his nose and drew his lips together. Tom knew that was *his* version of conceding a point. 'Even if you're right, Tom, and they're out there, we're not in a position where we can do much to help them.'

'Yes we are. We can go get them and bring them back here.'

'That's all we need, more mouths to feed.'

'It can be done. This country managed to live off its own resources for forty years . . . thanks to our foreign policy.'

Trent rolled his eyes.

'I'm just saying . . . we *can* do it. And if you want to be president of more than a dozen navy ships and nuclear submarines and twenty thousand refugees, we need to think nation-building. Bringing survivors together.'

Tom watched his friend digest that thought. They were guests of the Cuban nation. At first their hosts had insisted they remain on the south-west tip of the land and make use of the hostile and barren abandoned acres of Guantanamo Bay, suspicious of these American refugees. But humanitarian compassion had won over and the Cubans were beginning to cautiously suggest that Trent's people, with some adjustments, could be accommodated within their nation.

He knew exactly what Doug's dilemma was.

He's not ready to let America vanish. He's not going to let them absorb us. He wants to absorb them.

'A humanitarian effort, huh?' uttered Trent.

'And we get to decide who we rescue, Dougie. Only those healthy and fit enough. Those who can contribute.'

Doug raised an eyebrow. 'Americans?'

Tom shrugged. 'We can send some ships in both directions. Americans . . . Brits . . .'

'Ah, shit' He suddenly narrowed his eyes. 'Jesus, Tom . . . don't play me for an idiot. This is all about getting your kids.'

'I'm not going to lie to you. I'm holding on to a . . . a thread of *hope*, here.' He sat forward. 'That's all I've got. And, yeah. I hope, if we can get some ships over there, that they're amongst the people who've survived. But, look . . . we need people. We need to rebuild. We leave a rescue effort too long, and God knows how few will be left.'

Trent stared impassively at him. He wasn't even sure if the president was still listening to him.

'And we need more information about this virus. It's not just a virus. It's something different. It's *making things* for Chrissakes.' Tom stretched back in his chair and flexed his shoulders, only half aware that he was doing what his ex-wife used to call *roostering up*.

'Dougie, what if the outbreak wasn't the end, but just the start? What if this virus is something more? Something smart – something that's going to change, evolve? We need to get our crap together: we need people; we need smarts; we need resources.'

Trent nodded slowly as he waggled the pen still in his hand. Tom wasn't sure which angle was getting traction;

appealing to his vanity as a nation-builder, or appealing to his humanity. Doug had never had any children. He'd had trophy girlfriends, like his horses, trading up constantly from Ohio state pageant queens, to movie stars, to oil-money heiresses . . . but never a wife.

Certainly never a kid.

He put his pen down. 'Tom . . . old amigo, you're probably the closest thing I've ever had to a brother. You, me, and the other boys from section D. Right?'

'No man left behind.'

'Exactly. No man left behind.' He nodded slowly. 'All right . . . OK. Let's get some heads together and see what the hell kind of rescue effort we can put out.'

'Thank you.'

'Sure. *De nada.*' He winked. 'You go get your kids, Tom.'

CHAPTER 23

Freya put her hands on her hips. 'So what do you think of it all?'

Grace stood on the rooftop and cautiously peered over the battlements of the Norman keep. She gazed down at the moat and the grounds beyond, uneven and bumpy with the digging and filling, and the 'mine-safe' tracks making meandering lanes through the tall wild grass. Beyond that, the edge of the woods circled the grounds like another greater moat.

'Pretty cool,' she replied.

A fresh wind made the clothes on the laundry lines flutter and snap like medieval pennants and tossed Freya's long hair into her eyes.

'We're safe in here,' Grace added, and returned a smile.

'Unless the virus figures out how to make catapults or heavy artillery –' Freya laughed at her own joke – 'I'd say we're pretty good.'

Grace nodded as she continued observing, watching the people working just outside the castle walls and beyond the moat in the grounds.

Freya took the opportunity to surreptitiously study her. Grace looked like some comic book artist's idea of a villain, like Harley Quin, a duality: on one side innocent beauty; on the other, twisted and scarred. She could imagine some sick joke name for her character – 'Two Face Grace' – beauty and beast rolled into one.

In profile, Grace looked no different than Freya remembered her, except her hair was boy-short. Her long dark hair would have been burned away in that fire, and now two years on, this was as far as it had managed to grow back. Or maybe at some point in the last two years she'd cut it short.

She looked a little taller, but only a fraction so. She was still very small and slight for her age. Watching her observe the workers below, this was Grace as she remembered her. But older now. Older . . . and withdrawn, scarred both inside and out.

Only Freya and Leon knew where those burns had come from. But, as yet, neither she nor Leon knew what else Grace must have endured since then. Both of them wanted to ask, and both had agreed to let her talk about it when she was ready.

'You know, we thought you . . . were dead. Grace. Leon and me—'

'I escaped,' she answered. She turned towards Freya, revealing the damaged side of her face. 'The outside door wasn't locked. So I got out.'

'And you ran?'

She nodded. 'I don't remember much after that. Not for a long while after.'

'But I'm guessing someone found you, right?' Freya couldn't imagine she'd survived on her own.

'Yes.'

Freya dipped her head coaxing a bit more of an explanation from her. '. . . And?'

'And they looked after me. They made me better.'

'So . . . these people . . . where are they now?'

'She was called . . . *Hannah*.'

'OK. So where's this Hannah now?'

'Oh, she died.'

'And the others?'

Grace frowned slightly, one good brow knitting with one ruined one.

'You said "they"?'

'They died too. The virus crabs got them . . . all.'

Freya nodded. She sensed Grace was skating over things, giving just the bare bones of the last eighteen months. Freya studied her scars. They were deep. Horrible. What tabloids used to call 'life changing'.

She must have nearly died. Someone must have worked hard to keep alive, to keep those open wounds from becoming infected as they'd gradually healed. Someone must have grown to know her, grown fond of her and, in turn, Grace of them.

Then they, too, had died.

You poor, poor thing. But her aching sadness for Grace had been tempered by a concern. A *niggling* concern. A question she'd been wanting to ask Leon since they'd left Emerald Parks, but she never had, because Grace was dead and Leon didn't need to be asked. But since she'd arrived, the question had begun to resurface in Freya's mind.

What exactly DID you see in that sauna cabin, Leon?

Was it something? . . . Or nothing?

In the heat of that moment, in the rush of panic and adrenalin, had a shadow cast by Dave's torch become something it wasn't? A tress of knotted hair mistaken for some dangling viral appendage? Eighteen months ago Freya had been *almost* certain that Dave had murdered an innocent girl.

Almost certain.

But, looking at Grace right now, that final lingering doubt evaporated. She was real, no doubt about it. There was nothing she needed to ask Leon.

'Hannah was a German person,' said Grace.

'Oh, just like our Dr Hahn?'

'Yeah.' Grace smiled. 'I like Dr Hahn.'

'She's a very nice lady.'

'Are the others here as nice as her?'

'Hmmmm,' Freya hummed musically. 'They're a mixture.' She nodded over at the others doing laundry duty on the rooftop. 'That's Naga. She's quite sarcastic, which I guess is why we get on. The girl beside her is Denise. She's a good laugh.'

'What about the *men*?' Grace's tone hardened with suspicion as she said the last word.

Freya accepted she had reason to be wary. 'None of them are like, you know back at the *other place*. Leon's quite good friends with a guy called Fish. You met Corkie?'

'The one that saved me?'

'Yeah. He's an ex-army sergeant. Mouth like a potty,

you may have noticed. The old guy in charge is called Major Everett.'

'Is he nice?'

Nice. Freya wondered about that catch-all term. Perhaps she was using it to ask a more probing question. *Are we safe? Are they bad men like Dave? Or good men like Ron?*

'He's a good man. I think. Quite strict.' Freya laughed. 'And he sees himself as the Sheriff of Nottingham or a Ned Stark or something. You'll see that tonight at dinnertime. That is, if Dr Hahn's letting you out of the infirmary to join us?'

'Dr Hahn says I'm well enough now.'

Grace had been Hahn's sole patient for over a week, the doctor almost fulfilling a motherly role, feeding her, washing her, sitting with her every night after Leon and Freya had been summoned away to their beds by the 'lights out in five' warning blast of the horn.

They were in the main hall. A queue was already forming beside the fireplace. Tonight the room was filled with the smell of freshly baked bread as well as the smell of wood smoke, and the dogs were yapping incessantly for scraps. Freya was about to ask Dr Hahn whether she could have some extra painkillers for her hip when Everett joined them both.

'The girl looks a lot better than when she first arrived,' he said.

'She is much stronger now,' replied Dr Hahn.

'Poor child. Do you know what happened to her? Has she told you?'

'Only what Freya and Leon told us.'

Everett sucked his teeth. 'Disgusting. Truly disgusting. You'd think with most of humanity gone there'd be a little more tolerance and compassion going round among those who were left.'

Everett turned and picked out Grace standing in the queue with a bowl in her hand. 'By the way, Doctor, I presume you've done her bloods?'

'Her blood did not react to my test.'

'Of course. And no other health concerns?'

'She has been on antibiotics, but, actually, I think those are not necessary. Her scarring is fully healed. It will always be there and will always be tender to touch. But, apart from borderline malnutrition, she is all right.'

'I'm loath to put her on any duties yet. But I do feel it would be good for her to have some light chores to do. What do you think?'

Hahn nodded. 'I agree.'

'Good.' Everett nodded absently. 'Good.'

'So, Dr Hahn, anyway . . . ?' Freya continued. She'd got as far as saying she wanted to ask Hahn something.

Everett looked disapprovingly down his hawk-like nose at her. 'Young lady . . . manners?'

Freya pulled out a guilty shrug for him. 'Excuse me interrupting you, sir . . . Dr Hahn? Permission to speak?'

'That's much better,' said Everett warily. Although he suspected she was mocking him. 'I'll catch up with you

163

later,' he said, then excused himself.

'What can I do for you, Freya?' asked Hahn.

'Can you up the strength of my meds?' She patted her left hip. 'Last few days it's been aching quite a lot. I mean not, like, *that* bad, but more than it has in the past. I just wonder if with all the chores I have to do it's, you know, aggravating my condition.'

'I will make a note on my register to increase your daily allowance, Freya. Come and see me after dinner in the infirmary to remind me, just in case I forget.'

'Thanks. Will do.' Freya turned away and headed over to the queue, joining Grace with a bowl in her hand. 'So you're joining the general population at last.'

Grace looked back at her over her shoulder. Not quite getting her. 'Huh?'

'Down here, out of the infirmary.'

Grace smiled. 'It was getting boring up there.'

'Well, it seems like you're going to be joining a work group.'

'Do I get to choose?'

'I don't know. But I bet Everett sticks you in with me. That OK with you?'

Grace nodded.

CHAPTER 24

In the stillness of night, when the noises had settled down, the whispered conversations had come to an end, and the dormitories echoed with the regular rasping of deep and even breathing, was when Grace could most easily descend into her restless world.

She closed her eyes on the faint pall of light spilling in through the lead-lined windows from the floodlights outside and descended into herself. She had come to think of it as stepping from a room called 'outside' into another room called 'inside', a simple mental conceit that made the process of travelling from a macro universe down into a cellular one more comprehensible.

She was home again.

'Home' in many ways. Home in the comforting illusion she'd constructed of her bedroom back in New Jersey. Home amongst this ecosystem of entities that had come along for the ride with Grace to observe these curious humans holed-up in their fortress.

Grace liked coming to her interior world. She missed the intimacy of this micro community, with its communication that had no choice but to be honest. Communication that was more than just words; it was memories, smells, sounds, feelings, desires all conveyed at once in a rich cocktail. By contrast, in the outside world, talking felt like such a primitive and limited way to exchange ideas. Like using Morse code in an age of wifi.

It was tiring.

Here she felt relaxed, soothed.

She was home tonight for another reason, though: to comfort someone who needed her. Someone who was still very frightened and confused by her surroundings. She felt her presence nearby . . . a voice crying out in darkness. A wafting of sharp amino acids that clearly cried a frightened, 'Hello? Is anyone there?'

'I'm back,' said Grace softly.

'Grace? Grace! Is that you?' came the reply, clearly relieved.

'Yes, it's me.'

She created the familiar space of the infirmary in her head. Created herself as Dr Claudia Hahn would recognize her – disfigured by burn scars. One day, maybe soon, she'd present herself as she'd *once* looked, so much prettier with her long hair dark and wavy, and her skin smooth and pale.

But not yet. Familiarity was important.

She placed herself on the infirmary's gurney. Sitting upright on it, legs swinging over the side. And then she placed Claudia Hahn opposite, sitting on her examination stool.

Dr Hahn shook her head, her eyes narrowed behind her glasses, her forehead rumpled. She looked confused as she took in her surroundings. 'My infirmary . . . ?'

'Yes.'

'Grace? What is this? Am I . . . dead?'

'No, Claudia. You're alive. Like me.'

'But . . .' She looked around the room. 'But this is not real?'

'It's my *memory* of your infirmary. I think I got it mostly right.'

Hahn looked around and shook her head. 'Not quite.' She pointed at her desk, clear and organized. 'I am usually less tidy than that.'

Grace smiled. Encouraged that Claudia could joke with her.

'Can you help me to understand, Grace? I . . . am confused. I . . . The last thing I remember clearly is . . .'

'Dr Hahn . . . Claudia, you've been *absorbed*.'

She looked at Grace. 'You infected me?' It was a comment that floated halfway between a question and an accusation. Grace had had this conversation with Claudia Hahn the previous night, but then she'd been less 'there', her consciousness not fully assembled yet . . . less 'present'.

'I invited you to join us.'

'Us? Who is—'

'I know. It's all very difficult to deal with at first. But it gets easier, I promise.'

Hahn's frown deepened. 'But . . . you *did* infect me?'

'Yes.'

'But how is that possible? I am *immune*. I was taking the medication like everyone else.'

'Those chemicals make it much harder for us, but it's not impossible.' Grace held out a hand to her. 'And the truth is you and the others aren't taking enough to properly stop

167

us, just enough to slow us down.'

'Us?'

'Us.' She repeated the word, her hand still held out. 'You call us "the virus". But we're all family now.'

Hahn stared suspiciously at her offered hand.

'Those pills you take do hurt us. Those chemicals in your blood killed millions of our cells, but we managed to bring you over.'

'But . . . I am still . . . alive?' She shook her head as if she were trying to shake off a drunken stupor. 'Today – I think it was today, this evening, actually – was I not talking to you, to your friend Freya? I even spoke to Major Everett! Or was that all a dream?'

'No, you spoke to him and to Freya.'

Dr Hahn was frowning again. 'But how? If I'm *infected*?' She looked utterly perplexed.

'*They* are inside you now. They're a part of you. They're learning all about you so they can save you.'

Hahn's eye narrowed. '*They* . . . the virus?'

'The virus.'

Realization settled on to her face. 'God, no. Please . . .'

'It was exactly the same for me, Claudia. One of those small creatures "stung" me, some cells managed to survive in my bloodstream and they hung in there. Slowly they reproduced. It took weeks and weeks, but they managed to help me across to join them in the end. And all that time I was kind of confused, not sure what was real and what was not. It was like a long, weird dream.'

Grace stretched out and grasped one of the doctor's

trembling hands. 'There's nothing to be afraid of, I promise. You're still you. You'll *always* be you.'

'I don't want to die like this!'

'You're not dying!'

'I don't want to be –' she shook her head, trying to find the right word, then finally settled for Grace's – '*absorbed!*'

'They're just inside you, that's all. Today you *really* have been walking around, talking, being a doctor. No different from normal.'

'But am I still . . . a *human*? Not a—'

'A copy?' Grace shook her head. 'No. You're still *you*.' She nodded towards the door to the infirmary. 'Outside, in the Big World, you're asleep in that cot right next to mine. Right now, out there as well, I'm holding your hand.'

Hahn pulled back from her, then stared down at both her hands, touching them lightly together, fingertips tracing across her palm. 'This feels so real. Here, *I* feel real. But this is a hallucination?'

'It is what they call an abstract, but in some ways its more real than outside.'

'I do not understand this. *Where* are we right now? Where is *this*?' She looked around the not-quite-right infirmary. 'Am I *in* your . . . your mind? Or are you inside mine?'

'We're joined. So I guess you could say we're somewhere in between,' Grace replied. 'We're in the stream.'

'Stream?'

'That's what I call it.'

'*In* . . . you mean *blood*stream? We're in your *blood*?'

'*Our* blood. We're joined. Our hands are joined, melded. I've entered your stream.'

Hahn shook her head again. 'This is hard. Am I just . . . *cells*? Just cells floating in what? In plasma?'

'Uh-huh. I suppose.' Grace smiled. 'It's weird at first.'

'But how can I think? How can I talk? This is not possible. My mind is billions, *trillions* of cells linked together in a very specific way. Surely *who I am* is *that*! The structure of those cells!'

Grace shrugged. 'They understand which part of our mind is who we are, and which part of our brain is just, like, storage. Like how part of a computer is a processor, but another part is the hard drive.'

Hahn shook her head. 'I don't like this! I don't want this!'

'Give it time. It's weird, I know, but it does get easier. Then, soon, you realize it's the only way to be.' Grace smiled. 'It's *wonderful*.'

Hahn began to sob. 'Why? Why did you do this to me? Why did you infect me?'

'Because you were so kind to me. You cared for me. I like you, Claudia. It's my gift.'

'This?' She spread her hands at the illusion. 'This is a *kindness*?'

'You'll see that it is. Soon. You really will.'

'No.' She shook her head. 'No.'

'And I *had* to do it, Claudia. I had no choice.'

'Why?'

'The blood test. Do you remember what happened?'

Hahn shook her head. 'No . . . I . . .' She narrowed her eyes.

'That's OK, not all of your memory is assembled here. You did that salt test on my blood.' Grace shrugged. 'Obviously, I was *never* going to pass that test.'

Hahn screwed up her face, narrowed her eyes. 'No. Hold on. I remember . . . remember . . .'

Grace cut her short. Hahn's memory was going to be horrible. Grace sensed Hahn's cluster sending out chemical feelers for it, rummaging around for it like an absent-minded old lady in kitchen drawers full of junk mail and red-headed bills.

Grace enveloped the feeler and blocked it.

'It's OK. It's OK,' Grace cooed softly. 'It's been nearly a week now. You didn't tell anyone I failed. It's our secret.'

'My God, this is crazy. This is—'

'And we really can't tell the others, Claudia. We *can't* tell them about us.' She leaned forward and rested a hand on one of her shoulders. 'They'll burn us. They'll set fire to both of us if we do.'

'What about all the others?' Hahn stared at her. 'What is going to happen to the others?'

Grace hunched her shoulders. 'We're trying to decide what's for the best. That's what this is all about . . . what's best for them.'

Hahn shook her head vigorously. 'I will tell them. I am going to tell them!'

'Please don't.'

'You . . . you . . . *They* . . . can't do this to us! I can't let you infect them all!'

'Please!' Grace leaned her face closer to the doctor's until their noses were almost touching. 'Please?'

'This is not right. I have to tell them . . . I *will* tell them!'

'You know *they* are listening to us, don't you?'

Hahn looked around the illusion of the room. Her eyes darted manically.

'We're not alone – no one's ever truly alone in the stream,' said Grace.

'Grace, listen to me,' Hahn hissed, her voice lowered. 'Those people do not deserve to die.'

'I don't want to *kill* them. I want to *save* them. Don't you see?' A tear leaked from Grace's left eye and streaked down the scarred tissue of her cheek. Not for show. Genuine. 'Especially Leon . . . Freya. I love them. I *miss* them so much.'

'If you loved them, Grace, you wouldn't infect them!'

'Please?' Grace whispered. 'Say you won't tell anyone. Say it out loud. Say it and you have to mean it. You really have to *mean* it.'

'I cannot do that.'

Grace loosened her grip on the woman's shoulder. She sat back on the gurney and sighed deeply. 'OK . . . then we'll have to do the other thing.'

'Other thing? Grace . . . what is that?'

She shook her head. 'We'll talk again soon.'

CHAPTER 25

The 'proper' toilets in the castle were located downstairs off the main hall. Very posh, very modern ones with slate tiles and recessed ceiling lights. But they were no longer functional and were being used as storerooms.

The communal toilets were *now* located off the gallery floor. More convenient for those who had a weak bladder and needed a midnight piss, no need to tramp down the stone stairway and across the cold stone floor of the main hall, disturbing the dogs on the way. Just a tiptoe across the creaking wooden floor, past the women's dorm, past the closed door of Everett's 'campaign' room, past the laundry room and towards a large room that was now, as Fish liked to call it, the 'communal pisser'.

The latrine apparently used to be a function room where civil weddings were conducted and corporate strategies were explained before a PowerPoint presentation.

The conference table, lectern and chairs had been cleared out, and now there were half a dozen curtained cubicles set up inside the room.

Leon coughed once into his fist as he entered, as toilet etiquette dictated. No one responded. He had the latrines to himself. He swept aside the nearest curtain, lifted the yellow plastic lid of the 'Kampa Khazee', sighing wearily as he remembered Naga's latest whinge about men in this place not lifting the seats.

He did the decent thing.

The function room had tall glass doors that opened on to a paved balcony that protruded over the moat and provided what must have once been a beautiful view of the grounds beyond. Which made it the perfect place to locate the communal toilets; latrine duty involved dragging them outside, hefting them up on to the railing and emptying them directly into the moat below.

He finished his business, stepped out of the cubicle and went across to the glass doors, opened one and stepped on to the balcony.

It wasn't quite dawn yet, but the sky had already lightened to a metallic grey. If those floodlights hadn't been on down below, casting cones of sterile light across the lumpy ground, there would still have been just about enough light to see all the way to the distant tree line.

At this time – just before 'proper' dawn, with fingers of silvery mist withdrawing like phantoms – he imagined, before the virus, the trees would have echoed with chirrups and tweets from a dawn chorus of early birds.

Instead it was graveyard silent, save for the distant and soft rhythmic chugging of the generator powering the floodlights. He thought he could hear someone whistling a tune somewhere down below on the apron of ground that surrounded the keep. Probably the Kurdish guy, Omar. Omar seemed to know every Michael Jackson song ever written. Leon cocked his head, trying to catch the wafting notes, trying to recognize the tune. It sounded vaguely familiar.

He heard something else. Water sloshing softly. It was coming from further along the balcony, emerging from another open glass door. Curious, he took a dozen steps towards it and found himself looking into the laundry room. Just like the latrine, it had once been a function room. He could hear water sloshing around in a bucket. And the regular *fwip*, *fwip*, *fwip* of someone vigorously scrubbing something.

He coned his hands around his eyes, peered in through the glass and saw someone squatting on the floor of the laundry. The scrubbing sound and sloshing immediately stopped.

'Leon?' A small whispered voice. 'Is that you?'

'Grace?'

'Yeah.'

He pulled the door open and stepped inside. 'You OK? What the hell are you doing at this time?'

She didn't answer. He could see her poised over the bucket, perfectly still, like a small burrowing meerkat frozen by the sound of an approaching predator.

It looked like she was scrubbing at a bed sheet.

'Grace?'

'I had . . . an accident . . .'

'An accident?' He stepped towards her.

'Leo . . . please . . .' She held a palm out to him. 'Just stay there.'

'Hey, sis . . .' He ignored her and squatted down beside her. 'You all right?'

'Leon!' she hissed. 'Just go!'

He could see the glint of a torch on the floor beside her. Everyone had their own; every room had one. He picked it up and flicked it on.

'Jesus!'

The water was as red as a vat of cranberry juice. And there were dark, almost sepia-coloured stains on the sheet that were never ever going to come out. 'What the hell—'

'Leon!' She glared at him angrily. The eye on the ruined side of her face glinted harshly in the light of the torch. '*I said go!*'

'What happened?'

'What do you *think* happened?'

'I . . .' He looked at the dark, murky water. Unsure. 'Are you hurt? Did you cut—'

'Oh, brainiac, come on. What do you *think* . . . ?'

Then he got it. Belatedly. Stupidly. 'Oh . . .'

'Right.' She nodded.

'Ah . . . that's gross.'

'Thanks.' She resumed scrubbing the sheet. 'Little privacy then, bro, huh?'

He flicked the torch off again, stood up and backed up a step, trying to contain the queasiness in his voice. 'Uh, OK . . . I'm going.'

He wanted to find something funny to say. Something big-brotherly, witty, yet tender and supportive, but all he could come up with was, 'Crap. I guess it sucks being female, right?'

Oh, brilliant. Genius, Leon.

'It caught me by surprise. It's my first . . .' She stopped

scrubbing. 'Actually, do you mind? Can you leave, please?'

'Sure . . . I'll . . . let you . . . uh . . .' He retreated towards the veranda door he'd come through. 'See you at breakfast, then?'

Grace resumed her vigorous scrubbing as he stepped out into the cool dawn air and made his way along the paving stones to the open door leading back into the latrine room.

The end of the world might have been and gone, yet so many of the mundane, *inconvenient*, things in life still happened on a regular basis.

There was something oddly reassuring about that. About the awkward moment he and Grace had just shared. He found himself smiling as he made his way along the gallery towards the men's dormitory. Relieved. Proud. Reassured.

Looks like I've got my bossy little sis back.

CHAPTER 26

'First time?' Freya made a face. 'Poor thing. The first time it happens it's always totally traumatic. Fourteen is pretty late in the day for your first period, though.'

'She's small . . . Does that have something to do with it?' replied Leon.

Freya sighed as they both shuffled forward a step in the breakfast queue. 'What makes you an expert in female matters all of a sudden?'

'Just a guess.'

'Stress, trauma, poor diet, all those things have a bearing. And, bless her, she's been through all that and God knows what else over the last couple of years. Point is it's a really good sign, Leon. It means she's *mending*. It means her body has decided it's well enough to get on with the important things.'

'Porridge or bean stew?'

Freya looked at both bubbling pots dangling over the roaring fire. 'Is the porridge sweetened this time? Not salted?'

'Oh my days!' Danielle squawked indignantly. 'It was just a simple bloomin' mistake!' Danielle was, or used to be, the youngest member of the castle's community. Sixteen now, but fourteen when the world had ended. Yet sometimes she managed to sound like a cantankerous old housemaid from another century. 'The sugar pot wasn't labelled properly. It wasn't my ruddy fault!'

Last week, Danielle's group had been on kitchen duty, with Danielle, specifically, on porridge duty. The hall that morning had echoed with people making surprised gagging sounds as they'd tucked into her salty offering.

'Well, I guess I'll live dangerously and try your porridge . . . again.'

Danielle splattered a ladleful into Freya's bowl.

'Your heart's really not in this job, is it?'

She glared at Freya.

Leon ordered the same as her, and they found a space at the table. He looked around for his sister. 'Where is she?'

'She was still in her bed when I got up,' said Freya. 'She'll miss breakfast if she doesn't—'

'Ah . . . there she is.' Leon saw Grace coming down the steps from the gallery floor. He waved his arms to catch her attention.

Freya grabbed his arm. 'Don't talk about last night, Leon, OK? It's kind of personal and *very embarrassing* the first time.'

'Hey, c'mon. I'm not a complete idiot.' He waved to Grace again. She saw him and flashed a smile their way.

They watched her queue, grab a bowl of porridge and finally she joined them. Freya shuffled sideways to make a space for her between them. 'How are you feeling this morning, hon?'

Leon's jaw hung open and he spread his hands. *I thought you just said—*

'Leon told me what happened last night,' Freya carried on quietly. 'It's really crappy first time.'

Grace nodded. 'I feel horrible.'

'You should go talk to Dr Hahn. She might be able to get you excused from duties today.' Freya craned her neck to look around for her. 'Where is she?'

'I don't know,' said Leon. 'Not seen her yet.'

'Is she still in bed?'

Grace shook her head. 'No. I think she must've got up extra early.'

'Well, after breakfast, if you like, I'll come with you and we'll go up to her infirmary and get her to write you a note to give to Everett or something.'

'It's OK. You don't need to, Freya.'

'Hey, I don't mind.'

'No. Honestly. You don't need to. I'm fine.'

'You *should* be excused today. Seriously . . . it's not a good idea to—'

'I'll *go see her*!' Grace cut in tersely. 'OK?'

Freya recoiled slightly. 'OK . . . well, good.'

Leon met Freya's eyes, his eyebrows arched with surprise and a tight-lipped mouth struggling to keep a smile from spilling out.

Freya cautioned him with a quick frown. *Don't! Say! Anything!* And placed a hand on Grace's back. 'We'll come and check in on you later at lunchtime, if you like?'

Grace shrugged the hand off and spooned the porridge into her mouth without comment.

'Or do you want some space?'

Grace nodded, then ate in silence for a minute before finally sitting back and managing a grateful smile. 'I'm sorry for being crabby with you.'

'No worries,' Freya replied, and winked.

'I'll go see her,' said Grace. 'And I'll get a note . . . like you said.'

Grace slowly ate her breakfast, her head dipped, staring at the bowl on the table in front of her and hoping Leon and Freya would sense that she'd rather opt out of any breakfast chitter-chatter this morning. They got the hint and started talking about what work tasks they had lined up for the day and conducting a post-mortem on a flare-up that had happened yesterday evening in the female dormitory between Danielle and Denise.

Her mind drifted quickly on to other things. More pressing matters.

On Claudia Hahn.

Dr Hahn was upstairs right now. She was lying in the dark, narrow space beneath her dormitory cot. And she was no more . . . not in the 'outside world' sense, at least. She was gone. She was now safely absorbed – contained – within the 'inside world'.

The *thing* that was lying beneath the cot wasn't ready yet. If anyone had been bothered enough to trace the source of the faint yeasty smell, and ducked down on to all fours to look beneath her bed, they would have seen something *unfinished*.

A glistening in-progress project: a skeleton. The real bones of Claudia Hahn, slowly being encased in a thickening soup that had once been her soft tissue, rendered down to a bubbling pink broth during the night. And now the community of cells was working as quickly as they possibly could to reassemble a passable facsimile of her.

By lunchtime, Grace expected the internal organs would be completed, and muscle tissue would be growing like fungus along her abandoned bones. By mid-afternoon, the outer cells would be forming into a thin translucent layer of skin. By dinner time, the skin would have thickened and acquired a suitable amount of pigment to look convincing. The cells hard at work upstairs had learned lessons from other cells, which, in turn, had learned from other cells. Bones could be reused instead of attempting to create a tough resinous skeletal frame, which was the most time-consuming part of the fabrication process. Better still, another shortcut that had been learned over the last year: the keratin-based components, hair and nails, could also be reused. The cells that comprised the skin of Hahn's scalp had been left untouched and remained anchored to her skull. Last of all, in the final hour of the project, it would be absorbed, carefully replaced, cell by cell, with remade skin, each hair follicle preserved in place.

Grace had dealt with the stained sheets on her bed. And her chance encounter with Leon earlier this morning had actually been helpful. If there had been any doubts in his mind that she was the sister he once knew, that she was human, then it seemed those doubts had been dispelled.

But she was still going to need to dispose of Hahn's bloodstained pyjama bottoms and T-shirt, and then help her put on her day clothes. The copy of Claudia Hahn was going to need a few more hours' preparation to ready itself for interaction with the others. To learn how to move like she had; to recreate the timbre of her voice. There was no doubt about it, those here who knew her well enough were going to notice she was behaving oddly, differently. Not sounding quite like her old self.

But, then, none of those people had yet encountered a convincing remade human. Their only experience had been with crude copies from months and months ago.

None of them have any idea how well we can do this now.

CHAPTER 27

'No – let me go talk to her first,' said Freya.

'I just want to see how she is.' Leon flicked the crumbs of the energy oat-bar off his lap. The others in his work group were still eating theirs, and there was another quarter of an hour before the afternoon work-session horn was going to be sounded. That morning his group had been out in the grounds digging up the remains of the potato crop. Everett was determined that every last scrap of food nearby be brought into the castle in case the virals returned to try their luck again at getting in. It had been drizzling all morning and his hands, arms, sweatshirt and jeans were all caked with mud.

'Girl talk.' Freya gave him that *you wouldn't understand* look of hers. 'She won't want to talk about it with *her brother*, Leon. Trust me.'

'Oh, jeez . . . Fine.'

Freya planted her hand on his shoulder. 'We're somewhat complicated, us ladies.' Then pushed herself up. 'I'll catch you later.'

She made her way into the keep, across the main hall. It was filled with the clatter of crockery being gathered from the long tables and stacked for washing up, and Danielle's droning, echoing voice as she bitched about people not bringing their bowls back to the kitchen hatch.

She took the stairs up to the gallery, then crossed the floor to Hahn's infirmary. She knocked on the door. 'Dr Hahn?'

No answer.

She knocked again, waited, then tried the door handle. The room was locked. Which was unusual. Hahn's 'my door is always open' mantra, which came at the end of every medical briefing, was clearly not in effect today.

She's probably with Grace.

She made her way across the gallery floor to the women's dormitory, expecting to find the doctor sitting beside Grace's cot chatting away with her. The two seemed to have become very close over the last couple of weeks.

She pushed the door open and poked her head in. 'Dr Hahn?'

There was no answer. But she saw Grace in her bed, lying on her side, knees drawn up and her blanket pulled over her. 'Hey, Grace . . . you OK?'

She tiptoed over in case Grace was asleep.

Grace stirred and yawned. 'Hey, Freya,' she replied blearily.

'How're you doing?'

'I got tummy cramps.'

'Ouch . . . hate those.' Freya placed her walking stick on the floor between the cots and sat down heavily on Dr Hahn's. The springs creaked under her. 'It's usually, like, just for the first day, then it gets better. What did Dr Hahn say?'

'Oh, she said I should stay in bed today.'

'Yeah, I thought she probably would.'

'She said I was still quite weak, and then having this happen too . . .'

'I guess she's let Everett know you're off?'

'Uh-huh. Think so.'

Freya leaned forward and stroked Grace's forehead lightly. Her fingers were close to the ridges of scar tissue. 'That's not tender?'

'It's nice,' whispered Grace. She closed her eyes. 'Mom used to do that.'

Freya listened to the rustle of her even breathing. There was a slight wheezing sound and she wondered if that was a result of scarring inside her throat or nasal passage. She had a flash of memory of that day back at Emerald Park, the screaming coming from the storeroom and the gleeful baying of David Lester.

It had seemed like some medieval witch hunt – supposedly civilized, educated humans reduced to simple-minded tribal savagery. The memory brought with it the smell.

That horrible smell. A whiff of diesel and . . .

Freya clenched her eyes shut and opened them again, as if the simple gesture would scare the memory back into its cage. The smell still lingered, though. An unpleasant meaty odour. It reminded her of the time she'd been on a crowded bus on the way to school, the warm tangy odour of a Cornish pasty drifting through the bus. It had made her tummy rumble with hunger until she'd worked out it was the B.O. wafting off the big hairy man standing right beside her. The same smell . . . one moment, delicious, the next *revolting*.

She realized it was coming from Grace. The girl needed a wash. She wasn't the only one in the castle, to be fair. There were one or two, male of course, who didn't like splashing themselves with cold water, and left it far too long between visits to the washroom. This, though . . . *this* was really quite unpleasant.

She needs to wash more.

'Freya?'

'Yeah?'

'Thank you for coming up to see me.'

'Hey, that's OK. I told Leon to wait till later. He wanted to come up too.'

Grace held out a hand. She wanted it held. Freya shuffled forward so she could reach it. The soles of her trainers made a *snick* sound as they unstuck from the tacky floor.

'Ugh . . . what's that down there?' She was about to reach down into the dark space and feel the floor, but Grace grabbed her hand first.

'I *love you*, Freya.'

She froze. Surprised by that. 'Well . . . I love you too, sweetie.'

'I mean it. I love you. And Leon.'

'I know. He . . . he really struggled when he thought you were gone. For a while I was worried he'd end up doing something stupid.'

'I wouldn't blame him,' said Grace. She opened her eyes and looked up at her. 'I miss how it all used to be.'

'Me too.'

'It's really . . .' Grace frowned.

'What?'

'Really hard to keep on going.'

Freya squeezed her hand firmly. 'You shouldn't think like that. We made it. We survived.'

'Do you think there's a heaven?'

'What?' Freya laughed uncomfortably. 'Grace . . . c'mon, lovely – this is a period, that's all. You're not going to die!'

'Everyone dies, Freya. One day they do.'

'Yeah, true . . . but I'm in no hurry. Nor should you be.'

'I . . . have nightmares. Nightmares about *burning*.'

'God . . . Grace, I can't even begin to imagine how—'

'I don't want to die like that.'

'No. No you won't. I promise you, me and Leon are going to keep you safe. We're never going to let you out of our sight again.'

Grace smiled. 'Thank you.'

She closed her eyes again, and Freya listened to the soft rustle of her breathing for a while.

'I wonder what it's like,' Grace whispered presently.

'What what's like?'

'Being infected by that virus.'

'Jesus . . .' Freya shook her head. 'You're in a grim mood.'

'I saw someone dying of it.'

'We've all seen that.'

'No . . . I mean the first bit. When it first gets hold of you.' Grace opened her eyes again, but this time she was staring past Freya at the row of arched windows at the end of the dormitory. 'There was this man . . . and this woman. They were with us when we escaped from the train.'

Freya knew the train story. Leon had told her all about that.

'They seemed . . . *happy*.'

Leon had said that too. Like they were drunk or stoned. *Endorphins*. That's what Freya had told him: the human brain's mercy moment, flooding itself with a feel-good chemical when it knows the ship's going down for sure and there's not a hope of escape.

'I'm not going to die that way,' said Freya. 'If I knew that thing was *in me*? I'd grab a gun, or if I couldn't find a gun, I'd jump out of a window.' She pressed her lips together. 'Me and Leon, we made a pact, you know, if that happ—'

'But . . . what if it was . . . *nice*?'

Freya's face crumpled with incredulity. 'Nice?'

'Uh-huh.'

Freya leaned forward, her trainer *snick*ing again as she moved her foot. 'What the hell *is* that?'

'Dr Hahn spilled my soup earlier.'

Freya wrinkled her nose. Maybe that explained the smell. She resumed what she was going to say, clasping both her hands firmly round Grace's.

'*I'm* going to survive this virus. So are you, and so is Leon.' She realized her voice was beginning to wobble with emotion. Much more of this and she was going to go all mushy.

Not now, girl.

'However, if it comes to it –' *this* she needed to say out loud like a renewed vow – 'you know, if it comes down to a choice, I'm *not* going to die *that way.*' She shook her head. 'Not the virus. Not that way.'

The horn sounded for the end of lunch break.

Freya's intense expression vanished like a switch had been flipped. 'Jeez . . . enough of the morbid talk!' She patted Grace's hand. 'We're safe right here. Get some rest. Because I'm pretty sure Everett's *not* going to give you a day off tomorrow as well.'

She reached down for her walking stick, picked it up and realized the handle was tacky from the spilled soup. She wiped it on her jeans, then pulled herself up.

'I'll bring Leon up with me later, OK?'

Grace nodded. She watched Freya as she made her way out, a lopsided walk that looked tiring to endure, watching her until she disappeared through the door and closed it behind her.

Then she cried.

I'm so sorry.

CHAPTER 28

Leon saw them sitting in the far corner of the roof on the collapsible chairs someone had taken up from one of the function rooms. The spotlight perched on its tripod by one of the corner battlements would remain on all night, but the lights-out horn – due in about fifteen minutes – meant they'd all have to head downstairs to their dormitories, even so. Only the knight on watch duty would be allowed to remain up here.

Freya waved him over to join them.

'How is she?'

Leon sat down in the chair she'd saved beside her. 'Asleep.'

'Poor thing.'

'She was complaining about stomach pains.' He looked at Freya. '*Woman thing* . . . it's not *that* bad normally, is it?'

Naga overheard that. 'Yup. It is. She should get Dr Hahn to give her some Nurofen. If we've got any left.'

'Where is Hahn?' said Leon. 'I haven't seen her all day.'

'She's around somewhere,' said Freya. 'She was sitting with Grace earlier today.'

Fish held out one of his battered Nintendos to Leon. 'Fancy a thrashing before bed?'

He shook his head. 'No, it's all right.'

'Doesn't have to be *Mario Kart*. I've got *Pokemon*?'

191

'No, I'm good, thanks. I'm exhausted.' Leon had been digging in mud all day, squatting in the dirt, groping for spuds. After dinner he'd had to hose himself down with cold water and change into spare, uncaked clothes from the laundry pool. Right now he was wearing clothes he'd never have dared wear before: a checked 'dad' shirt and dark jeans with bright yellow double-stitched seams down the legs. He felt like a dork.

'I was talking to Gosling earlier,' said Naga in a lowered voice. 'Apparently they got ambushed by virals again. Not just ambushed . . . but *set up*.'

'What do you mean "set up"?' asked Fish.

'Tricked. Lured. They set a trap.'

Leon looked at her. 'Trap?'

'Uh-huh. Used some weak-looking ones to lure them away from the trucks to a stash of food, then some much bigger ones went straight in to trash the trucks.'

'Jesus, that's smart,' said Fish.

'That's exactly what he said. They were trying to cut off their escape.'

'Anyone hurt?'

'Luckily no.'

'The trucks?'

'Well, they drove both back, so . . .'

'That sounds coordinated,' said Fish. 'Planned, for sure.'

'Do you think these crabs have –' Naga shrugged – 'I don't know . . . *leader crabs*?'

The idea sounded ridiculous to Leon. From his experience of them, the things swarmed dumbly like army ants.

'What, like, brain crabs?' Fish snorted. 'Big wobbly brains on legs?'

She could see he was mocking her. 'Maybe. Why not?'

'It's more likely a form of crowd-source intelligence,' he replied. 'Like you see with schools of fish, or flocks of birds. Simple rule-set behaviour that each individual follows, but, applied to a crowd of individuals, it starts to look smart. Starts to look like a strategy.'

'Oh, I think the virus has a strategy,' said Freya. 'I mean, it's built a whole network of roots for starters.'

Fish tucked away his Nintendos. 'Which is exactly what a tree does. You wouldn't call a tree smart, though, would you?'

'It doesn't even need to be particularly smart,' said Leon. They all looked at him. 'If just one of those roots manages to grow across the moat, or up the wall, it's gonna be game over for us.'

The bedtime horn finally sounded.

'On that cheerful note,' said Fish. He got up and folded his chair to take downstairs.

Naga did likewise. 'Come on.'

'You go ahead. We'll catch you up,' said Leon.

Leon waited until they were both beyond earshot, helped Freya on to her feet and began to collapse their chairs. 'I haven't seen Dr Hahn all day, have you?'

Freya shook her head. 'I went to get some meds earlier. No sign of her.'

'I hope she's OK.'

They watched the others disappearing down the steps from the rooftop.

'Leon?'

'Yeah?'

'You're right, you know.'

'About what?'

'One of those roots . . . that's all it'll take.' Freya tucked one of the collapsed chairs under her arm and reached for her walking stick. 'And if Naga's right and the virus really did set a trap for Corkie's men, then . . . it sounds like it's starting to learn to make plans.'

Leon shuddered slightly. It might have been the cool breeze across the rooftop, or it might have been the chilling effect of her words.

He looked at her in the gathering gloom, ignoring the knight who was waving at them across the rooftop to get a move on. 'You're suggesting we leave?'

'All I'm suggesting is . . . let's not get too comfortable here.'

Grace waited until Leon had left the dormitory and the sound of his footsteps echoing across the gallery floor had receded. Downstairs in the main hall she could hear the dinner-duty group cleaning up noisily.

A part of her hated the secrecy, hated keeping things from Leon.

Once upon a time in another life, things had been different. She'd had her busy social life, and Leon had had his, for what it was. They'd been no closer than any other brother and sister. They hadn't really had that much in common. The only time they'd really interacted was when she'd nagged at him for being such a loner weirdo.

At middle school, on the regular occasions they passed each other in the hallway between lessons, Grace surrounded by her gaggle of friends, Leon invariably on his own, they'd barely made eye contact.

Since Mom and Dad had split and they'd moved to the UK, however, they'd grown closer. Even though Mom had asked Leon to look out for her, walk her to school, she'd been the one looking after him. He wasn't adjusting. He wasn't coping. She could see him receding further and further into a shell of his own making.

And then the virus struck and they'd lost Mom . . . and Dad. Grace realized now that in the aftermath, Leon had become the surrogate parent. Had stepped up finally and become her big brother, her protector. And she finally understood how much she loved him, depended on him. Understood how strong he really was.

And now it's my turn to look after him . . . again.

The bedtime horn had sounded. A few minutes from now, the women of this community would be coming in and the dormitory was going to get busy.

She sat up, hurried across to the open door of the dormitory, pulled it shut and then dragged the nearest bed a couple of metres across to obstruct it. Not as good as locking it, for sure, but if someone barged in it would delay them a second or two.

She hurried back to her bed, ducked down in the narrow

space between hers and Dr Hahn's, and lifted the dangling grey blanket.

The process was nearly complete. She could see in the gloom beneath the bed that the colony of builders had assembled a working frame around Hahn's bones: muscle tissue and tendons. Across most of the carcass the first thin membrane of skin had knitted together, forming a gelatinous yet transparent seal. They would require several more hours to grow the additional layers needed for the membrane to become an opaque and convincing facsimile of human skin.

She reached under the bed and rested her hand lightly on the cadaver's arm.

The head jerked sharply and turned to face her. Milky eyes without lids stared at her unflinchingly. Grace could see thick arteries pumping beneath the waxy skin, weaving across the mottled yellow bone of Claudia Hahn's skull. They pulsed and bulged subtly like insect pupae, working more industriously than any normal human arteries to deliver resources to where they were needed as rapidly as possible.

Grace pulled on the arm gently, careful not to damage the fragile first layer of skin.

'Come out.'

The cadaver flexed uncertainly. All four limbs called to action but as yet unrehearsed in their function. She helped it pull itself out from the narrow space beneath the bed. Sticky mucus-like strands of dead and redundant cells snapped from its back like the strong adhesive of duct tape. The body struggled to pull itself on to its hands and knees. Grace steadied it as the thing wobbled weakly, like a recently roused coma patient trying to comprehend the pitiful state of its useless atrophied limbs.

'Come on,' she whispered supportively, knowing that collaboration was taking place on a vast scale; billions of cells still linking up to their colleagues, attempting to comprehend their tiny role in a macrocosmic endeavour.

She pulled aside the blanket on Hahn's bed revealing clean sheets now, but ones that would probably need to be cleaned again in the morning. She hefted the upper half of the body on to the bed. The cadaver's legs scissored and kicked uselessly on the floor, unable to support the weight of its body just yet.

Grace lifted the first leg on to the bed, and pushed with all her strength against the base of the thing's spine. The cadaver understood what was being asked of it and flexed the bony claws of its hands, grasping at the bed sheet and pulling to assist her.

Just in time she managed to roll it over on its side and lift it on to the bed. She could hear approaching footsteps on the gallery floor. She quickly pulled the blanket over the thing's body, lifted its head up and stuffed a pillow under it. She pulled the blanket right up over the shoulder, up to where a half-formed ear was still in the process of knitting a cartilage frame. Grace quickly smoothed Hahn's blonde hair down over the ear, covering it up.

The door to the dormitory banged open against the corner of the bed, and Grace heard a voice beyond squawking in complaint.

She took one last look at Hahn in her bed and tugged the blanket up a little higher until all that was visible was the thick feathery tresses of her hair.

'Coming!' said Grace. She hurried across the floor and shoved the bed aside. The door swung inwards and she saw Danielle standing outside with her hands spread wide with a *WTF?* look on her face.

'Sorry, I—'

'Did you move that bed across on purpose?'

She nodded guiltily.

'It's not your personal bedroom, you know, Grace?'

'I just wanted some privacy, that's all.'

'Yeah, well, we all have to live here, not just you.'

Grace stepped to one side to let her in. She could see the others coming up the stairs from the main hall, the rest down the stone stairway leading from the rooftop.

'And shit!' Danielle huffed loudly, wafting a hand in front of her face. 'Maybe you should go use the washroom sometime soon.'

Grace held a finger to her lips. 'Shhh.'

'What?'

Grace pointed to Hahn's bed. 'Dr Hahn's trying to get some sleep.'

'We've all had a hard day.' Danielle swept past Grace and headed towards her bed. The other women bustled into the dormitory after her. The room, so quiet all day long, now echoed with a dozen voices talking over the top of each other.

Grace saw Freya and Leon come down the steps from

the roof, saw them exchange a few words and a brief hug. Then Freya caught up with Naga and they both joined the other women heading towards the dorm.

Freya saw Grace standing beside the door, smiled and waved. 'Hey there . . . how are you feeling?'

'Much better.'

'You look better.' They stepped inside and Freya noted the occupied bed in the corner. 'Ah, there she is! I need to see her about—'

'Claudia's sleeping,' said Grace quickly. 'She's not feeling too good.'

'Uh, what's up with her?'

Grace reached quickly for an answer. 'Migraine. A really . . . really bad one.'

'Oh. Poor thing.'

Naga clapped her hands together like a schoolteacher. 'Hey! Come on. Keep it down, ladies!' She nodded towards Dr Hahn's bed. 'The doctor's trying to get some sleep!'

'Well excu-u-use me,' huffed Danielle on the way out again with a wash towel over her arm.

Freya walked with Grace towards her bed. 'You coming with me to go get a wash?'

'Not tonight. I'm still a bit . . . you know.'

'Sure.' Freya wrinkled her nose slightly. 'But it might be a good idea in the morning?'

Grace nodded guiltily and smiled. 'I know.'

Freya draped an arm round her shoulders and planted a sisterly kiss on her forehead. 'Glad you're feeling better, hon.'

CHAPTER 29

In the almost complete darkness of 'lights out', the transition between the 'world outside' and the 'world inside' was almost unnoticeable.

The sounds of the dormitory – whispered chattering across the room, someone snoring loudly – gradually receded and were drowned out by a momentary roaring, the auditory processing cells of Grace's mind turning inward and 'hearing' the deafening bustle of activity. Red blood cells traversing the arterial highways like Manhattan rush-hour traffic, white blood cells weaving among them like canary-yellow New York cabs.

The senses Grace used for the outside world – compartmentalized into sight, sound, smell – blurred boundaries within her. She could 'smell' the passing strings of chemical traffic, packets of genetic data rushing to where they needed to be, 'hear' the microcosmic geometry of the world around her, like a bat senses its cave. 'Taste' the cells of her own consciousness coalescing, being shepherded together like schoolchildren on a field trip, to move as one extended block of awareness.

She navigated herself towards the place she needed to be, sensing trace cells that pointed the way to her location. And moments later the leading edge of her cluster recognized the first timid cells of the person she needed to talk to, orbiting round their core cluster like wary scrapyard dogs.

Grace constructed the illusion that had become their regular space.

Once again she was sitting on the infirmary gurney, and there, sitting on the stool beside her, was Dr Hahn.

'Hello, Claudia.'

'Grace.' Her voice sounded different this time. Less confused, less lost. 'They've been telling me things.'

'Do you know what's going on right now? Outside?'

Hahn nodded. 'I've been remade.'

'That's right.'

'And they've shown me so many other things.' She shook her head and a dreamy smile eased itself on to her lips. 'It's a whole . . . incredible . . . universe inside us?'

Grace grinned. 'It *is* incredible, isn't it?'

'It . . . It's . . . wonderful. They showed me . . .' She gazed out past Grace over her shoulder. Grace sensed Hahn reaching out beyond the illusion of the infirmary, replaying for her mind's eye some of the things she'd glimpsed.

'We're not alone. We thought we were. But . . .' Her eyes focused again on Grace. 'I understand now. I see . . . "outside" we live such lonely lives. All alone, isolated. We move around in our own solitary . . .' She struggled to find the right word. Then she had it. A way she could explain herself. 'Like *islands*. Lonely, remote Pacific desert islands. But in here we're all *connected*. One big land mass.'

Grace encouraged her with a nod.

'I never understood how . . . *sad*, how lonely my life

201

was.' She shook her head. 'I feel so sorry for Claudia.'

'You're still Claudia. You're just a *new* Claudia. A Claudia Hahn that *understands*.'

'She was blind, deaf, mute. She had no idea. No idea how beautiful life really is.'

Grace knew exactly what she meant. She could sense the emotion coming off the woman in waves. She had experienced the exact same moment of realization. To be 'human' was to exist in a bubble, a small world sealed within a wrapping of skin, a carpet bag of carbon atoms. Competing ruthlessly, sometimes brutally, with other lonely 'bubbles'. A caveman existence. Fighting, squabbling, killing, eating. Micro-world fighting micro-world in order to survive long enough to pass on a genetic baton to offspring like some bizarre, cutthroat relay race. Only then, having passed the genetic baton along, to become completely redundant, no longer necessary to anyone. And, from there, to eek out a pointless existence until chromosome telomeres had worn down to exhausted nubs, and new cells became old cells, and decay and death eventually followed. Grace was pleased that Claudia Hahn now saw that too.

Life . . . as it was.

There was no death in here. No selfishness. No jealousy. No tribal rivalry. No wars. No genocides . . . No brutal slayings because of the colour of a skin, the choice of a lover, the name of a god.

'I feel loved, Grace. For the first time . . . I actually feel *loved*. Is it crazy for me to say this?'

'No.'

Hahn leaned forward and placed a hand on hers. 'Thank you. Thank you so much.'

'I want to *help* the others too,' Grace replied. 'Most of all Leon and Freya.'

Hahn nodded. 'Yes, of course!'

'This afternoon I spoke with—'

'This afternoon?' Hahn laughed and shook her head. 'Afternoon. Evening. Day. Hour. These are strange things that mean nothing to me now!'

'I know.' Grace chuckled along with her. 'Time's so weird. Sometimes it seems faster on the inside, sometimes much slower.' She carried on with what she wanted to say. 'Freya visited me earlier and we talked. She said something that really frightened me.'

'What?'

'She'd kill herself rather than join us.'

Hahn cocked her head. 'I understand why. It was very frightening. At first.'

'Her and Leon. Both of them. They've agreed to kill themselves.'

Hahn sensed the waves of emotion coming off Grace. She got up and sat on the gurney beside her and hugged her.

Leon's seen far too much of it. Seen the process up close. Seen Mom die. Seen Ava, the lady on the train and that other man changing slowly. He's terrified of it.

She wanted them both to join. To give them what she'd already given to Claudia. A new life. *Immortality.* But she was terrified of losing them, terrified of what they'd both do if they became aware that they were infected. She could give them *this*, but only if they were alive. 'They' – the virus – were not magicians; they could adapt life, but they couldn't reverse death. If Freya and Leon did something stupid, they were going to be gone.

Forever.

Dust.

She turned to Hahn. 'Claudia, will you help me?'

'Of course.'

'It means returning.'

'Where?'

'Out there.'

Hahn took a long, deep breath. Grace could hear her thoughts like a one-sided telephone conversation spoken too loudly in a quiet room. Here was her home now. Here was a wonderful place. Here was love. But Out There . . . ? It was lonely, cold. A desolate existence in contrast to this chemical commune.

'Please, Claudia.'

Hahn eventually nodded. But Grace had already sensed her answer.

'Of course, I will help.'

CHAPTER 30

Fourteen Months Ago

'This is insane!' Tom Friedmann stopped halfway across the USS *Gerald R. Ford*'s deck and turned to look at his assistant. 'We need every goddamn ship we can spare. Particularly *this* one!'

His assistant was an earnest young ensign, who seemed to have miraculously kept his navy whites crisp and utterly spotless so far. 'Sir, the president was completely adamant about this. None of the navy vessels will be allowed to go.'

Tom banged his fist on the notepad he was carrying and looked around. The carrier's deck four months ago had been an untidy sea of civilian refugees. Now it was civilian-free. Two of the ship's complement of F-35C jet fighters were on the deck being prepped for launch, the yellow-jacketed catapult officer making last-minute assessments on the wind speed and checks on the electromagnetic catapult.

The *Ford* was keeping two jets in the air around the clock, circling the clustered ships like sheepdogs herding a skittish flock.

'Jesus. The *Ford* is the *one* ship we need.' Tom looked around at the enormous deck. God knows how many civilians they could bring back aboard her. She was vast up top, and vast below. Not just people, but perhaps supplies:

food, medicines, machinery. They could pack thousands of tons of payload aboard her and bring it all back to help out here.

'The president's not going to budge an inch, sir.'

Tom already knew that.

Four months ago, Trent had put him in charge of coordinating the rescue attempt, a task that was no more complicated than his last job collating Dow Jones share trends and compiling weekly briefing documents. Except it had been made difficult by the roadblocks Trent kept putting up. He had been dragging his heels on the resources Tom was going to be allowed to play around with. From the whole mixed-bag fleet of navy and merchant ships, he was down to six cargo vessels and a cruise ship. And absolutely no army personnel whatsoever. None.

Dougie had been clear about that point during their face-to-face a couple of days ago. He had about six hundred pairs of boots ready to hit the ground at a moment's notice. He wasn't going to let Tom take a single one of them away on a mercy mission.

'You want to go find survivors? You're not going to need any firepower, *amigo*. Trust me.'

'Dougie, we'll need medics! We'll need organization, *military* organization. And you know what? If enough people have heard our shout-out broadcast and made their way to those rendezvous locations, we're going to need troops to keep order!'

Douglas Trent leaned forward and rested his thick forearms on the desk. 'Tom, I'm gonna be real nice about this, because you and me, we go back. We're a couple more shitty exchanges away from the Cubans kicking us off this island. I'm going to need my boys. Every last one of 'em. Now, if you want to hold back on this mercy mission until we've got things sorted here, then—'

'Jesus, Doug, we need to go now! *Right now!* If anyone else out there managed to survive this goddamn nightmare, they're going to be struggling!' He banged his fist on the desk.

Trent's face suddenly hardened. His watery blue eyes glinted sternly beneath his bushy eyebrows.

'You *ever* raise your voice like that to me again, I will knock you down.'

'For Chrissakes, listen to me, Doug—'

'No, *you* listen.' Trent stood up and leaned forward over the desk, bracing himself on his knuckles, his lips parted to reveal a tidy row of small clenched teeth, a primate's territorial snarl. 'You saved my ass twenty years ago. I won't ever forget that. And for that you got your swanky well-paid job and all your connections. You got to live in a real nice neighbourhood, send your kids to nice schools. You got a navy chopper lifting you out of a shitstorm. And –' he lifted a hand and swished it above his paperwork – 'you get to sit at Caesar's table. But my gratitude isn't an endless eat-all-you-want buffet. Do you understand me?'

Tom stared at him. To nod mutely right now was to bring an end to the relationship they'd had all these years, to acknowledge absolutely his subordinate position.

So he'd walked.

And that's how he'd left it. He'd decided to give the president a day or two to calm down before attempting to get another face-to-face with him, but since then Trent had been too busy to see him. Tom had sent his young ensign with a handwritten plea to allow Tom the use of the *Ford* only.

Just the one ship.

Tom looked around at the hum of activity on deck, the red high-vis jackets of the ordnance crew backing away, having checked the jet's payload; the yellow and green jackets verifying the catapult's readiness with the pilot, cryptic hand signals and nods exchanged above the din of the engines revving up for a take-off.

At least, for the moment anyway, he had the president's permission to take a small flotilla of civilian ships.

If he decided to go right now.

They're over there. They're alive. Hurry.

Every morning when he woke up, that's what he assured himself. If there were any survivors left, his two kids and their mother *had* to be among them. He'd given them half a chance with an early heads-up, and all three of them had been popping pills of one sort or another at the time.

They have to be OK.

CHAPTER 31

'You say the pain is getting worse?'

Freya nodded. 'In my hips and legs mainly. It's obviously much worse when I move, but even when I don't it's there, constantly.'

Dr Hahn nodded slowly. 'Do you remember what type of condition your GP diagnosed?'

'Just multiple sclerosis, really. I know there are types. My mum did all the googling about it.' She shrugged. 'She could've told you everything you needed to know about it.'

'What about your energy levels? Are you feeling more easily tired?'

Freya had been. She'd been finding it harder to get up in the mornings, a steadily increasing battle of willpower to pull her body out of bed and get dressed. She'd been putting that down to getting less sleep at night because of the constant aching – that and the fact that every day she was working in the kitchen or doing the laundry. Both incessantly physical tasks.

A cumulative fatigue – that was her own optimistic layman's diagnosis.

'Yeah, I guess so.'

Hahn nodded again. 'Hmmm, this is to be expected, I'm afraid, Freya.'

'How much worse do you think my MS is going to get?'

'Obviously proper diagnosis is done in several stages in order to measure the rate of decline. So this is difficult for me to say. Have you experienced any periods of relapse? Or perhaps a plateauing of your condition?'

Freya cast her mind back over the last three years. So much had happened since that morning her doctor had dropped this bomb on her. It was difficult to compare one day to the next. The last three years had included the end of the world. There had been no such thing as a typical day. Not, that is, until the last couple of months.

'Not really . . . It's always there.'

'And you think your condition is worsening?'

She wondered if Leon could answer that better. Would he admit to Dr Hahn that he was finding her speech noticeably more slurred? He hadn't mentioned anything to her, or was he just being kind?

Freya nodded reluctantly. 'I think so.'

Dr Hahn gently tapped the tip of her pen on the surface of her desk. 'Freya, I would say you are very, very unlucky . . .'

No shit, Sherlock.

'I suspect you have PRMS: progressive-relapsing multiple sclerosis. It is the rarest kind; five per cent of MS sufferers have this form of the condition, and it is the most aggressive.'

'I'm going to die of it one day, right?' She remembered asking that very same question a long time ago.

'Not from MS directly. It is a condition that only affects the quality of life. We can manage the discomfort with painkillers and anti-inflammatories. But the fatigue . . . I'm afraid this is not something I can help you with. You'll be able to do less and less as your condition deteriorates.'

Freya huffed out a laugh. 'Well, I've always been a lazy cow. So no change there, then.'

Dr Hahn unlocked her medicine cabinet, rummaged around inside and pulled out a box of pills. 'These are much stronger than the ones we all take.' She held the box in her hand, seemingly reluctant to pass them over. Her eyes were narrowed, her brow furrowed. Thinking hard about something. The kind of expression Freya liked to think of as the *Did I leave the gas on?* face. Freya studied the doctor's thoughtful expression. She noticed Hahn looked slightly different this morning. She couldn't put her finger on what it was that had changed.

Did her face looked slimmer?

Freya finally cocked her head. 'Doctor? You OK there?'

'Sorry . . . I . . .' Hahn shook her thoughts away. 'I was wondering if there *was* another way . . . I . . .' Hahn shook her head again, that somewhere-else look clearing as quickly as a passing cloud. 'I am sorry, Freya. I was just . . . My mind was wandering.' She smiled sadly. 'I am also quite tired.' She handed the pills to her. 'You must take one a day only, please.'

'Dr Hahn gave me some stronger pills for my hip.'

Grace, Leon and Freya were sitting and watching Gosling and one of the other knights, Royce, working on the truck that had been attacked the other day. The hood

211

was propped up and Gosling was bent over, his head and shoulders inside, cursing and muttering as he tried to replace a length of torn rubber hose with a new undamaged section and a D clamp.

'I might go see Hahn and ask if she'll give me something extra too,' said Leon. 'My head's been pounding recently.'

Grace felt herself flinch at that comment. She knew that *this* – Leon's migraines, Freya's MS – could pose a problem. Claudia Hahn had been dutifully handing out those 'dud' vitamin pills for six days now, assuring everyone they were just a different brand of painkiller. Another week and hopefully the medicines in everyone's blood would be diluted enough.

It has to be quick. Very, very quick. When the time came to make a move, Grace needed them all to become infected at the same moment. She needed everyone to succumb as quickly as she'd seen those people fall on the railway tracks.

All at once . . . and no warning signs.

'You OK, Grace?' asked Leon.

'Uh-huh.' She smiled quickly for him.

'You looked like you were miles away there.'

'I was . . . just thinking about Dad.'

'You think he's still alive?'

She shrugged. 'I hope so.' She looked up at him, relieved for the change in conversation. 'What do you think, Leo?'

'Dad?' He frowned. 'I think if anyone else survived, he'd be one of them. You know what he's like.'

'You know what I think?' cut in Freya. '*Of course* others

212

survived. Actually, I think a ton of people must have survived.'

'So where are they?' Grace looked up at the sky. For once there were enough patches of blue to call it a nice day. 'Surely we'd have seen a plane or something by now. Or heard something on the radio?'

'Well, *we're* here,' said Leon, 'and who knows about us, right? We're not broadcasting on all frequencies.'

'Precisely.' Freya nodded. 'I'm thinking, you know, at least one complete *country* somewhere must have survived.'

'It came down everywhere, didn't it?' said Grace. 'Those flakes. I don't think a whole country, no matter how small, would have escaped it.'

'There was that message,' said Freya.

Leon shook his head. 'I think Everett's right. That probably got sent in the weeks after the outbreak. It's old, old news now.'

'What message?'

They looked at each other and both realized at the same time that no one had mentioned it to Grace.

'Me and Freya, we thought there was a rescue fleet coming.' He shook his head at how naive and hopeful that sounded. 'We came across this radio station and heard a message being broadcast.'

'What was the message?'

'Rescue ships, Grace. Coming to Southampton.'

Freya looked at Leon. 'You know what I think?'

'I suspect you're going to tell me.'

'I think Everett's full of crap.'

'Why?'

'I think he knows we're right, but he doesn't want everyone bailing out of his little kingdom.'

'That's crazy.'

'Is it?'

'You make him sound like *Hitler*.'

'Maybe he is. Maybe he's a total power junkie? A weirdo with a total hard-on for being the Sheriff of Nottingham.'

Leon made a face. 'Or maybe he just doesn't want people peeling off on their own and heading out and then getting jumped by snarks?'

'Yeah, right. Leon, you do know the only radio in this castle – the *only one* – is sitting in his study?'

He saw where she was going with this. 'Oh, come on.'

'That's what Naga told me. The other radios the knights have are shortwave or something, but the one in his study is, like, a *proper* one.'

'And you think he sits in there every night tuning in to radio stations around the world?'

'Maybe he does.'

Leon snorted at the thought. 'So if you think he's keeping that from us, go and ask him.'

'You mean go up and say *Mr Everett, I think you might be a power-mad sociopath who's been lying to us all. Can I check your radio, please?*'

'Well, not like that. But . . . just ask him nicely.'

'Seriously?'

Leon nodded. 'I'll come with you. We'll just ask him if we can try out his radio.'

'Jesus, think about it, Leon. If he *has* been lying to everyone here, what do you think that'll achieve? Where do you think that will lead?'

Leon *clupped* his mouth shut and pursed his lips thoughtfully.

'Exactly. We get kicked out on our own. And then we're totally stuffed.'

'So what do you suggest we do?'

Freya hunched her shoulders. 'I don't know. I'm not suggesting we *do* anything. All I'm saying is that *maybe* that signal, that message, wasn't old news. *Maybe* that signal is still going out, every day. And we're a bunch of idiots sitting here in this fake castle waiting for those snarks to finally figure out how to get in.'

CHAPTER 32

He sleeps in there.

Grace listened carefully to the sounds of the castle at night. Even after the last of the women had finally stopped whispering and dropped off to sleep, the place seemed alive with noises. The gentle thrum of the generator outside, the soothing *shhh* of the breeze stirring the distant treeline. The men's and women's dormitories playing an orchestra of snores and wheezes.

The building itself creaked, the floorboards across the gallery particularly so.

She saw Hahn waiting for her outside Everett's study door, as they'd arranged. Grace held out her hand and grasped the doctor's wrist. As their skin touched, it began to liquidize and meld together. The vein at the base of Grace's thumb opened and spilled information across the join between them into an artery in Hahn's wrist.

Information exchanged in perfect, still silence. They both closed their eyes to concentrate.

Freya says he has a big radio in there.

It is an old army one, Grace.

And it could be picking up messages from many other survivors?

Everett has said there has been nothing on it for over a year.

Freya thinks he's lying.

Why would he do that?

He is afraid. Too afraid to leave the castle.

Hahn was no longer a frightened and confused guest in this new microcosmic world. There was no need to construct the familiar environment of the infirmary. Her fluency in the chemical language was improving, if not yet complete.

Claudia. We/they have to know for certain if there are other survivors. Especially enough others to be able to put together a rescue plan.

There was mention of a message when those two first arrived. But Everett was certain it was old. What if there are other survivors, Grace? Can't they be left alone?

It's important. They have told all of us that their work could be destroyed, undone, by survivors if there are enough of them. Those who are left could still be dangerous.

What are we going to do?

I need to know if there are radio messages.

Everett was dreaming about the good ol' days. Not about the time before the virus came, but the time five years before that. When he'd been a *somebody*. A self-made rags-to-riches man.

Good times while they'd lasted.

His woolly consciousness slowly spun itself together. He was vaguely aware someone was talking. At first he was certain it was the tail end of his dream. But then he heard the soft, almost whispered, voice speaking to him again and he realized he wasn't alone.

'Everett?'

He blinked his bleary eyes open. The room was not wholly dark. A glow from the floodlight outside leaked in through the lead-lined window and cast diamond shadow patterns across his study.

'Who—' he started to grunt.

A hand clapped tightly over his lips and a small dark figure loomed over him.

'Shhhh . . . It's me, Mr Everett.'

The voice was small and childlike . . . and familiar.

'Yes, it's me. Grace. Stay still,' she answered his widening eyes. 'Claudia, is there a light?'

A moment later the lamp on his 'campaign' desk clicked on and Everett jolted in his bed.

It was the girl, all right, crouched down beside his cot and leaning over him, her face so close he could feel her breath on his cheeks.

But she was transformed horrifically. The burn-scarred side of her face appeared to be melting, as if the flames that had once caused those marks had returned. Strands of pastel-pink flesh were dangling from her cheek and jawline like drizzled icing from a cake, swinging and finally dropping in thick gelatinous globules on to his bare, hairy chest.

'Jesus . . . B-bloody . . . You're a bloody krak—' he started to say. She pushed her hand more firmly against his mouth, shutting him up.

'You have to be very quiet,' she chided him softly, 'or you'll wake the others.' Another hand came into view. It was a hand only in the sense that it was located at the end of her wrist. He tried to focus on it to comprehend what he was seeing.

Where a young girl's pink Mini Mouse watch strap might have been, her skin had changed from a pale hue to an angry inflamed septic red. Where the ball of her thumb should have been, the skin had torn as if she'd been stabbed by a serrated blade, and dark rivulets of blood were trickling from the wound.

The ragged flesh of the cut moved with a will of its own, parting like theatre curtains as something bulged and pushed its way forward. He could see it emerging, a growth small and lumpy. For a second he thought he was witnessing the knobbly end of her ulna bone pushing through. He'd seen something like that during a rugby game once: a shattered knee cap and the shards of a femur poking through the skin.

The thing emerged from the wound and continued extending towards his face. He struggled under the girl's small hand, but she was surprisingly strong.

Another figure came into view. It was Dr Hahn. 'Don't resist,' she said. 'You need to sit very still, Major Everett.'

The bloody protuberance unfolded, flower-like, in turn giving birth to a tiny spine that glistened cleanly and swept forward to rest just a few centimetres short of his bulging eyes.

'We don't want to hurt you,' said Grace. 'I promise. But

we do want to ask you something. And you have to be very honest.'

He glanced from her to Hahn, meeting her gaze, hoping the doctor was somehow waiting for the right moment to step in and put a stop to this.

'My brother said there was a radio message about a big rescue mission,' Grace started with a matter-of-fact manner, the tone of a little busybody settling a petty playground dispute between school friends. 'And he said that you'd told him that was all a load of silly nonsense because you've not heard anything on your radio.'

She lifted her chin slightly, looking down her nose at him like a disapproving schoolteacher. 'Now, you have to be honest with me, Mr Everett. Is that true?'

His eyes flickered back on to the sharp glistening spike hovering just in front of him, so close to him now he couldn't actually focus on the tip of it. It was a threatening blur.

'Don't shout the answer,' she said. 'Whisper it quietly. Were you telling the truth?' Grace lifted the pressure of her smothering hand ever so slightly.

'Yes! Yes! I was telling the truth—'

She pressed her hand down again to hush him. 'Hmm. I'm not sure I trust you.'

Everett glanced again at Hahn, his eyes pleading with her to help him. But she shook her head. 'I am with Grace, Major. Just be honest with us and we will leave you alone.'

Oh my God . . . She's one of them. They're both . . .

Hahn smiled. Guessing what he was thinking. 'Yes. We

have both been infected. But I am still very much Dr Hahn.'

'Be honest. That's all you have to do.' Grace lifted her hand again slightly.

'Please don't hurt me!' he gasped quickly.

She pressed down again to silence him.

'I think we're going to have to try your radio anyway.' Grace cocked her head. 'Can we?'

Let them. Jesus Christ. Let them turn it on. Let them play with it. They won't get anything.

He nodded quickly.

Hahn wandered from the bedside, across the study, to the table beneath his window. The army-green radio set sat in a metal carry-rack: a panel full of cryptically labelled buttons and a small LED screen.

She's no idea how to use the thing.

Hahn squatted down, inspected the panel for a moment, then found the power switch. She pressed it and the radio came alive, small green diodes blinking.

'Now what do I do?'

The hand was lifted from his mouth again. 'You h-have to hit the digital analogue mode button. Then the one n-next to it. That takes you through the f-frequencies.'

Hahn nodded and followed his instructions. 'There's no sound.'

Everett carefully raised a hand and pointed. 'H-headphones. There.'

Hahn picked up a heavy set of army headphones and pulled them over her ears. She began to turn the dial through the frequencies. In the quiet of the room, Everett could hear the steady hiss of white noise leaking out as she clicked through. He prayed he'd remembered to do *that precautionary thing* the last time he'd listened in.

'Is there anything?' asked Grace.

Hahn shook her head and kept turning.

'There's nothing out th-there . . .' Everett whispered. 'It's a w-waste of time.'

'Shhh,' said Grace. She pressed her hand down on his lips again to hush him.

A minute passed in silence, just the repeating click of the dial and an endless hiss, and Everett was beginning to hope there might be some way out of this for him. These two creatures might have just come here to learn the truth, and then having done so would disappear into the night never to return. Perhaps even leave the castle alone once and for all.

If only . . . God . . . He'd remembered to do it.

The girl was looking at him as they waited. 'I bet you're surprised at how good we've got at looking human, aren't you?'

Everett looked at Grace and nodded.

'Are you thinking there are others of us here?' She smiled reassuringly. 'It's OK, Mr Everett. It's just me and Claudia, I promise.'

Hahn finally pulled the headphones off. 'There *is* nothing, Grace. It is just white noise. Everett's right . . . there's no one out there.'

Everett did his best *not* to gasp with relief. The girl looked disappointed. He wondered if she'd been hoping to catch him out, to have enough justification to thrust that hovering spine deep into his right eye.

'Hang on, let me try something . . .' Hahn stood up, leaned over the rack and peered at the nest of cables emerging from the screw-in sockets at the back

No . . . Shit. No. No. No.

'What are you doing?' asked Grace.

'I'm checking to see if the cables are all plugged in properly.' She checked through them, one after the other. 'This one . . .' She leaned further over, squinting to try to read the socket labels in the poor light.

Everett felt his guts turn in a queasy loop.

'Not sure what this one is . . . but it is very loose. Almost completely unscrewed.'

Oh God . . . Oh please. No.

She twisted it tight, pushed the rack back, then squatted back down. The dial clicked once again as she began to turn it. Again, *click*, and the hiss of white noise leaking from the headphones.

Click . . . hiss . . .
Click . . . hiss . . .
Click . . .

CHAPTER 33

Leon stirred. It took him a few seconds to realize that he was actually wide awake, that his sleep had been disturbed by something real, not a dream. Then he understood what had awoken him. Noises were coming from outside, beyond the dorm's door and out on the gallery.

Voices. Several of them.

Feet clumped carelessly on the echoing wooden floor. He sat up. The dormitory was still mostly dark, just a faint glow of lethargic pre-dawn grey light spilling in through the narrow windows. He could see others sitting up on their cots.

'What the hell's going on out there?' grunted Corkie sleepily.

Leon could hear several female voices talking across each other. It sounded like a heated exchange. He assumed it was Danielle kicking off again, probably over a borrowed pillow or something, then he recognized Grace's voice, sharp and urgent, cutting across the exchange.

He swung his legs over the side of his bed, pulled on some tracksuit bottoms and a loose sweater. 'Something's going on out there!' he called as he hurried barefoot across the floor and pulled the door open to take a look.

The flickering beam of a torch cast distended shadows

across the floor and stone walls. He could see several figures gathered in the middle of the gallery, several more in the doorway of the women's dormitory, emerging like him to see what the hell was going on.

'What's happened?' Leon called out.

'Leon!' Grace cried. She hurried over to him and threw her arms round his waist.

'Hey! What's up? . . . Hey, Grace?' She was clinging to him tightly. He could feel her whole body trembling.

'Leon . . .' Naga's voice. She was the one holding the torch. 'She's really upset. She's manic! I can't get any sense out of her!'

He tugged Grace loose from him and hunched down so they were face to face. 'Grace! What's up? What's happened?' Her eyes were round and wide, her mouth the same.

Naga came over. 'I found her out here.' Naga shook her head. 'I think she's in shock.'

'Grace?' He grasped her shoulders and shook her firmly. 'Talk to me!'

'Sh-she-she's in there with him!' she managed to utter, her words almost incoherent.

'Who is?'

'C-Claudia. Killed!'

'*What?* Killed? Who's been killed?'

Corkie emerged from the men's dorm carrying his torch and cursing angrily. 'Jesus Christ! We're trying to get some bloody sleep in here!'

Leon tapped his sister's cheek lightly to get her to focus

back on him. 'C'mon, Grace . . . You said someone got killed? Who?'

'Everett!' she whispered.

'That's what I thought she was trying to say,' said Naga.

'Dr Hahn, Major Everett . . . Where are they, Grace?' asked Leon.

She pointed across the gallery floor at the door to Everett's study.

It seemed now that everyone had emerged on to the gallery, more torches adding to the confusing dance of shadows.

'Is she OK?' Freya's voice. Leon turned to see her limping over. She'd obviously got up too quickly to bother rooting around for her walking stick. She joined Leon and rested her hand on his shoulder to recover her balance. 'Grace? You OK, hon? You look like you've—'

'Everett's . . . infected . . . Hahn!' she cried out, finally managing to clarify things.

Infected. Everyone heard that word.

In the stunned silence Freya shook her head. 'Grace, sweetie, just slow down and tell us what's you've seen.'

'The virus!' She looked up at Freya, then Leon. 'It's in the castle!'

The gallery erupted with gasps of disbelief. Everyone staring at Grace.

'Grace, if it was in the castle—' started Leon.

'Everett . . .' She pointed again at his study door. 'He's one of *them*!'

'For Christ's sake!' snapped Corkie dismissively. 'Your

226

sister's a bloody pain in the arse.' He strode past them towards Everett's room and knocked heavily on the door.

'Major?'

The voices hushed down and they all waited in silent anticipation for the door to open and Everett to appear, bleary-eyed and grumpy at being rudely roused at such an unearthly hour. But there was no answer.

Corkie knocked again, harder. 'Major Everett?' He waited another couple of seconds, then tried the door handle. It was locked.

Then they heard it, muffled by the door but unmistakeable in the complete silence: a low keening moan coming from inside the room. It sounded like several blended voices, male and female, young and old – a small tuneless choir humming a discordant, rising note.

'Shit . . . shit!' hissed Corkie. 'Something's going on in there! Everett? Major? You OK?'

The wailing sound grew louder. More insistent.

'Do something!' snapped Naga.

'*Like what?*'

'Grace said Dr Hahn's in there too!'

'He's infected!' shouted Grace. 'He's infecting her!'

'Infected?' Corkie scowled. 'Oh, come on.' His voice sounded as if he were holding on to a hope that Grace was crying wolf. Then they heard something fall over and crash inside the room and the last of his doubt vanished. He turned round and picked out a few of his men. 'Gosling, Briggs, Royce, get a salt-sprayer and riot shields!'

'Yes, sir.'

'Hurry!' He took several wary steps back from the door as the wail grew louder and rose in pitch. 'And get some diesel!' he shouted after them.

The men's feet slapped quickly down the stone stairs and echoed across the main hall below.

The contortion of voices beyond the door could no longer be mistaken as human, as if whoever . . . whatever . . . knew what was coming.

Fire.

Something thudded against the inside of Everett's door, and Leon pulled Grace and Freya with him as he backed up several steps. He looked around at the frightened faces, stark torchlight picking out rounded eyes, mouths held wide open and silent. He found himself experiencing a fleeting recall of that nightmare moment back at Emerald Parks: everyone uselessly frozen, the only ones in motion those who were hell-bent on burning his sister like a Salem witch.

The door thudded again. Corkie jumped away. 'Everyone get back!' he barked.

'OhmyGod, ohmyGod,' whimpered Denise softly.

Leon felt Freya's hand grasping his arm tightly. 'Please not this again!' she hissed.

He nodded. Her memory of Emerald Parks was clearer than his. He'd been dazed, stunned by a punch to the head, and, mercifully, his recall of the last few moments had been a blur that he'd never since tried to revisit, pick through or make sense of.

The inhuman wail beyond the door rose and fell and

rose again like wind gusting across some desolate, bleak moor. They heard the clanking of the fire hydrant, below, the chilling sound of diesel sloshing in a jerry can, and the barefooted slap of Gosling, Briggs and Royce coming back up the steps, all three puffing heavily from the exertion.

Corkie took one of the shields from Briggs and a machete that the man had thought to grab too. He turned round and whipped the beam of his torch over the faces on the gallery, looking for Grace. He finally found her.

'You're sure both of them are in there, love?'

Grace nodded.

'Right.' He approached the door and knocked again one more time. 'Everett! Can you hear me? This is your last warning! Open the door or me an' the lads are going to kick it in!'

The wailing sound continued, rising and ululating, then dropping away to a mournful whimper. Leon wondered if that was Dr Hahn's voice. If Everett had infected her, then perhaps, just like that woman who'd been on the train with them, she'd gone into some sort of shock-induced trance . . . that god-awful moaning sound like some sort of lullaby or hymn.

The gallery waited in expectant silence for Corkie to make his move.

He decided he'd waited long enough. 'All right, stuff this for a game of soldiers.' He raised his bare foot up to waist height and kicked hard with his heel at a spot right beside the door handle.

The fake oak door rattled flimsily under his kick. The

veneer cracked and splintered. He raised his foot and kicked again and this time the door juddered inwards. The keening moan suddenly ceased.

Leon instinctively took another step backwards, drawing Grace and Freya with him.

Corkie picked up one of the riot shields standing on the floor beside him. 'C'mon, mate, let's stop playing silly buggers!' he shouted into the dimly lit room. He was about to step forward when something emerged from the grey gloom.

'Oh, *shit-shit-shit . . .*'

CHAPTER 34

The torch in Corkie's hand briefly illuminated the figure as it fell through the door, and Leon's impression of its size and shape was fleeting. It seemed to be two figures, or more accurately one and a half.

As the figure staggered upright, Corkie and his men backed up. Several torch beams converged as it hesitated there for a moment. Leon recognized bare male human legs: one still covered with pale skin and a fuzz of leg hair; the other a mess of jelly-like muscles and ligaments as its skin slewed off. Its groin was still covered by a pair of light blue-and-white-striped Y-fronts, though they were darkly mottled with smears and spots of blood. Its torso, however, was far less comprehensible; it was a contorted mass of bones and cartilage as two bodies seemed to be melded together.

From the right side of the torso, barely recognizable, Everett's arm had grown into a long serrated blade of tough resinous material, with short gnarled spikes and unfinished nodules bubbling off at irregular angles. On the left hand side of the torso, where Everett's armpit should have been, Leon could see a head welded into the flesh as if it had been forcefully rammed there, a nightmarish Siamese twin.

Hahn's face was still discernible, twisted upwards,

facing the ceiling. Leon could see the whites of her eyes as they rolled sideways, wide, confused, frightened. Her head was in effect morphing to become Everett's shoulder, but not yet completed. From the bottom of her head, the neck and the remains of Hahn's upper body flailed like a useless puppet, arms swinging. Her upper torso gave way at her waist to the flapping remains of her spinal column, her vertebrae still stoically held in place by frayed, knotted strings of nerves and arteries. One of her arms still seemed functional, and Leon watched as she raised her hand towards her face, flexed her fingers and stared longingly at them, as if saying goodbye to the last fragment of control she would ever have.

Everett's own head was perched on the end of a half-metre-long neck that was now bowed forward under its own weight. As they watched in a frozen silence, his head began to droop from the extended neck, like a plastic action figure held over a lighter flame. It sagged on sticky strands down towards the floor until finally they snapped like twine. The head separated and thudded on to the floor and the long neck recoiled and swung upwards.

Somebody screamed at Corkie to do something, and for Leon the illusion of time being slowed down to a glacial crawl suddenly evaporated.

Everything went into rapid motion.

'*Spray the bastard!*' bellowed Corkie. '*Spray it!*'

Gosling pumped the extinguisher's trigger and a jet of salt water spurted out across the gallery on to the conjoined figures. The response was instantaneous. Both mouths opened wide and screamed in synchronicity. Male and female vocal chords weakened by their rapid decay now sounded like recordings slowed right down: fluttering, loose and multi-timbral.

Everett's long, jagged claw-arm swung around in a vicious sweep that knocked the fire extinguisher clean out of Gosling's hands. Then swung back, barbed spikes lodging deep into his skull with a hard thud.

Gosling staggered backwards, clawing at his face, the spikes snapping deliberately, easily, like the delicate spines of a sea urchin. The claw-arm now swung towards Corkie and he quickly ducked down behind the riot shield. The shield *thrummed* like a plastic water butt under the hammer-blow impact.

'Briggs! Royce!' he shouted. 'For God's sake *burn it!*'

Briggs had the fuel in one hand, a shield in the other. He passed Royce his shield and started fumbling with the jerry can. The idiot was wearing cricket gloves for protection and was getting nowhere fast.

Leon pulled Grace's grasping hands off him and lurched forward.

'Leon! No!' both she and Freya screamed.

He snatched the jerry can from Briggs's gloved hands and grasped hold of the tightly screwed cap.

The Everett-Hahn creature's elongated, headless neck was transforming rapidly. From among the tattered strands, a knuckle of hard resinous material punched out and began unfolding itself into several long, jointed pincers. Corkie had his machete to hand now and was hacking at the claw-arm that had grabbed the top rim of his shield and was now stubbornly refusing to let go.

Leon's fingers were slippery with sweat. He couldn't get a purchase on the cap's ribbed surface. He frantically pulled his sweater sleeve down over his hand and tried again. This time the cap twisted.

'Watch out!' shouted Briggs.

Leon looked up just in time to see the newly 'born' pincers flexing and reaching out towards them. He ducked down as Briggs snatched the shield from Royce and raised it up to protect them both. The pincers clattered against the scuffed Perspex, latched firmly on to it and began to pull.

Briggs held on, bracing himself for a tug-of-war, his bare feet spread for balance. Leon spotted one of his feet too close to Everett's jettisoned head, brushing against the side of it. The head suddenly stirred into life.

'Your foot!' Leon yelled. 'Watch your—'

From Everett's wide-open mouth something darted out: a thin, slimy, hastily formed tendril, still gelatinous and fragile. It curled round Briggs's ankle. He yelped in surprise or pain and lifted his foot to swing and shake it from him. With his balance off, the pincers successfully yanked the shield out of his hands and tossed it to one side.

The extended neck quickly reared up above Leon and Briggs like a cobra, the pincers dancing and flexing in the air with balletic grace.

Briggs was weaponless. Leon had the fuel can. Royce was a step back from them both. Everyone else was backed up against the walls, and Corkie was on the far side of the creature, locked in his own struggle with the claw-arm.

Leon caught a glimpse of Hahn's wildly rolling eyeballs and wondered whether her sight was controlling the movement of everything, or whether each limb, each pincer, each tendril had a mind of its own.

He cowered as the pincers hovered in the air, flexing, and the neck drew back, ready to make its lunge.

Not at me. Not me. Not . . .

The neck whiplashed forward, the pincers whistling past Leon towards Briggs. He raised his arms to shield his face, and the pincers, each of them a metre long, closed around him like a penny-arcade grab machine.

Briggs wrestled with them, snapping one pincer easily, but the others, lined with little barbs, had a firm grip on his bare shoulders and back, and dug in. Leon saw thick tendons in the long neck flex beneath the waxy skin and knew huge muscular effort was at work.

The thing wanted to reel Briggs in like a fish.

Leon swung the opened jerry can and sloshed out an arc of diesel. It spattered uselessly on to the floor. He took a step closer and swung it again, this time splashing some on to the glistening skin of the creature.

'LEON!' Grace screamed behind him.

He sloshed more and more fuel, looking around for any other recently grown limbs the creature might use to attack him. Nothing seemed to be growing or emerging or ready to erupt from the mass, and there was only Hahn's very human, very feeble-looking forearm, hand spread as if she were waving at him. Or bidding goodbye.

He tossed the nearly empty jerry can on to the floor at the creature's feet and it gurgled a small puddle on to the floorboards.

'Light it up!' screamed someone.

But Leon didn't have anything, and Briggs was ensnared and being pulled in.

Corkie had given up holding on to his shield and now stepped around the creature. 'DO IT!' he shouted. 'LIGHT IT UP!'

'I can't!' yelled Leon.

Someone barged past him. Fish. He had a lit cigarette in his hand. He flicked it at the floor and pulled Leon back with him. The cigarette bounced, sparked, rolled and skittered towards the small puddle, coming to rest there and doing nothing at all.

Corkie meantime was hacking at the thick muscular neck pulling Briggs in. His machete had carved a deep fleshy trench. Another couple of hacks in the same place and he was going to do it . . . He was going to cut the man free.

The diesel ignited with a percussive thump.

CHAPTER 35

'. . . *Don't give up. Help is coming. Help is on its way. This message is aimed specifically at survivors in the United Kingdom and mainland Europe. If you are in Britain and able to travel, make your way to the city of Southampton. If you are in Europe, make your way to Calais by the first of September. A fleet of vessels from the New United States will be waiting for you. Medical help and emergency food supplies will be available there. Those requesting evacuation will be assessed. The ships will be there for two weeks only, leaving on the fourteenth of September . . . God bless you all.'*

. . .

. . .

. . .

'*This is President Trent of the New United States. Today's date for this broadcast is . . .* [Thursday, the eighteenth of July] *. . . My message to you is this: don't give up. Help is coming. Help is on its way. This message is aimed specif—*'

Corkie turned the radio off. 'All right. That's enough.'

They'd all heard the message half a dozen times already, and it was there to be listened to again and again, constantly looping, every day, every hour, every minute. He looked at the men beside him, then at the others sitting either side of the two long tables in the main hall.

'So Dr Hahn was right about that bastard sonofabitch. He was lying to all of us!'

Leon had got the story from Grace earlier that Hahn had revealed to her that she had misgivings about Everett.

Corkie looked down at Grace, sitting nearest to him. 'You should have come to me first, love.'

'Claudia wasn't completely sure about it,' said Grace quietly. 'She just had a . . . a . . . *hunch*.'

'All the same, you should have bloody well told me!' snapped Corkie.

Leon put an arm round her. 'Jeez, leave her alone. She didn't know who to go to.'

It was a gusty day outside and the only sound was the creak of the building mercilessly buffeted by the wind, its mournful whine pushing through the cracked open skylight, and a steady metronome *tack*, *tack*, *tack* of dripping water from the gallery floor above.

The mood in the main hall this morning was sombre. Silent and still. No bustling noises from the kitchen, no roaring fire, no bubbling broth. The castle reeked of burnt flesh, a savoury odour that might have had tummies rumbling with hungry anticipation if they hadn't known exactly what it was they were smelling.

The fire upstairs was out now. The gallery floor was soaked with water that had been tag-team carried in buckets from the washroom. And in the middle of the soaking, soot-covered floorboards sat a dripping, glistening black and dark brown *sculpture*. A nightmare statue comprised of twisted limbs and contorted, carbonized flesh. A surreal study of four human bodies . . . Everett . . . Hahn . . . Gosling . . . Briggs.

Mostly an undecipherable mass, but here and there parts that were horribly recognizable.

'You spoke with him every day,' said Naga. 'How come *you* didn't spot he was one of *them*?'

Corkie crossed his arms defensively. 'I don't know! He . . .' He shook his head. 'Everett seemed perfectly normal. Maybe he didn't *even know he was infected*.'

His words hung uncomfortably in the air.

'I'm going to say this out loud . . . because I know it's what we're all thinking,' said Freya. 'I guess we now know for certain it can replicate us . . . *and* can do it completely convincingly.' She looked down the table. 'So that means any one of us sitting here could be one of them.'

There was a ripple of unease. That's what they had all been thinking.

'We need to find out who's really human here.'

'What if Corkie's right?' asked Fish. 'What if we don't even know if we're one of them? Then what?' He looked around. There were heads nodding at that. 'Say, for example, I'm infected? What happens to me? Am I gonna get burned at the stake too?' He didn't like the look in their eyes and quickly defended himself. 'To be absolutely clear, I'm *not* infected, OK?'

'Salt water,' said Leon. 'We know it can't cope with salt water.'

'We *know* that?' said Naga. 'For a fact?'

'It works,' said Royce. 'We spray 'em and they hate it.'

'We all saw how it responded when Gosling sprayed it,' said Freya. 'And that's how Dr Hahn tested us all, mixing salt with our blood. Before we discuss what we're going to do next, we've all got to have a salt test. That's got to be the top priority.'

'*Discuss* what we're going to do?' Corkie cut in. 'There isn't going to be a bloody *discussion*, ladies and gents, because this isn't a bloody town council meeting! Love it or shove it, I'm next in the chain of command!'

Fish snorted sarcastically. 'Chain of command? We're not in your little platoon, mate.'

'We need to stay a cohesive unit. That means—'

'You're not even real soldiers,' said Naga. She cocked her head as she let her gaze settle on the knights flanking Corkie. 'None of you are, or *were*, soldiers. Am I right?'

Some of them managed to hold her accusing glare, while others looked away. She'd hit the truth with at least some of them.

'It doesn't matter what my lads once were,' said Corkie. 'I've trained them to fight these bloody creatures, and they do it well. You people want us to carry on looking after you, then I'm afraid, love, it's me who's going to be in charge.'

'Well, that depends on whether I agree with what you decide to do,' said Naga. She nodded at the radio sitting in its carry rack on the top table. 'I'm for leaving.'

'Me too,' said Fish.

'Go out there?' cried Danielle. 'You're flippin' mental! Seriously! No way I'm . . .'

Others raised their voices. There was an almost even split between those who wanted to stay and those who wanted to go. The hall filled with competing exchanges.

Corkie shouted above the noise to shush them. 'All right, enough! Enough!' He banged his fist down on the table. 'Everyone SHUT UP!'

The noise settled down. Corkie waited until he had complete silence. As he waited for their voices to hush, Leon noticed the man was on the edge: the slightest twitching of his head, the flexing of his right hand. He remembered his headmaster Mr Mareham's words of advice.

Brittle. Watch him. He'll snap.

'We're gonna do what you suggested,' Corkie said, glancing at Freya and Leon. 'Do this salt test, and when we're done with that . . .' He shrugged. 'I'll put it to a bloody vote. Stay or leave.' He spread his hands. 'Whichever way that vote goes, we're all doing it.' He looked around at everyone. 'That's it.'

The testing was done in an order that told Leon everything he needed to know about where they stood in terms of Corkie's trust. Corkie took charge of the process. He went outside and returned a few minutes later with a large bucket of stagnant water he'd scooped from the moat and a jerry can full of diesel. He set both down on the head table. He tested the ten remaining members of his platoon first. They stood in an orderly queue and he dipped a mug into the rancid bucket for each of them.

'C'mon, lad, one big glug of that shite and you're done,'

he urged them each in turn. One by one they swigged back the contents and, as they did, Corkie examined their faces closely. Leon wondered what Corkie was looking out for. What the hell were they expecting to see? Someone's head explode? A tentacle suddenly erupt from their forehead?

That ridiculous thought, mixed with the Russian-roulette tension, nearly made Leon laugh. He suppressed it. An out-loud laugh right now would've made him sound manic.

With each noisy gulp, the atmosphere in the hall momentarily froze and settled back down to a perfect silence.

The last of them tested, Corkie nodded at his men and gestured for them to stand to the left of the room. 'Drissell?'

'Sarge?'

'You've been promoted to corporal.'

The man nodded.

'We'll get you a bloody badge later. Meanwhile –' he nodded at the jerry can of diesel on the table – 'have that ready in case we need to use it quickly.'

Drissell came forward to stand beside Corkie, unscrewed the cap and set it down again, both hands resting on it, a box of matches set down on the table and ready to use. He looked ready . . . He looked ready to pick it up, swing it and douse anybody who came near.

'Right, then,' said Corkie. 'Let's get this done. Form a queue.' The people in the hall milled reluctantly together and a snaking line began to form.

Except for Fish.

'Look. I'm not doing this!' he said. He glanced around for others to stand with him on this. 'This is completely insane!' He turned to face Corkie. 'We haven't even defined what a *positive* result is yet!' He pointed at Drissell standing there with the jerry can ready to swing, and, from the look on his face, eager to do it.

'Before we go any further . . . what exact response from one of us means we're under suspicion? Huh? And what does that even mean – "under suspicion"? Does it mean Drissell lights us up straight away?'

'Shut up, Fish!' Corkie barked. 'Let's just get this over with.'

Fish picked out Leon for support. 'Leon, mate? C'mon this is crazy!'

'Maybe Corkie's right. The sooner we're done with this the better.'

'I . . . I . . . W-what if I *have* been infected? What if it's already in me?' Leon could see Fish was trembling. He could hear the terror in his voice. 'I don't want to *burn to death*!'

'You'd know,' said Freya coolly. 'Everett must have known. That must have been why he was lying to us.'

'Or he was just frightened of h-heading out there! Like, you know, I'm frightened right now of that frikkin idiot holding a gallon of flamma—'

'Fish! SHUT UP!' snapped Corkie. 'You get in line or I swear I'll shoot you and light your body up right now!' Leon noticed him place a trembling hand on the holster strapped to his belt.

He's not coping well with this, thought Leon. *He'll be fine, right up to the moment when he snaps like a dry twig.*

Leon placed a hand on Fish's arm. 'It's OK. You're going to be fine. It's the same deal for all of us. Best just get in line like he says.'

Fish nodded. 'Yeah . . . yeah, I s'pose.'

'Come on.' Leon led him to the back of the queue. 'Just relax.'

'This is totally insane, Leon.'

Freya and Grace joined them both at the rear.

'Fish,' said Freya, 'for God's sake, just take it easy! I think it's safe to say you'd *know*. You'd flippin' well know if you were a . . . a . . .' She didn't know what to call the creatures. She laughed uneasily. Her laugh came out sounding awkward and unsettling.

The queue began to shuffle slowly forward. The hall was quiet now, conversations few and whispered as person after person took the mug from Corkie and slurped the rancid, salty moat water.

'As far as I could see,' said Freya, 'Everett kept himself to himself. He kept everyone at a distance.'

Leon looked at her. 'Meaning?'

'Meaning, maybe he *knew* he wasn't quite right? That the less he interacted with others the less chance he had of giving himself away. Maybe that's what Hahn noticed. Maybe that's why she got suspicious, right, Grace?'

Grace didn't respond. Leon noticed his little sister looked worried.

'It's OK, sis. We'll be done pretty soon.'

'I'm scared, Leo.'

'It's fine. It's gonna taste like crap but—'

'Literally,' added Freya. 'We've been emptying the latrines into it.'

'And probably give us all diarrhoea and—'

'Dysentery. And Hepatitis B,' added Fish. 'This is a *bad* idea. Hahn would never have allowed this.'

The queue continued to edge slowly forward. Those who had swigged the water were gathering with Corkie's men over on the left side of the hall.

Grace reached out and grasped Leon's hand tightly. He could feel her trembling. 'But what if Fish's right?' she whispered. 'What if it can infect us and we don't even know about it?'

He looked down at her. She looked terrified. The unscarred side of her face was ashen.

Jesus, with good reason, especially after what she's been through.

'Grace, I can't see how a person *wouldn't* know. This thing kills you. Turns you into a puddle of goo.' He squeezed her hand. 'You ever been a puddle of goo?'

She shook her head vigorously.

'You'll be fine then, sis.' He winked and smiled. 'I promise.'

At the head of the dwindling queue, Danielle swigged from the mug, then squawked loudly in disgust. 'It's frikkin rank!' she cried. She made a big show of gagging at the taste, but it was clear she was relieved beyond words.

Corkie shooed her away impatiently. 'Next!'

'Leon, if that psycho –' Fish pointed at Drissell – 'decides for s-some reason that I'm a viral, you gonna vouch for me?' Fish looked as pale and terrified as Grace. 'Freya?'

'Well, are you? A viral?' asked Freya.

Fish went goggle-eyed at that. '*What?*'

She smiled. 'I was joking! Just trying to lighten the mood.'

He cursed. 'Th-that's not even f-funny!'

'Fish, come on, you're being ridiculous. You need to calm down.'

'I don't want to *burn*, Freya!' Fish's voice had changed from a whisper to a whimper.

'Calm down!' Freya glanced at Grace. 'You're frightening her.'

They followed the shuffling queue. There were just a dozen people ahead of them now.

'I'll go first, Grace, OK?' said Leon.

Naga was at the front now. She reluctantly took the mug from Corkie and, after catching a whiff of the water, she shook her head vigorously and passed it back. 'I can't . . . I'm going to be sick.'

'Just bloody well drink it!' Corkie muttered, thrusting the mug back towards her.

She stepped back from the table. 'I can't. Really. I can't . . . I'll just throw it up. Look, this is absolutely bloody ridiculous. There's got to be a better—'

'DO IT!' Corkie's voice, normally so deep, like a sack of gravel sliding across the back of a flatbed truck, was suddenly cracked and high-pitched. In a flicker of movement, he whipped his gun from its holster and had levelled it directly at Naga's head.

She yelped in surprise.

'DO IT!'

'Oh, G-God!' she stammered as she stared at the muzzle of the gun. 'I'm telling you! *I'll be sick!* I'll throw it right back up!' She turned to Drissell. 'Please . . . if I throw up, it doesn't mean I'm—'

'Drink it, just like everyone else!' he said quietly. 'Or I will shoot you right now.'

Leon could see Corkie was right on the edge, teetering, the ticking of his head more pronounced now. He could see the tendons in the hand holding the gun fidgeting under the skin, his index finger twitching and flexing against the trigger.

Crap. He's losing it.

'Naga,' called out Freya. 'Just hold your nose and toss it back! Think of it as a Jägerbomb!'

Her joke seemed to do the trick, pulling the moment back from the brink.

'Aye,' said Corkie. 'Like a really shitty warm Newcastle ale.'

Naga nodded, pinched her nose, lifted her head and emptied the mug into her mouth. The room seemed to freeze for a moment as everyone watched her response. Naga had her hand politely to her mouth just in case she threw it back up. But after a little mild heaving she seemed to be OK.

Corkie waved her aside. 'All right, off you go. Now you lot,' he said as he looked at Leon and the others.

Leon stepped forward to go first, took the mug from the man and brought it quickly to his lips. Instantly, he could understand why Naga and everyone else had recoiled from it. It stank of old pond water, an eggy, crappy, rotten odour that screamed NOT. FOR. DRINKING. EVER.

He stopped breathing through his nose, tipped the water into the back of his mouth and swallowed it down as quickly as he could.

'Mmmm. Tasty,' he said.

'Go, on . . . move along, son.'

Freya was next. She took the mug from him, stared at the brown-stained liquid and pulled a face. 'Your home brew sucks, Corkie.'

'Just drink it!'

She did as he said and puffed her cheeks out after swallowing. 'Think I'm gonna vom this up.'

It was just Fish and Grace left now. Leon noticed Corkie looking at his man, a not-so-subtle double-check to make sure Drissel was ready with the fuel for Fish's turn.

He thinks Fish is infected.

Or . . . Grace?

'I'm not infected . . . I'm telling you,' said Fish. 'I've never been out of the castle grounds. I've never been out on one of your foraging trips. I'm—'

'Shut up.' Corkie pushed the mug at him.

Fish took it and stared at Drissell, holding the can in both hands, drawn back and ready to swing it.

'OK, OK . . . just don't, you know . . . be too f-frikkin eager to throw that stuff on me?'

The hall had gone completely silent and Leon realized Fish's earlier protestations had condemned him in the eyes of everyone.

They're expecting a positive.

'Fish . . . just drink it!' called Freya. 'You're gonna be fine!'

Fish nodded, closed his eyes and gulped the water drown. The main hall was perfectly still. The wind gusted and moaned softly far above them. They waited as Fish kept perfectly still, statue still, eyes clenched shut. One of the castle dogs whimpered unhappily beside the dark, unlit fireplace.

Finally, he opened his eyes . . . and managed a relieved smile. 'Actually, I think I'm OK.'

A collective sigh rippled around the room, the release of breath held in by everyone for far too long.

'Move over to the others,' said Corkie. He dipped the mug into the nearly empty bucket and presented it to Grace. 'Now it's your turn.'

She took it from him in both hands, drew it up to her lips without any hesitation, lifted her head and tipped it into her mouth.

She grimaced at the taste. 'You thought I was infected, didn't you?' Her small voice seemed to fill the main hall.

Corkie stared down at her. 'Well, we found you in a place crawling with those bastards, and I don't know anything about you.' He shrugged.

She handed the mug back to him. 'So, now it's *your* turn.'

He took it from her dipped it down into the bucket and brought the mug up to his mouth. He turned towards the crowd gathered to his right so they could all clearly see him taking his turn, then tipped it back, glugged a few mouthfuls and slammed the mug back down on the table.

'Urgh . . . that's rank!' He rolled his eyes and gasped.

Somebody snorted out a laugh – the sound of pent-up tension finally released – and it spread. The atmosphere in the hall changed in a heartbeat, and the room came back to life once more, echoing with the sounds of conversation and relieved laughter.

Drissell stood down, screwing the cap back on to the jerry can and setting it on the floor.

Corkie placed the gun back in his holster and closed the flap. 'Right, everyone shut up! We've got to discuss what we're going to do nex—'

He stopped mid-sentence, his hand clenched in front of his mouth.

CHAPTER 36

Corkie grabbed at his stomach with one hand and steadied himself against the top table with the other. He belched loudly.

'Oh blimey, that's coming right back up,' he muttered.

He swallowed repeatedly, fighting with himself not to retch, but after a few seconds of stoic resistance he finally doubled over and vomited on to the stone floor at his feet.

'Oh, see?' crowed Naga. 'After all that bullying and threatening, it's *you* who ends up throwing up like a girl!'

The hall filled with a mixture of laughter and exclamations of relief that it hadn't been them.

Corkie slumped down on the bench. He stared at the puddle between his boots. It was the same tea-brown liquid he'd just swallowed, mixed with the remnants of last night's broth.

'Bloody hell,' he grunted. He looked up at everyone with a grin and a hint of shame and contrition on his ruddy face. 'Well now, *that* caught me by—'

He convulsed again, a jarring muscle spasm that rolled up from his belly like a racing tidal wave. He quickly leaned forward on his elbows to make sure that whatever was coming out cleared his legs and boots.

A dark jet of vomit spurted out of his mouth in an arc that spattered the floor in front of his boots. Not just a thin brew of bile and moat water this time; it had bloody substance. The hall had gone deathly quiet again. The atmosphere of impish mirth had evaporated instantly and given way to a growing concern.

'Sarge?' Drissell stepped forward. 'You all right, mate?'

Corkie wiped his chin as he stared at the thick puddle before him. 'I don't remember eating that.' He laughed. 'And where's the bloody carrots, eh? There's always—'

He convulsed again and another thick rope of vomit erupted from his mouth. The new addition was stained a deep crimson, almost black, and unlike the rest it didn't spread into a pool, but remained as a solid chunk in the middle.

'That doesn't look good,' said Drissell.

Corkie groaned in pain. 'Shit!'

Leon felt Grace squeeze his hand. He looked down at her and she shook her head. Her expression matching what he was thinking.

He's infected. He's one of them too.

His groan became a sudden shrill bellow of agony as he threw up yet again, this time a freight train of bloody chunks.

'Oh, shit!' yelled Fish. 'Those are his frikkin organs!'

'OhmyGod!' screamed Danielle.

'It's him,' shouted Naga. '*He's* infected!'

The silence in the hall was gone and everyone reacted, drawing back from him. Royce, closest to Corkie, looked at a loss as to what to do – comfort his sarge with a supportive pat on the back or run for his life?

'Burn it!' screamed someone. 'BURN IT!'

Leon looked around. *It?* The poor bastard had gone from a *him* to an *it* in a heartbeat.

Drissell's indecision ended. He gave his sergeant a wide berth, picked up the can of fuel and began unscrewing the cap. Corkie meanwhile had collapsed off the bench and rolled forward into the mess of his insides. He was crouched there on his hands and knees, bellowing in agony.

Drissell came round the table and stopped short, hesitating. Not quite so keen now to fulfil his role as diesel-thrower.

'DO IT!' shouted Naga.

'Oh, God, don't look!' gasped Freya. She turned towards Leon and Grace and threw her arms round them, pulling them into a tight huddle with Grace in the middle.

Drissell swung the can and sloshed fuel over Corkie's back.

The sergeant reacted instantly, sitting bolt upright. 'No!' he screamed. 'Not like this!'

Drissell swun the can again.

'No! No. No. No!' Corkie's hand flailed at his holster.

Drissell dropped the can at his feet and fumbled frantically to pull out a lighter. 'Sorry, Sarge, sorry, sorry!' he cried.

He had the lighter out now and was holding it to a twist of paper, clicking to get a spark. Just as he got a small blue flame, a shot rang out and Drissell's legs buckled beneath him. He collapsed like a puppet cut from its strings, knocking the jerry can over . . .

. . . The twist of smouldering paper fluttered down to the ground, seemingly in slow motion.

It touched down, turning damp-dark as it slowly soaked up the diesel, finally turning damp at the end where the lighter had caught.

The diesel ignited with a soft thump.

The hall, which seconds ago had been a dim, gloomy, haunted-house grey, was now alive, bright with the orange of flickering flames.

Leon watched over Freya's shaking shoulder as Corkie's silhouette thrashed around in the middle of the flames, the hall filled with the harrowing sound of his screaming. He untangled himself from their three-way huddle, left Freya and Grace behind him and hurried forward.

His eyes had caught the reflective glint of Corkie's gun, flung to one side. He ran over, scooped it up, and without a thought one way or the other, right or wrong, he aimed and fired.

And fired, and fired.

Until the gun clicked uselessly in his hands.

The figure finally, mercifully, collapsed amid the flames, which were now towering high enough to lick at the floorboards of the gallery above.

He found himself staring just like everyone else, transfixed with horror at the pyre. He was sure Corkie was dead, but there still seemed to be movement among the flickering flames. Silhouetted forms, shuddering, quivering instinctively trying to escape the searing heat. He thought he saw something the size of a fist pulling itself desperately towards the edge of the fire, one finger elongated, hastily grown into a spindly leg, struggling to pull itself out of the flames.

There was another percussive thump as the remaining fuel inside the jerry can erupted and a thick oily mushroom cloud billowed upwards and bathed the wooden planks above.

It's all going to go up.

'Everyone out!' shouted Naga. 'Out! Out! NOW!'

The slack-jawed inertia that had rooted everyone in the hall to the spot and rendered them passive, foolish observers, was suddenly dispelled and panic stirred them all into action.

There was a surge of movement towards the doors that led outside. The hall was beginning to thicken with black smoke. It had started pooling beneath the ceiling but was now descending down towards them like a blanket of fog.

Leon looked around for Freya and Grace. He saw several people stupidly hurrying up the stairs to the gallery floor, presumably to grab important keepsakes, and hoped they'd have more sense.

He felt a hand tug at his arm.

'I'm here!' said Freya. He turned to see her looking frantically around. 'Grace . . . She was with me a second ago. She was just . . .'

Leon saw his sister, making her way towards them from the corner of the hall, stopping and starting as she dodged around others running across her path. He watched her pause to look at the flickering flames.

'GRACE!' he shouted above the roar and crackle of burning.

She seemed hypnotized by the sight.

Or in shock.

The first of the floorboards above cracked with a loud snap and clattered down on to one of the long tables, sending up a bonfire shower of sparks.

'GRACE!' He started towards her, but then someone grabbed her roughly by the arm. It was Danielle. She had an armful of things she'd managed to grab from the dormitory. She jerked Grace forward by the arm as she barged her way through people zigzagging across the hall.

'Yours!' she gasped as she pushed Grace towards Leon, then headed with the flow towards the main doors leading outside.

Another floorboard cracked and fell.

'Shit . . . Let's go, go, go!' gasped Freya.

They joined the back of the chokepoint of people pressing through the main doors. Leon had always wondered how pile-ups like this happened with fires. Now he understood. These doors opened inwards and the press of bodies against them had hampered the opening of them.

One was now finally, fully open, but panic was tangling everyone up in the tight space, a squirming many-legged, many-armed beast struggling to squeeze its ungainly shape through the narrow gap.

The air behind them was thick, choking and lethal. Ahead, through the one open door, fresh air gusted in as if they were standing in a wind tunnel, pulled in hungrily by oxygen-starved flames.

'Come on!' Leon screamed hoarsely, along with everyone else.

They pushed and squirmed through the gap and finally found themselves emerging outside. They staggered away from the door towards the trucks, collapsing on to the ground in a choking, coughing sprawl.

Leon thought they were the last ones out. But a minute later he caught sight of a figure through the open door It was staggering around in the main hall, doubling over and zigzagging to avoid the sporadic crashing of falling floorboards.

He lost sight of it, then, a moment later, Fish appeared in the doorway and lurched out leaving a trail of smoke behind him.

He looked around, patting out embers that had settled on his hair and shirt, before hurrying over to join them. He had a tartan backpack slung over one shoulder. He collapsed on the ground beside Leon, coughing up sooty phlegm and gasping for air.

Leon wanted to ask him if there was anyone else stuck in there. But the question was rendered pointless as an enormous crash from within pushed a plume of flames and a cloud of sparks out through the open door.

Not any more.

The gallery floor had collapsed.

'You . . . idiot . . .' wheezed Leon. 'What was so important you . . . nearly . . . got . . . ?'

Fish pulled out a Nintendo DS from his tartan bag and waved it at him, unable to say anything as he hacked up sooty phlegm on to the ground.

CHAPTER 37

'Grace, I just want you to know how proud of you I am.'

She looked up at Dad. He'd been waiting for her outside Davison Middle School's gym hall along with the other parents, all huddled together for warmth against the cold, gusting November wind.

The other kids who'd performed this evening were flooding out to be greeted by their own very proud parents, who'd seemed intent on catching every possible moment with their smartphones.

'You were fantastic.' Dad squeezed her shoulders. 'I can tell you put a lot of thought into that.'

She had. A lot. She'd been working on that dance routine with her friends for months. The backing track had changed several times, and Grace had had to take charge of their small troupe after Natasha Baumstein had stormed off due to 'artistic differences'.

Mom hadn't been able to make the Thanksgiving concert. She'd had to fly back to England to help Grandad deal with Grandma's cancer scare. And Leon, as always, had other plans. So it had been just the two of them this evening, Dad filming her on his iPhone and grinning at her proudly from the front row as she and the girls did their energetic dance routine to Jessie J's latest track.

That was the last time she could genuinely say she

loved him. The big revelation, the BIG ROW and the bust up between Mom and Dad was just a few weeks away.

So this particular memory of him was tender and precious.

'You're such a clever girl.'

It was the last time she remembered desperately wanting him to be proud of her.

'Thank you, Dad.'

'You showed them. You managed to show them all.'

Grace was aware that her memory was being used by *them*.

'It was so hard.' She shook her head. 'It actually hurt. Hurt so much, it felt like I was burning up on the inside.'

'But you were strong . . . and very brave not to show it.'

'I knew it was coming. So I had time to prepare.'

The salt test. Leon's suggestion. When he'd blurted the idea out, she'd known there wasn't going to be any escaping it. And she had to pass the test, or . . .

She just *had* to pass it.

She didn't know how to do it . . . just that she needed some kind of protection, and *quickly*. Equally, she didn't know how to instruct her heart to beat or her lungs to work, or blood to flow . . . These things just happened. She had to trust that the community of *colleagues* inside her would know what to do to save them all.

As she'd queued, standing between Leon and Freya, she'd felt things happening inside her. She could sense the builder cells urgently converging in her throat, her trachea. She'd fought an urge to hyperventilate as the lining of her throat thickened, the airwaves contracting and beginning to affect her breathing. She'd fought the urge to gag as she'd felt something alien rapidly swelling inside her gut.

Given more time, *they* might have been able to completely isolate her from the agonizing sensation of millions of cells dying as the salt water flowed over and through them.

That brackish, rancid, toxic water had burned as it entered her mouth, burned its way down her throat, and burned as it passed through her small intestines. It was burning its way through the small protective pouch of cells in her stomach – a gut within a gut – before she'd had the chance to stagger away and evacuate the dying mess of throat and stomach lining into a corner of the main hall.

As the fire consumed the hall and panic reigned, she'd had the chance to cough up a thick gelatinous string of blood and mucus: millions of microscopic lives selflessly given to ensure the survival of the whole colony – spat out in a heap on the stone floor.

She'd been hoping, assuming even, that the silly man, Corkie, would test himself first. And, if he had done, the ensuing chaos might have ended the testing right there. But it had happened as it had, giving her body just enough time to save itself. The best thing was that if Leon and Freya had had *any* doubts at all about her before, they certainly didn't now.

And there was Claudia's sacrifice to acknowledge. Her body was gone, her bones, her hair and nails, the last forensic fragments of who she used to be. Now, though,

Claudia's *essence*, her consciousness, lived on within the biochemical universe of Grace. It had been a willing sacrifice. Claudia had understood what they needed to do. Everett needed to look guilty. Needed to be the guilty one. The distraction.

There were other fallen comrades too. The small community that had been slowly growing inside Corkie, for example. Given a little more time, Corkie, like Claudia, would have begun to understand and accept . . . and embrace this new form of life. But, and this is where the tragedy lay, he was never going to know that. All that was him had gone, burned away.

Grace looked up again at the illusion of her father. 'I'm doing the right thing, aren't I?'

He nodded. 'If the survivors can send fleets of ships . . . if they can do that . . . what else can they do?'

'We have to know, don't we?'

'Of course we do, Grace. You have to go and see.'

She glanced at the other girls in her dance troupe, now climbing into the warmth of their parents' cars, others hurrying off to catch the subway home.

'We have to send word to all the others . . . tell them what I'm doing, right? Let them know I'm going to try to board the ship?'

He squeezed her hand. 'You're quite right, we do. But first things first, little monkey. Fancy a McDonald's on the way home?'

*

Leon looked out of the back of the truck as the countryside rolled by. Every now and then he found his gaze resting on the driver of the truck behind them – Royce.

Royce was 'in charge' of the soldiers now. The conceit that they were 'actual' soldiers had slipped away like an embarrassing idea for a fancy-dress theme that no one was bothering with any more. He hadn't promoted himself to 'corporal' or 'sergeant', wasn't insisting that anyone call him *sir*, but by default, being the oldest and hardest-looking of the knights, he'd assumed the role of their leader.

Their eyes met through the mud-spattered windshield. Leon acknowledged Royce with a quirk of his eyebrows. Royce constantly had a face like a balled-up fist, even when he smiled.

He scowled back.

They were heading south, heading for Southampton. Towards something that had become much more than a glimmer of hope – something real, reinforced every day by that looping broadcast. The wording of the message had stayed exactly the same each time they listened, but the date was revised by an automated voice.

And, Jesus . . . Trent. *President* Trent. Was that *Dad's friend*, Trent?

He knew the two of them went way back. They'd been in the army together. Served alongside each other in Iraq. Leon had met the man only a couple of times: once at the opening of some college building that he'd paid for, and once at a garden party. *His* big-ass garden. *His* expensive party. Leon had hated seeing Dad being all deferential to the man, bowing and scraping before him, laughing too loudly at his crap, crass jokes. Leon had even once witnessed him swat his mum's behind, like he wanted to make the point he 'owned' her as well as Dad.

President Trent, ladies and gents. When the hell did that happen?

Although Leon had only met the man twice, he'd seen his face pretty much every day. There'd been a framed photo at home on the wall beside the stairs. A picture of Dad and Trent and several other guys in their unit. Young men pumped up with the sense of their own invulnerability, sitting on the blackened carcass of an Iraqi tank. Second Lieutenant Douglas T. Trent, Staff Sergeant Tom Friedmann and three other young bucks.

Freya nudged Leon and leaned towards his ear. 'You OK?'

He nodded. 'You know the guy making that radio announcement?'

'It's the president, isn't it?'

Leon nodded. 'Did I tell you he's a close friend of our dad's?'

Freya's eyes narrowed suspiciously. 'Yeah, right.'

'No, I'm not messing. Dad and him were in the army together.'

Her eyes rounded. 'Seriously?' She looked to Grace for confirmation, but she obviously hadn't heard him over the rattling growl of the truck's engine, and, anyway, her gaze was far away, taking in the overgrown fields receding on

264

either side behind them and the procession of abandoned cars on the hard shoulder.

Grace had been like that for the last couple of days: withdrawn, saying hardly anything. Leon was worried about her.

'How does your dad know the president?'

'Old army buddies from the nineties or something.'

'Wow. And now he's the prez?'

Leon shrugged. 'He was already something in the government. A secretary of something. And he's, like, billionaire-rich . . . or he *was*, anyway.'

Freya thought about that for a moment. 'Then maybe your dad *is* alive still? You know, if he has connections to the president? And the US is together and sorted enough to launch a rescue fleet?'

'*New* United States,' he corrected her. 'And *new* president. That sounds to me like they didn't completely escape the plague. Some sort of crap went down over there for sure.'

'At least they've got a government. Our useless lot just disappeared. But it's pretty hopeful, right? About your dad?'

'Maybe.'

He looked out at a field of broccoli stalks, rows of stubby green heads that had gone to seed and been overrun by tall nettles and cow parsley towering over them, seeming to bully them into submission. It never ceased to surprise him how quick nature was to step in, how soon hard road surfaces buckled and cracked and sprouted weeds, how quickly untended window boxes became drooping jungles that turned the sides of buildings into vertical wild gardens.

Just two years and nature had grabbed it all back from mankind.

Their journey down to Southampton so far had been slow. They had a fortnight ahead of them, if the dates in the radio message were still accurate. It was the third week of August now, and they had until September. Even though the roads were regularly plugged by snarls of abandoned cars demanding detours, this was Britain, not the sprawling US. *Nowhere* was weeks away over here.

They were going to get there with plenty of time to spare.

The mood of everyone aboard the trucks had lifted a little from the despair and panic they'd felt in the aftermath of the fire. They'd had to lower the bridge and withdraw to the far side, and from there they'd spent a day and a night watching their fortress slowly burn to the ground, leaving them out in the open, vulnerable, exposed, with no one, it seemed, in a fit state of mind to step forward and take charge of the situation.

Over the last few days, Naga seemed to have finally emerged as the unofficial 'civilian' leader, with Royce in reluctant command of the remaining knights. He seemed increasingly happy to defer to her with each new decision that needed to be made.

Naga had made the call that the only thing they could do now was head for Southampton and hope for the best.

As they'd driven slowly away, they'd all been expecting

the worst: to be overrun at any moment by swarms of giant crabs, drawn by the belching noise of two overladen trucks; to witness the English countryside turned into something alien and ghastly, a landscape of pulsating viral roots linking and branching and giving birth to endless hordes of nightmare creatures.

Instead there had been only a handful of distant sightings.

This morning, for example, as they'd set off at first light, they'd spotted a solitary crab watching them. Leon guessed it was about the same size as the ones Corkie's men had fought when they'd rescued Grace, the size of a large breed of dog, or a small pony. It had bobbed there, just a hundred metres away at the edge of the weed-tufted forecourt, swaying on spindly limbs. None of them had any doubts that it knew they were there.

It was clearly watching them.

Then it had turned and scuttled nimbly away into the nearby trees.

Leon wondered how the virus organized itself. How it was structured. Were the crabs their version of knights or soldiers? Or were they like attack dogs, 'trained' to kill? And what about the human manifestations – Everett and Corkie . . . Had they somehow been a part of the virus's ecosystem, *avatars*, created by the virus to spy on them?

Or had they simply been unaware hosts?

He wondered if the virus had any kind of hierarchy at all, or whether it was just some sprawling cooperative of organisms united by one simple principle – anything other than its own kind was the enemy and theirs to destroy.

Leon was certain Corkie had had no idea that the virus was sitting dormant inside him. But Everett? Had the man been infected all along? One of *them* from the very beginning?

If so, if they'd known, they might have been able to overpower him somehow, restrain him in some way . . . and then question him.

Question him? Leon shook his head at how ridiculous that sounded.

How do you talk to a virus?

CHAPTER 38

They came across it without warning, driving through a village that could once have been the setting for some cosy Sunday-night drama. The village green, big enough on which to play cricket, had become an acre of untamed prairie grass, and the decorative flower baskets outside the post office drooped long roots like unkempt hair, having long ago given up any hope of finding water.

The narrow road they'd been driving along took a sharp left turn round a bandstand, and there it was. No warning signs. No hint of what was coming, that something so catastrophic and so large had struck at the heart of such an innocent-looking rural idyll.

The front truck lurched to a halt and everyone in the back lurched with it.

Leon banged his head against a tarp strut. 'Ow!'

With the truck's rear cover on, no one could see what was ahead. But they heard Fish, on driving duty, through the partition. '– the effin' hell is THAT . . . ?'

Leon, sitting at the rear of the truck, was the first to stand up and clamber over the tailgate. He dropped down on to the narrow road and stepped to one side to see what was blocking their way.

He spotted the tail fin first: tall, white, unscratched, with the British Airways logo still patriotically displaying its swipes of red and blue.

'What is it?' Freya called down.

'Plane,' Leon replied. 'A crashed one.' He took a few more steps to the side of the road to see round the truck. The tail fin curved down to merge with the rear half of the fuselage, which looked unblemished and undamaged, until, catastrophically, it was. There it went from gleaming and smooth to a twisted, buckled and frayed mess of cables and exposed rows of passenger seats. 'A *big* crashed one,' added Leon.

The driver-side door opened and Fish stepped down. Leon joined him and for a moment the pair of them stared in awe at the wreckage. The wings were gone, sheered off. The plane must have come in from their right, aiming optimistically for the fields beyond the village on their left.

'You think it was trying to land?' asked Leon.

Fish nodded. 'Tried . . . and nearly did it too.'

Others were dropping down from the back of the two trucks and soon they all stood together in silence, listening to the tick of the trucks' engines cooling down, and trying to comprehend the scene of violent impact before them. Presumably it had happened a couple of years ago.

Naga broke the silence. 'We passed a left turn a couple of miles back. We can get round this mess.'

'We should look it over,' said Fish. 'There might be some things worth scavenging. Bottled water, sealed food.'

She frowned. 'Why? We're just a day, if that, from Southampton.'

'What if there's no one there . . .' Fish looked around

at the others sheepishly. 'Yet?'

Leon nodded. 'He's right.' They had pallets of food and bottles of Evian in the trucks with them, but they were getting through them quickly. Any opportunity to scavenge, particularly from an easy target sitting right in their path, was worth a few minutes of their time.

Naga relented. 'Ten minutes only.' She looked around. 'And just a few of us. Leon and Fish, take Royce with you.' She made sure they took a fire extinguisher and a gun.

Leon, Fish and Royce left the rest beside the trucks, taking a moment to stretch their legs. They made their way towards the wreckage of the plane, stepping over twisted fragments of metal, partially scorched and melted shards of plastic. Up close, he could see rows of seats still locked in place and canted at an angle as the plane appeared to have twisted along its length. They were all still occupied. Carbonized bodies were strapped in like crash-test dummies, one or two leaning forward in what looked like the brace position.

'Flash-fried,' grunted Royce. He looked at them. 'They were burned so quick they kept their pose.'

'Just like the Romans in Pompeii,' added Fish.

Leon turned to his right, towards the rear of the plane. The roof of the fuselage was still intact from here all the way back to the tail, but he could see into some of the gloomy interior, where shards of light angled down from the regularly spaced oval windows. The rows of seats were filled with blackened corpses all the way to the toilets at the back.

Every seat taken. The last train out of Dodge City.

Fish bent down and scooped something up from the ground. He held a scorched fragment of paper in his hands and squinted to read what was on it. Leon looked around and saw that the ground was littered with papers, most partially burned at corners and edges, the print faded and blurred by exposure to two seasons of rain and snow. He saw the cover of a British passport nearby and wandered over to pick it up.

'Theresa Redmond, MP.'

Fish picked up another. 'Jeremy Bolland, MP.' He looked at Leon and raised an eyebrow.

Leon looked around and found another one nearby. 'Simon Hurst, MP.'

'The government,' grunted Royce.

'Looks like it,' said Fish. He found another passport. 'Yup, another MP.' He had a hard smile on his face. 'So *this* is where our government ended up.'

'Figures,' said Royce.

Fish shook his head. 'They locked down the airports for the rest of us peasants, then tried to do a runner themselves.' He laughed coldly. 'Well, this is a fantastic example of poetic justice for you.'

Leon looked up at the rows of carbon-black bodies welded to their seats, to their seat belts. 'You think they burned *after* crashing?'

Fish shrugged. 'The wings are sheered off. That's where the fuel is kept . . . I think. Maybe on impact those tore off and –' he gestured at the scorched interior of the plane – 'that was the result.'

Leon had a thought. 'I wonder if it was brought down? You know, shot down?'

'By one of our jets?' Royce looked at Leon. 'Or was it one of *yours*?'

Leon looked at the wreckage, avoiding the man's glare. Royce had the bulgy-eyed look of the kind of lifer you'd definitely not want to share a cell with.

He slapped Leon on the back. 'Relax, mate.' And wheezed out a laugh. 'If it was a Yank jet, then sod it. Good luck to 'em.' He chucked the passport he was holding back into the seats above them. It clattered down through several rows and finally lodged against one of the seat's arms.

They returned to the trucks twenty minutes later. At the back of the plane in the rear galley they'd found some bottled water and a catering pack of honey-roasted peanuts: *80 x 250g – Always check for nut allergies before opening.*

About a handful of nuts each. Not a great haul.

As Leon clambered up, Grace hovered at the back of the truck and gazed at the distant wreckage. 'Were there people . . . in that plane?'

'Yeah. Lots.'

'Oh. The poor, poor, things.'

'Freya?'

'Uh?'

'You were saying earlier about the British government disappearing?'

Her eyes widened. 'Leon, you're kidding me!'

Royce clambered into the truck. 'Looks like it was the whole bloody lot. The entire bleedin' House of Commons.'

He turned and offered Grace his hand to pull her up. 'There you go, sweet'eart. That's how real life works. When the ship goes down, it's the bloody captain and his mates who get the lifeboats. The rest of us buggers have to swim.'

Leon helped him lift Grace. 'You look pretty pleased about that.'

Royce sniffed. 'Just confirmed what I always suspected, mate. One rule for 'em, one for us.'

Grace stood outside the toilet door. It was a door very similar to the one she'd once been dragged towards by her mom.

She recalled their panic-stricken retreat across a forecourt of coffee tables and cheap leather chairs, much like this one – another service station on another motorway.

She stared at the sign above the ladies' toilet. Last time she'd stared at a service station toilet door, she'd been running from *them*.

Now she *was* one of *them*.

She pushed through the door into the ladies' toilet. No hissing of cisterns. It was silent and still . . . and it stank. The other women in their group had used all three cubicles many times over since they'd parked up earlier that evening. They were all asleep now, stretched out on the coffee-shop chairs, along carefully lined-up rows of burger-bar bucket chairs, or on sleeping bags on the cold, hard floor.

A forecourt that wheezed and rustled uncomfortably.

She pushed a cubicle door open, pulled the seat down and sat on it.

It was time to gather her thoughts and compose a message.

She pushed the left sleeve of her cardigan up, careful to make sure it wasn't going to be stained by what she was about to do. She closed her eyes and descended deep into herself.

For old time's sake and because this was a final farewell, they were both back in Dr Hahn's infirmary. Claudia Hahn was sitting at her small desk, Grace on the gurney, swinging her legs once again.

'Hey, Claudia.'

'Hello, Grace.'

'It's time to go. Are you ready?'

Hahn nodded. She looked keen. If Dr Hahn had constructed this illusion, Grace suspected there might have been a suitcase with a train ticket sitting proudly on the top by the handle.

'I can't wait to explore the bioverse. To meet everyone out there, all those minds,' said Claudia. 'Perhaps I will find my family too?'

'Perhaps.'

Bioverse, Hahn's name for it. Grace thought it was a very good one. Perhaps on Claudia's travels her term would catch on and spread, like its very own virus. Like some sort of internet meme.

'How will I know where to go?'

'You don't need to know. You'll be carried.' Grace smiled. 'Just like taking a taxi.'

Hahn nodded. She looked troubled though.

'You feel bad about what happened,' said Grace, more as a statement than a question.

'Yes. Mr Everett wasn't really a bad man. Just—'

'Frightened. And dishonest.' Grace leaned forward. 'What you and I did was absolutely necessary. Our friends would still be stuck in that castle until they eventually ran out of food and starved.'

'Poor Everett never got a chance to become part of the—'

'I know,' cut in Grace. 'But life is unfair. Think of every person who lived and died before *they* came. What about them? Gone. Forgotten. Dust.' Grace decided to soften what she'd just said. 'I'm sorry, too, that he didn't get a chance to join us.'

'What are you going to do when you get to Southampton?'

Grace absently stroked the lining sheet on the gurney. 'I think the best thing I can do is to learn as much as I can about the *remainders*.'

'Why bother? Why don't we let them be?'

'*We* need to know how dangerous they are. Are they a threat to us? Do they have any big bombs?'

'Nuclear?' Hahn said.

Grace nodded. 'The thing is, the man in charge of them is a close friend of my dad's.' Grace shrugged. 'If I could get close to him . . .'

'You'd infect him?'

She frowned as she wrestled with the details of her

276

fledgling plan. 'I think . . . if he could just understand, if I could get him to understand how wonderful this is, how kind *they* are—'

'That will be very hard, Grace. The infection process appears so frightening. The unknown is terrifying.'

'A handshake . . . just one touch. That's all.' She tapped her fingers on the bed. 'Then, after a few weeks or months, he'll begin to understand. Like you did. Like I did.'

'There will be tests. Lots of tests to make sure you're not infected. They must also know about salt, about the painkillers. They may have other ways, more effective ways, to screen for infected hosts.'

'If they find out I'm a host, then . . .' The prospect of ending up like Everett, burning *again*, made her shudder involuntarily. 'If I'm . . . if I can explain what I am very carefully and why I'm there, maybe they will want to talk with me. They—'

'They will use you as a guinea pig, Grace.'

'No, as a . . . a . . . What's the word? Inter . . . ?'

'Intermediary?'

Grace smiled. 'That's the one. If the president learns that the virus can communicate, that it doesn't mean any harm—'

'They will *incinerate* you. As soon as they discover you are—'

'I have to try. If they do have bombs, they could burn us all. Millions – no *billions* of us, like you and me now, people of the *bioverse*.' She shrugged. 'I can't ignore that.'

'You are a brave girl, Grace.'

'That's the message I need you to share: "I'm going to try to talk to the remainders".'

'Who will I tell that to?'

'Any of them. News spreads.' She managed a smile.

Hahn stood up and came over to the gurney. She put her arms round Grace. 'I will miss you.'

'I'll miss you too.' Grace hugged her tightly. 'I hope you find your family, Claudia.'

'And I hope you find your father.' Hahn let her go and stood back. 'Will I ever see you again?'

'I'm out there too. Parts of me. Echoes of me.'

Hahn looked around the room. 'In the end we are all just data, aren't we?'

'I think that's what we've always been. It's just that now, finally, we've all been linked up.'

A chemical signal gently informed Grace that the carrier was almost ready. 'It's time to go, Claudia.'

'Take care.'

'I will.'

The illusion of the room slowly wavered and faded, and Grace surfaced once more into the gloomy interior of the toilet cubicle. The end of her left forearm and hand looked as though she had plunged them deep into the whirring blades of a food blender. Bloody viscous strings of flesh drooped from the bones of her hand down to the floor, where they had congealed, and almost finished forming into the components of a small crablike creature.

The supercluster of cells travelling in convoy through her arteries had now dropped down through this conduit of flesh and into the creature.

Your taxi awaits.

She smiled at that thought.

Grace sensed Hahn's departure. Like the umbilical cord of a newborn baby, the flesh separated and began to slowly withdraw back up into the skeletal remains of Grace's hand. She bent down, scooped up the little creature with her good hand, opened the cubicle door and wandered over to the bathroom's small window.

Again, she experienced a fleeting sense of déjà vu as she looked up at the wire-mesh glass. She lifted the support arm, opened the window a crack and pushed her hand outside into the cool night air. On her palm, the crab glistened darkly, its pearl carapace still covered in the darkness of her own blood.

'Goodbye, Claudia,' she whispered softly, then turned her hand over.

She came back to the cubicle, sat down on the toilet seat once more and waited patiently for the flesh on her left hand to reknit itself. The donation of biomass was only small, less than a fistful. The cells that were converging to reform muscles, ligaments, tendons and skin over the borrowed bones of some other poor long-gone child were coming from all over her body.

She went back to her sleeping bag an hour later, exactly the same height as she had been, the same frame, just with a tiny fraction less soft tissue enveloping it.

CHAPTER 39

One Year Ago

'Ah, you decided to come.' Trent extended a big hand above his desk and smiled at his visitor. 'How's your English?'

'How is your Spanish?' his visitor replied.

'*Yo . . . hablo . . . poco.*' Trent gave up struggling and shrugged. 'It's pretty crap to be honest.'

'Then we should have this conversation in English, I think.' The visitor ignored the extended hand and Trent let it drop to his side.

'Sure. Why not? Take a seat, President Questra.'

'I will stand, thank you. This will not be a long meeting.'

Trent glanced at the guards flanking the President of Cuba, then at Tom and grinned. 'Oh well, perhaps you're right about that.'

'The Partido Communista de Cuba empowers me to speak and negotiate on their behalf,' said President Questra.

'Unlike Congress who are a complete pain in the ass,' Trent replied. 'Or once were.'

'President Trent, I will be frank with you. The people of Cuba took pity on you and your American refugees and offered you a safe haven. You are our guests, and as such we expect your behaviour to remain—'

'Ramon, let me stop you there.'

Questra frowned at the interruption and the uninvited familiarity.

'Look, let's you an' me cut all the diplomatic bullshit and get to the point, shall we?'

'The world is now a much smaller place, President Trent. Apart from the coalition based around New Zealand, and one or two other small island nations, it appears that we are all that is left of humanity. We have to work together if we are to create a vaccine, if we are to rebuild the world—'

'Well, I couldn't agree more, Ramon.'

'The PCC and myself have consulted. There is concern that there is a potential for . . . *difficulties* to develop between your people and ours. It therefore makes sense to merge your people with ours. To naturalize them as—'

'Turn Americans into Cubans?' Trent shook his head slowly. 'Not gonna happen.' He leaned back, taking the weight off his fists, standing up straight. 'But, you know, I totally agree with you – we've got to pull in the same direction or we're not going to make it. We're all in the same boat, and we *are* gonna be screwed if we carry on squabbling like we have been. So yeah, Ramon, we do need to think about pulling our strings together.'

Questra shook his head, anticipating where this was heading. 'Trent, you must understand you will *not* be invited to be a part of the Partido, or the Council of Ministers. There is absolutely no possibility of this happening.'

Tom noticed a flicker on his friend's face. He knew that

look. *Rage*. Rage, with a lid screwed firmly down. Only Tom had glimpsed it.

So this is Doug's fallback position? Some kind of partnership authority . . . two presidents ruling side by side.

Only, Questra had shot that down before it had even been placed on the table.

That's not good. From years of knowing him, Tom was well aware that no one said 'NO' to Doug. It was the unwritten eleventh commandment. You broke that one at your own peril.

'Ramon, I don't want to *join* your government. In fact, I've got a counter proposal I'd like to share with you.'

Shit, where's this going?

Tom could see Dougie was smiling politely, but he could hear the edge in his voice.

Easy, Dougie . . . take it easy.

'I've done my homework, Ramon. And here's where we stand. I'm the leader of a nation that's been whittled down to just over twenty-three thousand citizens. We have a fleet of seventeen ships and six submarines. Nine of those ships are navy ships. One is an aircraft carrier with eighteen fully operational fighters. I have at my disposal five companies of marines, some special-forces units and just under six thousand navy personnel. But you know what?'

He sat down in his chair.

'You really don't need to worry about any of that. Because I have thirty-seven nuclear warheads at my disposal.' Trent clacked his tongue like a poker player laying down a hand of aces. '*Thirty-seven*. Nothing really in Cold War terms, perhaps. But certainly more than enough to completely *glass* this shitty little island.'

Jesus. Tom looked at the Cuban leader and saw that his face had lost a little colour. All the same, Questra managed a casual smile. 'You would not do such a thing, Trent.' Questra's voice remained low. 'You rely on us for water, for food. We know you have few supplies of your own.'

'We have more than enough supplies to keep us going. Certainly to keep us going long enough to sail over to the Malvinas, maybe the Azores.' Trent winked at the Cuban leader. 'There's more than one way to skin a cat.' He hunched his shoulders and spread his hands. 'But you know what, Ramon? It's nice here. We'd rather stay, you know, if that's OK with you?'

The Cuban remained silent.

'And since we'll be staying, like you said, we really do need to consolidate. Pull together, instead of pulling in different directions. So, then, we get to my counter proposal. Your party will surrender its control over the people of Cuba—'

'This will not happen, Trent!'

He leaned forward again, his voice just a touch calmer, and colder. 'I have six submarine commanders ready to set sail at a moment's notice.' Trent tapped the phone sitting on his desk. 'One word from me and they start prepping those warheads.'

'This is a foolish bluff.'

Tom felt his stomach lurching. *Jesus, Dougie, you've taken this too far.*

'You are a fool, Trent! You are a *dangerous fool*!'

'Uh-uh . . . let's not name-call.' Trent wagged a finger at him. 'Just being pragmatic. Tough times, tough measures.'

Trent extended his large hand again. 'Whaddaya say?'

The Cuban leader ignored his hand, turned and left the room, his guards turning crisply and following him out.

'Jesus, Dougie!' said Tom after the footsteps had receded down the hall. 'What the hell have you just done?'

Trent looked sharply at him.

'What if he does something? What if they take you seriously and mobilize their troops? For Christ's sake, Doug . . . you won't do it? Right? You're not going to—'

'Relax, they won't do a thing.' He frowned. '*This* is why I needed all our ships right here, Tom. *This* is why I've been trimming back your mercy mission for the last few months. It's not that I don't give a shit about any other survivors out there.' He looked at the doorway. 'It's just that I knew those sons-of-bitches were going to come asking for the rent sometime soon.'

'Doug . . . reassure me here. If they do call your bluff, tell me, please, *tell me* you *aren't* going to actually launch goddamn nukes?'

Trent looked at him with an expression of utter bemusement on his face.

'Of course not, *amigo*. Of course not.' Then suddenly scowled as if even the idea of asking that question was a hurtful erosion of their friendship. 'Come on, Tom, now that would be *insane*.'

CHAPTER 40

Progress had been frustratingly slow this morning. Leon and Freya could hardly hear each other speak over the laboured drone of the trucks' struggling engines. The radiator – attacked by those crabs – had been patched but not wholly repaired. It kept leaking, and every hour they had to stop and refill it. He could tell when the hour was nearly up because the overheating engine started to judder and stall. There had already been four 'radiator stops' and three 'complete stops' where everyone had had to bail out the back and help with the task of pushing dead cars to the side of the road. The tyres were mostly flat, but the wheels still turned. Give it another five years, Leon guessed, and they'd be rusted rigid. Then the only way through these traffic graveyards would be with a tank or a bulldozer.

They'd been back on course for a while when the truck suddenly ground to a halt again, everyone lurching with it. A collective sigh chorused down both sides. Another car graveyard, no doubt . . .

'*People!*' Naga's muffled voice cried out from the driver's cabin.

They looked at each other. 'Did she just say . . . ?'

Naga's voice again. '*There's other people!*'

They got up quickly and shuffled to the back, taking it in turns to drop down on to the road. Leon helped Freya off the truck and then joined the others as they spread out either side of the front truck and stared ahead at the logjam of vehicles.

It took Leon a moment to spot them because of the hazy glare of daylight, but also because there was absolutely no movement. Finally he picked them out standing among the cars – a group of children of various ages. It looked as though they'd been in the process of attempting to clear a path through the blockage, but now they stood inert and wide-eyed, staring back silently, like some long-lost tribe of Amazon Indians encountering outsiders for the very first time.

Naga stepped down from the cabin ahead of them.

'Hey there!' she called out. 'You kids!' she added as an afterthought. 'It's OK, we're not bad guys!'

None of the children moved. They continued to stare in a bewildered silence, like Peter Pan's Lost Boys – and girls – encountering grown-ups for the first time.

'They look weird,' said Royce.

Leon had to admit he had a point. There seemed to be something not quite right about them. Perhaps it was their perfect, frozen-in-the-headlights stillness.

Moss, one of Corkie's men, pushed past him holding a saltwater extinguisher. He took up position a few steps ahead of Naga.

'You kids OK?' asked Naga, hoping to provoke some sort of a response.

Finally one of them stirred. A tall, thin boy stepped forward. He had fine blond hair that had grown long, a greasy fringe dangling like a theatre curtain over his face. His eyes seemed to blink constantly behind it as if the day was far too bright for him.

Leon guessed his age to be a year or two younger than him, although it was hard to tell; his skinny frame could have been making him look years younger or older.

The boy reached into the back of a trailer. The trailer was tethered to half a dozen bicycles lying on their side in the road in front of the jam. Several tufted heads suddenly popped up and looked curiously out like puppies in a basket. Leon's first impression was that they *were* puppies.

But they were toddlers.

The boy pulled out a cricket bat that had a number of nails hammered through the bevelled willow, poking out threateningly from the varnished wood on the other side. He held it aloft in both hands, ready to swing it if anyone approached him.

'Are . . . you . . . *real* . . . p-people?' he asked slowly.

One of the toddlers peering out of the trailer answered that. 'Peeep-ol!'

Naga took several cautious steps forward. 'Yes, we are, love. We're real.' She held out her empty hands. 'We're not going to hurt you. It's OK . . . It's OK.'

The boy took his time regarding her.

'Look!' said Naga. 'I have fingernails. Hair. I'm real!'

The boy stared at her hands for a while then, slowly, he lowered the bat to a half-ready posture, still in both fists and still ready to swing at a moment's notice. He eyed Moss holding the extinguisher, and Royce holding a jerry can of fuel. 'Please . . . d-don't hurt us.'

'We won't,' assured Naga. She took another step forward.

'I . . . I had to l-l-look after them all,' said the boy slowly. His eyes darted from one person to the next. With the bat in his hands he looked like a guilty schoolboy explaining a broken window. 'Th-th-there was . . . n-no one . . . else l-left.' His stammer was achingly bad. He pushed through the words, tenaciously delivering a few at a time until he hit another hard consonant. 'N-no g-grown ups l-left . . . I . . . I had . . .'

Naga advanced towards him. 'It's OK, sweetheart. It's OK.'

The boy lowered his bat all the way until the tip of it clunked harmlessly on the road beside his feet. He was trembling. From where he was standing, ten metres away, Leon could see he was shaking and twitching uncontrollably.

'C-c-can . . . we . . . c-c-come . . . with . . . you?'

'Oh, love!' gasped Naga. 'Of course you can!' She quickly closed the gap between them and wrapped her arms round him. The boy towering over her was frozen and stiff at first. He looked confused, unsure, his rapidly blinking blue-eyed stare continuing over the top of her head, evaluating each of them in turn.

He began to wilt like an unwatered sunflower. His head, too big for those narrow shoulders, gently lowered until it rested on Naga's, his chin settling on to her dark hair.

He closed his eyes and began to sob.

CHAPTER 41

They were into Wiltshire now, having detoured off the M3 because of the frequency with which they'd been having to stop and clear their way through jams. They'd gone towards Salisbury along the A303, and after skirting the cathedral town were now heading south-east again, back towards the coast. On several occasions they'd passed through a vehicle graveyard with a pathway already cleared through.

An encouraging sign.

'Looks like we're not the first ones heading to Southampton,' said Freya. She gazed out of the back of the truck. They were moving slowly but steadily, not hampered by blockages, but slowed down to a walking pace by those who couldn't fit into the two trucks. They were taking turns to ride or walk, the youngest and weakest children, by common consent, being excused from the rota.

'Well, we may not be the first . . .' replied Leon. They could see marks on the road where vehicles had been dragged or shunted to the side of the road. 'But now I'm beginning to think we might end up being the last ones in line.'

'We'll be fine.' Freya elbowed him. 'We'll get on a ship.'

Leon glanced at his sister. Grace was one of those walking behind the truck. The children they'd picked up – there had been nearly fifty of them – had merged into their group. Some were too poorly and malnourished to walk, some just too young.

Leon noticed Grace seemed to be getting on with the skinny blond boy, the children's reluctant leader. His name was Jerry. Leon had heard a bare-bones sketch of his story from Grace the last time they'd stopped for a toilet break. Jerry was fifteen, tall for his age, and under different circumstances might have been bulkier. Dad would have said he had the frame for a quarterback. He just needed to throw some more meat on it.

The kids had all been in a children's hospital in London, a famous place called Great Ormond Street. When he'd shrugged at the mention of the name, Grace had tutted at his ignorance. Although Leon was pretty sure she'd not heard of it either until five minutes ago.

When the virus had struck, it wiped out everyone but the patients, the majority of whom, of course, were on analgesics of one kind or another at the time. Jerry, thirteen when it had hit, had been the oldest surviving patient. Being the eldest, he'd become their leader by default.

He'd told Grace that for the last two years the children had sheltered in the hospital surviving on the scraps they could forage from the surrounding city, fighting off the 'creepers', as they'd called them.

Leon studied the boy. He had the gaunt look of someone who was ready to cave in. Those rapidly blinking eyes, the head tremors, the stammering . . . He looked as if he'd been just about managing to hold it together for the sake of the little ones.

Originally there'd been about a hundred of them, Grace had told Leon. Over half the children under Jerry's care had died – some because of the illnesses from which they were already suffering, but many others from simple things like septicaemia or malnutrition. And, of course, others had been jumped and killed by the creepers. Leon wondered how he himself would have coped with such a burden. It had been hard enough having just Grace to worry about in those first few months after Mum had gone. But to have so many children looking to you for their survival, every minute of every day? It was no wonder poor Jerry looked like a battle-scarred old man.

Then, just like Leon and Freya had, one day the children had stumbled across something on a foraging trip: an emergency command and control centre, still running on a trickle of electricity coming from somewhere, and a crackling radio broadcasting the American president's message.

Leon watched his sister and Jerry walking together, knuckles almost brushing as their hands swung loosely by their sides, heads leaning in to listen to each other as they spoke, and realized that there was some chemistry going on down there.

A virus of a different kind.

'You thinking what I'm thinking?' said Freya.

He turned to her, and she was smiling. More a mischievous smirk.

'You think?'

She nodded. 'I think.'

Leon looked back at them and realized he was actually evaluating the boy's suitability for his sister. He saw their loose swinging hands begin to slow down and synchronize, bump gently against each other, fingers cautiously extending and tangling. And he couldn't help smiling for her.

At that moment Grace caught his eye and glared when she noticed Leon was watching them. Leon gave her a cheeky wink then made an exaggerated show of turning his back to her.

'Giving those crazy kids a little space, huh?' asked Freya.

He nodded. 'We have stage-one hand-holding going on!'

CHAPTER 42

Grace knew, or was almost certain she knew, way before she felt the warmth of his skin against hers. As their fingers tentatively entwined for the very first time, the cells from her sweat glands were already on the surface of his skin, embarking on a covert mission of discovery.

And so, in turn, were his.

Less than a minute after first contact, one of his cells was in her bloodstream and being approached by her body's endlessly patrolling security guards, her version of white blood cells. An exchange of amino acids later, and 'friend' status was established. Within another minute the invading cell had been carried along the arterial transport system up to a primary data-gathering cluster for closer examination and confirmation.

Chemical messages released, absorbed, tasted and understood in nanoseconds.

Grace turned to look at Jerry, and at almost the same moment he stole a glance back at her, blue eyes meeting brown.

Around them the others were all walking too closely for Grace and Jerry to talk aloud, and the truck's belching and complaining engine was far too loud for them to whisper.

However, through their clasped hands they spoke. A conversation slowed down to almost human standards as intelligence clusters phrased questions and passed them on to data-carrier cells, which flowed into the pulsing stream, through the connecting tissue that was now gluing their hands together and onwards up to the receiving cluster to listen to.

[You are infected. I thought ---- were.]

Grace smiled. {Thought you were too. Are you the only one in your group?}

[No. We all infected.]

Grace couldn't help turning to look at him. {All of you?}

The communication wasn't perfect. She sensed he was using different chemical combinations and concentrations to her. A variant of their language. Like an accent.

[I had no choice. Infect all.] He looked up at the youngest children sitting in the back of the truck in front of them. [Many of them were ---------- of --------- when I got -------- it ---------- so they -------------]

{Jerry, can you adjust your carrier sequence? Some of your messages are becoming fragments I can't understand.}

Jerry nodded. A moment later he came back to her. [Is that better?]

{Yes. Much better.}

He'd also adjusted his chemical carrier to match hers. [You get so used to talking within your own colony. You develop your own language.]

Grace nodded. {Like different accents and slang words, I suppose.}

[Exactly.]

{Tell me again . . . about the children?}

[Most of them were dying of cancer and other medical conditions. When I got infected . . . when I finally became aware I was infected, I realized they would die if I didn't try to save their lives this way.]

{You did so much more than save them.}

[I know.]

Grace sensed regret or sadness in the taste of his last message. {You did the right thing, Jerry.}

[It was hard at the time . . . They were terrified.]

That message came with a visual memory attached. For a fleeting second Grace glimpsed a gloomily lit hospital ward. Tall Victorian sash windows barricaded with upended beds, slits of daylight slanting down into a dark space full of dirty sheets and mattresses, a floor covered with opened and discarded tin cans, human faeces collecting in corners. And blood . . . so much of it. Grace could see dozens of pallid young bodies scattered across the ward floor in various stages of decomposition, a grotesque massacre of children, with just a few left cowering in one corner, hugging each other, screaming in terror at the slaughterhouse scene before them . . . and Jerry, approaching them, looming over them in whatever terrifying manifestation he must have been in, slowly descending upon them.

Grace felt their terror in his memory. Felt their horror and felt the reluctance on his part to give them this *gift* . . . because of how traumatic the moment of transition was going to be.

His memory triggered one of her own. She remembered

being little more than a toddler, getting an injection in her arm for something. She remembered crying and screaming, her and all the other boys and girls in her elementary school class. Even though she knew it was a good thing, a medicine to keep them all safe from nasties, she'd been terrified of that tiny little glinting needle sliding into her upper arm. It had been the terror of . . . *anticipation*, of seeing those 'treated' before you, of counting down the victims ahead of you in the line.

Jerry's memory was a thousand times worse than hers. Those poor children . . . waiting their turn.

{Oh my God . . .}

[It was . . . *difficult*. We were all in one small space together. It was attack them all at once or do nothing. I had little choice.]

{It was the right thing to do . . .} she sent. But the following thought tagged along with it: *Could I have done that?*

[You do what is for the best, don't you?] replied Jerry. [You help. You preserve life if you can. Even if the way to do it is . . . terrifying for the person.]

{Change can be really, really hard.}

[Harder for some, much easier for others. My change was gradual. It was easy for me. I didn't realize I was infected for a long time. Then *they* began to show me things.]

{It was the same for me. Dreams at first . . . then the explaining.} Grace looked at him. {You ever wonder who *they* are? Where *they* came from?}

[Perhaps it's God? Maybe this is where the idea of heaven and God came from? This virus?]

{You mean it's been here before?}

[Perhaps. I don't know. I do know *they* care for us. They want what's best for us. No matter how frightening this has been, the plague when it first arrived, the *creepers*, the fighting to stay alive – all those things – beyond all that, this has been about what's best for everyone.]

Just like the nice young doctor who came to her elementary school with his bag of scary shiny needles.

[You know what makes me really sad, Grace?]

{What?}

[All those people, even the animals, who lived out their short lives then died before the virus came along. All gone. All those wasted lives. All those wasted memories.]

Grace felt Jerry squeeze her hand. She turned to look at him and she saw beneath the loose locks of his unkempt fringe, his blinking blue eyes. He looked so sad.

{Yeah. You're right. That's really horrible to think about.}

Jerry changed the subject. [What about you?]

His message arrived without any context. {What are you asking me?}

[Is it just you in your group or are there others?]

Her method had differed so much to his. Perhaps she should have done the same, infected them all at Everett's castle. One night of butchery and bloodletting and the nasty business would have been done with.

But, then again, there would have been flames. So

her approach had been cautious.

{It's just me . . . and one other.}

[That's dangerous. It has to be all.]

Grace knew what he was saying. She knew that better than anyone. Their paranoia was like a forest fire: one suspicious sign, one odd look, it seemed, and the fuel came out.

[You need to save them all. All at once. No mercy. It's the kindest thing, Grace.]

CHAPTER 43

'Lieutenant Tidwell . . . talk to me, son. What do you see?'

Lieutenant Dan Tidwell stared through the tall iron bars of the perimeter fence out at the six lanes of El Malecón highway. Those six lanes were usually sparsely populated with vehicles running on rationed gas. The highway was normally just sun-baked concrete that bordered the study in rich blues that was Havana's idyllic sea view.

Right now, though, the highway was more than just an empty concrete apron. A column of tanks and armoured personnel vehicles was rolling menacingly up it towards the American embassy's grounds.

Tidwell pulled up his field glasses, counted the vehicles approaching them, and made a rough estimate of what was coming their way.

He thumbed his radio on. 'I'm looking at a couple of mechanized brigades, BTR Forties, Fifties carrying men, backed up by, I dunno . . . maybe a dozen, T-sixty-twos.' Tidwell knew President Trent had done his time in the marines. Twenty-five years ago or thereabouts, he'd been a lieutenant just like Tidwell. The president would know his hardware shorthand and what Tidwell and his men were facing . . . and probably knew exactly how they were feeling.

Shit scared and unable to show it.

'Just hang in there, son,' replied Trent. 'You keep those assholes off my lawn, OK?'

'We'll do our best, sir.'

'Thank you, Lieutenant. Stand by for further orders.'

Tidwell lowered his field glasses and turned to his men. Two sections of marines carrying nothing but M27s and one FGM-148 Javelin between them. For a defensive position they had pretty much squat, nothing more than some flimsy iron railings, some shitty dried-up bushes and a couple of sandbag horseshoe positions for cover.

'Buckle down, guys. Looks like the Cubans are gonna dump a whole load of whoop-ass on us. Ross, Farez, get that launch tube set up. At least we got a shot at taking out one of their goddamn tanks.'

'Sir!'

Tidwell tucked away the binoculars into his pouch and took several steps back from the iron railings. *Shit* . . .

He doubted they'd even get a chance to fire the javelin. If they were smart, those sons of bitches were going to pull up those T-62s into a tidy line across the highway and shell them until they were mincemeat and rubble.

'Lieutenant? This a "for real" situation?' asked Corporal Gant.

'It is.'

Standing orders were to hold the ground. Fire on anything that got within range. He turned and looked back at the severe glass-and-concrete embassy building. The president was in there still. He could have bolted for the docks, leaving him and his men behind to defend the last bit of functioning US territory left in the world.

But he hadn't. That meant something.

And if the POTUS was staying put, Tidwell and his boys were going to dig in like bloody-minded little ticks on a dog's back and hold this hard shitty scrabble ground for as long as possible.

'This is frikkin crazy, sir!' said the corporal.

He had a point.

'Frikkin crazy it certainly is, Gant,' replied Tidwell.

He watched as several of the BTRs came to a halt and spilled troops from their rear. Roughly a company's worth of olive-drab revolutionary guards spread out either side of the highway, picking their way forward, running from cover to cover towards the embassy compound.

Crazy. The world's population reduced to what? Their ragtag fleet and this island? And, God knows, maybe one or two other small pockets elsewhere . . . and, still, it came down to a shooting match between Us and Them.

'Doug! Dougie! For Chrissakes, pick up the damned phone and talk to them!'

The only other man in the room was a marine sergeant. Tom noticed him stiffen and wince at his over-familiarity with the president. He gestured at the window. 'They're not playing around any more!'

Tom was sure Trent could see the convoy of vehicles like a long, fat olive-green python sliding down the highway from where he was standing behind his desk. It was pretty goddamn impossible to miss. Like a Red Square parade, except with a warm tropical backdrop.

The phone was ringing incessantly on Trent's desk, an old-fashioned bell-and-hammer trilling that didn't sound as if it were going to stop any time soon.

'If you don't talk, they're going to shell us!' said Tom.

'Relax, *amigo*.'

'Relax?'

The phone stopped ringing.

Trent had his fingers steepled beneath his chin, his lips pursed pensively. 'They're calling our bluff. This is just them pushing to see how serious we are.'

Our bluff? Tom absently shook his head. *It wasn't 'our' bluff – it was yours.*

Trent had the military radio in one of his big hands. On one frequency he had those poor marines down in the compound; on another he had fleet command. His thumb was absently tapping the frequency dial.

'Dougie, this is crazy. We're going to be exchanging fire any second now – over what? A flag? Over what-the-hell-nationality we get to call ourselves?'

Trent narrowed his eyes. 'Ideology. You want the last nation left on earth to be a communist one?'

'You serious?'

'Deadly serious. You want that, Tom? Because if we roll over on our backs now, that will be it. No more USA.'

'Look, frankly, I don't give a flying crap what flag we have to salute—'

'You hear that, soldier?' barked Trent.

The marine nodded obediently. 'Yes, sir, Mr President.'

Trent glared back at Tom. 'Staff Sergeant Friedmann . . . you took a goddamn oath thirty years ago to honour your country, your flag and your president. What the hell was that, then? Huh? Some cheap frat-house oath? Just a bunch of bullshit words?'

'Look, Doug, I'm not doing this with you now. We're friends. You're my friend first, my president second.'

'I am your president first,' Trent said slowly. 'You'd do well to remember that.'

'Jesus . . .'

Tom studied his friend's impassive face. It was like a shopfront closed for business: shutters down, blinking neon nightlights on. *Come back tomorrow, folks.*

I know what this is about, thought Tom. *This isn't about ideology.*

Tom knew Douglas Trent better than anyone; better than any of his trophy girlfriends or Republican buddies. What he'd always admired about the man was his open cynicism. None of that *In God we trust* crap. None of that *Four score and ten years ago* dewy-eyed patriotism. He knew how the world worked for those in the know: money and influence. The holy duality. From the moment he'd stepped into the duplicitous world of politics, he'd been the *I don't talk bullshit – I talk business* character.

This isn't about patriotism. This is about him. This is his ego.

Trent's fist was clamped round the radio like some grubby mitt round a baseball.

'Doug, this isn't about our flag . . .'

Trent glared at him, and Tom sensed that this might be the very last time he'd ever get to use his friend's first name. 'You have to let this go.'

The sound of the first gunshots echoed up from the compound.

Lieutenant Tidwell could feel the vibration through the sandbag he was cowering behind as a dozen rounds smacked into it. It was like sitting on one side of a punch bag with Mike Tyson on the other.

Keeping our heads down . . . while they outflank us.

Tidwell waited for a pause in the gunfire, then stuck his head up like a meerkat. Through the railings, beneath the shadows cast by a row of stunted trees, he could see figures jogging to his left, heading for the embassy's front entrance. Tidwell had a section of men manning the concrete sentry post there. Far better cover than here . . . and far tougher for them to dislodge the guys dug in there.

Right *here* was where Tidwell would've picked to break in: iron railing and bushes – that's all that separated the USA from Cuba right now. Easy pickings. The flanking manoeuvre was clearly a feint.

He felt something hum past his face, like some high-speed insect on a *can't stop now* errand. The sand bag beside him suddenly spat sand into his eyes and he ducked back down again.

'Shit! Shit! Shit!'

'You OK, sir?'

'I'm good, I'm good!' he shouted above the rattle of

304

gunfire. 'Got grit in my eyes.' He swiped at his eyes with the ball of his hand and rapidly blinked until tears started rolling down his cheeks. 'They're moving to the left, towards the entrance!' he yelled as he tried to deal with the intense stinging in his eye.

'Should we reinforce—'

'No, stay put!' He fumbled in his webbing for the water bottle. Found it, blindly unhooked it and uncapped it, cocked his head back and poured the warm water on to his face, blinking frantically to dislodge the grain of sand beneath his eyelid that right now felt like a goddamn bastard-bitch of a flint boulder.

He got it. Blinked again to double-check. Gone. He shook the water off his face.

'We stay right here! They're trying to get us to spread out.'

Tidwell could hear the growl of an engine nearby being zealously revved. Then heard the rattle and clank and squeal of rusty tracks beginning to turn on their wheels.

'Incoming!' shouted Farez.

Tidwell poked his head over the bags again and snatched another half-second appraisal before ducking back down. One of the T62s had been using the distracting small-arms fire to make its way down the Malecon highway over the decorative flower beds towards the perimeter fencing.

A plain and simple plan, knock down the railings, flatten the bushes and pull back, leaving a handy breach for the Republican Guards to spill through.

He leaned back on his haunches to get a look into the

sandbag horseshoe next door to see if Farez and Ross had the javelin set up and ready to fire. He caught Farez's eye and saw him tapping at his wrist – *need more time*. Ross was huddled down with the launch's bulky tube balanced on his right shoulder; they were still waiting on the thermal-targeting system's coolant to green-light a *good-to-go*.

He cupped his mouth. 'Fire when you're ready!' he yelled across the gap.

'Yes, sir!'

The rattle of gunfire coming at them from an increasingly widening arc was clearly designed to keep their heads down, to keep them from launching anything at the approaching tank. Over the noise he could hear its growl and clanking. It was growing louder . . . closer.

Still leaning backwards, the small of his back aching to change position, he waited for a thumbs up from Farez. Finally he got it.

Tidwell cupped his mouth. 'We'll give you covering fire in ten seconds!' he yelled across the gap to them, then pulled himself forward until he was leaning back against the sandbags.

He looked at Corporal Gant and the other four marines waiting to get into the fight. 'Don't bother aiming . . . just pray and spray, OK?'

They nodded.

Tidwell mentally counted down the last five seconds, then . . .

'NOW!'

All six men rose together, poking as little of themselves above the sandbags as possible, but enough all the same to present as targets. They unleashed a spattering of volley fire across the parched lawn, through the iron railings and into the shaded flower beds beneath the trees.

Tidwell saw the Cuban soldiers dropping down and scrambling for cover. As far as he could tell, none of their un-aimed shots had found a target. Nonetheless their volley had the intended result, sending them diving to the ground.

There was a lull.

Ross clambered to his feet, levelled the launcher's thermal targeting reticule at the approaching T62 until he had a lock on, then dropped back down out of sight. He levelled the javelin straight upwards and launched it. The missile popped forward out of the launch tube like an embarrassing misfire. A momentary, fifth-of-a-second pause later the missile's propellant kicked in and it soared into the clear blue sky like an eager greyhound released from its trap.

Tidwell watched it arc sharply in the sky above them. It did the tightest turning circle it could given its ferocious speed, a tidy vapour trail a hundred metres up then straight back down again.

The blast was so close that the percussive wave hit them at almost the same time as the light flash. He felt their sandbag emplacement wobble precariously. Then the boom. Too slow to cover his ears, he knew his hearing was going to be screwed for the next few minutes. The roar of the skirmish now reduced to a muted white noise, he watched as, seconds later, charred and jagged fragments of the tank clattered down around them, along with lengths of iron railing.

Shit.

He chanced another quick look over the sandbags. The chassis of the T62 was burning ferociously just a few metres short of the railing it had been rumbling towards. Their perimeter barrier, however, was gone. The javelin had done the tank's job for it.

Frikkin marvellous.

The enemy was in.

The windows in Trent's office rattled furiously in their frames. Trent, Tom, even the marine sergeant, ducked instinctively at the sound of the blast across the compound.

Tom hurried over to the desk, picked up the deck phone and held it towards Trent. 'Jesus Christ, call them! Before we lose the connection!'

Trent stared at him, blue eyes icy beneath his bushy blond eyebrows. For a moment Tom wondered whether he was considering ordering the sergeant to arrest him or, worse, shoot him.

Instead he snatched the phone from Tom's hand, and dialled a number.

Outside, the lull after the explosion was populated with the staccato crackle of gunfire.

'Yes,' said Trent after an agonizingly long wait.

Then another damned wait.

The gunfire was increasing in volume and intensity. He could hear orders being barked in the rare interludes, the marines out there sounded as though they were being beaten back from their positions, withdrawing from the compound and into the building itself. He looked at the marine sergeant, who appeared increasingly desperate to leave the stuffy confines of the office and get out there to help his comrades.

Finally, Trent's impassive face stirred into life as someone took his call.

'Yes, it *is* President Trent speaking . . . Uh-huh. Yes . . . to President Ramon Questra. *Directly* to him, please.'

Tom sighed with relief. He was torn between wanting to hurry over to the window to get a clearer picture of how much more time their marines could buy them, and staying right where he was, watching Trent as he offered up their surrender.

Don't say anything stupid, Doug.

His friend looked up from the ink blotter on the desk in front of him as he waited patiently. He noticed Tom gripping the edge of the desk and glaring at him . . . and winked. 'It's OK, I got this covered, buddy.'

'Doug, just be careful,' said Tom. It was all he could think to say right then.

Trent held up a finger to shush him. 'President Questra?'

On a quiet day, from where he was standing Tom might have heard the deep voice of the Cuban leader leaking from the old-fashioned earpiece. Not today.

Trent was listening, nodding. Then finally drew in a

breath to reply. 'No. No . . . No. I'm sorry, Ramon. I'm really sorry but that's completely unacceptable.'

Tom spread his hands. *For God's sake, what the hell are you—*

Trent held up his hand to stop him from talking. 'Ramon . . . Ramon! Be quiet! I'm the one speaking now!' He had quietened the Cuban leader.

He took in a deep breath and pursed his lips. 'I want you to know this for the record, for goddamn posterity – *you're* the stupid sonofabitch who pushed the situation to this. This is entirely on *you*.'

In his other fist, Trent still had the military radio. He thumbed the frequency dial and lifted it quickly up to his other ear. Phone on one side, walkie-talkie on the other, Tom suspected the man would have paid anything right then for a photographer to be here in the room to capture this moment, to capture his majesty, his command . . . his coolness under fire.

Trent spoke one word into the radio. 'Go.'

Then back to the phone. 'Ramon? Did you hear that? That was me giving the command. Why don't you go take a look to the east?' He placed the phone gently back in its cradle and the walkie-talkie down on the blotter. He smiled at Tom. 'Now, old friend, we'll see where our chips fall, shall we?'

'*What the hell have you gone and done!*'

'What needed to be done.' Trent walked round the desk towards the tall glass doors of his office that led on to the small balcony outside.

'Then what?' asked Royce.

Naga stretched her arms back behind her and uncrossed her legs. 'I don't know. I really don't know.'

'The message has today's date in it,' said Royce. 'It's not old. It's good.'

'The date is automated,' said Fish. 'The Stephen Hawking style being the *big* clue there.'

Royce cocked his head, trying to figure out if Fish was having a poke at him.

Fish continued. 'We have to prepare for the possibility that this is going to be a disappointment. That when we get to Southampton docks we're going to be looking at a lot of nothing.'

'I know,' said Naga.

'And possibly a lot of other people looking at nothing,' said Leon.

Heads all turned his way.

'I'm just saying. We heard the message. These kids heard it too. Others will have. We might get there and find hundreds, maybe *thousands*, of other people just sitting there, waiting for somebody to look after them.'

Leon looked around. 'All of them needing food and water. If we just rock up with our backpacks . . .' He didn't want to elaborate on that point in front of the younger ones. 'I just think we need to be prepared for, you know, a whole bunch of different possibilities.'

'We've got about a dozen firearms,' said Royce. He looked around at the other men, his fellow knights. 'And proper trained-up lads ready to use them.'

'Look,' said Leon. 'I'm pretty sure there's a rescue attempt going on. But just in case we're wrong, *just in case* . . . we need some kind of contingency plan, right?'

Naga nodded and the foyer went silent. Nobody seemed to have one ready.

'If it's bogus, we'll have to start over,' said Danielle. 'From scratch.' Her eyes suddenly widened. 'What if we could find a ship and sail it ourselves?'

'Anyone here secretly a marine engineer?' asked Fish, looking around. 'No? What about a pilot? Or a navigator? No? Bugger.' He shrugged and shook his head sarcastically. 'Otherwise a brilliant plan, Danielle.'

'Hey! I'm just trying to offer some ideas!'

'Well then, idiot-check them using your inside voice first, OK?'

'Fish, come on,' chided Naga. 'Stop winding her up.'

'A ship isn't *that* bad an idea,' said Leon. 'I mean, it's not like we have to sail it anywhere. The point is that it'd be like the castle – it's sitting on salt water, right? It would give us some degree of protection.'

Royce looked at him. 'So if we turn up and there's no US Navy waiting for us, we just go and set up camp on a ship?'

'Right.' Leon nodded. 'We base ourselves on a ship and we can forage from there.'

'For how long?' asked Naga.

Leon shrugged. 'If there's any rescue attempt, I guess that's where it would come to. Eventually.'

'Our plan B is just wait and hope?' said Fish.

'Southampton's a *big* freight port, isn't it?' said Freya.

'Which means there must be thousands of those freight containers full of, like, stuff. It's got to be a better place to forage than Oxford was. And –' she looked up at Leon – 'as he said, a ship's just as good as any castle.'

Naga was nodding at that. 'So that's our plan B. Plan A is get rescued. Failing that, we make Southampton our new home.'

'And what if we turn up and half of England is sitting right there?' asked Royce. He shrugged. 'Even if there're rescue ships waiting, are they going to have space for all of us?'

'If there were that many people left, I think we'd have come across more than just these children on the way down,' said Freya.

'Yeah.' Fish nodded. 'I don't expect it's going to be like Glastonbury or anything.'

'But there could be *thousands*,' said Royce. 'And if there're no rescue ships, what if they all have the same idea? Setting up camps on ships and all foraging in the same place for the same food and water?' He spread his hands. 'We're gonna end up fighting with all the others for scraps. I say, if there's no rescue, then we got to go somewhere else.'

'Hate to admit it, but knuckle-head might be right,' said Fish.

'Piss off of my side, you pasty-faced tosser,' growled Royce.

'Royce has a point,' said Leon. 'It's something we need to consider.'

315

'We may need our trucks again,' Royce added. 'If we just abandon our trucks when we get stuck and walk the rest of the way in, someone else might nick 'em.'

'So, if we decide we can't drive any further,' said Leon, 'let's just send a scouting party forward to look-see first. Check out the situation?'

'Maybe you're right,' replied Naga.

'I mean it's not a plan as such.' Leon shrugged. 'It just seems like the sensible way forward.'

Leon sensed that no one else had anything to add to that. Heads nodded and cramped legs uncrossed and stretched out. Naga's Big Planning Meeting had ended up with nothing more than: *'We'll keep going till we're stuck, then go take a sneak peek ahead.'*

'All right, then – I suppose it's bedtime, everybody,' said Naga. 'Big day tomorrow.'

'One other point!'

Naga looked around and saw Fish had raised his hand as if this were a school assembly.

'Miss?' he added with a sarcastic grin.

'What is it?'

'Call me Mr Paranoid, but, uh . . . I'm just wondering when we were planning to get around to salt-testing our new friends?'

'The little ones?' said Danielle. She gestured at them – they were sitting on the hard floor like primary school kids waiting patiently for story time. 'Seriously? You want to jab needles into all of them?'

Some of the children whimpered unhappily at the thought of that.

'They may look sweet and cute an' all that, and we may all be feeling sorry for everything they've been through, but any one of them could be a carrier,' said Fish.

Naga looked like this wasn't something she wanted to deal with right now.

'N-none of them are infected,' said Jerry. 'I know all about the s-salt thing. We d-did that.'

'How? Blood samples? Did you do that?' asked Fish.

Jerry shook his head. 'Just salt . . . on our f-fingers. Then rubbing our gums.' He mimed as if he were brushing his teeth.

'So when? When did you last test this lot?' demanded Fish.

Jerry looked taken aback. His nervous blinking made him look fragile, but he surprised Leon with his curt reply. 'S-so when did they last test *you*?'

'Well, we all did it . . . what? Eight, nine days ago?'

'Ten,' answered Royce.

Jerry scratched his temple. 'So . . . ten days? Anything could have happened in t-ten days.'

'We're not doing this,' said Naga. 'We're not turning on each other.'

'We were all spooned up together last night, and the night before that,' cut in Freya, 'and as far as I'm aware no one's been turned into a slime monster yet.'

Danielle chuckled at that, a raucous laugh that made some of the children smile. 'Look, we're one day out from

Southampton. We might even get there in the afternoon. They'll have doctors and medical teams and probably much better, more thorough screening tests than we can do. And a much better way of dealing with anyone they catch who's infected.'

'Well, I'm not happy with that,' said Fish. 'I raised this yesterday and the day before.' He looked warily at the children.

'Weren't you *against testing* back at the castle?' said Freya.

'Yeah, so? That was before I knew for certain I was OK. We don't know about these kids.'

'Fish, if any of them were virals, we'd know by now,' said Naga.

'Well, I'm keeping my distance tonight . . . again.'

'Fine, you do that,' said Naga.

'Tomorrow, though – we're testing everyone before we set off. I insist . . . a salt drink for breakfast.'

CHAPTER 45

Fish hugged himself in his sleeping bag, balling up inside it as best he could to generate a critical mass of body warmth. He was lying on the floor of the truck, looking out at the night sky. It was clear tonight, the stars flickering faintly, and without the low ceiling of clouds the temperature had dropped. His breath was producing a faint plume.

He was beginning to regret his stubborn bravado.

Naga had tried to persuade him that sleeping inside the store would be perfectly safe and certainly warmer. And, as Freya had said, no one had dissolved during the night so far.

He consoled himself with the fact that, paranoia aside, the little buggers were simply annoying. Night-times had become disrupted by their whimpering, their mewling cries from nightmares, their snotty rasping breaths. The endless bloody fidgeting and toilet trips.

Even attempting to sleep away from them these last few nights, Fish's rest had been repeatedly broken by one or another of them.

So he was outside, curled up in the back of the truck in an empty car park, alone.

Admittedly, he was only three metres away from the shop's glass front, but far enough away that if one of those crab things snuck into the back of the truck with him . . .

He had a gun, which helped. Naga had let him take one with him. Although she said he was probably more at risk of blowing his own head off than being devoured.

He was beginning to feel horribly vulnerable and exposed out here. He pulled himself along the floor until his head was poking out of the back of the truck, and turned towards the camping store. The window had cracked in several places, frosted with granules of glass and a radiating spider's web of fractures, but through it he could just about see the reassuring glow of a couple of the solar-powered lamps casting light across a floor that heaved like a restless ocean surface with twitching bodies in rustling vinyl sleeping bags.

Those kids were probably no more likely to be infected than any of them. They would have been dosed to the gills in hospital. If a simple paracetamol every other day could scare the virals away, he imagined chemotherapy, or whatever else they were being blasted with, would be a permanent turn-off.

All the same, salt worked. It had flushed out the one bogeyman lurking in their midst, *Corkie* of all people. Fish tried his best not to replay that moment in the grand hall.

My God. Corkie had *actually* vomited up his guts. Almost literally turned himself inside out.

Uncomfortable with his head exposed in the open for any nearby scuttler to see, he wiggled like a caterpillar all the way inside to the far end, resting his back against the partition and the small slide-hatch to the driver's compartment.

Tomorrow this would all be over. Tomorrow they were going to come across navy ships and buzzing helicopters and soldiers in biohazard suits and medical staff ready to check them out and inject them with some miraculous vaccine that was going to keep them immune forever. And there'd be electricity and generators, hot-water showers, even.

A taste of the old life again. A return to civilization.

A silhouette appeared at the end of the truck.

Fish lurched. 'Who's that?' Stupidly, his arms were deep down inside the bag by his side. He started wriggling frantically to free them and reach for his gun.

'Me! Fish, it's me, Grace.'

He heaved out a fluttering sigh. 'Shit, you scared me!'

'Sorry. Can I come up?'

'Yeah, sure.'

She clambered in and picked her way down the truck, sitting on one of the benches beside him.

'The brats keeping you awake?'

He heard her huff wearily. 'They *are* so noisy, aren't they?'

'I didn't sign up to be a childminder. I'm hoping tomorrow we can hand them over to someone else to look after.'

'You really suspicious of them?'

'Only in so far as I don't know for sure if your friend, Jerry, has really actually tested any of them.'

Grace leaned in towards him. 'Do you think he was lying earlier?'

'I don't know, but I'm thinking the smart thing to do first thing tomorrow is give them all a spoonful of salt each. We'll *all* do it before we set off. Thing is, if we turn up at Southampton and there are soldiers and stuff . . . and one or more of us gets flagged as infected, maybe they'll think the lot of us are. That'll be it, then. No evacuation for any of us.'

'Yeah . . . maybe.'

'And it has been over a week. I think we should be testing ourselves at least every other day and frying anyone who starts puking bloo—'

'No one wants to end up like Corkie. I guess if I was secretly infected and I didn't know it yet, I wouldn't want to find out the way he did.'

'True.' Fish suddenly felt bad about this conversation. Leon had explained those burn scars on Grace's face and body – a childhood accident – and here he was casually saying 'frying'.

'Sorry, Grace. That was insensitive of me.'

''S OK.'

'But I am concerned. If they do find one or more of us is carrying the virus, what are they going to do with us? Makes sense to do a quick check tomorrow before we set off. I'm sure Leon and Freya will back me up. And you?'

'Sure.'

'If we all just insist, then Naga'll go along with it. Won't take us long to do anyway. Ten, twenty minutes and we'd all be done.'

'And will you be the one to burn those children? If any

322

of them are infected? Will *you* do it?'

He hadn't actually thought that far ahead. He was kind of assuming that Royce or one of his knuckle-dragging mates would do the honours. 'If there was no one else, I suppose. If it came to it. Yeah, I suppose if—'

He flinched instinctively as he heard the rustle of movement. Something sharp and jagged was suddenly there on his face, clinging to his cheek and digging into his flesh. He opened his mouth to scream but Grace's hand slapped down heavily over it. Behind his back, he heard the hatch to the driver's compartment slide quickly aside and something nudged him forward, pushing through the gap like a python sliding into the back of the truck.

'I'm sorry, Fish,' she whispered.

Fish squirmed to free his arms from the bag, shook his head from side to side to shake her hand off his mouth and dislodge the thing that was clinging to his cheek.

The 'python' pushing at him from behind was an arm. It reached round the bag and clamped tightly across his chest, holding him firmly against the partition. A very strong arm. He wondered if it was Royce.

He was pinned, his arms uselessly trapped, and the assault rifle sitting by the side of his sleeping bag.

'Fish,' whispered Grace, 'we have to do this. We can't do that salt test. *I* can't do that salt test . . . not again.'

We? Grace? Grace is infected?

He fought to stay calm, to appear calm, to assure her he wasn't about to scream out. Then mumbled softly against the palm clamped over his lips, a sound reassuring her that it wasn't going to turn into a cry for help the moment she lifted her hand. He did it again and he felt the weight of her hand lessen as she eased the pressure from his lips.

'Grace . . .' he whispered. 'You're . . . you . . . ?'

'Yes, I'm infected.'

Stay calm, Fish. Stay calm. Talk. Reason. Discuss. He desperately needed to find his way into a conversation with her, a conversation that would keep her talking, hopefully lead to some sort of negotiation.

'Since when?'

'Since a long time ago.'

He looked down at the arm crooked round his chest. 'And who else? Is Leon?'

She shook her head. 'Jerry – he's infected. All the children are too.'

'The children?' He managed to nod calmly. 'Then, shit, I was right. I . . . I thought so.'

'The thing is, if you convince Naga to do those tests, we know how it's going to end up, don't we? It'll be horrific. There'll be flames, and burning, and screaming, and . . . those poor children—'

'But they're not real children, Grace. They—'

'They're more real than they've ever been. I know you don't see this yet. But you will.'

'See what?'

'Shhh . . . Keep your voice down.'

The arm round him flexed and tightened. Through the material of the sleeping bag he could feel lumps and bumps stirring along the arm.

He nodded. *Keep calm, fool. Keep her talking. Say anything . . . Just keep her talking.*

'Grace, look, I'm not going to ask her to test everyone tomorrow. I'll say she's right. I'll say we should just let the rescue people do the—'

'Fish, I can't risk letting you go. I can't trust you won't go straight in there right now and warn everyone about us.'

'I won't! I promise!'

'You will.'

'Oh God . . . Please don't h-hurt me, Grace.'

'I don't want to hurt you. I really like you.'

Fish smiled; he tried to make the moment seem funny. Once before, a long time ago, he'd managed to joke his way out of a knife-point mugging. Made the mugger laugh . . . and in that moment he'd been released, allowed to go on his way again, along with his wallet.

Make her laugh. Make her laugh.

'Didn't your mum ever tell you, good friends don't dissolve each other?'

Grace smiled. 'I want to give you something . . . a gift. I know you don't want it now, but once you've got it you'll understand.'

'Grace, please – come on . . .'

She covered his mouth again with her hand. 'You have to be very quiet now, Fish. I promise this won't take long.'

He felt the deadweight on his left cheek stirring to life again. He'd almost forgotten it was there, but now it moved carefully. He could feel tiny prick after tiny prick as something with miniature legs scaled the cliff of his cheek up to the wet rim of his eye.

'I want you to join us as quickly as possible,' Grace said quietly. 'There's a fast way and a slow way. It got me really slowly. It took weeks and weeks before I realized I was one of *them*.'

Oh, Jesus . . . He could feel the creature's tiny limbs exploring, testing the rim of his eyelid. He began to struggle again.

'My first *visitors* had to fight hard to survive in my bloodstream. They had to conquer my body gradually, bit by bit, and, even though I didn't realize it, there was a battle going on inside me. My body did all it could to resist, to fight back. It didn't understand *they* were only there to help. My body was just plain stupid. Just billions of dumb cells that didn't know anything.'

He felt her other hand stroking his cheek gently, wiping away the tears that were streaming down from his aggravated eye.

'The sooner they get into your *head*, the sooner they can explain themselves, and then you'll see for yourself that they're not our enemy – they're our friends.'

He felt a tiny, sharp, tugging sensation. He felt the small creature lifting his eyelid, pulling it out just a fraction, a few millimetres, then squeezing itself into the gap.

'And the quickest way to get to you, Fish, I'm so sorry, is this way. It's through your eye.'

He screamed against her hand and she pushed down harder to muffle the sound.

He felt the creature working its way downwards,

burrowing around his eyeball. At first it felt like a large bit of grit, or a dislodged contact lens, but as it progressed it felt bigger and bigger, like a jagged shard of flint, scraping and wriggling to get behind his eye.

Suddenly, he felt a sharp, searing pain, like a white-hot stiletto blade plunged deep into his ocular cavity, deep into the tender cluster of nerves leading to his brain.

He lurched in his sleeping bag, legs kicking out and drumming against the floor of the truck as he fought against the agony. Grace was saying something, but he wasn't listening. He was far too busy experiencing the most excruciating pain he'd ever encountered in his life.

'That pain, Fish, it's just a crawler – just like a little taxi – but he's carrying very important passengers. I want you to listen to them.'

Blinding agony.

CHAPTER 46

Do you hear?

The impossible discomfort, the searing agony was a distant memory now. Someone else's memory, someone else's problem. Fish was in a different place now. Somewhere calm, dark and quiet, and mercifully free of pain.

Do you hear?

He had no idea how he felt. There were no words to describe it. 'Disembodied' was a close one. But then disembodied implied a sense of nothingness, no substance, like being some disconnected ethereal spirit. He didn't feel like that. On the contrary, he felt connected to everything. To something vast, but he wasn't quite sure what it was yet.

Do you hear?

The voice that had been repeatedly, patiently, asking that question sounded genderless. He was vaguely aware that it didn't actually sound like anything. That he wasn't hearing a sound so much as sensing the question in another way.

'I hear you,' he replied.

That is good.

The voice sounded reasonable. Like someone he could talk to, get some answers from.

'Who are you?'

What you hear is *thought*. Who we/I are/is ......

The next word became a taste on his tongue. The nearest comparison he could come up with was that it reminded him of the taste of Bovril. Fish understood the 'name' had become a flavour, because using a word he didn't understand would have been pointless. It was a form of synaesthesia: the brain reinterpreting stimuli from other senses, like bats 'seeing' sound.

'You're the virus, aren't you?'

A collective representative entity. Yes.

'In my mind?'

I/We am/are a supercluster – that word came with the Bovril taste on his tongue again – *connected with your linguistic processing. Conscious reasoning.*

'I'm infected now?'

No answer. Perhaps that was too dumb a question. He had another one to which he had to know the answer.

'Am I going to die? Am I going to be dissolved ... turned into mush?'

No harm to you. We/I wish to help.

'Well then get out of me!'

There was no answer to that either.

Autonomous supercluster structure 'Fish' – his name was accompanied by the sudden taste of sardines on his tongue, a *literal* interpretation of his nickname. That taste quickly changed to something else, something sugary-sweet, as if the virus were, just like him, learning a new language – *is unaffected at this stage.*

'Am I still alive? Am I still human?'

Unchanged. Yes. Framework is unaltered.

'Why have you left me unaltered? Not that I *want* to be altered. I just—'

Awaiting instructions from supercluster-designate-representative.

Another flavour arrived on his tongue, something indescribable that had a hint of vanilla to it. He instinctively, somehow, knew the flavour meant *Grace*.

This morning everyone had woken and rallied early with a palpable sense of excitement mixed with foreboding. Today was the day that was going to end with them all knowing whether this nightmare was finally over . . . or whether they were going to have to dig deep, find a new home and start again on the long-term business of survival.

Naga was keen for them to get going. There were granola energy bars and energy drinks in the store. They all had one of each, clambered aboard the trucks and set off.

The engine of the lead truck growled to life, and those who were walking wearily shouldered their bags and backpacks, ready to resume what would hopefully be the final day of their journey.

. . . [We don't have much time left, Grace.] She felt Jerry squeeze her hand as they trudged in silence. [If rescue is waiting for us, we will all be tested and discovered and destroyed. Which is why we have to act soon. Now.]

{Jerry, this is more important than us.} She turned

wordlessly to look at the children walking behind them. {There's a much greater community out there. It's all of us. Billions of lives. Humans and so much more.}

[I know.]

{I was called to a . . . I suppose you'd call it a 'conference' or something. We discussed the next stage of their plan.}

[What is their plan, Grace?]

She sensed Jerry's exasperation. {They haven't told you?}

[Only that they want what's best for us. My connection to the larger community has been limited. They seem to trust you more than me.]

{Or perhaps they feel sorry for what happened to me? The point is that there are stages to the plan. I don't know what the next stage is, but I do know *they* are really worried about the number of people who have not been *included*.}

[*Infected.*]

Grace hated that word. It sounded harmful. It sounded malicious. {*Invited.*}

[There can't be that many. Virtually everyone died in the first stage.]

{They have been gathering information. Just bits and pieces of knowledge about how many remain out there. That radio message, for example, they need to know how many are left and whether they might be a threat to us.}

Jerry looked at her suspiciously. [You're planning something?]

{I sent a friend with a message for them.}

She imagined by now Claudia would have made her

way, escorted by guide-clusters through the network of tributaries, to where the main concentration of superclusters had converged. If *they* had something that resembled Congress, that was it.

Her message would have been heard by now, and they would understand what she was hoping to achieve.

[What was the message?]

{I think there's a way I can reach out to the remainders.}

[What do you mean by 'reach out'?]

{I mean talk with them.}

[They won't want to talk. They'll want to destroy you.]

Grace knew that all too well. She didn't need Jerry to remind her how quickly rational thought could give way to knee-jerk panic.

[As soon as they find out what you are, you know they'll destroy you? Why do we need to talk to them anyway? Their days are numbered. They're obsolete.]

{We need to find out if they're a threat to us.}

[How would they be a threat?]

{If they have weapons? What if they're working on some sort of 'cure'? That radio message . . . it means enough of them survived to manage a rescue. It means they're organized. It means they're dangerous. You heard the message too. Isn't that why you were heading down here, to learn more?}

[No.] Jerry looked at her. [We knew the message would draw the remainders out into the open.]

{Make them easier to attack?}

[Of course.]

She sensed Jerry didn't like how his reply made him sound.

[We just want to help. You can't explain it to them, that this is for their benefit. You have to just get on and do it.]

{I think we have different goals, then.}

[Grace, we should absorb everyone right now. Before we encounter any more people. Merge our clusters, produce child fabrications as bait and generate a large number of creepers . . .]

He was talking about the larger crustaceans. They called them [. . . . . .] The name was a taste that vaguely reminded her of peppermint. The nearest translation of the meaning of that taste was *gatherers*.

[This road is where others have already come, and more will. We could intercept everyone right here. It's a perfect opportunity.]

There was some sense in what Jerry was suggesting. Whatever small bands of people were left alive and yet to travel down to Southampton were likely to come this way. But how many had already passed through?

And, far more importantly, how many people had come to rescue them? How many ships? From which countries?

How many *remainders* were left out there?

That was the danger to them.

Humanity living, planning, organizing . . . preparing. Fighting back like an immune system.

She had to stop them.

CHAPTER 47

Their slow, plodding journey by truck came to final full stop just after midday. As their short convoy passed a place called Eastleigh, the M3 branched off, leaving them on a double-lane A-road heading into Southampton city centre. Shortly after, they encountered the tail end of a far more recent traffic jam – a mixture of trucks and vans, and in one case a touring coach, all of them quite clearly abandoned over the last few days. Their tyres were not sagging and cracking or completely flat; there were no mini-jungles of long grass and nettles growing beneath them.

There was a hastily written sign propped up in the rear window of the SUV in front of them.

Responding to US rescue. Have walked from here. Roads blocked from this point on!

Naga called everyone out of the two trucks and they assembled together in the space between them.

She was smiling. Leon noticed a lot of them were, including Freya.

'So there you go, ladies and gents. It's definitely not just us making the trek. There are others too!'

A cheer went up.

'It doesn't necessarily mean there's a rescue party waiting for us,' said one of Royce's men.

'Well, actually, I think it probably does, Osman,' Naga

countered. 'Otherwise whoever parked up those vehicles ahead of us would have come back for them and they'd have gone elsewhere.'

'Or there'd be a sign,' added Freya. '*No rescue, folks. Just a big waste of time.*'

Osman was going to say something else, but Royce talked over him. 'I agree with her.' He nodded at Naga. 'People wouldn't have dumped their vehicles unless there was a good reason. What worries me, though,' he added, 'is that there could be thousands ahead of us. We might have to fight our way on to those ships.'

Naga tutted. 'It's not some cretinous Jason Statham movie, Royce. We're not going in guns blazing. I'm sure there'll be UN troops. I'm sure there'll be some kind of registration and processing, and probably a fair bit of queueing.'

'Naga,' interrupted Freya. 'Last night Leon suggested we scout ahead, before we commit?'

Leon nodded. 'We should see what the situation is before we just leave our trucks and supplies behind.'

'Yes I suppose so, but I don't know.' Naga wrinkled her nose. 'We're so-o-o close now, I'm thinking we might as well just walk the last bit.'

'We don't know what's happening in Southampton yet,' said Leon. 'We should at least get a look first.'

'Leon's right!' said Grace. She shrugged her shoulders as if that alone made her point. 'We should be careful.'

Naga gave that a moment's thought and then finally nodded. 'All right, Leon. Just go and take a quick look, then come back and let us know what the situation is. I suggest the rest of us go through what supplies and personals we've got left in the trucks and work out what we're taking and what we're leaving behind.' She clapped her hands together. 'Come along – off your bums, everyone!'

The meeting broke up and Leon headed for the rear of the leading truck where his rucksack was stashed inside along with dozens of others. He climbed up, rummaged through them until he found his, then dropped back down on to the road.

'I'm coming.'

Leon turned to see Freya, Grace standing beside her.

'Uh . . . maybe it's best you just stay here, Grace.'

'I'm coming,' she said firmly.

Freya laughed at her firmness and looked at Leon. 'You going to argue with her? I've already tried.'

'Grace, I'll be an hour or two, tops. It's gonna be OK.'

'I'm coming.' She turned to look at Freya. 'And you are too.'

'Huh?' Freya looked surprised. 'I am?'

'Yes. The three of us.'

Leon shook his head impatiently. 'No, come on, Grace. Don't be silly.'

'I'm NOT being silly!' she snapped at him. 'The three of us are going together! That's final.'

'I don't know how far we have to go. And Freya's legs . . .'

Freya shrugged. 'I'm not that bad. I could actually do with stretching them a bit.'

'See?' added Grace. 'She's perfectly fine.'

336

'Oh for . . .' He rolled his eyes. 'OK.'

'And Fish. He's coming with us too.'

'Jeez, Grace, who suddenly put you in charge of things?'

'Fish,' she said again. 'Two girls – we need two boys . . . to protect us.'

'You don't need protecting – you need gagging,' said Freya.

Leon looked across at Fish, who was looking even more vacant than usual, staring bleary-eyed at the commotion of backpacks being passed around him. Leon guessed his protest-camping outside last night had left him sleepless and exhausted. All the same, if another guy were needed, he'd rather have Fish than that surly-faced Royce.

'All right. What about your new boyfriend, Jerry? I suppose he's coming along too?'

'He's *not* my boyfriend,' she replied. 'And no . . . he's staying right here.'

Leon turned to Freya and she spread her hands with a *What're you gonna do?* look on her face. *Lovers' tiff?*

'I do believe The Grace hath commanded,' said Freya.

'Right.' Leon swung the strap of his backpack over one shoulder. 'I better go let Fish know he's coming along and see if Naga will let us grab a couple of guns.'

He headed across the road to talk to her.

Freya leaned against the back of the truck and called to Denise. 'My backpack . . . just there. That one, the red one. Can you toss it over?' Denise pulled it from the pile and slid it along the floor of the truck. 'Thanks.' Freya picked it up and shrugged the straps on to her narrow shoulders, then grabbed her walking stick, leaning against the tailgate. 'You seem really fired up this morning, Grace.'

'I'm excited.' She smiled. 'We're finally going home.' She cocked her head at Freya. 'How are you feeling?'

'Good.' Freya grinned. 'Actually *really* good.' She patted her left hip. 'Dr Hahn gave me a stash of some mega painkillers and it seems like they've been doing the job, since . . .' She let the rest of her sentence go. Change of subject. She shot a look at Jerry, who seemed to be holding court with the children he'd come with. 'You two lovebirds fallen out or something?'

Grace shook her head. 'Nope.'

'Only I noticed a lot of hand-holding the last couple of days and I couldn't help thinking—'

'He's *not* my boyfriend, all right?'

'Fine.' She raised a hand in surrender.

'Yes, that's not a bad idea, Leon. Take a couple of guns to be safe,' said Naga. 'See Royce. He'll sort you out.'

'Thanks.'

Naga reached into the open passenger-side door of the truck and pulled down an unfolded map from the passenger seat. She opened it up, kneeled on the tarmac and spread it out. Leon got down beside her.

'So I'm guessing if there's a big processing camp or something like that, it'll be over here where the quays are. I think that's where the cruise ships used to dock, so maybe they'll be using the buildings there to process passengers coming aboard.'

'Right.'

Naga guess-measured the distance across the map with her thumb. 'What do you think? About six or seven kilometres?'

Leon frowned. 'What's that in miles?'

'Oh, you Yanks and your imperial. That's about half in miles. Say four miles. So, four miles there, just look OK, don't do anything else, then come back, all right?'

'Yup.'

'You taking Royce or any of the knights with you?'

'Taking Fish.'

'Really?' She shrugged. 'He's not going to be much protection.'

'He's better company. Anyway, we're scouting, not fighting.'

'What about virals? Do you want to take a fire extinguisher? Just in case there are any lurking around?'

'Sure.' The damned things were heavy, but he could take it in turns with Fish to carry it on his back.

Naga looked at him. She smiled and patted his hand. 'I've got a good feeling about this. I'm so glad you two turned up at the castle.'

'You'd have come across someone else heading down to Southampton, eventually,' said Leon.

'I suppose so.'

She looked down at the map. 'I just hope we're not the last ones to arrive, like Royce said. That would be totally rubbish, wouldn't it? *Sorry ladies and gents, no room left. Try again next year!*'

Leon nodded. 'That would suck.'

'Anyway, don't dawdle. Hike there, take a look and hurry back.'

'OK.'

'I guess we'll see you in two or three hours. Be careful, Leon.'

'Will do.'

CHAPTER 48

Leon led the way, surprised at how energized he felt, how eager to complete the last few miles of their eventful journey. Before the virus came, he guessed, the entire journey would have taken just a few hours on a good traffic day.

It had taken him and Freya seven months.

The road into the city centre looked like so many others: Terraced houses fronted by small gardens that had grown tall and wild. Road tarmac cracked from the big freeze of the last two winters. Here and there the mouldering humps of uncollected dead leaves piled in the blown-open doorways of newsagents and off-licences.

And, just like every other dead town these days, it was no longer a horror show of rotting corpses and tendrils of slime. That time was long gone, leaving behind mere mummified parcels of bone, cloth and hair. And buildings patiently accepting their gradual dereliction as a matter of course: Nature's scruffy piecemeal conquest of what had always been hers.

He realized he was pulling ahead of the others and stopped and waited for them to catch up. Freya's walk was looking easier than usual. She was dragging her left foot slightly, but it seemed the action was less uncomfortable today. She looked better than she had for quite some time.

'How're you doing?'

'Surprisingly well,' Freya replied. 'To be fair, I've been sitting on my butt for a week.'

She looped a hand through his offered arm and they continued walking down the abandoned road. 'I was actually expecting to see more life than this,' she said. 'You know, more general activity.'

'There's been *recent* activity. Look.' He pointed at drag marks in the road and a chalkboard braced against a chair on the pavement. *Head towards quays. It's safe. No recent signs of virals*, was scrawled on it. In the corner was yesterday's date.

Freya nodded. 'I was hoping it would be like the approach to a festival or something. Lots of stewards pointing us in the right direction: this way to whatever, that way for toilets – that kind of thing.'

'And hot-dog vendors on the pavement?'

She smiled. 'Yes, please.'

Leon looked around. 'You'd think we'd hear something, though. A public-address system or something.'

'I know. It's pretty unimpress—' Freya dug her fingers into his forearm suddenly. 'Oh, shit!'

'What?'

'You hear that?'

Leon cocked his head. Nothing but the gentle stirring of the small stunted trees along the pavement.

'A hissing. Listen!'

He tried again, then heard it, very faintly. *Tish-tish-tish-tish,* like a small dog panting frantically.

Freya stopped walking and tugged Leon to a halt. She glanced around the deserted road at the terraced houses, some with kicked-open doors that led into dimly lit interiors; at the abandoned cars and vans on the pavement, some of them hidden up to their headlights by tall tufts of nettles and grass.

A hundred different places for those snarks to hide and wait.

'You thinking what I'm thinking?' she whispered.

Fish was getting used to the strange transition from Inside world to Outside world. It only took the desire: a simple thought expressed clearly, and it seemed to happen. Far less trouble than getting up from an armchair, opening the back door and stepping into the garden.

I wish to be in . . . and so it was.

I wish to be out . . . and so it was.

He experienced the peculiar transition of his 'consciousness' as being carried from one place to another, piggy-back style, by some friendly servant who never grumbled at the task.

He was dimly aware that in the way time was measured in the outside world, it was just last night that Grace had overpowered him and thrust that horrific little invader into his eye. But *within*, in this womblike existence, it felt like days, weeks even. Apart from those first few agonizing moments, the memories of which were quickly fading. Since then, it hadn't been a *frightening* experience. Bewildering, perhaps, at first. But not frightening.

For the first few 'weeks' they had kept him inside. In the dark, as if in a dungeon. But not alone. *They* had been there with him, answering his questions, assuring him they meant no harm. Grace had come to visit him, to let him know this wasn't forever.

Then the light had been switched on and he'd found himself in his bedsit back in Morecombe. There was his desk, his MacBook and his HP laptop, the grimy sash window with its view across grass-tufted dunes, the gravel and silt beach, the cold grey sea and the decrepit-looking Morecombe pier in the distance. And Grace, sitting cross-legged on his unmade bed. She'd told him she'd read all his memories like a book and made this 'scene' so that when she finally turned the light on, he'd feel a little less freaked out by everything.

Fish had told her. He got it immediately. He understood what this was. 'It's like the internet. Like virtual reality.'

'I guess so. I never thought about it that way.'

'A biochemical version,' he'd added, wandering over to his desk, running his fingers across the clacking keys of his keyboard. 'More real than anything digital.'

'Yes. Give it a little more time, Fish, and you'll soon learn how to move beyond your own memories.'

She'd told him how his trillion-cell body was like a little world; even just his billion-cell mind was a continent he could explore. But, beyond that, the bodies and minds of countless others were an infinite universe. To step out of this into the 'real' world was to step into a much smaller, more limited, place of possibilities.

Fish had adapted quickly, accepted and embraced his new reality.

It's like virtual reality but way . . . way . . . way . . . better.

By the time the first light of dawn had risen and everyone was stirring on the floor of the camping shop, Fish had been ready, like Grace, to travel between inner-space and outer-space. Only it was outside that now felt insubstantial and *virtual*.

He was walking beside Grace. A dozen steps ahead of them were two people for whom he felt more affection than he had for anyone in his old life.

I was such a loner. So lonely back then.

He watched Leon and Freya walking at Freya's pace, her arm linked through his, their heads close together as they talked in hushed tones, and he wondered why the hell they insisted on remaining just friends. They seemed to be like boyfriend and girlfriend in all ways but one.

Not that he had a great deal of experience in that department.

'I hope you forgive me now,' said Grace.

His thoughts evaporated. 'I do.' He smiled at her. 'You were right. It's incredible.'

'Fish . . . I wanted you to come with me because there's something important we need to do.'

'What?'

'I need to talk with whoever's in charge of the human remainders.'

'Talk?'

'They don't know what you and I know. They've just seen the horrible things, the early stages when the virus acted more simply, more brutally. They're scared. Like we were once.'

'We're not just scouting ahead, then?'

'No.' Grace shook her head firmly. 'We're not going back.'

Fish shook his head. 'Yeah, but you said *talk*? If they test you, or me . . . I mean . . . the second they figure out we're virals, they'll kill us.'

'If I can explain to them that the virus can talk, can reason, can—'

'They'll burn you the second they find you out.'

'We have to try,' she replied calmly.

Up ahead Freya and Leon had stopped suddenly. Both of them frozen still. Grace and Fish drew up beside them.

''Sup?' said Fish.

Leon was grimacing, listening for something.

'Leon?' whispered Grace.

'Shhhh!' Leon held out a finger. 'You hear it?'

She couldn't hear anything. Then all of a sudden a faint whispering *swish-swish-swish* that was gradually getting louder. The sound was changing as it increased in volume, changing from the *swish* of a horse's tail, to a *thud* . . .

Then, suddenly, it burst from soft to loud, became deafening: a *thwup-thwup-thwup* from above. They all looked up at the cloudy sky to see a helicopter swooping low over the rooftops across their road and beyond those on the far side.

346

Leon instinctively shoved his arms up into the air and waved them desperately.

'Down here! We're down here!' he bellowed, as if they could hear him.

The helicopter veered off its tangent and slowly began to swing back around towards them.

'They've seen us!' shouted Leon. 'They've SEEN US!'

Freya let go of his arm and balled her hand into a fist and punched the air. 'Frikkin yes!'

Grace looked pointedly at Fish. *We have to act as though we're not infected for now.*

She jumped up and down excitedly and waved her hands like her brother. Fish understood and followed her lead.

The helicopter had circled back and was now hovering above them, the downdraft from its rotors pounding them hard and stirring all the dead leaves and loose detritus up into an excited cyclone.

But it remained where it was. Not descending, just hovering. Marking the spot.

Then finally over the roar of the helicopter's engine and rotors they heard something else. They turned to see an army truck pull up thirty metres away and a dozen soldiers in white biohazard suits spill out of the back, guns raised, shouldered and aimed squarely at them. The helicopter quickly moved off, the deafening noise beginning to lessen as it tilted and sped away across the rooftops.

A voice came from behind the Perspex visor of the nearest soldier, but it was lost in the noise of the receding helicopter. From the gestures he was making, it was clear that he wanted them to put their hands on their heads and kneel down.

Freya, completely unintimidated by the dozen gun barrels aimed her way, whooped with unrestrained joy. 'Yes! We're saved!'

The gestures again, more exaggerated, more insistent.

She held her free hand out in a gesture of submission, then braced herself against her walking stick as she struggled down into an uncomfortable kneel. The others followed her lead.

'So –' she huffed from the effort – 'what the hell took you guys so long?'

CHAPTER 49

Naga had everyone ready to move for when Leon and the others got back. They all had their backpack or shoulder bag on or beside them on the ground, each one loaded with a couple of litres of water and several tins of food.

There was still a fair amount of their stuff sitting in the backs of the trucks. It felt foolishly reckless just leaving it all behind, but if help was waiting just a few miles away, then it didn't seem to matter any more.

And Leon was almost certainly coming back with good news. She could have sworn she'd heard the chopping sound of a distant helicopter coming from somewhere over the city.

The mood among them had lifted, a stark contrast to the sombre and sullen collective that had set off from the smouldering ruins of the castle. There were smiles and laughter for the first time in what seemed like ages. Danielle notably amongst them, for once laughing instead of griping about something or other. She watched some of the former knights – Moss, Crouchman, Hester – sitting on their helmets and playing cards.

Several others were making the most of this downtime to stretch out and rest their aching legs and sore feet. Patrick had taken his trainers and socks off, and Osman was busy checking his old feet for infection, replacing padded blister plasters where needed.

Royce was sitting on the tailgate of one of the trucks rolling a cigarette.

Denise had just finished brushing the tangles out of Rachel's long frizzy hair and was starting to plait it. Naga smiled at that; for the first time in a long time, someone was actually concerned with their appearance.

Naga's gaze finally settled on their new friends, Jerry and his brood of waifs and strays. They were clustered together away from everyone else, beyond the low centre barrier of the road, where there was a little more open tarmac to move around. It looked as if he were organizing a game for them to play while they waited for Leon's return. They were gathered tightly around him, listening intently as he talked.

She was so impressed by Jerry. He was so good with them.

He was what? Sixteen? In the good old days ... *before* ... her only experience of boys that age had been surly-faced little thugs hidden beneath their hoods, only looking up from their iPhones to sneer an acknowledgement at the rest of the world.

She wondered if Jerry would have been like that, but here and now, having been handed such a burden of responsibility, he'd become someone else altogether: a pied piper for orphaned children. Peter Pan with his Lost Boys and Girls.

The children had largely kept to themselves since they'd hooked up several days ago. She didn't blame them. Her group of mostly adults were complete strangers to them.

She saw Jerry spread his arms out wide and the children surged in towards him. Their painfully thin arms wrapped around him, and his around them.

Group hug? Oh God, that's adorable. Naga smiled as she watched them snuggling in tightly, all squirming to get closer, like teenyboppers around a pop star, but without the screaming or cheering. It was a perfectly silent group hug.

Oddly silent.

She cocked her head at the strangeness of it: no giggles or '*awww*'s or even that self-conscious '*mmm*' sound that people feel the need to make alongside a hug. It was decidedly peculiar.

The pressing of bodies together looked more intense now, more purposeful than a display of affection. It was starting to look more like a rugby scrum. She saw someone's pink rucksack drop to the ground amid the forest of scrawny legs. Among the legs she could see the silhouette of one of the youngest ones, a toddler of two or three, being carelessly buffeted and knocked by knobbly knees.

They need to mind the littlies.

'Hey kids!' she called out.

None of them looked her way.

'Jerry!' she called again. 'You've got little ones in the middle getting squished in there!'

Jerry didn't respond either.

She wondered what the hell they were playing at. Maybe it wasn't a group hug after all, but some stupid game. She

351

made her way across to the central barrier and swung a leg over.

'Jerry . . .' she called again. 'You need to watch out for the babies . . .' She pointed at the road beneath their huddle. She caught a glimpse of pale mother-of-pearl shellac and hair-thin legs scuttling across the broken tarmac, around a tuft of weeds towards her.

A viral. One of those miniature ones they hadn't seen in a long while. Then she saw another one, zigzagging quickly across the road. She saw more, one after another, a line of them, like an ant trail, leading back to the squirming mass of children, weaving around and through that copse of skinny legs, emerging from their shadows like freshly hatched spiders from a deep, dark forest.

She was about to yell at them to scatter when her eyes caught other details . . .

. . . an ear dangling from the side of a girl's head, attached by a jelly-like string of flesh.

. . . a small dismembered chubby hand lying on the road, fingers still curling and flexing.

. . . a yellow T-shirt twitching from protuberances beneath, sprouting crimson stains.

Oh my God . . .

And in the middle of the dark forest of legs, she saw the silhouette of a baby sitting on his padded bottom, jawbone slowly swinging like a pendulum and descending into his lap from spittle-thin strings of mucus.

She tried to scream. Not bothering to try forming words, just a shrill bark of noise to warn everyone to run . . . but nothing more than a hoarse wheeze came out.

The mass of children collapsed inwards from the middle. Legs no longer functioning as viable supports for the mass of loosening, jellying tissue sagging inwards under its own weight. The silence was broken by the spatter of organs on to the tarmac and a growing moan coming from those children whose vocal chords were still intact: a deep-pitched mournful sound, like the pitiful lowing of cattle awaiting slaughter.

Naga noticed that the 'ant trail' of crabs scuttling towards her had quickly escalated into a thicker stream. And from the growing slush pile of organs on the ground, even more were emerging.

She felt the sharp sting of one of them sinking a serrated-edge spine into her ankle. Felt another sting as a second leaped for an ambitious hold further up her calf.

She screamed, finding her voice second time around.

'RUN!'

Naga staggered backwards towards the central barrier, bumped into it, lost her balance and toppled over its corrugated-iron lip. She landed heavily on the far side, winded from the backwards tumble.

She turned her head to look back under the rusting barrier, ignoring the scratches and scrapes across her face from the gravel. She saw, from low down, from her right-next-to-the-ground perspective, what appeared to be a tidal wave of glinting, wire-thin limbs, sharp barbs and ragged surgical pincers racing towards her.

A second later they were upon her.

CHAPTER 50

'Why won't you guys say something?' Freya looked from one masked face to the next. The soldiers were all wearing thick, white biohazard suits with hoods that appeared to have their dark semi-opaque eyeholes integrated into them. As seamless as possible. Airtight. All she could see of their faces was the occasional glint from their eyes.

'Say something! You can't just stare at us!'

Once again they were in another truck. This time they were sharing it with a dozen faceless armed figures. There were no patches or markings on the biohazard suits. No indication that they were army or not. No indication that they were even American.

Leon looked across the space at Grace. She gazed back at him calmly. He wasn't sure if that was relief on her face or resignation. Beside her, Fish looked far less comfortable about things. One of his legs jiggled, heel tapping the floor.

He imagined Fish was thinking that these people might be Russians or something. That they were destined for some grisly concentration camp. Leon knew that's how Fish's mind worked.

'Jesus, do you guys even speak English?' shouted Freya.

Leon placed a hand on her arm to calm her. 'It's OK. We're safe now whether they speak English or Russian or Martian.'

He leaned forward to the soldier sitting opposite him. It might have been the one who'd gestured for them to kneel and put their hands behind their heads, but since none of them wore any markings at all, he couldn't tell.

'There are others with us,' Leon said loudly. 'About a hundred and twenty.' He nodded out of the back of the truck. 'Back where we came from. Where the traffic blockage is.'

The head turned briefly to look the way he was pointing, then turned back to face him.

Leon tried a different tack. 'There've been others like us, right?' he persisted. 'Others arriving on foot here? Recently?'

No response.

'We have to go back for our friends. At least let them know what's going on!'

Still nothing.

He sat back, exasperated. 'I don't think they understand English,' he said to Freya.

'So not American, then,' she added. 'OK.'

'Clearly.' He settled back and looked out. Behind them a dirty and deserted city centre was beginning to show signs of life. They passed a patrol of troops at the roadside, all white biohazard suits and assault rifles. Several of them were dragging a large cylinder on wheels, and another was holding a hose and liberally spraying a blue-tinted liquid over everything, like a gardener watering his lawn.

Another truck rolled past them, heading back the way they'd come. Leon wondered if word had been passed on and it was on its way to get the others.

Their truck slowed right down to a crawl and vibrated as it ran over something. Leon saw a metal grid like a cattle grid had been laid out across the road. He saw chain fencing, more soldiers in biohazard suits, yellow ones this time, and then, as the truck swung round and came to a halt . . . people.

Civilians. Hundreds. Possibly even thousands . . . all milling around between rows of tents and Portakabins.

The soldiers in the truck spilled out of the back, army-issue boots smacking down hard on quayside concrete. One of them beckoned for Leon and the others to follow them.

Leon looked around as soon as he was out and down. They were standing in the middle of a vast stretch of Southampton quays. Freight-loading cranes towered over the expanse like giants, but casting a looming shadow over them and across the rows of tents, cabins and the perimeter mesh fencing was an enormous aircraft carrier.

Leon scanned the vast blue, grey and white stripes of paint along its hull for an indication of whether it was American or not. He saw an '03' painted in multistorey white block lettering, and craning his neck stiffly to look beyond the lip of the launch deck he saw the very top of the control tower, topped with aerials and radar dishes and a flag fluttering in the offshore breeze.

Red with yellow stars.

'It's Chinese,' he said.

'Ah,' replied Freya, 'well, that explains the lack of stimulating conversation.'

Grace and Fish joined them, looking around at their surroundings.

'So many people,' Grace said, looking at the civilians.

'Hey! You!'

They turned at the voice to see a yellow suit approaching them, assault rifle slung over one arm, clipboard tucked under the other. At least this one had a full Perspex visor. Leon could see a face behind the reflective plate.

'You folks need to come with me.'

Freya looked at him. 'You don't seem to be Chinese.'

'United States Navy, ma'am,' he replied. 'Now, will you folks please follow me?'

CHAPTER 51

Tom Friedmann signed the form as best he could, wearing his thick, black neoprene gloves. He handed the clipboard back to the lieutenant. Any fool could have forged that nondescript scrawl and authorized the resource allocations on the sheet.

'Thank you, sir.'

Tom nodded and watched him jog back down the mile-long quayside towards the far end of this vast fenced encampment where the Pacific Nations Alliance ships were all birthed. The largest of them, the Chinese aircraft carrier *Jiangsu*, loomed over Southampton like a giant grey, white and blue multistorey car park.

Down *their* end of the quayside, the US presence was far less impressive. Despite two false starts and very nearly a complete cancellation, Trent had allowed Tom to take only a couple of destroyers and seven cargo ships. One of the destroyers and five of the cargo ships were moored up in Calais right now, running a similar rescue operation for mainland Europeans. That gave him just under two hundred navy personnel, about fifty medically trained civilian volunteers and one platoon of marines.

The rest of the navy and military boots were back in Cuba, busy enforcing Trent's presidency.

Tom stepped out of the tent, his onshore 'office', and

into the tepid, pallid daylight. He looked up at the scudding clouds and recalled one of the many times he and his ex-wife had flippantly played the *my country's better than yours* game. She frequently used to win with the *well, at least we're not all packing firearms like the A-Team* argument. However, he felt he was close to a draw with *the weather's always so goddamn insipid and grey*.

Once again he scanned this end of the camp for his children's faces. He wondered if he'd even recognize them now. It had been three years since he'd last seen them. Grace had been eleven. She'd be fourteen now and Leon nearly nineteen.

If they were still alive.

He shut that down quickly. *We don't go there. They're alive. We frikkin well know it, don't we, Staff Sergeant Friedmann?*

The 'processing camp' was divided in two: a coil of barbed wire ran down the middle, cutting it neatly in half. On one side, US marines patrolled; on the other, Chinese, New Zealand and Australian troops took turns.

Tom was irritated by the lack of trust between them. They should have been pooling resources, working together to feed and process the Brits who'd turned up here. But the Pacific Nations Alliance now viewed what remained of the US with extreme caution. The detonation of a tactical nuclear warhead thirty miles out to sea off the coast of Havana hadn't been missed over there. They viewed the hostile takeover of Cuba as an illegal act, an act of terrorism, and the use of a nuke as a warning sign that the only other surviving nation on Planet Earth was dangerously ready to throw its weight around.

The PNA, frankly, wanted to put a safe distance between themselves and Trent's 'America Version 2.0'. And Tom really couldn't blame them for that. But here, far away from that idiot, they should be coordinating more.

This should be *one* processing camp. Instead, here was this long barrier of spiralling razor wire, a symbol of distrust because that hothead had wanted to make his point with a fifty kiloton warhead.

They needed to be sharing their limited resources. They should have been working together to decide which tested and properly evaluated evacuees were going in which ship to which nation.

Mistrust was hampering their efforts.

Both groups had arrived here two weeks ago. The PNA ships had arrived several days ahead of them, and the quayside had already been crowded with nearly a thousand people waiting for rescue. All of them fast running out of food and water. The first order of business had been constructing the perimeter, setting up the mesh fences, the watchtowers. He'd argued for one compound, but the PNA fleet led by the *Jiangsu*'s captain, Xien, had insisted on setting up the border.

Tom had spent the last week in negotiations with his PNA opposite numbers – Captain Xien from the Chinese navy and Admiral Kemp from the Australian navy – discussing how the Brits were going to be tested and sorted. The PNA, more specifically, the Chinese, had been doing some useful groundwork on testing, while the US had been playing gunboat politics. It seemed they knew far more about this pathogen than anyone else. They had a test process they were prepared to share with the Americans: a blood test that checked for elevated levels of oestrogen and histamine, but which also mixed a small amount of salt with the blood. There was an active ingredient that responded to coagulation and turned the sample blue-ish. It wasn't perfect. The blue was dark; you needed to hold it up to a strong light to spot the colour change. But it was a damn sight more helpful than anything Tom's side had come up with.

Trent's parting piece of wisdom had been, 'If one of those Brits so much as sneezes, shoot 'em dead.'

Sharing the testing technique had been the easy part of the negotiations. The more difficult part had been discussing how they were going to divide up those that had been passed as clean. There was a temptation on both sides to cherry-pick the most useful: engineers, mechanics, doctors, dentists, and so on.

They'd managed to agree on a 'passport' design, however. It was a simple red credit-card-sized document, handed to those whose blood didn't turn blue. A digital photo and name. The Chinese carrier had a reprographics room, and their printing machines were running the passports off right now. The most important part of these hastily designed documents would be the space set aside for two further photos to be trimmed and stuck in: pictures of *two* distinguishing marks.

Tom knew the virus could make bugs. They'd seen images. This pathogen could make creatures. There was a microbiologist among the US personnel who didn't know how to categorize this thing. He didn't know which branch of microbiology expertise they could file it under: bacteriology, mycology, protozoology, phycology, parasitology, virology . . .

Out of exasperation he'd even resorted to using a line from *Star Trek*: 'This isn't life as we know it.'

It can make things.

Tom had seen with his own eyes the virus grow tendrils, like mould-growth, reaching out across the ground, spreading from the mush that had been a human body. He knew – they all knew – that it could do that, but from conversations with the Brits in the holding pen, waiting for the testing to start, they'd learned about the bigger creatures. Worse than that, the *copies*. Some of them had mentioned the virus attempting to produce a range of lookalike animals: dogs, cats, rabbits, deer. He'd asked if it were possible that what they'd actually witnessed were just infected animals that had somehow been partially liquefied, absorbed – whatever the damned correct term was – but had managed to survive. The interviewees had all seemed quite certain they were viral creations, mostly bad copies, yet lately *almost* convincing.

They'd learned about a root network. Just like those hairline tendrils but on a much bigger scale. Like tree roots, but thicker. Apparently this damned thing was linked up like a telephone network.

And then, the most unsettling of all these conversations, were the people who'd claimed that this thing had begun to mimic humans. At first Tom suspected he was hearing from the crazy few, the sort of idiots who saw a face in a banana and claimed it as a miracle from God. Survival paranoia. Fear and ignorance combined to create mythology. The very same recipe that produced barbaric 'treatments' and 'exorcisms' in West Africa, that once produced ridiculous headlines about the AIDS epidemic during the eighties.

But he'd heard the same crazy thing enough times. And if he could accept the virus was having a go at dogs and cats . . . then why not humans?

Photographs of distinguishing marks on the passports were agreed on both sides of the table to be the most important inclusion. Birthmarks, scars or tattoos. At least two. The Chinese had pushed for three, Tom had pushed for one, arguing that if some poor child was too young to have fallen off a bike or a skateboard, or get marked up with body art, did they really deserve to be left behind?

Two was the compromise.

The hardest of the negotiations had been to determine how they were going to process the passport-holders. Trent had given Tom a checklist for potential candidates: a scoring system taking into account health, skills, age, *race and political leaning for Chrissakes*. Tom had ditched Trent's memo as soon as they'd set sail. But healthy and young – or at least not too old – those were the criteria upon which he and Captain Xien had agreed.

Tom surveyed the camp. The holding pen was now

crammed with several thousand people yet to be tested. They had been held in there for over a week, and their relief and gratitude was turning into something else.

We need to get moving before we lose control of this.

In front of the pen, the testing tents had been set up, several dozen of them on their side of the camp divide, and many more on the other. Tom was pushing to start testing; Xien wanted to hold out for a while longer. Evacuees were arriving every day. The PNA had space for far more people than Tom's small flotilla did.

When they'd arrived, there'd already been just under a thousand waiting for them. The supplies they'd brought with them (if any) had run out and they'd been foraging from supermarkets and warehouses in the area. Over the last week that number had swollen to about six thousand. It seemed as though it was tailing off now.

On the US side of the razor wire, they had space for about nine hundred evacuees on the three ships. Xien and his translator had so far been coy about revealing how many they had space for, but talking to a more relaxed Australian navy officer, he'd discovered that they were looking to take on no more than two and a half thousand.

Between both fleets, they were going to be able to rescue only half the people gathered here. Which was news best kept to themselves.

He looked at the long holding pen and the people crammed inside, noses and fingers pushed through the wire, calling out to the marines standing guard in their yellow biohazard suits.

The cavalry's arrived, folks! But only for some of you.

Tom decided to take another tour around the camp, to check on the set-up of the last few testing tents and the wire fence 'corridors': one leading those who'd be given passports to another sorting area, and another leading the rest out of the perimeter of the camp to fend for themselves.

Half of you will be saved . . . The rest? God help you.

When their nine hundred were aboard, it was going to be time to set sail, leaving the rest of these poor bastards behind. That, he knew, was going to be most dangerous part of the operation. The moment the 'left behinds' figured out the ships were getting ready to depart, there was going to be bloody chaos.

It was going to turn ugly.

Which is why he wished there was a little more openness and cooperation going on. If Xien's fleet started packing up before they were done, Tom's marines were going to have to hold the line until they were ready to cast off.

He shook his head. This would have been a lot easier if Trent hadn't been such an asshole.

Tom muttered under his breath as he scanned the pen yet again for Jennifer and the kids, convinced they were in there somewhere. He'd given them the edge; they'd escaped London before the lockdown. Jenny's parents' home was the perfect rural hideaway . . . and he recalled her father had a shotgun too.

They made it. They survived.

He scanned the faces beyond the wire systematically,

his eyes darting from face to desperate, hopeful face, hoping to see Leon and Grace.

They're here. They HAVE to be here.

Tomorrow the testing process would begin. They had seven tents. Three examination booths per tent, so batches of about twenty evacuees at a time. The PNA would probably process twice that number. Altogether sixty people at a time. Allowing for half an hour per batch for blood testing, photographing distinguishing marks and filling in the passports, they'd be through the people in this pen in about two days.

Come on, Leon. Come on, Grace.

Tom was going to spend all day tomorrow on the pen gate as they let each group through. Watching the candidates like a hawk, theirs and the PNA's.

And, if need be, he was going to be standing there all through the night.

And the next day.

Because he knew . . . he just knew

CHAPTER 52

What the hell have we gone and done?

They were stuck in a wire cage the size of a couple of football pitches. Along each of the four sides soldiers in yellow and white hazard suits were standing guard. At all four corners, towers had been improvised, using freight-loaders, their crane arms fully raised. On top of each one a wooden pallet served as a platform and two soldiers manned a sweeping floodlight.

Leon watched a solitary figure in yellow slowly stalking the far end, clipboard under one arm and just a metre or so back from the mesh.

He wasn't sure what was concerning him more: the menacing, faceless guards, or the cram of humanity sharing their cage. He had no idea how to judge numbers. There were easily thousands in here, though. The concrete ground was occupied from one side to the other with people standing or sitting, with bivouacs made from coats and jackets. The pen reeked of human faeces. The guards had provided basic latrines in one corner of the pen, but there was no getting away from the smell.

The sky was beginning to darken now and the glare coming from the floodlights was more noticeable.

'Any sign of the others yet?' called Freya.

He turned to her. Leon had managed to find a vacant

space along the mesh that gave him a view of that cattle grid and the entrance to the camp. Freya was sitting on the ground a metre back. 'No.'

Leon had been fully expecting them to turn up here at some point today. It's not like they were far away, and he was sure Naga would have sent someone else in to see what had happened to them. The afternoon had drifted by and was now waning.

'Maybe they've decided not to come,' he added.

A woman to Leon's left looked at him. 'You just arrived this morning, love?' She had a mop of wild and wiry grey hair held in check by a baseball cap.

'Yeah.'

'We been here a week. It's a bloody disgrace, treating us like this. Like effin' animals.' She nodded out through the mesh at the figures patrolling the fence. 'Bastards.'

A siren sounded from one of the four watchtowers. Leon flinched at the noise. 'What's that?'

'Feeding time at the zoo,' the woman replied. She nodded her head. 'There . . .'

Leon followed her gaze and saw about two dozen soldiers in white hazard suits escorting a convoy of seven forklift loaders towards the pen. The forklifts were stacked high with crates. As they approached, the soldiers guarding the entrance began to wave their arms at the people inside to back up from the gate to allow the forklifts in. They were getting little cooperation, and Leon noticed the woman beside him shaking her head.

There was a heavy rattle of gunfire over their heads

368

from the guard tower beside the entrance, and the angry crowd ducked, cowered and withdrew.

'People are going to start getting shot if this keeps up,' she muttered.

The gate clattered to one side and the soldiers were first in, waving the crowd back with their guns. Behind them, in the space created, the forklifts rolled forward, deposited their loads on the ground then slowly reversed out, the spinning yellow lights accompanied by warning beeps.

'There's no bloody organization here,' she said. 'It's absolutely disgusting. There's people been stuck here for days and got nothing to eat yet.'

The soldiers withdrew and the entrance gate rattled closed again. The crowd surged forward as one, and Leon's last glimpse of the crates was of a man clambering on top of the nearest stack and tearing at the cardboard and packing tape with his bare hands.

'Like I said . . . feeding time at the zoo.'

It was cold, made even more miserable by the rain drizzling down from the dark overcast sky. The floodlights sweeping the pen picked out the rain in thick, glistening beams.

'OK, so I'm going to write a letter of complaint to someone once this is all done,' said Freya. 'Mind you, to be fair, I've been to rock festivals that were almost as shit as this.'

Leon put his arm round her shoulders and tugged at her to shuffle up. They were sitting under his anorak in the rain in a pen that reeked of human crap, and yet he realized he was OK with that; if he could feel the body warmth of Freya right next to him, that would do him.

Do you love her, MonkeyNuts?

Of course, Dad. She's great.

Then tell her, for Chrissakes!

She bum-shuffled closer then rested her head on his shoulder. 'Grace is working her magic again, I notice.'

A few metres away, Grace was squatting down with some other folk, Fish beside her. They seemed to be deep in conversation.

'Getting the camp gossip, I guess,' said Leon. 'Where's everyone come from? Who's just braved Crap Corner to go have a dump?'

He felt Freya's shoulders jiggle beside him.

'I guess they weren't expecting this many people,' he said after a while. 'I'm sure we'll get sorted soon.' He felt rain pool on his brow, then run down the bridge of his nose. 'Real soon, I hope.'

Freya nodded at the Chinese aircraft carrier. It had loomed over the quay like a joyless multistorey car park during the day. Now that it was dark, the lights glaring brightly on every deck made it glow like some sort of dystopian shopping centre. 'I'd say there's room for everyone here on that big old bugger alone.'

'Destined for China.'

'I've always wanted to visit there.'

The woman from earlier appeared in front of them. She squatted down and pulled out her pac-a-mac to shelter her legs from the drizzle. ''Ello again, love,' she said to Leon.

'Hey,' said Leon.

From beneath her mac she pulled out a couple of cans with ring-pull lids. 'I'm not sure what's inside 'em, but it's better than having nothing.'

'Oh, hey –' he took them from her – 'that's really kind of you!'

'Yeah,' said Freya. 'Thank you so much.'

'Ah, that's OK. There's cans being passed all around. Us Brits aren't complete savages.'

'Agreed.' Freya nodded. 'Dunkirk spirit. Toodle-pip an' all that.'

'Oh, and I thought I'd let you know . . .' She leaned forward. 'There's a rumour going around that they're starting to load people aboard the ships tomorrow.'

'I'm guessing they'll be testing us or something?' said Freya.

The woman shrugged. 'You know about the virus-really-hates-salt thing?'

Leon and Freya nodded.

'So it'll be pork scratchings all round for breakfast.' She cackled at her own joke.

'Are you with anyone else?' asked Leon.

'Oh, aye. A load of us were making a go of things outside Chester. We heard rescue was coming so we all convoyed down. I was starting to worry this was a big mistake. We were doin' all right where we were, really.' She looked up at the glowing aircraft carrier. 'But if the rumour's true . . . then, well . . . we'll be sorted.'

She stood back up and adjusted her mac once

more. 'Enjoy supper, you two.'

'Hold on!' Leon emerged from the snug warmth of their anorak and stood up. 'What's your name?'

'Cora.'

'I'm Leon. And this is Freya.'

Freya smiled. 'Hi.'

'Nice to meet you both,' said Cora.

Leon gave her a quick hug. 'Oh . . . oh, dear me,' she chuckled awkwardly as she patted him lightly on the back. 'So you're a hugger . . . OK, all right.'

'Thank you for the food.'

'That's uh . . . that's quite all right,' she said, pink-faced. 'Anyway, I better get back to my brood.'

They watched her pick her way between huddled circles of figures until she was lost in the rain-glinting crowd.

'Nice lady,' said Freya.

He nodded. 'That kind of thing . . .' He let the words go.

'What?

'Random stranger kindness.' He puffed. 'That's what makes us worth it.'

Freya's eyes narrowed. 'I really don't do schmaltzy-sentimental.' She made space for him as he snuggled back under their cover. 'But I suppose I can make an exception for an idiot like you.' She kissed him quickly on the cheek. 'Now then . . . dinner?'

CHAPTER 53

'All right, can everyone hear me?'

Tom gazed at the faces all the way along the mesh fence, crammed into every space available, with yet more faces peering over shoulders. The microphone and the PA speakers had been borrowed from the aircraft carrier. Tom wasn't sure which Chinese character indicated on, off or mute. All he had to guide him was the small LED, which showed green right now.

'Can you people hear me?'

He heard his words bounce back from somewhere. It was on. And he saw a few heads nodding. To his side he thought he heard Captain Xien utter, 'Tough crowd.'

Tom almost did a double take at him. *The crafty bastard DOES speak English.*

He turned back to the people packed into the pen. 'All right, then. I know it's going to be hard for you folks to hear what I'm saying with this damned mask on, and the address system ain't great, but bear with me.'

'We're going to be testing you all for symptoms of infection, and then we'll be allocating about two-thirds of you to be taken by representatives of the Pacific Nations Alliance, and one-third of you to American Cuba.

'How we're doing this is as follows: we'll be processing batches of seventy-five at a time. Fifty will be tested and processed by PNA personnel in those tents over there.' He pointed at a row of tents beyond the razor wire, dividing the camp in half. Since people were going to be escorted to and fro all day long, the barrier had been pulled to one side.

'And the rest in our tents here.' He pointed to his left. 'We'll be taking blood and testing for high levels of oestrogen and histamine. And I'm sure a lot of you are aware of the salt test. We'll be testing for coagulation.'

He was relieved this was a public address and not a question and answer. The question all of them must be wanting to ask right now was what happens to those who fail the test.

'After testing you will be issued with one of these . . .' He held up one of the red passports. 'These are your Willy Wonka tickets off this island. They'll be filled in with your name, age, profession and/or qualifications.'

Tom opened the passport. It was plain red cardboard folded in half. On the inside were spaces where that information would be written, and spaces for four photographs.

'Your photograph will be taken. But more importantly . . . and this is *very important* –' he let the speakers echo that and fade away; he needed them to hear this next bit clearly – 'we will require every person who passes testing to have at least two distinctive features that can be photographed. The list of features that may be included are surgical scars or scars caused by injury, but not burning scars. Body art. That means only tattoos, not piercing holes. Birth marks caused by pigmentation and not vascular marks. So distinctive or large moles, sometimes called cafe-au-lait marks or Mongolian spots. Red markings such as macular stains, haemangiomas and port-wine stains will not be allowed.'

'Once you've had your red passport completed, you will be escorted along guarded channels to our ships or the PNA ships.' Tom pointed to a corridor that had been constructed from the rear of their testing tents to the quayside. The corridor was made of flimsy two-metre panels of fencing that had been cable-tied together to form a continuous walkway to the waiting boarding ramps. The panels wouldn't stop anyone determined to clamber over them, or stand up to anyone intent on flattening them, but they would help control the flow and separation of people. Tom didn't bother pointing out the other channel that led out of the camp.

Keep it positive.

'We anticipate that each batch will take about forty-five minutes to an hour to process, which means, folks, I need you all to be patient and well behaved. I assure you, everyone here *will* be tested and evaluated.'

He lowered the microphone from his mask and then fumbled with the slide-switch until the LED blinked red. The last sentence was a lie. A sickening one. As soon as they had their quota and the PNA had theirs, that was it. Time to leave.

Once again he scanned the long row of hopeful faces pressed up against the mesh in the vain hope he'd recognize one of them.

'Hold still, please.'

Tom watched as the medical crew from the USS *Gerald Ford* processed their second batch. In each tent they had a gurney set up with a wheeled medical trolley beside it. They had one shoulder-high partition as a concession to modesty and functioning as a plain backdrop for face photographs. A spotlight with a diffuser loomed over the partition.

Beyond it, two other people in the tent waited their turn, guarded by four marines, while the first one to be tested rolled up her sleeve. On the floor, tucked out of view was a pump, cylinder and hose. The cylinder contained a particularly nasty and strong blend of sodium hypochlorite. Beside that they had improvised a flamethrower, a fire-retardant blanket and a tazer.

Stun. Spray. Burn. Extinguish.

They'd all been drilled on what to do in the case of a positive result. The medical officer would raise a hand and signal them, then back out of the tent. The marines would do what needed to be done, as quickly and quietly as possible.

The last thing they needed was a sudden outbreak of panic. The last thing he needed the penned-in crowd to hear was gunshots and screaming.

The testing process was going to work until, all of a sudden, it didn't. Like all great military plans, it looked fine on paper. It was just waiting for the first road bump to shake it to pieces.

The medic was busy taking blood while another staffer was asking the young woman on the gurney her details and writing them into the passport.

'Name?'

'Shelly, Maisy, Gower'

'Gower . . . spelled Golf, Oscar, Whisky, Echo, Romeo? Is that correct?'

'Uh, yeah. That's it.'

'Birthdate?'

'Fourteen, third, ninety-six.'

'Uh, ma'am . . . you mean, third, fourteen?'

'Fourteenth of March, 1996.'

'Understood. Occupation?'

'I . . . well, I was a degree student when the—'

'Majoring?' The medic looked up through her mask, pen poised over the cardboard.

'Huh?'

'What subject?'

'Oh. Contemporary Dance and Drama.'

Tom watched as the medic finished extracting Shelly Gower's blood sample and then squirted one drop into an analyser for the oestrogen and histamine tests, and another drop into a petri dish filled with a saline solution and a pigment-triggering catalyst.

'Can you tell me two identifying marks we can log and photograph, ma'am?'

The young woman lifted her jumper at the back. 'I got a tattoo at the top of my bum. See it?'

The medic nodded, picked up a digital camera, took a

shot of it, then entered a description on to the passport.

'And I've got this small scar on my knee.' She rolled up the left leg of her khakis until a pale knobbly knee emerged.

'That's fine, ma'am,' said the medic. She took another photograph, then wrote down a description.

'And . . . I got, like, this raspberry-shaped mark thing on my . . .'

Tom walked out of the rear of the tent and peered into the next one. A middle-aged man with a thick, dark beard and an arm tattooed from wrist to armpit was being examined. He glanced at the other two waiting with the marines to be tested next, and sighed again.

Don't you give up hope yet.

Tom stepped out and poked his head into the next tent . . .

CHAPTER 54

Leon and the others were standing in a queue. He'd been fully expecting to be jostled and pushed around the entrance to the pen. But instead he'd been surprised to find everyone had calmly formed one long snaking line. A number of people had even appointed themselves as stewards, indicating where the queue should double back on itself and keeping an eye out for 'corner jumpers'. The woman from last night was one of them: Cora, barking out instructions like a collie herding sheep. She smiled and nodded at Leon and Freya as she walked down the line.

'I reckon it's going to be quite a few hours,' Leon said.

Freya braced a hand on his shoulder and craned her neck. 'Yeah.'

Leon looked around again, hoping to catch sight of Naga and the others. 'Hey, Fish, have you seen any sign of our lot this morning?'

Fish looked as though he were about a million miles away, eyes wide and glazed over.

'Fish?'

He was holding Grace's hand. She looked equally blank-eyed and distracted, but she stirred, aware that Leon had spoken. 'No,' she answered for him. 'I don't think they're going to be coming, Leon.'

'Well, they're going to miss this if they don't get a move

on,' said Leon. He continued looking around at the faces in the queue. In the last few months he'd come to know some of them – Naga, Denise, even Royce – well enough to care what happened to them. 'We should have agreed on what to do if we didn't report back.'

'Naga's not an idiot. She's probably sent Royce and some of the knights already. Or maybe all of them are walking in.' She started looking around. 'They'll be OK, Leo.'

He looked through the mesh at the soldiers standing and watching. Some white-suited, some yellow, all of their faces hidden behind tinted visors or round goggles. He wondered which one had made the announcement. It had been hard to hear exactly what was being said. The speakers blasting out from each corner tower had echoed over each other, making the instructions almost unintelligible.

He'd got the gist of it, though. Blood tests and body marks. As they shuffled forward a step, he catalogued what he had to show. No tattoos. No birthmarks. But there was an appendix scar, a faint circular patch on his arm from an MMR jab he'd got at school and one wart on his knuckle. Leon wondered whether Grace's scars would qualify as one identifier or more. Maybe they'd need something else. 'Grace, haven't you got three moles clustered together like Mickey Mouse?'

Again, she looked lost, somewhere far away. He waved a hand at her. 'Grace?'

She blinked and stirred. A flash of irritation flickered across the unscarred half of her face.

'Jesus, Grace – Fish – what is it with the pair of you?'

'Aw, leave 'em alone, Leon,' said Freya. 'They're tired. So am I, for that matter. I didn't get a wink of sleep last night.'

Leon was tired as well. But not totally zoned out like them. They needed their wits about them this morning. Not daydreaming. Not shuffling along like zombies. 'Grace, Fish – you heard the guy? You'll need two identifying marks. Grace, what have you got?'

She cocked her head and glared at him with feigned indignity. 'I'll be telling the doctor, not *you*!'

'So there!' Freya chuckled. 'You tell him to mind his own business.'

'Name, please, sir . . .'

'Joseph Anthony Garret.'

Tom checked the watch strapped round the outside of his suit. It was eleven thirty. They'd been at it for just over two hours now. They were actually making good progress, working through the waiting evacuees quicker than he'd expected. They were on the fourth batch now, which meant that once this lot were done they'd have one hundred vetted British people billeted aboard their ships.

One hundred done. Eight hundred to go. Sixteen more hours of this, provided there were no hitches or speed bumps. So far there hadn't been a single positive result, which was pretty much what he'd been anticipating. If this virus really . . . *really* . . . could mimic humans as some of these Brits had been claiming, surely they'd be far too obvious. And, even if they looked convincing, surely they wouldn't understand verbal instructions, or be able to partake in a conversation, give a name or a date of birth or a previous profession?

Mimic humans?

The idea sounded ridiculous. Far more likely that it was the manifestation of panicked minds. These people had been hanging on for nearly two years. Most of them in remote, isolated enclaves, no contact with the outside world, perhaps even convinced they were the last humans left alive. No wonder these poor bastards had been jumping at shadows. One person hollers 'wolf', and all of a sudden that wolf becomes a very real thing in the minds of those within earshot. Two years of survival. Two years of holding out on their own, and fighting off viral creatures that certainly were for real . . . Tom wondered if he'd have fared any better.

'And your date of birth, please, sir? That's month, day, year.'

Leon weaved his way through the long snaking queue on his way back from the toilet corner. He'd hung on as long as he could, then checked with an old biker who was unofficially stewarding their section of the queue that he was OK to go for a leak and keep his place rather than going to the very back of the queue.

He scanned the faces he passed, still hoping to catch sight of Naga and the others. He hoped to God they'd finally figured out what had happened, that they'd been picked up and rescued.

He rounded another bend in the winding line and spotted Fish. But not in the queue. He was standing to one side of it, close to the pen's fencing. He appeared to be with a group of about fifty or sixty people.

Leon stopped. 'Fish?'

No response.

'Fish!' he called again. 'What're you doing over there?'

The group seemed to be huddled together and holding hands like some sort of impromptu prayer meeting. He walked towards them. Close up, he could see some had their eyes open and were staring dull-eyed at seemingly nothing. Others had them shut, as if deep in prayer or meditation. No one was talking and they were standing unnervingly still, men, women, children alike.

They didn't appear to be members of one particular survival group. Leon had noticed over the last two years that hard survival had begun to make people who'd endured it together look vaguely similar. The learned habits, the layers and methods of protection defined to some degree how they dressed. This gathering of 'parishioners' looked as though they'd come from all corners of the United Kingdom.

'Fish! Hey!' He slapped his friend's back gently to make him jump, partly because he was annoyed that Fish had just wandered off and left the girls unguarded.

Fish remained inert. His eyes cracked open gradually and he turned slowly to look at Leon.

'Fish . . . what the hell are you doing?'

He frowned and for a moment it seemed he didn't even

recognize Leon. Then the stupor cleared from his face and he smiled. 'Hey.'

Leon looked around at all the others, stock-still and utterly silent, hands clasped. He cocked a brow. 'Who're your new . . . umm . . . friends?'

He noticed Fish was holding hands with a middle-aged Asian man on one side and a large round-shouldered guy on the other.

'Leon . . .' Fish hadn't seemed to have heard the question, or was choosing to ignore it. 'This has to be goodbye, mate.'

'What?'

'I like you. Both of you.' Leon guessed he was talking about Freya. 'But I'm gonna say goodbye. I'm with these people now.'

'What's wrong with you? You can't just—'

'Leon!' Fish hissed under his breath. 'You have to go! This is not a good time!'

'What's going on?'

'Just go!'

Leon reached down to grab one of Fish's hands.

'DON'T!' Fish snapped angrily. 'GO!' There was something in his wide eyes and the hardness of his expression that suggested the next time he said 'go' it was going to come with a shove.

'OK . . . OK . . .' Leon raised his arms and hands in surrender and backed up a step. 'You know where we are.' He nodded over his shoulder. 'In the queue over there, but we're getting quite near to the gate so . . .'

Fish nodded, the hardness melted away. He tipped

him a nod and offered a faint smile. 'See you around, mate . . . soon.'

Tom watched the three evacuees leave, clutching their red cardboard documents as if they were winning lottery tickets. A marine waved at them to follow him along the marked channel towards their ships.

One hundred and seventeen passed, he calculated. They'd rejected only about half a dozen people so far. Not because they'd found a viral *imposter* – which, frankly, he was beginning to suspect was a load of paranoid hokum – but because they hadn't got enough acceptable identifying marks to log. Tom had been tempted to step in and overrule his medics at one point. It had been a nine-year-old girl for God's sake – of course she didn't have any bloody tattoos or scars. But then if he started bending the rules, making allowances and exceptions, berating his personnel for following orders to the letter, this process was going to descend into chaos.

Watching the little girl being escorted into the 'rejected' channel without the card had been hard.

With some of the others, though, the ones who grumbled angrily, ungratefully, at their week-long incarceration, the lack of creature comforts, he'd been tempted – *God*, he'd been seriously tempted – to fail them. Every person issued with a red card meant one less space aboard for Leon and Grace.

The next three candidates were led in. Tom glanced at their faces then excused himself to check in on the neighbouring tent. He stepped in to find the process was already underway with the first candidate.

'Name please, ma'am?' asked one of the medics, passport flattened out on her clipboard and pen in hand.

Another one was busy uncapping a new syringe.

'Name? Please?'

'Uh . . .' The woman looked confused, as if she'd been turfed out of a comfy bed two minutes ago and was still trying to figure out if she were awake or not.

'I need your name, ma'am. First, middle and last.'

The medic with the syringe slipped a pressure band over the woman's bare forearm and cinched it tight.

'Martell. J. T.,' the woman replied sluggishly.

'Uh . . . ma'am, that's my colleague's name.' She looked at the name badge taped to the front of the hazard suit beside her. 'I actually need *your* name.'

The other medic was shaking her head irritably as she stared at the pale arm. The pressure band had been tightened, but she was struggling to find a vein. She cinched it tighter and looked again, but found nothing into which she could tap.

'Miss . . . are you or have you ever been a heroin addict?'

The woman was staring at the glistening needle poised above her skin, which hovered like some bird of prey looking for a hapless scurrying field mouse below.

'Miss?'

Tom noticed the other two candidates she'd come in with were shuffling uncomfortably: two men, one black, one white, both in their thirties, he guessed. They took a step towards each other. He saw them reach out and clasp hands tightly.

Well, OK . . .

'Miss, I need you to look at me and listen!' The medic, Martell J. T., was getting frustrated. 'I can't find a vein we can use in your arm, ma'am. So we'll need to try the other . . .'

She loosened the clip on the pressure band and tried to slide it down her forearm. But it was stuck.

'Uh, hold on.'

The woman's skin seemed to be stuck to it. 'I guess that was on pretty tightly. Just bear with me . . .'

Martell tugged at the pressure band a little more firmly. This time it slid easily down her arm, but the woman's skin peeled away with it, tearing all the way down her forearm like wet tissue paper.

'*What the* . . .' The medic stared at the exposed muscles and tendons, a perfectly flayed arm dribbling dark strings of viscous liquid on to the woman's jogging bottoms.

CHAPTER 55

'But why's he gone and abandoned us?' asked Freya. 'Was it something I said?'

Leon shook his head. 'Fish has been acting weird for the last couple of days. I don't know what the hell's wrong with him.'

'He said he was just going for a pee,' said Freya. 'He just wandered off, didn't say anything about leav—' She stopped and looked at him. 'You don't think he's . . .' Freya left that question hanging in the air.

'Come on. Seriously? When? How? He's just . . . I don't know, being an asshole, I guess. Which is a shame, 'cause I kinda like the guy.'

'No, Leon. No.' Freya didn't accept that. She shook her head. 'He *has* been really distant and weird since we got here. Thinking about it, even before that. When we left Naga and the others, he wasn't saying much. I thought he was sulking about something. Maybe sulking about being overruled by Naga. You know, when he said about testing the kids?'

'Maybe.'

Freya glanced at Grace. 'What's he been like with you? You two have been getting quite clo . . .'

Grace was staring intently at something outside the pen. Freya and Leon followed her gaze. There was a commotion

388

going on inside one of the tents. The steady clinical illumination by strip lights inside had made the canvas material of the tents glow like a row of Chinese lanterns for the last few hours, but now one of them was flickering, the colour changing from a sterile cyan to a modulating amber.

Leon saw a tall shadow diffused against the canvas moving in front of a light source. He thought he saw the material of the tent bulge and quiver as something bumped against it from within.

Then they heard it, a gunshot.

Followed by another.

'Shit!' hissed Freya.

Leon finished her thought. 'They've found one.'

The material at the top of the tent began to darken. The steady glow of the cyan strip light suddenly winked out, leaving just a flickering amber glow within, casting tall distorted shadows that reminded Leon of American Indians dancing around a campfire. The material right at the apex of the tent gave way and ribbons of flame burst out through the ragged hole.

The tent was on fire, spreading, exposing the metal support frame and the goings-on inside. He could see an impossibly tall figure, seven foot, eight foot, staggering around with tongues of flame rising from it, a silhouette that looked like a totem pole of human arms and unfolding claws and spines.

Then something started inside the crowded holding pen. He heard screaming and turned to see a wave of movement making its way through the long, winding queue.

'What's going on?'

Leon's attention was drawn in the direction of Fish, a hundred metres away with his new weird, silent, hand-holding buddies. All heads were now turning that way. Something was happening over there.

People backing away, with cautious *What the hell?* retreating steps quickly escalating to *get me the hell out of here* scrambling.

Over the heads and shoulders of the mass of fleeing people, pushing past and tangling with each other, he saw what was causing the stampede.

Another top-heavy many-limbed totem was rising from the crowd like some parade-day effigy hefted up for all to see. That was the last thing he glimpsed before the surge of panic hit them like a tsunami.

Everyone coming at them at once.

Everyone heading toward the pen's entrance.

Leon floundered in the press of bodies, picked up and carried forward like debris on a furiously surging river. He twisted left and right, desperately trying to keep sight of Freya and Grace.

He could see the top of Freya's head being pushed in the same general direction, but a growing number of people were filling the space between them, separating them.

'Freya!' he shouted across to her, but then everyone was shouting. Leon's voice was lost in the cacophony of panic. He could see her looking at him, eyes locked on him.

I see you, Leon . . .

He nodded. *As long as we keep sight of each other . . .*

The white biohazard-suited soldiers guarding the entrance made a stoic effort to hold their line, first firing a warning volley of shots into the air, then as the surge of people spilled through the opening in the fencing and the weight of bodies collapsed the panels either side of the entrance, the soldiers began to fire directly into the crowd.

Too little too late.

They were quickly overwhelmed, guns wrestled from their hands, some of them shot by their own weapons, some clubbed to the ground, some just left empty-handed and ignored as people streamed past them.

Leon found himself propelled outside the pen. He staggered out of the flow of people to an empty space beneath the corner tower guarding the entrance. He scanned the stream of faces pouring by, hoping desperately to spot Freya and Grace as they were pushed out past him.

Tom had collapsed on to his butt, fighting his respirator for air. Panting hard as he sat on cold concrete and watched the testing tent twenty metres away burn like a ritual pyre. It had all happened so quickly.

. . . *The woman's skinned arm moving suddenly.*

. . . *Those two men holding hands.*

. . . *One of the marines in the tent spiked by a long, jagged spear from behind.*

. . . *The tip bursting out of his chest and his biohazard suit . . .*

. . . *The woman thrusting her freshly flayed arm at the medic . . .*

. . . Something bloody exploding from the palm of her hand on to the medic's face plate.

. . . Gunfire.

The other marine had reached for the gasoline, ignoring the whole carefully discussed and rehearsed routine:

1. Taser target
2. Burn
3. Extinguish
4. Bleach everything.

The tent suddenly reeked of carelessly sloshed fuel. The two male candidates he'd spotted holding hands seconds ago began to *merge* into some bizarre swirling mess of dripping white and black skin from which hard-edged limbs were beginning to rupture and sprout.

Tom had staggered backwards out of the tent, continued staggering backwards, not able to turn his back on the unfolding, flexing nightmare, not able to run for his life, only to keep taking idiot reverse steps until finally he collided with something, lost his balance and tumbled heavily on to the ground.

He was panting with exertion, with fear, in shock for perhaps thirty seconds before he pulled his wits together and sat up.

The tent was fully aflame. The two-man nightmare was staggering around on fire, flailing its long articulated limbs at the marines who were firing automatic volleys at it. Tom saw something flick out and lasso one of his men, wrapping itself round his neck and dragging him in towards the flames.

He became dimly aware that there was gunfire going on elsewhere in the camp. He pulled himself back to his feet, not an easy task with a heavy air cylinder on his back.

The pen . . . Oh, shit, the holding pen.

He saw the flood of people surging out of it and realized there was no hope of regaining control.

Freya lost her grip on Grace's hand. She'd let go for a nanosecond to protect her face from some idiot's swinging elbow. Then back again, expecting Grace's small hand to still be there, to fold round her own, but she was gone.

Freya looked around her.

No sign.

Leon was five, six metres away from her. She could see him trying to get close to her over the turbulent sea of heads and shoulders.

'GRACE!' she screamed. 'I LOST HER!' But her voice was just a drop of water in a deafening waterfall. Somebody shoved her roughly from behind and her useless left leg buckled and betrayed her. Freya collapsed to the ground and instantly felt boots, trainers, wellies stamp on her hands, her wrists, the small of her back as she became nothing more than uneven ground for unthinking feet to traverse.

She pulled herself up into a tight foetal position and waited for what seemed like ages, waiting for the flow of crushing feet to thin out enough for her to try to pull herself up. Finally, there was enough room for people to spot her on the ground and step around her. Painfully, with difficulty, she manoeuvred herself into a kneeling position, then, by reaching out and grabbing on to some random arm, she managed to get back up on her feet again.

Behind her, she heard screams . . .

Not human ones, but that inhuman wailing chorus she'd heard at the castle. She followed the flow of movement towards the exit, and was finally spat out past the wire-mesh boundary, nearly tripping over the white-suited body of a soldier. She looked left, right, expecting to see either Grace or Leon somewhere ahead frantically looking around, waiting for her.

But nothing. No sign of either.

Leon? Grace? Where the hell are you?

She twisted one way, then the other, suddenly so aware of how useless and vulnerable she was on her own.

She staggered past one of the burning tents, and past another from which half a dozen suited soldiers had spilled out. She expected at least one of them to stop her, level a gun at her, but they hurried by, passing on both sides of her as if she weren't even there.

No plan of action now – every man for himself.

She kept going. Without her walking stick, her left leg was dragging like an anchor on a gnarly seabed. She kept going alongside the row of tents, not really sure why she was heading in this particular direction.

She stopped and cut into the space between two tents.

To her right, the entrance to one flapped open, and on impulse she stepped into it, hoping to find someone in authority to help her, to at least tell her what to do. Where to go. To tell her what was happening.

Inside it contained what she'd expected to see: medical equipment, a gurney, syringes, blood samples, a bright spotlight on a stand . . . but no one left inside doing their job.

A small table had been knocked over and a clipboard and pen along with dozens of those little red passports the man had been waving around earlier that morning were scattered across the ground. She bent down and picked one of them up. It had a mugshot photo of a dark-haired female roughly her age. She suspected that clutching a red passport in her hand might save her from being gunned down by some panicking soldier with his finger resting too heavily on a trigger. She doubted, however, that it would get her past anyone bothering to inspect them closely.

She clambered awkwardly towards the far side of the tent and an exit flap. She stepped out of the clinical glare of the tent and into drizzling grey daylight.

'STAY WHERE YOU ARE!' screamed a muffled voice.

Freya saw a yellow biohazard suit and a gun aimed shakily at her. She instinctively held both her hands up because that's what people did in movies.

'YOU BEEN TESTED!'

She realized he was looking at her raised hands, the card clearly held aloft in one of them. She understood it wasn't a question. It was a statement.

'Yeah . . . I'm good. I'm not infect—'

'GO . . . GO . . . GO . . .' The soldier waggled the muzzle

of his gun to the left. 'THAT WAY!'

Freya saw he was indicating a channel flanked by mesh panels.

They must have gone past me.

The surge of people streaming out of the pen was lessening now, and those left inside were pretty much the infected. Leon felt like an idiot just standing there. Grace and Freya must already be waiting somewhere else for him.

He scanned the open compound. It looked like footage of some sort of bizarre ComicCon sped up: people milling frantically in all directions with no clue which was the right way to go. To his right, tents were on fire, flames curling into the wet air. To his left, soldiers in yellow were huddled together in uncertain groups, some firing warning shots into the air, some impassively waiting for orders, and some still attempting to herd people back into the holding pen.

The American side was a shambles. There was no semblance of containment or order left; it had borne the brunt of the chaos.

Over on the Chinese-led side, there still seemed to be some sense of cohesion. Half a dozen white-suits were pulling loops of razor wire from the quayside across the open expanse of concrete. The border, which had been opened earlier to allow for the easier movement of people, was now hastily being dragged back into position. Leon could see more white-suited soldiers hurrying down the ramp from the Chinese carrier and forming into a long thin line, assault rifles raised and ready to use if the razor-wire barrier failed.

Beyond them, a significant number of people who'd escaped the holding pen were loose in the international half of the camp. Some were being gunned down, others randomly rounded up. He could see more personnel in biohazard suits streaming out of their row of testing tents, some of them carrying equipment. All of them hurrying towards the carrier's broad embarkation ramp.

Breaking camp. Game over.

They're leaving us.

Tom fought the urge to break down at the appalling sight in front of him. The whole thing had fallen apart frighteningly quickly – from the woman's skin peeling away like tissue, to the mass breakout from the holding pen – it must have occurred in less than a couple of minutes.

From order to anarchy in less than the time needed to boil a kettle.

Over the last week he'd become concerned at the sheer number of people who'd turned up and were still arriving. There'd been three mistakes that had led to this. One: he'd underestimated how many people would respond to the rescue broadcast. Two: there were not enough boots on the ground. Trent had let him take just one company of marines, which he'd had to split between Calais and Southampton.

The third mistake had been not believing the Brits when they'd said the virus could 'do people'. Frankly, that had sounded nuts. But now he'd seen it for himself. Those three test candidates in the tent had *all* been infected. They'd seemed aware of that and had been working together . . .

Holding hands . . .

The woman had been the distraction, while the two men had begun to merge.

Merging. Jesus. Merging into whatever the hell you'd call that tall frikkin thing.

His men had said similar creatures had been forming up inside the pen. Dozens of them, like mashed-together towers of flesh and bone, spitting out everything from vast crustacean-like pincers to curling lassoes of soft flesh.

'. . . Sir . . . SIR?'

Tom realized a number of his people – medical staff and marines – had coalesced around him and were looking to him for orders.

'– everywhere, sir!' barked a muffled voice.

The air was filled with the percussive rattle of gunfire. The Chinese troops had formed a defensive line where the barbed-wire barricade had been pulled back into position. They'd given up firing warning shots into the air and were now picking off people who'd managed to scrape their way through the coils of wire.

There was a distant thud, and a lazy cloud of oily smoke rose into the sky as a stash of gasoline went up in one of the many burning tents.

Looking across the concrete into the abandoned holding pen, Tom could see something he knew he was never, ever, going to be able to *un*-see, picked out in the merciless glare of the floodlights.

An area like marshland, like a swamp, a small bubbling lake of fluid, from which leg bones, ribcages and various undigestibles protruded like reeds and wetland roots. The virus was consolidating, working its way through its brand-new victims, *processing* them as they'd hoped to process the survivors. A bubbling witch's brew of molten skin and glistening tendrils snaking out across the hard ground, seeking further outlying pools with which to unite, absorbing, consolidating.

In the middle of its mass he could see movement beneath the glutinous surface, like bubbles of steam in a thick porridge trying to break through and burst.

What's going on over there?

As if in answer, the surface suddenly ruptured and Tom saw movement of a different kind, no longer the languid undulations of a lava lamp, but a frenetic fidgeting of glistening sharp edges, points and spines . . . spreading as fast as a bloodstain across a crisp white shirt.

I've seen this . . . Shit, I've seen this.

The CCTV footage from that religious cult.

Those spidery things. Coming this way. *Swarming* their way.

You've lost this one, Tom. Get going. Now.

'We're leaving!' shouted Tom above the din. 'Everyone back aboard!'

They were slow to respond, or perhaps hadn't heard him. He jabbed a finger towards the loading ramps of their three ships.

'. . . RUN!'

CHAPTER 56

Grace wandered slowly across the chaotic quayside, almost serenely, like some slack-jawed tourist marvelling at a theme-park recreation of Armageddon, untouched, unaffected by it all and amazed at the spectacle around her.

She finally came to a halt and found herself looking up at the daunting structure of the vast Chinese aircraft carrier, a glowing leviathan of endlessly stacked decks and floodlights that shone down unrelenting on the Southampton quayside like some visiting extraterrestrial mother ship.

Dimly, she could hear voices, gunshots and screaming. Dimly, she sensed movement all around her. Dimly, she felt the thud of a stray bullet tear through her thigh. Nothing to concern her. The wound would coagulate, a thick resinous layer would coat and fix the fractured femur within hours; the skin would reknit. She had no idea whether the shot had been aimed at her specifically or meant for no one in particular.

It didn't really matter anyway.

Behind her, she knew the thin white line of soldiers was being overwhelmed by the thick tidal wave of *carriers*. Their guns were useless weapons, as ineffective as trying to swat at a cloud of mosquitos with a baseball bat.

Nearby, a group of tested-and-passed evacuees were being hustled towards the loading ramp by a mixed group of Australian and Chinese soldiers.

The last, lucky few.

They hurried towards her, then either side of her, as if she weren't even there, scrambling desperately to board the ramp to safety.

She could see that the carrier was beginning to move excruciatingly slowly, not exactly a quick getaway vehicle. She could hear klaxons wailing, warning amber lights flashing and spinning either side of the ramp. It was beginning to slide and bump along the concrete, nudging boxes and crates into the water as it inched along.

She was ushered on to the ramp with the others and felt the harsh skittering vibration of the grinding metal walkway beneath her feet. She could feel the transmitted deeper vibration of the ship's engines back-pedalling furiously away from the shore, turning the water around the vast grey hull into a boiling white froth.

This was not how it was supposed to go. But then she wasn't in charge. No one was really in charge. She was one of many, part of an enormous community, a family even – everyone wanting the same end-goal, but with differing opinions on how they should get there.

She'd wanted the face-to-face encounter to be a calm and measured one: Grace speaking on behalf of the virus to some person in charge who would represent what was left of mankind.

A meeting of civilizations.

A peaceful discussion of intentions, of what the future held. She'd been hoping to present herself to someone In. Charge. Of. Things. To calmly reassure him, or her, that, *yes*, she was infected, but that, *no*, she wasn't about to explode into a million little bugs.

She wanted to talk. That was all.

She'd had a plan, not even a plan . . . just a *hope* that she could reassure those people left alive on this planet that they had absolutely nothing to fear. That, yes, change can be scary, change can *look* scary. But ultimately, if one doesn't change, one slowly dies. That there really was nothing to worry about . . .

Despite the 'messy' appearance of transition from one form of life to another, it was nothing to be afraid of. In fact, it was something truly wonderful.

Life . . . was changing.

Life . . . was being reinvented.

Life . . . *was being Reborn.*

TO BE CONTINUED . . .

ACKNOWLEDGEMENTS

I'd like to thank the team at Macmillan for helping me get this out there. Firstly to Venetia Gosling for her deft application of editor's margin notes, and secondly to Samantha Stewart and Lucy Pearse for their forensic copy-editing. And thirdly to Debbie Chaffey for going through this book line by line, hunting for gremlins to squish. Without you four, this book would be half what it is :)

ABOUT THE AUTHOR

Alex Scarrow used to be a rock guitarist. After ten years in various unsuccessful bands he ended up working in the computer games industry as a lead games designer. He now has his own games development company, Grrr Games. He is the author of the bestselling and award-winning TimeRiders series, which has been sold into over thirty foreign territories. He lives in East Anglia. *Reborn* is the second book in the Remade series, and Alex is currently working on the explosive final instalment.

Visit his website at www.AlexScarrow.com

A virus that can think, a teen boy who
was never cut out to be a hero,
and a promise to a dying mother to protect
a younger sister – no matter what.

**THE TENSE THRILLER FROM
THE BESTSELLING AUTHOR
OF TIMERIDERS**